SCARS OF THE SUN

A LIGHT IN THE DARK
BOOK TWO

NOELLE UPTON

Cover Art by Julia Saxton (Instagram: @j.sgrey)

BEFORE YOU READ

Dear reader, thank you so much for picking up a copy of *Scars of the Sun*. These characters blossomed from small seeds I planted in *In the Light of the Moon*, and I hope you find them just as fun and engaging as much as I do. This novel has been edited, but if you find any errors, please let me know.

And if you need it, below is a list of content/trigger warnings:

- Mature and explicit sexual content
- Mention of self-harm and suicide attempt throughout
- Explicit violence
- Gore
- Explicit language
- Mentions of past child abuse (physical, verbal, and emotional)
- Mental health struggles including depression and PTSD
- Classist language/statements
- Slut shaming language/statements

I tried to handle these themes with care, but know that healing from a mental health crisis and from childhood abuse are central to this book. Please take care of yourself as best as you see fit.

If you are so inclined, please feel free to send me any reactions and/or questions while you read. I get such a kick out of real-time thoughts and conversations with my friends and would love to hear from you! You can email me or send a DM on Instagram any time.

Again, thank you so much for reading, and I hope you enjoy!

For all of those with lists. I see you and am so proud of you.

And for the love of skater boys.

PROLOGUE

Haunted, honey.

The woman—witch—beside the beautiful one cleared her throat. "We ordered online. Should be under the name Orion." But my mind felt like static had settled over it, like a weighted blanket that demanded my calm and my attention. The wariness that had snapped to the forefront of my mind when they'd walked in was flattening.

The skin around her eyes was sunken and puffy at the same time. The way she curled inward speaking of a desire to disappear. But there was no missing the flat turn of her full lips or the light flush on the tops of her cheeks. What was she feeling? Did she sense the undeniable *pull*? Was I hallucinating?

Her expression remained vacant, and I shook myself. No. A strong, flitting physical attraction at most.

I busied myself with my actual job, trying to temper the calculating instincts that called me to react to the supernatural females before me. My shifter blood recognized all of theirs. Even if they were Wolf in nature.

A young pup, a non-shifter, and a shifter mate.

Without a word, I went back to the kitchen to retrieve the

order that was indeed under the name Orion. Which, in of itself wasn't fucking good. Based on the research I'd done about this town, the local Pack Leader was of the same name. I wouldn't be lucky enough to encounter such a random coincidence, would I?

In the short minute or so of me putting a container of bread-sticks and sauce in a bag and stacking everything up, the familiar chill of resignation was settling over my shoulders. I'd been here for nearly six months which was the usual signal that time was up. There could be no settling. Not if I wanted them to catch up with me.

Two sets of eyes—one brown and the other that rich and light honey—settled on me. The pup's light green, however, was pinned onto the styrofoam to-go cup filled with suckers that I'd put beside the register. It was stupid, and had turned out to be more for me than anyone else. I'd just finished a blue raspberry one before they came in, working dough beneath my hands and losing myself to the hours of the slow evening.

She was tall enough to reach it, the little girl with brown skin like her mother beside her and tightly coiled red hair, but maybe she needed the external permission? At her age, I would have just stretched on my toes to grab at least two or three. The need to ask permission to so much as take a deep breath had been beaten into me years later.

I plucked one randomly from the cup and extended it toward the pup whose entire face broke with glee.

She and her mother thanked me, to which I didn't respond. Balancing their food in my hands, I transferred the two pizzas and breadsticks to the non-shifter Wolf that I was trying very hard to ignore.

Until the tips of our fingers brushed, the scrape of her finger-nail as light as a butterfly kiss. Electricity, fire, ice, raced up my arm, and I tried my best to stifle the flinch. And... the purr that was forming at the base of my chest.

We locked eyes for an inhale that stirred my blood. On the

exhale, the tingles were continuing to fizzle, once again demanding I take notice.

The three of them walked out of the door as images of peeling back her layers of apathetic gray to understand what terrors she was experiencing underneath ran through my mind. Would they match my own? Would the faint hint of sweetness bloom once I was let in past the taunting sour of her winter grapefruit scent?

I watched them go, all plan to get the fuck out of town banished to the back of my mind. No, it wasn't right yet. No matter if I'd never let myself stay in one place this long in eight years. The decision didn't even feel like me—it was already made. Like the one to leave the farmhouse at ten, then to smuggle myself out of hell at seventeen. Every town, every odd job, every temporary connection. The intrinsic sense of rightness hadn't failed me yet, not truly.

My phone pulled me out of my trance, still staring out of the window after the red SUV they'd arrived in was long gone.

BLOODSUCKA

Yo. Still up for rehearsal tomorrow?

Right.

Accepting Ty's invitation to replace their old guitarist had, logistically, felt like a ridiculous whim, but that same certainty had pushed me to agree. Breaking out my Iceman for more than idle strumming during my lone hours in the evening was surprisingly… fun.

I texted back, telling him to count me in, and returned to the kitchen to join Parker who'd finally returned from his smoke break. It was only the two of us tonight, and I wasn't with that 'I'm the manager' bullshit to get out of work, so I made myself useful by cooking alongside him and taking orders as they came in.

But I saw a halo of black wispy curls every time I blinked. While I dropped wings and fries into spitting oil, I envisioned her spread beneath me, the bare, long legs I'd seen firsthand wrapped around my waist. Was her smile big and loud or small and shy? Was her laugh a melodic trill or a raspy bark?

If I tried, would I be able to set ablaze the ghosts that haunted her?

"No mames," I cursed to myself while I shoved an extra large pie into the oven. *I need to get fucking laid, that's what I need to do.*

PART ONE

CHAPTER ONE

RAMONA

One of the many therapists I'd seen recently suggested making a running list to turn to when shit got dark.

I was no longer in as much of a dull fog as I'd once been and found myself taking note of the things that gave me that bright feeling, even if I never wrote them down. Now, I swept the back of my hand across my brow and waved back at a grinning Dahlia. She tottered toward a makeshift kitchen set on the other side of the room while Ollie was already sitting and playing with a group of babies his age.

Number Seven.

Wrangling them both into the car then into their Montessori school was both harder and easier than I'd thought it would be. Harder because the newness of my presence was already wearing off, and my brother's children weren't just excited to see me anymore. Ollie had cried when Sylvie handed him to me this morning, and Dahlia had pouted and whined when she realized that she wouldn't be staying at home with Sylvie and me. But we'd made it. I'd buckled them into their car seats, drove my brother's SUV all the way to their school, and gotten them into the building without losing one of them or any serious injury. *I could imagine myself doing this for a while.*

"Hey! Ramona, right?" A deep, friendly voice shoved the darkening clouds threatening my mind. I blinked and looked up at the man—male—grinning down at me. His honey blond hair was a little mussed, and his tan skin was smooth and lightly freckled. The faint hint of wildness entwined with the more bland human scent was enough to highlight his shifter heritage. His nostrils flared a little as he took an inhale, his shoulders relaxing on the exhale.

Mine did the same. "Um, yeah. Why?"

He pursed his lips and turned back around to where the kids were playing. The male's broad shoulders somehow looked soft and warm beneath the rugby-style shirt. When he looked back at me, he seemed a little more uncertain, but his friendly demeanor didn't fall. He waved a hand toward Dahlia who was now leading some other children in cooking some make-believe dish. "I'm a student teacher for the older kids, but Sylvie mentioned you'd be here to drop off Dahlia and Ollie today."

I looked him up and down, noticing the way he nervously swept his palms over his slacks. When I met his eyes again, the first non-shifter Wolf I'd ever really spoken to, I felt my body take notice of the large, sculpted muscles that blended with the delicate kindness that radiated from his face.

Exacerbated by the gray muck of the past few years, I hadn't felt even a nudge of attraction for another person in years, and since I'd been in Antler Pointe, I'd been too preoccupied with making the most of this... new life. At least to pay attention to anyone that wasn't my family.

Ordinarily, I'd balk from the overly-familiar way this male spoke to me, but I forced myself to stay facing him and soften my tone. "Okay. Did you want to talk about something or...?"

He lightly smacked himself on the side of his head, and I had to admit that the gesture was… cute. "I'm being so weird," he muttered to himself, and I tensed in anticipation. His large palm stuck out stiffly toward me. "My name's Delaney."

Nervousness was pouring off of him, enough that even I could smell it, faintly bitter. But when I fit my much smaller hand in his, it cleared almost immediately, and a giant puppy dog smile spread across his face. Good god, the guy even had dimples. "Nice to meet you. Uh, is there something I can help you with?"

Delaney dropped my hand and nodded excitedly. He lightly grasped my arm and pulled me further away from everyone else milling about, starting their day at school or dropping their children off. Normally, I'd struggle or rip a stranger's hand off of me, but he seemed nice.

His wide eyes and long lashes blinked, and I found myself leaning in. He kept his voice low. "Sylvie said that you'd be there tonight."

I released a breath after his meaning seeped through my frazzled thoughts. "Y-yeah. Are you a member?"

A noticeable blush colored Delaney's cheeks, and he nibbled at his bottom lip. "Not yet. But I want to be. Are you?"

I shook my head. "No. This will be my first meeting. If you know Sylvie, you know who my brother is, then."

Somehow, Delaney's eyes got even wider. He nodded gravely, like it was some terrifying honor to be sister of the Pack Leader. "I-is it okay if I sit with you? During the meeting?"

My brows nearly rose to my hairline as I took in this large male—I honestly wouldn't have been surprised if he was a football player or something—who was staring back at me like a scared kid on their first day of school.

The Antler Pointe Pack was a group of shifters, mostly Wolves, and their mates that resided on this stretch of land. I wasn't too familiar with pack customs, but I knew the basics from what I'd gathered being around my brother. Especially these past weeks after moving in with his family.

They met every other week, with one full moon run each month. At their last meeting, O had put it up to a vote for the pack to allow me to attend their meetings, which I hadn't asked him to do but was silently grateful for. The two meetings I'd had to sit out involved me and an empty house. A year ago, that would've been welcome. Amazing even.

Now... I was getting better, but I didn't completely trust myself.

"Sure, I guess. If you want."

Big, solid arms brought me in, and I found my cheek smushed into Delaney's chest. Orange and vanilla, his scent wrapped around my stiff body as I tried to figure out whether to return the embrace or wriggle out of it.

During my deliberation, he dropped his arms and grabbed his cheeks that were red again. "Oh god, I'm sorry. I'm just so relieved to know someone that's going. I've been worrying about it since Sylvie gave me the news."

My skin didn't feel like it was crawling with ants, and his wide, remorseful stare was apology enough. "S'okay."

Delaney glanced over my shoulder, back to where all the children were congregating for the start of their day, and nodded decisively to himself. When he looked back at me, he gave me a soft smirk. "Awesome. Thanks, Ramona. I'll see you tonight." Then, his lips twisted. "Um... can I hug you again?"

My lashes fluttered in surprise, and when his shoulders fell a little, I found myself nodding woodenly. I wasn't going to just kick the large puppy when he was already vibrating with nerves.

This time, I wasn't squished. Just held for a moment that made me feel so calm and full, my own arms wrapped around his back to return the embrace. He was like the morning rays of summer sunshine.

We mutually untwined our arms, and with a last dopey smile at me, Delaney said goodbye. My gaze followed his retreating form that went to start his day, and my chest and belly felt warm, like after eating a favorite meal from my childhood.

Number Eight.

All the way to the car, I pondered the exchange. There was certainly something nice about the body contact—*Am I touch starved?* Was it possible to be when I now had little Wolf pups climbing on me more often than not?

The leather seats of the car burned the backs of my thighs, and I rolled the windows down as I pulled out of the Montessori school. My brother was at work, my sister-in-law gone to a coffee shop to work on her new book, so what was there for me to do?

After grabbing my own coffee and saluting a typing-away Sylvie, I stopped by the pharmacy to pick up one of my prescriptions I had sent here when I moved into my brother's home. After that, there was nothing else to do *but* go home. I knew no one else in town, didn't have anyone worthwhile to get to know.

A blue-stained tongue flitted through my mind, but the image was watery, seen through two panes of glass as we drove away the first night I arrived. Much clearer, though, was his scent. Clove and chiles. Humid nights and spice to roll around in, to revel and be loose in.

I refused to just walk around town until I caught a whiff of it. Even when I caught traces, stating that he was still *somewhere*, what the hell was I going to say if we collided? He'd said no words to me, just done his job, and we'd left.

No, I reasoned with myself, *I need to concentrate on being here, helping my brother's family, and just—moving.*

I pulled into my brother's preferred spot in front of the cabin and cut the car off. The sun was fully bearing down, now, with no clouds to shield me from its burning. My skin was slick beneath my hoodie, and it only barely started cooling when I walked into the icebox that was Orion and Sylvie's home. The scent of it rang strongly of them and their children, and temporarily swirling with... me. It was easy to point out, the thing that only barely belonged, but I was grateful to have a space that was *warm*.

Typically, I posted up on the couch with a book or the TV turned to whatever that could hold my attention. The garden out back was Sylvie's domain, with me only her bumbling assistant, so I didn't dare touch it while she was away. My brother's work shed beside it was locked when he wasn't around, and I knew fuck all about carpentry or woodworking.

There were enough books to keep me occupied for a century or two, but, somehow, it felt like I'd already made it through half of them. I wandered the house aimlessly, feeling the smooth wood, cold tile, and soft rugs beneath my bare feet. Picked up stray toys when I encountered them then returned to my march to keep moving.

They said idle hands are the devil's playthings, and when I crossed through the kitchen again, I felt dark, self-serving desires take hold. I knew where everything was, now, and it would be so easy. With no one home and my quick healing, no one would have to—

I ran out of the house, into the blazing summer heat that felt far too early for May. I let the soles of my feet burn on the patio, my bare legs be slapped and marked by the sun. And when my phone started ringing in my back pocket, only to be an incoming call from my *mother*, I flung my phone away from me. It landed with a soft thud, in the grass somewhere, but there was no way I could handle her, no way I could not reveal where I was or that I'd left everything. And then she would guilt and shame and pull it out of me what I'd done, what I'd tried to do. Then she'd be unbelieving at the same time as trying to drag me back, and it would suffocate me. I could feel it plugging my throat now, going into my lungs, and, and—

My fingers scrabbled at the neckline of my hoodie while my legs carried me to the shimmering water just some feet away. Running, now, I pulled it over my head, felt the phantom-tender scrape against my forearms. At the edge of the lake, I flung down my sweatshirt and unbuttoned my shorts, jumping out of them, uncaring, just needing to feel something, to get the dark haze *off*.

The water wasn't cold, but it was far cooler than the air around me. I kicked up a raucous splash, naked and barely conscious in my panic. With desperate mental hands, I tried my best to pull up my list. The soft lake floor squelched between my toes, usually a wholly unpleasant sensation but now something to cling onto. I went and went until only my head was above water.

"O-one," I recited once it finally, finally became tangible. "The first sip of coffee in the morning. For the taste and ritual of it."

I released my feet from the bottom of the lake, moved my arms until I was floating on my back. I let my front bake under the sun and fought for another breath.

"Two," I said with a hoarse, tear-filled whisper. "A pile of soft blankets and pillows after a hot shower. Three, being called 'Mona'."

I filled my lungs to their capacity, emptied them till there was nothing left. Imagining a square and following the borders with each draw. "Four. Being 'Auntie Mona'." That one elicited a tear that became the water of the lake, accepting and holding my secrets and weakness.

Stuttering and bobbing with the tranquil water, I felt the urge I almost succumbed to shrink and fall back. For now. "Eight. A..." My lip trembled, so I puckered my lips to force the next exhale. "A hug from a stranger."

I was past the point of judging myself for how pathetic it sounded, just let my confession get carried into the leaves hanging above and started again. I recited it like a chant, a prayer, while the world turned and shifted and moved around me. Fish swam below, the birds flew above, and I waited until I felt all the bends of water around my skin. The drops seeping across my scalp and up the sides of my neck.

It could've been minutes. Could've been hours, but when I finally emerged with my list tucked away again, I retrieved my clothes with pruny but steady hands. I refused to look anywhere else, bear witness to other parts of me, lest having to dive into the water again to shock my system.

I reluctantly took up my phone after reminding myself that my brother and sister-in-law also couldn't get in contact with me if I left it in the yard. And the girlish hope that… Dad might call, too.

My shower was long, scalding, and after fully enacting Number Two, I indeed lay down on the guest bed with one of Sylvie's books in hand. Darkness that wasn't mine was welcome, and I reread the story of female rage and gore while I kept myself bound in softness and calm.

CHAPTER TWO

RAMONA

Whatever I'd thought a pack meeting was going to look like, the actual thing was way more pleasant than I had imagined. I kinda just pictured Wolves sitting in the woods surrounding a fire in the ground, eating from a deer they all just killed or something. With my mother barely acknowledging that part of herself at all, and my lack of ability to shift altogether, my firsthand knowledge of Wolf customs was slim.

I recrossed my legs, careful to not bunch up the blanket I sat on. We, actually. Delaney did indeed want to sit with me during the pack meeting, and he had made a beeline to sit beside me. Now, he was leaning forward, hanging on every word that was spoken by my brother.

The meetings rotated locations, to give all who wanted the honor of hosting an opportunity, apparently, and we were now in the sprawling backyard of a Wolf named Tina. Her place was pretty swanky, and the large fire pit we all sat around crackled.

Not every meeting was mandatory, so I didn't think this was everyone, but there were about fifteen members in attendance tonight and about five pups that were running around and playing in the soft grass. Another Wolf named Bill had taken the reins on grilling for everyone—regular burgers and hotdogs, no deer carcasses—and I lifted my own cheeseburger off the paper plate beside me to take a bite.

My brother, Orion, sat on the other side of the fire with his mate, Sylvie, beside him. The bright yellow and orange flames of the fire and the pink tones of the sky above made his pale skin and hair look blushed. I knew from photos and old memories that his father had been more my complexion, but my brother inherited the fair coloring from our mother.

"Now that we've all settled with our food, it may be best to give introductions to welcome our newcomers, as well as to give pack members opportunity to get to know them better." Sylvie shot him a bright smile while my stomach clenched at the thought of having to stand up and speak. "Unless, of course, you all don't want to. I must admit that I'm not the biggest fan of meet-and-greet activities."

A few members chuckled, but no one opposed.

My brother nodded and briefly met my gaze before doing the same with Delaney on my right. I heard him suck in a breath as if Orion was going to lunge or something, and he let loose a relieved exhale when Orion dropped his gaze to the fire. "I am Pack Leader, but you may call me Orion. I've been Leader for three years following the resignation of the previous leader. My father's family led the establishment of this pack, and I am grateful to be given the opportunity to follow in their footsteps. I'm also a professor at Antler Pointe College in the English department. You may come to me with any concerns you have—"

"Just don't call him unannounced unless it's an emergency!" A teenaged Wolf shouted and received another round of laughter. My brother's disdain for talking on the phone was pretty much legendary, and apparently everyone in the pack knew it, too.

Surprisingly, my brother's lip twitched as he rolled his eyes before continuing. "My mate will formally introduce herself, and our pups Dahlia and Oliver are over there playing. All right, who's next?"

The teen that teased my brother scrambled to his feet and stood like he was giving a presentation at school. "Hey! My name's Harrison..." And one by one, the pack members introduced themselves to me and Delaney. It was a bit overwhelming, having the attention on me, but it was nice sharing it with someone else. And, at least, I had something else to occupy my headspace. My fingers pulled anxiously at my sleeve cuffs as I tried my best to nod along to the group of elders that ended the exercise. The reverent hush that befell the circle for them made the expectant turn of every eye to Delaney and me that followed even more terrifying.

A nervous hand clutched mine, fingers squeezing almost painfully but not quite, and I felt my near-panting calm. When I found my brother's light green eyes over the flames, they were planted somewhere on my face, but the small nod of encouragement combined with Sylvie's smile my way made my stomach relax even more.

Just as I opened my mouth, Delaney cleared his throat and started, fingers still holding mine. "H-hi everyone. I'm Delaney, and I'm a student at APC. I wanted to thank all of you for allowing me to attend this meeting. I've been wanting to find a pack again, and I'm very happy to be here." My eyes scanned the gathered Wolves and their mates, taking in the many smiles that returned Delaney's sunny demeanor. *Well,* fuck, *how am I supposed to live up to that?*

I was panicking, worried I would say the wrong thing or make an ass out of myself, and it wasn't until a reassuring squeeze of my hand brought me back to the present. All eyes were on me.

"Um..." I wiped my free palm on my bare thigh, felt sweat prickle at my temples. "Hi everyone. My name's Ramona. I'm staying with my brother and his family," I gestured a hand to O and Sylvie, "and am grateful to be here." That was enough, right?

Judging by the nods and redirecting of attention toward Orion, it was. I sighed. There was no fucking way I was going to remember everyone's names, so their faces and scents would have to do.

My brother took a pull from his beer before continuing the meeting. The sky had continued to darken, the last tangerine rays of the sun just a sliver on the horizon now, and I batted at a mosquito that landed on my ankle. "Before I turn it over for other matters, today, we welcome Ana and Jasper to our meal tonight, following their first run since their punishment has been lifted." Something about the ticking in my brother's jaw and the solemn nods of two Wolves in particular told of a much larger story that no one piped up to explain.

Add that to the running list of things I needed to ask Sylvie about.

"Lastly, myself and a few of the elders are meeting with representatives from the Serafim Group next week. It should just be a courtesy introduction, as they are looking to engage in business on our territory. But we will update you at the next pack meeting."

A middle-aged Wolf with thinning red hair and a barrel chest sat forward. "Any word on that Jaguar? I've seen him down at Vinny's a few times." A few Wolves began murmuring to each other, but the excited lurch and hammering of my heart made it difficult to parse through all that they were saying.

My fingertips tingled with wisps of electricity, calling back to my first evening living in Antler Pointe. Black eyes and the harsh glint of facial piercings were interwoven with the scent of dense brush and spice. With heated nights that were just as likely to intoxicate as they were to heal.

My weeks had been filled with gardening, reading, and family time, so I hadn't caught another glimpse of the shifter. Sure, I could've gone to Vinny's at any point to see if I'd be lucky enough to see him, but then what would I have done?

What was one touch? One—barely—interaction that was even

more brief than the quick intimate touches and conversation with the male who was still holding my hand.

"No word to me, though I don't know if others have had interactions with the Jaguar," my brother replied. When Sylvie, Dahlia, and I had returned home from picking up pizza that night, Orion had been mildly curious about the new shifter in town, but that'd been it.

The red-headed Wolf gave a grunt that was one of the most wolf-like sounds I'd heard all night. "I don't like it. He should come pay respects, at least." Ah, there was the territorial nature I'd been expecting. Not that I thought *all* Wolves would be mindless, but there was a reason packs had the reputation.

When the male looked me up and down with a confused frown, I realized that I'd been scowling at him, eyes narrowed as he insinuated something unsavory about the jaguar shifter. *Who I didn't even fucking know.* I broke our stare to watch my smaller hand being swallowed by Delaney's. When I raised my head, he appeared to be hanging on what my brother said next.

Without so much as a flinch, Orion addressed everyone, including Delaney and me, "We can keep tabs on him, but so far, he's done no harm. Should he wish to join the pack or run permanently on our land, we will establish a more formal connection. I will not punish another shifter for just existing here." A wash of *dominance* settled over my skin, and it made my spine straighten. It wasn't fear, but a response at a cellular level to take notice of the decision being set.

I stared at my brother, wondrously. Though I couldn't change into a Wolf, the threads of otherness within me hummed, and the urge to bow tugged at my muscles.

With me, Orion was dry and teasing. With his mate and children, he was quiet and sweet. I was more than a little ashamed to admit that I hadn't quite been able to visualize my brother as a Leader, in the shifter sense.

His pinning green stare and the scent of Leader coming from him erased all of that. And I felt a new sense of pride at the stance he'd taken. He'd not only found his place but stepped up to take charge of a whole group of people. All these pack members looked to him for support and guidance, something I could tell that he took seriously.

And they not only accepted him—they embraced him for who he was. With the way they all responded to him tonight, leaning in with their attention and familiarity.

Shit, I wiped at a tear that threatened to spill over. If out of love for him or envy, I wasn't so sure.

The Wolf that'd spoken up dropped his gaze with a curt nod, and the air around us thawed. The sound of excited pup-babbling and chirping crickets filtered back in as the meeting continued with all the relaxed attitude of a summer barbecue. After the pups got bored playing their own games, they wandered over to us, and while Dahlia caught the attention of Sylvie, going on about some game they'd made up, Ollie came to me, dirt-caked hands outstretched.

My first pack meeting didn't have a formal adjournment, but the mood palpably moved from meeting to casual gathering. Some stood to mill about the yard with their beverages in hand, some called their goodbyes, and some reclined in their seats, content to continue socializing.

With my nephew in my lap, I felt at least more certain about what to do with my hands, and though my hold on Delaney was broken, he remained close. O had stood and began speaking in quiet, respectful tones to one of the elders who remained seated.

My new acquaintance blew out a breath while offering his finger to Ollie who grabbed it with the iron grip of a one-year old. "That wasn't so bad. Right?"

I tickled my nephew's little belly and hummed my agreement. "Nah, it was good. I think. Not sure how these things are supposed to go."

Delaney rested his elbows on his knees, curling his back inward to make himself smaller. "Well, in my experience, this was great. There's nothing like having a pack to depend on, but it can... go bad really fast."

Ollie cooed happily while I took in this guy that I'd just met today who'd all but decided we were BFF's. Or was I misreading things? Was he attracted to me? Was I attracted to *him*? If I was asking, maybe not. Right?

Ugh.

"Never been in a pack before."

He looked horrified. "Wha—really? I mean, I know we can't shift, but you've got one shifter parent at least, right?" When I nodded, he continued after a quick glance at O, "Your brother seems like a good Leader. Why haven't you been in the pack before now?"

My brow hung low over my eyes as I contemplated the question. Really, I wasn't opposed to the pack life. It was my mother who'd been determined to keep me away from that side of myself as much as possible. And with my abilities leaning more toward strength, healing, and heightened senses, there wasn't *that* much to hide.

"Ah... it's complicated. But I grew up with our mom who is... weird about it." Ollie started wriggling in my arms, pulling at my hold toward Sylvie who was coming our way. When she rounded the fire pit and plopped down in front of us, my nephew abandoned me without a thought.

Delaney didn't ask me to explain more, for that I was grateful, and turned to my sister-in-law with so much gratitude in his brown eyes that they almost glazed over entirely. "Thank you so much for inviting me, Sylvie. I missed this so much."

My sister-in-law, dressed in a swishy dress and sandals, waved off Delaney's words. Without a stitch of shame or propriety, she pulled down the neckline of her dress and guided her pup to her breast. Ollie quickly climbed into her arms, and she gently ran her fingers over his tawny cheek. "Oh, *pfft*. It's no trouble at all. Having new faces is a welcome change."

"Is there anything you need me to do?" I took note of more

people heading out, parents carrying sleepy pups toward their cars as nighttime descended upon us.

Sylvie caressed the soft black curls on her son's head while he breastfed. "Absolutely not. You've already helped so much. Is there anything *we* can do for you?"

Though she was kind, Sylvie was also astute as a mother-fucker, and the way she eyed me, as if peering under my skin to the taped-together heart underneath, threatened to let loose memories of staunch white and loud, overstimulating entertainment rooms.

The two of them said nothing, waiting for me to reply, but all I could muster was a weak, "N-no. I've got everything I need." That didn't feel like a lie.

Did it?

If I were being honest, the thought of returning to the guest room at Orion and Sylvie's cabin, with only the relief of a book or TV binge to knock me out, was making me feel like I was going to suffocate. My skin had been buzzing with restlessness tonight, after hours being crumpled up on my brother's sofa with a book in hand until it was time to pick up the kids. "Actually—do you know when that skatepark closes?" For some wild reason, I'd slung my skates over my shoulder when I fled my apartment in New York, and they'd been sitting at the foot of the guest bed. Apparently, there was no skating rink in Antler Pointe, and my brother's gravel driveway was impossible to practice on.

Sylvie's lips turned down. "Not sure, but I think I remember seeing people there even late into the night. You should be fine. Do you want one of us to go with you?"

"No, I'll be okay. Probably won't be out there long. It might be closed, anyway."

She began to gather her feet beneath her, maneuvering to stand without jostling Ollie who was looking like he'd fall asleep any moment. Delaney and I followed, gathering our things, and he made to start folding up the blanket. "Thank you again for having me. I don't have much going on outside of school, so I'll be at the next meeting—if that's okay?"

My sister-in-law softly rocked her torso from side to side. "Well, we were hoping so! And, I know you're busy at the school and all, but we could always use an extra set of hands with the garden. Ramona and I are there quite a bit."

I couldn't help but snicker. "Don't fall for it. She'll rope you into doing the grunt work while she and her witch friend use their powers for the cool stuff."

Sylvie's face broke into a massive grin, her laugh a lilting melody in the warm night. My lips twitched, but when I caught my brother drifting over like a moth to a flame, a full chuckle bubbled up from my chest.

O put his arms around Sylvie from behind, kissing the top of her head. He'd started sporting a short, trimmed beard since he started as Leader, and the fact that it still remained on his face was a shock I was still getting over. For all of my life, he'd had the same haircut, wore the same sort of clothes, and changed as little about himself or his surroundings as possible. Granted, his haircut and clothes were pretty much the same. But the beard and the look he gave me was like a new version of my brother that I was still just getting to know.

Delaney, who'd joined Sylvie and me in laughing at my joke, had curled even more into himself and cast his eyes downward. What was all that about?

Sylvie craned her neck to get a kiss from my brother, who returned it with a softness that felt too intimate to witness, however quick it might've been. When his eyes met my face, I tried to give a subtle jerk of my head in Delaney's direction, hoping he'd do something.

Orion sighed and straightened from embracing his mate. "We hope you come back, Delaney."

My new… friend sucked in a quick breath, frantic eyes darting back and forth on the grass at his feet. His skittishness was freaking me out a little, and Orion seemed similarly bewildered. His fingers tapped in their usual rhythm at his sides, a tell of when my brother was feeling some surge of energy or overstimulation. By the tightness around his mouth, this time, it was discomfort.

"Um, yes, I was just about to accept your mate's invitation to keep attending. And m-maybe help with the garden, too. If that's okay." I knew that he'd been nervous before, but this was a whole new level. What the fuck had his last pack been like?

Orion frowned. "Why wouldn't it be?"

Delaney bowed his head even further, seemingly panicking at how to approach the question. As if he was worried it was a trick. Before anyone else could answer, Sylvie stretched out a hand. "Honey, do you mind if I touch you?"

That got him to look up, though it was with more silent questions. I already knew what was coming, but his growing trust in my family, despite his hesitance, was clear when he shook his head, blond hair flopping around his ears. Sylvie cupped his face with the barest of touches, and my own body felt the phantom sensation of when she would do the same to me.

No one had bothered to explain the full extent of my sister-in-law's powers, but she'd brought me into a state of grounding calm more than a few times. I knew it was working when Delaney's entire posture relaxed, and tears shimmered around his eyes. My brother watched Sylvie, reverence and love abundantly clear in his scent. Bright and rich like chocolate covered strawberries.

"We're not the sort of pack that thrives on fear, honey. I know it'll take time to get used to, but we want you here. Both of you." She glanced at me, and I felt my own throat get choked up. Fuck, I needed to get out of here. There were too many feelings happening inside and outside of me for comfort.

Delaney stuttered a nod as Sylvie retracted her hand. He ducked his head, muttering a reverberating, "Thank you," to both my brother and his mate. "I'm gonna head out now, but this has been great. Really."

He gave us all an individual smile that had more of that sunniness, and I found myself shuffling my feet back and forth, trying to figure out how to excuse myself, too.

Orion beat me to it. "I heard you saying you wanted to go to the skatepark. Have fun." His dry tone might've sounded like a dismissal to anyone else, but I knew it was a gift to save me from getting dragged into more conversation with the pack members that weren't subtle in their eavesdropping on everything that just transpired.

He tossed me his keys, and I muttered something about seeing them back at the cabin before trying to calm my feet from a full on retreat. With the windows down, I drove the dark streets to the cabin to retrieve my skates before running back outside to drive to the skatepark. Though it read *Closed* at this time on Google Maps, when I pulled up, the white fluorescent lights were still on, illuminating the concrete and colorful graffiti that decorated it.

With my headphones draped around my neck, I kept my head bent toward my task of lacing up and selecting my usual warm-up playlist.

The park was bigger than I'd thought it'd be, with a large bowl in the center, a few ramps of varying sizes, and a multitude of ledges that were waxed and scuffed from use. I rolled over to an open area that was flat and felt the tightness in my muscles and lungs release. Though it'd been months since I'd skated, my body remembered, easily switching to skating backwards and forwards, creating my own path to follow. I crouched low, stretching my thighs, then started up a pattern of pivoting one-footed over and over. The soft indie song drove me, and the rewarding trickles of sweat trailed down my temples and the back of my neck.

Time ceased to matter, and neither did the other skaters that joked and whizzed through the air.

At least, until a familiar spice caressed the edges of my mind, like a tantalizing pass of a firm hand against my spine. Trying not to look like a thirsty idiot, I kept my gaze uncaring and casual while I made another revolution around my little area.

Was I drooling? *Shit.*

It was him. The Jaguar.

I was failing at feigning nonchalance, but who could blame me? He had his head thrown back, laughing at something his somber counterpart said, and his mischievous mirth lit up the air around him. Instead of up like the last time I'd seen him, his hair was down and framing his striking face like the most luxurious of curtains.

Without a care in the world, he grabbed the hem of his shirt and lifted it over his head. I swallowed and forced myself to do a couple spins to make it seem like I wasn't ogling him like a creep. When I righted myself, he and his friend were over near the bowl, clasping hands with some other skaters and chatting with their boards at their feet. What really caught my eye, though, was the extensive collection of intricate tattoos over his whole body. Skulls on the backs of his hands, a flower on the side of his neck, a detailed tree line wrapping around his arm. With his back and shoulder to me, I could see a large, black dragon scaling his spine like the golden-brown tower that it was. Which then made me think of doing the same, and I nearly choked.

Such a strong and immediate attraction to someone *never* happened to me. If I'd questioned for a second whether I wanted Delaney, nothing could compare to the way this shifter was short-circuiting all my mental faculties.

But it wasn't just his body that was calling to me. As solid and loose as it was. No, the way I could still see the glint of dark amusement in his black eyes, despite the distance of concrete between us, left me nearly panting for more. He'd been locked down at Vinny's that night, but as he shared a beer with his friends, I wanted nothing more than to be over there, to be… seen by him.

And when he turned over his shoulder, meeting my stare head-on and refusing to look away, I nearly fucking tripped over my own skates. The Jaguar grinned, white teeth looking blunt without a hint of the fangs I knew that he had. With a wink and a nod, he went back to his group, but for the rest of the few hours I stayed at the skatepark, I felt that same caress running down my back, my cheek, my neck.

CHAPTER THREE

RAMONA

I fought the urge to push my sleeves to my elbows, gritting my teeth as they, inevitably, became dirty from the garden soil. The sun was mercifully obscured behind a sheet of gray clouds, and I held the pruning sheers steady. With Sylvie's instructions in my mind, I snipped the stem of the ripe jalapeño pepper that had surpassed green and was beginning to turn red. I passed it from my gloved hand and tossed it into the wicker basket beside me.

"Aren't these usually green? Does red mean there's something wrong with them?" I asked absently, bobbing my head to the light music playing from the bluetooth speaker.

My sister-in-law remained facing the tomato plants that grew on wooden trellises against the old white house. I paused my harvesting to watch her run an assessing hand over the fruit. Though the warm weather and summer storms helped the garden tremendously, sometimes she would break out her powers to help the spoils ripen.

Or just for fun. Either way, I watched small, barely-there tomatoes turn into full, plump globes at her silent command. The breeze rustled the curls that escaped her topknot, as if an equally silent acknowledgment from the earth.

She barely had to give the tomatoes a twist before they released into her palm, and she placed them in her own basket. "No, when they turn red, the flavor changes a bit. Your brother likes the sweeter and spicier taste for certain dishes, so I promised that I'd let some ripen a bit longer for him this time."

I nodded, turning back to gathering all the peppers that were how my brother had requested. After riding with Sylvie to drop the babies off, we'd spent the morning at her grandmother's old house, where the air seemed charged, humming with some energy that I couldn't name. It wasn't unsettling, necessarily, but like the amplified version of how it felt to be around shifting Wolves or Sylvie when she performed a spell.

Though it was still blistering hot, the simple work held the fog at bay to where it was only tendrils of gray at the edges of my thoughts. Stirring and muttering despondence at all hours, all times. Here, though, it was overpowered. Even with my muscles tense from hours bent over tending to the plants, hot air pressing on me from all sides, I was... content.

At least, until I pulled my arm from the basket, settling in to snip off another pepper, and saw the giant fucking spider on the back of my hand.

"Holy fuck!" I squealed, trying to fling the ginormous black and yellow terror off of me. The embarrassing squeals and whimpers were inescapable, and apparently, so was the spider. The thought of squishing it was equally as unpleasant, and I shot up, stamping my bare feet and wiggling my arm, trying to get it off, off, off.

Sylvie came running over, hands outstretched. "What's wr—be careful!"

"No, no, please, get it off, that's fucking huge—"

"Shh, shh, she didn't mean it." To my express horror, Sylvie steadied my forearm with a touch that was strong enough to stop my squirming. She offered a palm, to which the spider quickly retreated and settled. To take that a step further, Sylvie passed a gentle fingertip over the spider's back, *and leaned her ear closer to it.*

I shook out my arms, knocking off the imaginary spiders that were crawling all over me. Sure, the depression was far from my mind *now*, but it was replaced with watching my sister-in-law whisper and listen to the vile thing. Was this worse? Yeah, this was worse.

Sylvie nodded down at the spider, as if they'd come to an agreement, which was crazy. My heart was still threatening to beat out of my ribcage, and when she extended her arm a little, to let me get a better look at the thing, I scrambled back a good three steps. Or ten.

"This is Petunia. She said she's sorry for scaring you." I swatted at my arms again, making sure there weren't like— fucking *eggs* or something on me. "She's lived here for a while now. Since Josie and I enhance the garden through the winter, she's survived the past two freezes here and helps us a lot by munching on the pests."

My hand was absolutely not shaky when I ran it along my scalp, trying to calm my breathing. "This is crazy. Sylvie, you're talking to a spider who could have *killed me.*"

The spider was crawling around her forearm, like it didn't have a care in the world. No, I knew crazy, and this was down-right insane.

"Uh, it's about as crazy as your brother and mother being able to turn into wolves. And I *am* talking to her. She was just curious. She was born here, and she's never met someone that's afraid of spiders before." *Petunia* trailed down to Sylvie's fingers that were a shade or two darker than mine and stayed still while Sylvie lowered her back into the garden bed. I kept my eyes on the black and yellow thing, making sure that it continued to wander away from me.

Realizing that I'd almost scrambled out of the garden area completely, I took a step closer. Sylvie laughed, and I frowned, slowly returning to my basket. "You know, Ollie lets her take rides on his shoulder while he runs around."

Just the thought of that made me shudder and compulsively check that mine were spider-free. "And my brother allows that? You truly have him in your thrall."

She fluttered her fingers in my face, giggling loud and light when I batted them away. "You better believe it."

I scoffed, and after triple checking that no spiders were laying in wait, I got back to work while Sylvie wove through the plants, boosting with magic any that looked like they needed a little something. Which, there wasn't much, but the heat these past few days had been pretty brutal with summer in full swing. The garden behind the cabin was tended more regularly, but from what I understood, this was her grandmother's garden, a decades-old endeavor that she was determined to keep thriving.

After I had a basket full of jalapeños, the plants had all been watered and pruned, and we were both slick with sweat, our rhythm was broken by Sylvie's phone ringing.

I gathered our tools, packing up for the day.

"Okay, baby. Are you sure you're okay?" That got my attention. Orion and the elders were supposed to be meeting with the Serafim Group today. I'd overheard my brother discussing more details about the shifters who were looking to open a few locations of their business on Antler Pointe Pack territory, and I was guessing by the concern in Sylvie's voice, it hadn't gone as well as they'd hoped.

Fully leaning into my eavesdropping, I stilled and could make out what my brother was saying on the other end. The acoustics of the call were as if he was in the car. He sighed. "I'm fine. We're going back to Vera's to discuss all we learned today. Are you sure you don't mind picking Dahlia and Ollie up from school?"

"Of course not. Do you need anything?"

His blinker clicked beneath his voice. "No. I love you."

Sylvie's smile was soft as she fiddled with the delicate gold necklace she wore. "I love you, too, baby." They exchanged more routine information before hanging up, about when O expected to have dinner ready and their desire to both read to the babies tonight, and I mentally added this to my list. Number Ten felt heavy, in a good and somber way. My brother, though busy with all his responsibilities, was happy and loved, and it was a blessing to be witness to it.

I screwed my face like I'd tasted something bad—*that spider has truly fucked with me.*

She hung up with my brother, and once we had all our things put back in the small and neatly organized shed, we locked up the house and filed into Sylvie's car and started toward the Montessori school. Full, dark clouds started to push away the lighter wisps that'd covered the sky earlier. Even with the windows up, I could feel the thickening in the air with the impending afternoon storm.

Flyers reminding parents of the quickly approaching end of the school year lined the sidewalk and entryway leading inside, and a worried thought lodged in my throat before I swallowed it back down. Sure, I wouldn't be taxying the babies to and from school, but summer break would involve having to entertain them even more, right? Yeah, no, it'd be cool.

We were allowed back, closer to the main space that held the most play and learning areas. All the furniture was child-sized and a pale wood that provided a subtle undertone to the splashes of colorful toys, books, and plants that lined the windows. The older children had more formal classrooms, and I absently remembered that Delaney had said that was the age group he worked with.

"Mama!" There were at least two children shouting for their mothers, but I could pick out Ollie's voice and scent anywhere. It was a perfect combination of my brother and Sylvie's—a calm and cloudy winter morning just before snowfall.

He was an early walker but managed to not fall as he tottered over to us. Dahlia must've heard or sensed our arrival because she was quick to make her way over, beating Ollie with her much more coordinated sprint. Her scent was slightly different than her brother's, the height of a cold and bright afternoon.

We checked both children out for the day and made our way to the car. They babbled excitedly, Dahlia in full sentences and Ollie with his own baby noises and screeches, and I settled into the passenger seat, content to listen and let their happiness stand in for my own.

While rain sprinkled lightly upon us, I helped Sylvie get them in the house, their snacks prepared and presented, and coerced them both to short naps to tide them over until bedtime. Dahlia, thankfully, didn't fight it, but she tried to stall as we walked her to her bedroom.

"Auntie Mona, what are those?" She pointed a little finger that I followed toward the front door. I craned my neck to see what was new, what she might not be able to identify, and all I came up with were my pink roller skates. I supplied her with the name after picking her up. Her lips pursed in toddler contemplation, and I startled with how much she looked like my brother. Her red french braids bumped against her shoulders as I walked her down the hall and into her room. "Can I try?" she asked while I tucked her on top of her comforter and reached for her blanket at the foot of the small bed.

"Well, they're my size, so they're too big for you." I braced myself for her to start begging to have her own pair, but instead, she pouted and nodded sleepily. I gave her a quick kiss on her head and left her to sleep off the hours at school.

But as Sylvie and I sat on the patio, enjoying the last patters of the quick summer storm, I kept turning over what Dahlia said. I'd gotten my first pair of skates when I was around her age. While I'd learned in the smooth, sprawling driveway at home and at the rink, I might be able to teach her the basics at the park.

Eventually, my brother came home, greeting me with a grunt and Sylvie with a kiss before he started his own routine that helped him reset after a day of work. When he came back outside with his two wide-awake pups, I watched him play and tire them out all over again in the yard.

We ate dinner out there, sandwiches with homemade bread and fruit and chips. Number Five was one of my favorites, and I focused in on the scents of my brother's land. The people, the earth, the heat. Let it fill me until there was no room for anything else.

"Did Vera's go well? Is everything all right?" Sylvie asked while the kids ran about the yard, trying their best to catch fireflies. Dahlia tried to direct her brother who just swatted aimlessly at the glowing insects.

Orion leaned back in the patio chair and ran a hand up the back of his neatly trimmed hair. "As well as it could've. We declined their initial request, but that's not to say they'll be leaving anytime soon. The elders selected Jasper to be our eyes and ears while their representatives are in the area."

I saw a muscle tick at the corner of his jaw as he informed us, but I had little to no context about what could cause such a stir of irritation in him. Sylvie nodded along, though, so it must've been something she was well aware of. "What are they wanting to do?"

Orion's arms rested on the tabletop, fingers tapping away at the metal in a steady and fast rhythm. "To do business here. An office location and a bar as far as everyone will be aware. But I reached out to other packs, and they're known for... darker dealings. Human and otherwise. I don't want to bring that here."

Sylvie rested a hand on his back and offered a reassuring smile. I watched as tension left my brother's shoulders, his tapping somehow taking on a calmer, happier note than the palpable distress from before.

"Sounds like you made a good decision, O. Don't want them running like... vampire-grade guns or something. If that's even a thing. Wait—" My eyes widened. "*Is* that a thing?"

Orion pursed his lips and thought for a moment. "They're mostly shifters. But supernatural-grade weapons and drugs seem to be how they make the majority of their money. If our contacts are to be believed. They've twisted the arms of many packs up and down the east coast. Roping them in one way or another."

A knot of sympathy twisted in my stomach. How my brother had been able to juggle all of his responsibilities was a mystery to me, let alone dealing with a fucking—shifter mob. I didn't think the Pack Leader life was easy, but this was starting to sound dangerous.

"Well, you've got a witch that gossips with spiders and a sister that's at least reliable in a brawl. It'll be fine." Not like a few years of boxing and marital arts were much of a match for fighting shifters with guns, but that and a little levity were all I could offer.

In a rare moment of humor, O snorted and rolled his eyes. The smile that ghosted his lips spoke volumes. "It's better than nothing."

"Hey!" Sylvie shot him a narrow-eyed look. "I'll start snatching out hearts, and then maybe you'll give me my flowers."

I had no idea what the fuck they were even talking about, but Sylvie and I were able to get my brother distracted enough from pack stuff, even drawing out a few chuckles. And when the kids came over with fireflies cradled carefully in their palms, we cooed over their efforts.

Yes, Number Five was one of the best.

CHAPTER FOUR

RÍO

"You put any up by your place?" Tyler picked through the stack of flyers for our show and stapled one to the bulletin board by the skate spot entrance. There were a bunch of old, tattered flyers from shows and events passed, and I ripped them down while he stapled up a few more for good measure.

"Yup." I balled up the trash and tossed them into the big, overflowing can on our way inside. I dropped my board to the ground and hopped on, kicking lazily against the concrete to keep moving forward.

Until I caught a whiff of wintry sweet and sour, that was. Then, I almost stumbled and wiped out over fucking nothing. Ty glanced up at me with his own board tucked into his side. He raised a brow, silently asking me what the fuck was wrong with me all of a sudden, but I didn't give a response.

My chest was tight as I tried to restrain myself from looking over at the Wolf girl and keep my Jaguar from doing something reckless just because she was here again.

Usually, she arrived at night, but a few days ago, she'd started to come earlier in the day. Maybe she'd been doing that for longer, but work mostly had me tied up at this hour. What did it say about me that I made sure to be here, at this time, on my day off? And drag my nocturnal friend with me for reinforcements.

He groused about the heat and pulled his hat lower on his brow. Good thing the legends got that part wrong, because I'd feel bad if my stupidity and his being a decent friend made him burst into flames. "Fucking hot as shit," he grumbled while we found a bench that was in the shade. Luckily for me, Tyler was high up enough as the owner of his family's funeral home that he pretty much went into work whenever he felt like it and took care of things from home if he wanted to. Left him free to skate when I had the itch but also needed the backup.

To give me the confidence to finally talk to her or keep me from doing it, I still wasn't sure.

"You got me here, so let's hand these out, too." There was a decent crowd, despite it being in the middle of the day, but I guessed that was thanks to it being summertime. Teens, college kids, and townies were shooting the shit and dropping into the bowl. Grinding on the rails and working on their latest tricks.

Now that I'd joined the band, it was back to performing after their last guitarist moved away. I'd never really played in one before, just messed around on my Iceman alone, but I had to admit. It was nice, and Brody and Jess were cool, too.

Tyler and I split up with a stack of flyers each. I dapped up a few skaters I recognized, talked up our show that was next week and featuring three other bands. And what of it that my arc around the park brought me closer and closer to the girl with the prettiest pair of legs I'd ever fucking seen? Her tight jean shorts ended right below the curve of her ass while her hoodie covered everything else but her neck, face, and hands.

Those honey eyes hadn't looked up at me at all, but was I hallucinating the stiffening of her shoulders as soon as I'd caught sight of her and the pup on the far side of the park where the ground was flat?

The pup with red pigtail braids and a green helmet to match her skates and pads was clinging onto the Wolf girl's hand as she walked them in slow circles. The little girl couldn't have been older than five or six, but she was catching on pretty well. The first time I'd seen them, she was still getting used to standing on shifting wheels, but now, she was able to shuffle along while her aunt guided her across the smooth surface.

I absently handed out more flyers while listening to what the Wolf girl was saying, clear as the deepening sky above. "You got it, Dolly. Yup, remember what you need to do if you wanna slow down? Yeah, yeah, good job!"

A smile pulled across my face as I listened to her teach and encourage the pup. A guy I'd given a few pointers to on his kick flip asked about the show, so I talked about our newest set, pulled out my phone so he could hear a little bit of our latest song.

He nodded along to the music and took a picture of the flyer I held out so he'd remember the details. Jess ran the Instagram profile she'd convinced Tyler to agree to us starting, so I directed him to that. I was gonna have to figure out how to make sure my photo didn't show up on the page or any of the videos, and I cursed myself again for my bright fucking ideas causing more problems.

When I turned around to seek out the next person to invite to the show, I froze and had to clench my jaw. Tyler was talking to her. He was gesturing to the flyer, talking about the bar we were performing at, and my feet were already marching me closer to them. When his eyes lifted to track my advance, he pointed at me, dead center in my chest. "Yeah, here's our new lead guitar right here."

And then she looked up at me, those eyes lighting mine up like golden rays of sweet and decadent honey. Her braid cascaded down her chest, curly tendrils plastered against her temple with sweat. She blinked a few times, chewed on those luscious lips I just wanted to bite and lick and—

A loud squeak snapped against my trance, and the pup was

sprawled out on the concrete. She took a tumble over her wheels, and even though her pads certainly took the brunt of the fall, I could already smell the welling of tears before she started to whimper. Probably more out of surprise and embarrassment than pain since we shifters were pretty tough.

Her aunt shot down to the ground, checking her over for injuries, and I crouched a few feet away, unable to not respond to the little girl looking around with wide, leaking eyes. Her lip trembled while her aunt petted her back and gave her reassurances.

"Hey, pipsqueak," I cooed. "You're all right."

They both turned to look over at me. The Wolf girl glared for a second, like I was being a dick and making fun of her niece. But I pressed on. "Fallin' hurts, but I've seen you learning fast. We all wipe out, and it can be scary. But you've got it. Yeah?"

She sniffed and wiped a scraped hand over her cheek. Luckily, it wasn't bleeding. She nodded and managed to give a shaky smile. Mine in return was wide and encouraging. Even though I healed fast, falling was definitely something you had to get used to, and she'd just started. I extended my fist her way, and she perked up, turning around fully to do the same. "You're a skater, now. Which means you're brave. We gotta be pretty special do this stuff and get back up every time we wipe out." With the Wolf girl and Tyler both boring holes into me with their stares, I slowly led the pup through a simple handshake. She was the youngest kid out here, one of three females, and the only one with safety gear on.

We did the handshake I made up on the spot—a fist bump, two claps, and some finger wagging before a final dap—a few times more before she seemed to have the hang of it. "All right, pipsqueak. Remember the right way to fall, and do what she says. 'Kay?"

The three of us stood, and the Wolf girl took extra care to steady the pup back on her wheels. With no more tears, she beamed up at me. "'Kay."

Tyler cleared his throat, and the Wolf girl was still eyeing me warily as she snatched the flyer from his stack. "Yeah. So, the show will start at eight, but doors open at seven. See you around." She nodded as Tyler pulled away, and I hesitated. She was gorgeous, proper with the elegant way she always twirled on her skates. Even with her perfectly white sneakers and designer hoodie today, she had a depth that I was itching to dive into.

The pup started to pull on her hand, trying to urge her to keep going with her lesson, so I forced myself to take a step back. It was for the best that I put some space between us. She watched me go, heart a quick patter in her chest that matched mine. "See ya around, rich girl."

Her lashes fluttered before settling on a sharp look and delicate sneer. Her gaze swept me up and down, and her heart started beating an even sweeter, faster pattern. My nose was good, and that cold grapefruit darkened with wisps of desire that had me downright grinning.

I spun on my heel, leapt onto my board, and rolled after Ty. I wondered if she would taste just as sweet and sour, too.

CHAPTER FIVE

RAMONA

"**Y**ou really don't have to come if you don't want." I chewed at my lip while I watched Sylvie work the edges of her hair into stylized little curls and loops. She set down the little toothbrush she'd been using and tied a satin scarf to set her edges.

"*Pfft*, are you kidding? I haven't been to a show in forever. It'll be fun!"

My lips threatened to curve up into a smile, but I just managed to tamp it down. I leaned against the counter in Sylvie and Orion's bathroom and watched my sister-in-law start on her makeup. She rifled through a black makeup bag and pulled out an eyeshadow palette and a tube of mascara. She opened the palette and glanced at me in the mirror before us. "Are you not going to get ready?"

I looked down at my ripped denim shorts and sweatshirt. Sylvie was still in her sweatpants and t-shirt, but I'd seen the slinky dress she'd laid out on the bed. "Uh, I—I thought this was good?"

It was a metal show at a dive bar downtown, so I hadn't even thought about dressing up. But watching Sylvie apply reds and blacks around her eyes made me start to rethink my strategy. It'd been so long since I'd wanted to… be noticed. And there was no denying that my sister-in-law was beautiful. Unnaturally so. Would I just look like a washed up slob next to her?

Sylvie smoothed mascara over her lashes, and with the grungy eyeshadow she'd applied, her eyes looked hauntingly large. "Tell me something." I tensed. She took a dark liner, traced the contours of her lips, and blended it with a red-tinted gloss that made her look even witchier. "While I was giving Dahlia a bath the other day, she mentioned you acting funny around some guy at the skatepark. This show wouldn't have anything to do with him, would it?"

The back of my neck began to sweat, and I had the irrational urge to run away. Who knew my niece would be a little traitor?

She rolled her eyes when I refused to answer. "Do what you want, but if you'd like help getting ready, I'd be more than happy to."

Eyeing the makeup on the counter and the pretty yet simple enhancements Sylvie had done to her face, I bit my lip. When the shifter's friend had handed me a flyer for their show tonight, I didn't even want to admit to myself how eager I'd been. To see him aside from the glimpses I got of him flying through the air and laughing with his buddies. Maybe I'd be able to sit with him at the bar. Or… I didn't know, do *something*.

"I don't, um. I don't have a lot here, but that'd be cool, I guess."

Sylvie's eyes almost fucking sparkled as she grinned, and I had to again fight the urge to run. My mom had long ago given up trying to fuss with my hair and force me into clothes that she deemed ladylike and appropriate, so I was tensing for this experience to be more of the same. It wasn't that I didn't like getting dressed up, but the times I *had* let other people dress me or do my makeup, I'd never felt like myself.

Sylvie guided me to sit on the closed lid of the toilet and

looked over my face and hair with lips pursed. Coming to some sort of conclusion while I tried to look anywhere else but her, she asked, "So, what kind of look would you want to go for?"

I blinked rapidly, trying to catch up to the question. "Ah… something simple, I guess?"

She nodded. "M'kay. Your eyes are really pretty, so I was thinking about some dark eyeshadow to make them pop. How do you feel about blush?"

I gaped like a fish and croaked, "It's fine."

"And your hair? Do you feel better with it down or up?"

It was in a mess around my shoulders, right now, but thinking it through, I felt a little more confident when I let her know that I wanted it down. The shifter had only seen me with it pulled back in a braid so far, and I wanted to do something different. When I'd been able to tame it, my hair could look decent, at least.

Sylvie nodded again, brow furrowed like she was on a mission, and she darted out of the bathroom without saying a word. I watched her leave and heard a rustling in her bedroom. Before she came back, a little pattering on the wooden floor preceded Dahlia sticking her head into the doorway and giving me a curious look up and down.

Her mother came back with a short skirt and a black, long-sleeved shirt in her hands. "How about this? I think they'll fit you."

She moved closer toward me, clothes extended in my direction, and I reached up a hand to touch the silver accents on the skirt. They were simple but striking enough to not be boring. Thankfully, she'd picked up my wearing full sleeves without asking any questions about it, and I swallowed the thick lump in my throat. "Yeah, that looks good."

Sylvie gave me a kind smile, and I understood what my brother went on about when he mentioned his mate's sweetness. And it was rubbing off on me, because I felt my own smile rise in response.

She draped the clothes over a free area on the counter and

turned back to me. "Sweetheart," she spoke at Dahlia behind her, "can you go get me your hair stuff from your room, please?"

Dahlia let out a little, "Okay," and scampered out of the room while Sylvie started running her fingers over my hair. The big, dense curls were a far cry from my mom's pin-straight locks, and if I wasn't entrusting them to the hands of an experienced hairstylist, it was easier a lot of the time to just plait them out of the way.

Sylvie retrieved a glass spray bottle from the wooden cabinets beneath the counter and held it up to me with a questioning raise of her brows. I bit my lip and nodded, and she got to work.

After she wet my hair, Sylvie slowly started on my curls, and when Dahlia came running back into the bathroom with a jar of curl cream in her little hands, Sylvie began smoothing the product into the strands. Though there were some nasty knots in there, her fingers were gentle, and at some point, I'd closed my eyes, relaxing into the way she worked on my hair.

"Oooh." Dahlia's voice broke my trance, and I fluttered my eyes open to find Sylvie twirling her finger around the shorter locks framing my face. She then took large handfuls of my hair, scrunched them to encourage the curls, and let them fall around my shoulders and down my back.

I still hadn't looked at myself in the mirror, but I continued to stay still while Sylvie went to her makeup bag and pulled out a new brush and swiped it in a pot of shadow. I closed my eyes obediently and tried my best to keep still.

Luckily, Sylvie wasn't like Mom or the makeup artists she hired over the years, because it took about five minutes for my sister-in-law to brush the color on my lids and swipe some liquid blush on my cheekbones. Lastly, she dipped her finger in a jar of Vaseline, and I tilted my mouth up toward her. She dabbed it on my lips and pulled back.

She looked at me with a satisfied grin, and Dahlia's face was a cute echo of her mother's. Sylvie opened her hands toward me, and I looked at them, confused. After a moment, I settled my palms over hers and let her bring me to a stand. She pulled me back toward the mirror, but I hadn't been prepared for *this*.

My hair fell in buttery ringlets around my face and cascaded down my back and shoulders. Black shadow smoked around my eyes, making their light color sharper, and the delicate blush made me look more alive, somehow. I didn't remember ever admitting to Sylvie that I had a weird aversion to anything other than balm on my lips, but she'd somehow known what to do. The Vaseline made my lips look poutier.

I examined my face and hair, tilting my head this way and that, admiring what Sylvie had done. My hair would dry, getting softer and bigger, but the way she'd set it left the smile on my face. For once, I was done up, *and* I felt like myself. The makeup didn't swallow my features or comically exaggerate them.

With an encouraging pat on my back, Sylvie steered Dahlia out of the bathroom and closed the door to let me change.

I unbuttoned and unzipped my shorts first, switching them out with the miniskirt that was a good fit. My hips were a little narrower than Sylvie's. If I had to guess, the skirt was meant to be higher on the waist, but on me, it settled around my navel. I lifted my sweatshirt a little, and did a little turn in front of the mirror. My legs looked nice and long under the short hem, and it hugged my ass in all the right ways.

Satisfied with that part, at least, I took a deep breath, and pulled my sweatshirt up and over my head. I eased it slowly, trying my best not to ruin my makeup or my hair, and tossed it to the floor. My lace bralette was pretty but not anything special, and the silver bellybutton ring I'd gotten in a rebellious fit at seventeen matched the decorative details on Sylvie's skirt.

As much as I tried not to look at them, the deep scars running along my inner arms were an ugly sight. I shoved on the shirt as quickly as I could while still being careful to not ruin Sylvie's hard work.

It was oversized and cropped at the same time, and the boxy silhouette was familiar and comforting. The hem of the shirt just met the waistband of the skirt, and when I twisted or raised my arms, a sliver of my belly showed. At least that wasn't a part of my body that I was insecure about.

After a few more twirls in front of the mirror, I opened the door and stepped out into Sylvie and Orion's bedroom.

Sylvie was doing her final twirls in front of a full-length mirror near the closet, and Dahlia was running up and down the length of the wall of windows, engaged in her own imaginary play. When I made a few tentative steps toward her, Sylvie turned her head and gave me another approving grin.

"I'm so glad the clothes fit. You look great!" Her praise made me blush, and I hoped the redness was disguised by the makeup she'd put on my face. Sylvie smoothed a hand over the sleeveless dress she'd put on that hugged her curves and ended about mid-calf. A pair of combat boots rested against the double doors to the closet, so I figured those were the shoes she'd decided to go with.

She gave herself one last once-over and grabbed a small fanny pack that'd been thrown on the large bed. I almost laughed at the outdated thing, but when Sylvie buckled it around her waist, further accentuating her curves, and settled it into place, the snicker died in my throat. It was black, to match our outfits, and I had to admit. It looked good with her dress and was a smart way to avoid holding onto a purse all night.

"All right, are you about ready?" She opened up and dug in the fanny pack. After checking her phone and putting it back, she bent down to pick up her shoes. "We've got time to grab a drink and find a good spot, I think."

I tucked my hair behind my ears and took a breath. "Yeah, that sounds good. Just gotta grab my phone and wallet from the room."

"Okay. Come on sweetheart, Auntie Mona and I are gonna say bye to Ollie and Daddy then go to the concert."

We left the bedroom as I grumbled, "It's not really a concert."

I heard more than saw Sylvie roll her eyes. "A show, whatever. I'm the one who actually likes heavy metal, you know."

After retrieving my things from the guest room, I followed Sylvie and Dahlia up the hall and into the living room. The light of the few lamps turned on in the large space was low enough to be cozy, and the record player that ran at nearly all hours of the night played my brother's preferred mellow Motown rhythm.

Orion was sitting with Ollie before the unlit fireplace. They were both on a little play mat with toys strewn about, and Ollie was in his pajama onesie. Even though it was almost his bedtime, my nephew looked cheerful as he lifted and rattled a brightly colored ring before tossing it to the floor.

Dahlia pattered over to her brother, but Orion stilled at the sight of Sylvie beside me. He rose to his feet, and it was like they were the only two in the room. My brother was in some sort of weird trance.

When his tongue swiped at his bottom lip, I'd had more than enough and made my way to the little bench near the front door.

While I laced up my boots, aside from the music and the soft noise of Dahlia directing Ollie on how to play with his toys, I heard Orion and Sylvie's heated whispers.

"I *swear*, baby, if you ruin this dress when I get back, so help me."

"Why would I when you look like this in it?"

Sylvie scoffed. "Because I know you won't want to bother with the tiny zipper, and you've ripped to shreds plenty of my clothes at this point. I'm on to you, Dr. Gealach."

"Well, what if I just lift it up, then?" *Aanndd* that was my cue. Though I'd never admit it to him, I was extremely happy that my brother had found a mate like Sylvie. But, my god, they were disgusting to be around sometimes.

"You ready, Sylvie?" I hollered over to them and stood. Luckily, I'd packed my old, worn-in boots during the frantic dash out of my apartment back in New York. With my arms still wrapped in bandages and my head foggy, I'd frustratedly ripped through my clothes, stuffing my go-to's in my bags and only snagging the shoes that were sitting by the front door. Faced with piles of expensive fabric I'd hardly worn, I couldn't see the point of… any of it.

The shifter not even asking me for my name at the skate spot was one thing. But the accurate nickname made me feel all kinds of annoyed and frustrated.

Sylvie and my brother made their way over while my niece and nephew stayed bickering and giggling in the living room. Orion and Sylvie both had evident blushes on their cheeks, and I didn't even want to fucking know. I'd been living alone long enough to kind of forget what it was like living with married people. And though the soundproofing they'd done a few years ago was good, it obviously couldn't be absolute, what with having kids.

"Okay, baby, I love you." Sylvie smacked a kiss on my brother's cheek, and we switched places on the bench. Her boots looked about as old as mine, and when I took in both of our outfits, I realized for the first time that we were matching.

She stood, and I patted my pockets before my brother opened the door for us. "Pssh, never opened the door for me before," I muttered on my way past.

"I open it for Sylvie," he said with no other explanation or pleasantry.

"Bye, Mommy! Bye, Auntie Mona!" Dahlia yelled from inside, and Sylvie and I called our goodbyes back.

"Be safe, you two. Call me if you need me to come get you."

Sylvie walked to the driver's side of her shiny red car, and the door unlocked at her touch. After reaching inside, she unlocked it the rest of the way, and I slipped into the newer SUV. The leather was still warm against my bare legs, and as soon as she pushed the start button, the air conditioning and music blasted in our faces.

We both flinched, and Sylvie turned some knobs until the volume was comfortable and rolled down the windows. With a few glances in the rearview, she turned us around to proceed up the drive and toward town. The sun still hadn't fully set, and the burnt orange color in the sky chased us through the dark cast by the lush canopy of trees. I sucked in the air that raced past us and tasted the aroma of my brother's homeland. What was it like to belong so deeply somewhere that the land sang to the same melody as your soul?

Even Sylvie, who, as far as I knew, wasn't tied to the land in the way Orion's family through his father was, had some sort of pull to it. It was almost like the trees, the brush, and the *essence* of the forest bended toward her, ready to listen. A small but bright smile was pulling at her lips, and though she'd slicked her hair up as tightly as possible, a few strands bobbed and swayed as if answering back.

She skipped to the next song on her playlist and a harsh guitar solo filled the speakers. I tucked my hair behind my ears. "Going to a metal show in a mom car is kinda weird," I deadpanned.

Sylvie released a tinkling little laugh. "My idea of a Wednesday night, if you ask me."

She shoved me lightly on my shoulder as she turned onto the road leading to town. A few cars sped past us, and I could practically feel my hair growing in volume as it air-dried. "Are you sure you'll be able to peel yourself away from the crotch-goblins for a few hours?"

She shrugged, but instead of saying something smart back, she answered earnestly, "I've been out and about without them, but I'll miss tucking them in tonight." I remained silent, feeling bad for teasing her about something I had no idea about, and the heavy music filled the space between us.

We started to hit more and more traffic, and soon we were surrounded by buildings and shopfronts instead of clusters of trees and the odd house or private drive or two. My stomach began to flutter as we continued through the narrow downtown streets that were a grid of one-lane roads which was annoying and stupid. I drummed my fingers on my knee while we drove around, eyes scanning for a parking spot.

"There." I pointed at a lucky opening someone was pulling out of. After crossing a lane to get there, Sylvie pulled us in and shut the car off.

Before she could protest, I shot out of the car, pulling my slim wallet from my back pocket. With a quick swipe, I put as much money on the meter as I could, and after the confirming beep that the charge went through, I let Sylvie lead me down the sidewalk toward the dive bar.

I ran my hands over my front and back, making sure my outfit wasn't riding up or pulling in a weird way. After a minute or two, Sylvie made a turn and pushed open an old, beaten wooden door that led into darkness. Cool air settled over my skin, and the universal smell of alcohol and cigarettes made me feel nostalgic.

The walls were painted a dark umber, and band posters and weird knickknacks decorated the walls and side tables. The old couches and scarred wood tables were nearly filled with Antler Pointe townies.

A hand clamped around my fingers, and Sylvie pulled me in the direction of an empty curved couch in a deep fuchsia color. I tried to focus in on my anticipation instead of the thin thread of disgust at the less-than-clean furniture that met the skin of my bare legs.

"Okay, what do you want to drink?"

I floundered, trying to think of all the possibilities, but I apparently was taking my own sweet time, because Sylvie just nodded and patted my leg. "Okay, I'll get you a beer. Be back!"

Before I could insist that I treat *her* to a drink since this was my excursion, after all, she was already lost in the crowd that was filling the bar floor. I scanned the space, feeling out of place until glancing at my outfit and realizing that, okay, my sister-in-law did know what she was talking about. Everyone was dressed in black and denim, the makeup was sparse or dark, and the looks were somehow severe and good-natured at the same time.

By the time Sylvie wound her way through the crowd and back to me, she'd already been stopped a few times to chat, and her smile was pulled high.

"Okay, I just got you one of my favorites. Hope it's okay." I took the proffered can and was met with a light and tangy fizz, like blackberries.

"Yeah, this is good. Thanks. I'll get the next round."

She waved my offer away. "Hush, I kept my tab open."

Well. As I was planning a way to pay her back, the lights around us began to dim, and a round of cheers and hollers started in a wave, cresting in a few screams when the members of the band began to step out.

The drummer and bassist I didn't recognize, but next came the pale, soft face of the vampire who'd given me the show flyer at the skatepark. His eyeliner was heavier now, making his eyes sunken craters to offset the softness of his round cheeks and tapered chin. A ladder of piercings up his ears and one in his lip set off the look as he sauntered to the microphone, center stage.

My eyes ran frantically back and forth on the stage, *where is he where is he*—"Thanks for coming out." The vampire's voice was deep and raspy. "We're Concrete Executioners…" He cut his eyes to the side of the stage, and I watched his pinched brows relax. "And this first one is 'Forget Me Not'." Just as he announced the first song, the one I'd come for, the Jaguar I'd dragged myself to the bar to see, ran onto the stage with a purple guitar slung across his front.

The bassist started strumming a rumbling beat, with the drummer following in step, and the jaguar shifter took his place on the right of the stage, back straight and cocky smirk on.

I was entranced, the loud, scratchy music scraping against my ears, but all I could take in was his form, easy and confident holding his guitar. Long fingers working the strings with practiced ease.

His gaze lazily swept the audience that nodded along to the heavy beat, and it felt like my heart was just at the back of my tongue. My muscles vibrated with more than the reverberation from the amps, and when his black eyes, creased with joy at the music he created, met mine and held, I stopped breathing altogether.

Like he had every time at the skate spot, he grinned. This time though, as the band handed the song over to him and the drummer to carry the bridge, he didn't let me go. As if the song was an enchantment to root me in place. To paralyze and open me up for him to *see*. And when he threw his head back, laugh bobbing his throat, in perhaps joy at what he'd discovered, I felt it in the deepest parts of me.

CHAPTER SIX

RÍO

The crowd wasn't half bad for a Wednesday night. I still was getting used to playing with this band, but they were good people as far as I could tell. As soon as Tyler'd found out that I played, he wouldn't let up until I finally agreed. This was only my second show with the Concrete Executioners, but so far, it was a fun way to spend my hours outside of work. And it gave me another reason to maybe stick around longer than I'd originally intended.

My fingers flew across my purple Iceman, and the thrumming calm made me feel high. The raised stage space wasn't much, but the lights on us and the ear-splitting music we made was *almost* better than sex. My boot tapped against the old rugs that lined the floor, and when Tyler handed the bridge over to me, my mind further slipped away. The crowd clapped and shouted while I let my fingers slide and stepped further to the edge. My hair fell over my shoulders, and when I reached the crest of my solo, I raised my chin.

The faces around me were darkened, slightly obscured, but as

I scanned the crowd, I locked with honey brown eyes smoked out with black.

With her hair down and makeup on her face, I almost didn't recognize the girl that'd started bringing the Wolf pup to the skatepark. The one who'd come into Vinny's those few weeks ago.

But those sweet, haunted eyes were the same. The lightness and pull in my chest flittered, and a chuckle boomed out of my chest. To hear her breath hitching and scent the distinct swell of that sweet and sour scent of hers that made my mouth water.

Tyler stepped back up to the microphone to finish out the last chorus of the song, and I couldn't help winking at the beautiful girl as we started up the next one.

The rest of our set went well with minimal fuckups. Though, it wasn't for lack of trying, at least on my part. Luckily, I'd put in enough practice over the years, and we'd rehearsed quite a bit prior. Because the majority of my attention kept drifting over.

After the first song, she looked more shy, dropping her gaze whenever I met it, but the deep flush on her cheeks was more than enough.

Soon, the set ended, and we were free to watch the rest of the show or leave. So, instead of doing the sensible thing, I hung around, watched the other bands from a corner of the bar that Tyler had commandeered, and continued to drift my gaze to the rich girl. My nose kept catching the thread of her scent that begged me to grab on and find my way over to her.

Jess leaned forward on our table. "You guys going to Finn and Jason's?"

To my surprise, Tyler agreed and threw back his shot of whiskey without even flinching. Brody was nodding and already fucking drunk, so there was that. Alex was here, too, giving Tyler hopeful glances that he was either outright ignoring or completely unaware of. "I'll go." He was a nice guy that was Jess's childhood best friend and made sure to come to most of our shows.

The three of them turned to me, but it took me awhile to notice they were waiting for my response. The people around us began to applaud, but I was too caught up in my own head, seeing those light eyes every time I blinked.

Brody's nudge on my shoulder snapped me back to the people that were way easier to leave. "Uh, sure."

"Did you see that girl from the park?" I whirled around, catching that bloodsucking motherfucker giving me a tiny uptick of his lips like he was just so fucking observant.

A small amount of my old self slipped out, voice chilling. The pressure of the bodies and music around us pressed against my skin, but instead of making me tense, my body reacted in the opposite direction. To be loose, prepared to move in any direction necessary, was instinct. "Don't know what you're talking about."

Should've expected a vampire to face me like this and not give a shit. I supposed that having more years than most of us led to few surprises. And probably a lot of boredom. "I'm gonna go invite her," he said to my horror and stood. I forced myself to tense, to clench my teeth hard in my mouth to keep the fangs from emerging to tear out his throat. For again approaching what was mi—

I needed to get high. Or drunk. Or fuck someone.

Alex sent me a kind smile, and I took him in for a second. He was pretty, with long, brown hair. He was dressed down more today, with a t-shirt and jeans, but his lips were glossy, and I knew that they'd taste like cherries.

Too bad he was hung up on Tyler. We'd fucked around once or twice already, but I could tell we both had the mutual feeling that nothing would come of it.

He turned back to his conversation with Jess, and I took a sip of my beer. Where the fuck was Tyler? What was he saying to the one that I was obsessing over sinking into? Literally and figuratively.

The second band ended their set, and the crowd met them with resounding cheers and clapping while Tyler wove his way back to us. His usually flat expression held a glint in his brown eyes, but I wasn't gonna give him the fucking satisfaction of asking about her. There was no reason for me to put *more* roots down here. Despite what every other part of me was screaming and craving for. I'd given them enough by dangerously extending my stay here.

He bypassed us and went to the bar, just to be a fucking asshole. So, I purposely faced the stage and was *not* burning to hear her answer. No, cause it didn't matter. As soon as we left here, I was going to find *some* hole to fuck. I didn't give a shit about gender or whether it was a mouth, pussy, or ass. The release I needed was going to happen, or I was going to inch closer and closer to seeking relief in a far stupider way. Like eviscerating my friend or finally getting a taste of the Wolf girl.

Tyler eventually made his way back after stopping to have conversations with people I knew he couldn't stand or barely knew. Something he'd never normally do. I was straight up not looking at him when I sensed him beside me again. The leather couch we shared dipped as he sat. I waited. And waited, not hearing one note of the music that was thundering through the speakers. He slammed his glass down once more, draining another Jameson. "She said she'd think about it."

The empty room I found was a stuffy solace between all the noise and people trying to talk to me. Normally, I would relish in it. Drink and smoke and laugh until I had a faint buzz going and let it drive me for the night. But every time the goddamn door opened, I was looking for her. I'd walked around outside twice already, trying to convince myself that I was *not* disappointed she'd decided not to show up.

So, I did the reasonable thing and found Alex who was also not making any headway with Tyler. My friend was on the hunt for dinner, or maybe a fuck too, and he yet again wasn't responding to any of Alex's advances. When I'd whispered in the nice guy's ear, asking if he wanted to go somewhere, he'd nodded gratefully and let me lead him in here.

The kisses along my neck were soft, albeit a bit sticky from his lipgloss. My half-hard dick was slower to respond, but it was steadily hardening, especially with the way Alex was straddling me as we sat in front of the window. Our cocks were both trapped in our jeans, and the friction of his against mine made us moan and press closer together. And I steered my mind away every time I thought about his vanilla and rainy day scent filling my lungs. That it was the wrong one.

He went on to slide down my lap, kneeling between my legs, and I helped him undo my belt and fly to pull out my dick. His hand slowly jerking my shaft to full hardness brought a small groan out of me that was almost eclipsed by the noise outside. Steps moved past the door, and we both turned our heads that direction at the distinct, slight rumble of Tyler's voice.

Alex kept jerking me. "Uh. Do you want me to talk to him for you?" Was I really offering this while the guy was about to suck my dick?

He shook himself and refocused on my cock in his hand. "No. It's fine." And he sucked the head into his mouth.

"Shit," I grunted at the wet suction and closed my eyes. He was obviously distracted, not like last time we'd done this, but my hand in his hair served as a bit of a reminder to keep going, to take more. My heart beat faster, and Alex licked at the slit of my cockhead, bringing out a louder reaction.

It took me longer than it should've to notice the door ripping open and just as quickly slamming shut, what with Alex trying to take me to the back of his throat.

But as soon as the air settled, when I was able to take a breath as he bobbed his head up and down on my cock, I had to focus on silencing a roaring purr that'd begun churning.

It was her, the Wolf girl.

CHAPTER SEVEN

RAMONA

I stumbled down the hallway, barely tipsy, and the darkness, pounding music, and scents were assaulting my conscious thought. It was kind of bullshit that I got these downsides of shifter abilities without the actual benefit of being able to turn into something. Though I'd come to terms with it some time ago —because what else was I supposed to do?—it was still irritating. Unless I could find really strong stuff or something designed for non-humans, regular alcohol just brought on a faint buzz at most.

The smell and smoke of weed hung heavy in the air, nearly choking me, and the body odors and cheap perfumes and cologne were giving me a throbbing headache. Following half the bar to this party wasn't my best idea, but I would never admit to my sister-in-law that I should've headed home with her after the show ended. Though I didn't expect Sylvie to come with me, the way she'd been at the bar had me kind of hoping. I didn't have kids of my own, but I could kind of understand her desire to return home to them even after only a few hours. Even when she trusted my brother wholeheartedly to take care of them. That weird envy tightened my chest, and I spotted someone with a bottle of something in their grip.

They were already stumbling, so they didn't put up much of a fight when I snatched the alcohol from them and took a long swig. It didn't burn, but a warmth started blooming to chase away the pang of wanting what O and Sylvie had.

When I shoved the bottle back toward the dude I'd taken it from, he snickered and eyed me up and down, like he was impressed. Now that I'd stopped, he looked like one of the members of the band—maybe the drummer? I'd only been paying attention to the jaguar shifter, to be fair.

Two things I wouldn't admit to anyone. That he'd been the only reason I went to the show and that I'd been searching the party for him. My sense of smell was good, but it was mediocre in shifter terms. Or else I would've been able to find him.

But what would I even do once I did? Yeah, he was cool at the skate spot, but seeing him on that stage was a whole different experience. He'd been intense in a totally different way. Cooly charismatic, and when he'd pinned me with those black eyes, I had to catch myself from inching closer to the stage. Again—to do what?

The drummer leered at me, pushing himself off the wall opposite and opening his mouth to say something. Before he could utter a slurred word, I turned and shoved my way into the nearest room. Luckily the door wasn't locked, and I shut it in his face.

I sighed in relief and tugged down my mini skirt. The raging music vibrated the walls and the floor beneath my feet, and I tried to breathe through the burgeoning ache behind my brow. Sweat clung to the back of my neck, and I lifted my dense hair off of it.

Someone grunted behind me, and I stilled. Yeah, it was probably stupid to enter a room and just stay facing the door. I cursed myself in my head and whipped around, dropping my hair so that it flopped on my back.

I'd stumbled into a bedroom, looked like, and it was bigger than I would've thought for the small house on the edge of downtown. I still didn't know who it belonged to, and I guessed it didn't matter.

The curtains draped over the window on the other side of the room were closed, but not all the way, and a sliver of light from outside cut across the space. It was dark, but not nearly enough to stop me from snapping to the sight in the corner. My heart picked up, and I would've been embarrassed if I weren't stunned stupid.

The shifter I'd been looking for was sprawled lazily in an armchair beside the window, which seemed a bit weird since there was a bed, made neatly, that he'd clearly bypassed. But he obviously didn't care with his jeans opened and someone between his legs.

Whoever it was had long, lighter brown hair and was wearing a version of what most people around here were wearing. Their t-shirt, jeans, and boots looked thrifted or really worn in, and they were working over his lap. The fact that I'd missed the obscene slurping and moaning sounds was testament to how off-kilter I felt. The few parties I'd gone to in high school had been either disastrous or just uncomfortable, so I'd avoided them like the plague in college. Which wasn't really that hard when you had no friends. But still.

The shifter had his eyes clenched closed, but I would've been surprised if he didn't know I was here. The way his brow was creased didn't seem completely in the throws of pleasure, frustration somewhere in there, too.

"Faster," he directed and palmed the back of their head.

I didn't think I was into voyeurism or anything like that, but there was something spellbinding about the way his limbs were draped powerfully in the seat while still holding a certain grace. Like it was a throne, but not for a king. More like a wicked prince.

His hair was down like it'd been at the show, and now that I was focusing, his unique blend of chile and clove filled my nose. My fingers twitched over my sleeve cuffs, but my feet stayed rooted to the scuffed floorboards.

He winced and opened his eyes to shoot a look at the person

in his grip. "Watch the teeth." They mumbled something back that sounded like a, 'sorry', but they had his dick in their mouth, so. That was just a guess.

Instead of closing his eyes again, he slid them to me, and my heart picked up even faster. Was he mad that I'd walked in on him?

We stayed staring at each other while he got his dick sucked, but it wasn't nearly as uncomfortable as I thought it would be. No words formed in my throat, but I also didn't feel the need to force any out, either. His facial piercings may have looked too heavy on someone else, but on him, they went right along with his sharp jaw and nose and the prowling way he moved throughout the world. On his board or on stage, he was the most interesting person I think I'd encountered. Ever.

Whoever it was that was kneeling at his feet gave a moan that seemed out of some bad porn, and I couldn't help tearing my eyes away from his to glare at them. The noises they were making were annoying, and they obviously weren't doing much, because he seemed pretty far away from coming. Not that I had much experience with that, but, whatever.

A snort had me looking back at the shifter, and he was smirking at me. His short fingernails, painted a deep purple that looked black in the darkness of the room, stayed buried in the person's hair, but his attention was all on me. "Think you can do better, rich girl?"

Maybe the alcohol was affecting me more than I'd thought, because without thinking, I snarked back, "Probably."

His brows rose, and a delighted smile made him look downright devilish. It made me relax and feel jittery at the same time. Even when the pet name still annoyed me a little bit. It was outshined by actually *having* one, though.

He swiped his tongue across his bottom lip in a way that was far from the leering glance I'd gotten in the hallway. He nodded down toward his lap, and the fluttering in mine was what drove me forward and around the bed.

I had been around him enough at the park that I was used to the way my shifter blood reacted to his—with wary interest. Like with like but different enough to prepare for danger. With the way I kept seeking him out, I was either a fan of that dangerous feeling or I was growing addicted to the warmth it caused. Maybe a little bit of both. I loved my brother and his family, but each moment I'd had around this guy was like pops of excitement amidst the steady calm I'd been experiencing.

And like, fuck it, I'd wanted to be alone with him. Maybe I didn't envision sinking to my knees beside someone else, but I was going with it.

Our eyes stayed locked, and his lids lowered in want. I didn't think I was ugly or anything, but it was definitely a confidence boost to see him look at me in a way he wasn't looking at the one beside me. They'd pulled back on the shifter's cock and were giving indulgent licks and tonguing kisses.

The shifter reached up his other hand and hesitated. My lashes fluttered up at him. He somehow managed to strike that balance of beautifully masculine, and I rested my touch on his leg. His skin was warm, even beneath his jeans, and when he finally caressed the back of my head with his tattooed hand, I bit at my lip to hold back a needy moan. I was out of my depth, but instead of panicking, for some reason, his black eyes swallowed me to the point that I felt tightly embraced. I'd never sucked a dick before, but with him looking at me the way he was, I felt confident in a way that I wouldn't have otherwise.

The person beside me had a different idea of what was going on, though. They grasped my face and slammed their lips to mine. They had some kind of lipgloss on, and the remnants of cherry on my tastebuds stood out to me, along with a musky, bitter taste that was unfamiliar but easy to identify.

The kiss wasn't terrible, and I was already turned on enough that their tongue sliding against mine wasn't all that bad. My arousal, though wasn't spiking because of them. My hands tightened on the shifter's leg, and his grip stayed in my hair while I made out with the person who'd been giving him an unsuccessful blow job. They moaned into my mouth, and my hand slid to rest on their knee. Their leg was skinny, and thankfully, they smelled like clean rain instead of musty body odor like half the people at the party.

The shifter used his grip on both of us to pull us apart, and I blinked a few times to adjust to the low light again.

"Go back to the party, Alex." I glanced back up at him, and that frustration was on his face again.

Alex pouted up at him, but he just patted them on the cheek and pulled me closer between his feet, effectively shoving them out of the way.

With a huff and a toss of their hair behind their shoulder, Alex did just that and made a point of stomping out of the bedroom and slamming the door.

The shifter rolled his eyes before settling back on me. He smirked. "You can still back out, Princess. Wouldn't want you to ruin your makeup."

His mocking tone had me squirming, and I sat up to better see what I was getting myself into. Though I'd never sucked one, I'd seen a naked cock in person, but his was longer than my high school boyfriend's.

Oh, and there was a piercing in it.

The black metal was a sharp contrast against his golden brown skin. Yeah, Matt definitely hadn't had one of those.

He palmed the base and lifted his hard dick from where it'd been resting on his abs. He had a simple black t-shirt on, but I remembered the tight muscles I'd caught a glimpse of at the skate spot.

He moved to hold my chin, and he titled my head up while he leaned over me. Unlike Alex, he kissed me with a slow, thorough claiming that made me want to melt into the floor. I sank into his control and tasted traces of beer on his tongue. Mine teased against the piercing he had in there too, and my thoughts went hazy like I'd downed the rest of that bottle from earlier and smoked a blunt or two.

When he pulled back just enough to speak over my lips, his hair shifted to brush against my cheek. It was soft as silk. "You taste sweet and sour. Like candy." I scoffed but didn't pull away, and that sent him into a round of low chuckles that just made more wetness pool between my legs. He licked at my top lip a few times, as if he was tasting more of that candy flavor he'd said I had. "You don't have to, but I'm hard as fuck, so it's either that, or I'll take care of it. You can stay regardless, though."

He pulled back a little more so that I could see his eyes, lined with smudgy black and cloaked by thick lashes that were totally unfair. I nibbled at my bottom lip, trying to gain hold of any coherent reasoning. His eyes softened a fraction, and I wanted to hit something. I was a goddamn adult, and I wanted this.

"What's your name, Princess?" His voice and the gentle tapping of his finger on my cheek snapped my thoughts back to one definite path.

My throat gave a dry click, and I licked my lips to clear the way. His black stare broke to follow the movement, and I felt a bit stronger. Enough to say, "Ramona," without my voice cracking.

I gave another moan, sank into him again when he slanted his lips over mine once more. His teeth were sharp and perfect when he caught my lip between them, and my hands tightened on his calves. He broke our kiss, and I sucked in air that, at this point, I didn't even want. I just needed more of him.

"Mine's Río."

I felt my brows tighten and my lips jut out in a contemplative pout. "Like a river?"

He grinned and pet the back of my head like I was a pretty cat. "That's me. Always runnin'." And he chuckled at his own joke. My eyes rolled, and I gave a scoff. But that just made him laugh more. "So, what'll it be, Princess?" He went back to staring me directly in the eyes, head tilted to the side. It was almost threatening, how much he wanted the truth. There would be no waffling back and forth with him.

I took a deep breath, trying to force in as much oxygen as possible to keep me from going completely lightheaded. Was I actually going to do this? Suck a random cock at a random party in a random town on a random Wednesday?

"I've never seen a dick piercing before," I said instead. A bead of moisture rested against the barbell that ran through the slit, and it seemed to be growing as I stared. My navel fluttered again, and thrill ran back and forth from it and between my legs. I couldn't imagine willingly inflicting that pain onto myself, but I was surprised to admit—it was hot. What would that feel like against my skin? Would it be cold or warm against my tongue?

He didn't react to my comment, and my face heated with the knowledge that he was still staring at me. But the drop of liquid was running down the head of his cock, now, and I leaned forward. I glanced up at him, hoping like hell he wouldn't make me actually say the words and just take my movements as consent enough.

I stuck my tongue out and swiped indulgently, wanting to feel the weight of him, the smoothness of the piercing, and the taste of his precum all at once.

He hissed, but didn't pull it away, and I went in for another lick. And another. He tasted wilder here. Like everything stripped away to reveal just the bare essence of him. It was weirdly good— no, addictive, and all of a sudden, my brain caught up to find myself sucking him further into my mouth. His cockhead and first inch or so of his shaft weighed heavy on my tongue, and the piercing tickled my flesh. But it felt oddly comforting, and I pressed up on my legs to get a better angle.

Río released the hold he had on his shaft and transferred his other hand back into my hair. He leaned back in the chair, and I steadied myself on his thighs. Remembering what he'd directed at Alex, I made sure to shield his cock from my teeth and took more of him into my throat.

"Shit, rich girl," he groaned.

I flicked a glare up at him underneath my lashes, hair curtaining the sides of my face. That nickname was infuriating but not enough to make me stop. Especially when he gave me a lust-filled grin and touched the tip of his tongue to a sharp canine.

My mouth sank further onto him, a little more than halfway, and I felt my body try to reject the invasion. My fingers tightened on his legs, but he didn't seem to mind. His hips were moving in small, aborted movements, like he wanted to shove himself completely into my mouth but was holding back. Spit pooled around my lips, dripping down my chin and the rest of his length.

I shifted again, this time grabbing the base. My head bobbed, and my necklaces tinkled with the movement. The nestle of soft, trimmed hair tickled the side of my fist. It was difficult to look up at him now, so I just closed my eyes to focus on the task of learning what made him feel good.

Judging from the fact that his hips would make a larger thrust, then another small one like he was losing the battle to keep on his restraints, I was on the right track. A light touch, warm and gentle, ran along my cheekbone and to my jaw.

I felt my eyes prickle, so I focused more on taking him the whole way into my throat. None of the books or fanfics I'd read over the years could've prepared me for how difficultly arousing this was. My throat was already being rubbed raw, my knees and legs starting to burn with strain, but my mind had never been emptier. More at peace. How fucked up was that?

Like what I'd read, I tried to breathe through my nose, but the lack of air was growing too much. I pulled back, sucking in precious oxygen. An even spicier aroma flooded my nose now that I could breathe, and while I flicked my tongue against the jewelry pierced through him, I let it wash over me. There were notes of his but also of mine, cool and hot twining and swirling together. Who knew it could be like this?

Río's back was thrown against the chair, but his body held a tightly coiled tension while he watched me like I was a mesmerizing snack.

He'd been about to open his mouth to say something, but the door banged open, startling me enough to make me pause for a moment before continuing to plant open-mouthed kisses on the leaking cockhead. My eyes stayed locked with Río's.

"Tyler's looking for you." I recognized Alex's deeper voice, no longer squeaking with indignation at being forced off their knees.

"Fuck off. I'm busy." Río leaned forward at the same time he pulled me away from his cock. His lips smashed into mine, claiming my mouth once again. A faint growl rumbled from his mouth into mine, and I let him take control. My lips and tongue reacted to his, moving and molding against them, but my thoughts remained happily empty.

Distantly, I knew that the door was open, the sound of talking and music much louder than it'd been before. But Río had moved his hand to cradle the back of my head, pulling me more tightly into him, demanding it, and I couldn't even begin caring who saw me on my knees for him. My mother could've walked in, screeching to high heaven, and I would've just gone back to sucking Río down my throat.

Suddenly, cool air kissed my lips instead of his hot ones, and my eyes cracked open at the vicious words in a tone I didn't recognize. "Don't make me tell you again. Get the fuck out." He wasn't yelling, but the way his lips pulled back in rage made me gasp.

Not in fear, though. A whimper escaped my lips, and his cock twitched in my hand. Río's head remained turned toward the door until I heard a sharp slam, sealing us in the room once more.

When he turned back to me, he blinked a few times, and his expression softened to the drunken lust it'd been before.

He tilted my face to the side, and I gave a high-pitched moan when he dragged the flat of his tongue from the corner of my jaw up to my hairline. My fist started jerking up and down on his cock, and he rewarded me with another swipe against my cheek.

The hard press of his tongue piercing amidst the wet softness of his flesh made me squirm, trying to find friction to relieve the want in my body.

Río nipped at my earlobe, hard.

I cried out, and my left hand shot to my lap. I parted my knees while he soothed the throbbing pain of his bite by giving small, tender licks.

"You're gonna touch that pretty little pussy while you finish sucking my cock, Princess." Another lick, and I gasped at the sweet pressure of my fingers against my clit. I didn't even bother pulling the soaked fabric of my underwear to the side, just moved my fingers fast and released another long, high-pitched whine. "And then you're gonna swallow every bit of cum that I give you and let me hear you scream while *you* come. Got it?"

It was hard to keep my eyes open at this point, let alone say anything coherent, so I just stuttered a nod while my hips and fingers moved frantically. Río gave me a quick kiss on my cheek before guiding my head back to his cock. He didn't even really need to apply any pressure, because I licked my lips and sank down readily.

I still wasn't able to take all of him, my throat spasming and gagging when he got too far, but I didn't have time to get embarrassed about it or wonder if I was doing the wrong thing. Each time it happened, he groaned, let me pull back to breathe, and then nudged my head back down after a moment or two.

His body tensed beneath me, and my fingers were circling fast and hard to chase my own release. Muffled moans went from my lungs to vibrate against his cock splitting open my throat, and then back out of his mouth as rough groans.

Before I could reach the height of my orgasm—it stayed just out of my grasp—he gave a breathy grunt. "Gonna come." I hollowed my cheeks, sucking harder, and was rewarded by a sustained growl and the heady sensation of cum shooting down my throat, straight into my stomach. I focused on swallowing, taking all the salty bitterness, but there was way more of it than

I'd anticipated. I pulled back, choking a little, and some of his cum spilled out of the corners of my lips and started down my chin.

"*Fuck*, that's a pretty sight." Río's tongue caught the lines of his jizz trailing down my face and fed them back to me. My tongue swirled around his, taking the slightly salty cum and swallowing it down like he'd wanted.

Once my face was cleaned, and my lips were thoroughly swollen from his rough kisses, he whispered over my mouth, "Need some help, Princess?"

My eyes opened, staring at his sharp face cloaked in darkness. A sliver of yellow light slanted across his brow, down his nose to his jaw, and it was enough for me to take in the shadows dipping across his cheekbones and flowing over his lips.

His forehead rested on mine, and a gentle pass of his palm down my front made me shiver. He lapped at the tip of my nose a few times, and my mouth dropped open as the back of his hand moved under my skirt and between my thighs. I wished I could see his tattooed skin against mine, but that fantasy was quickly erased when he slipped behind the waistband of my panties and found my clit with quick accuracy.

I found myself clinging to his shoulders, nails digging through his t-shirt while I pretty much humped his hand like an animal. He dipped his fingers inside of me to wet them and alternated between circling and gently pinching in a way that made me feel like I might fly so high that I'd float away.

"*Nnggh*." The noises I made didn't make sense, but I couldn't hold them back. I'd probably be embarrassed tomorrow, or even immediately after this was over, but it felt so, so good now. I'd never felt someone's fingers besides my own, never tasted someone besides myself, and I simultaneously wanted the pleasure to fucking break already and for it to never end. To always be this.

Río didn't bark orders, but he instead groaned assuring words over me. While my eyelids were clenched closed, I could feel his black eyes glued to me still. "That's it, Princess." And, "Relax, and let me feel you come all over my fingers," filtered through my awareness as I finally crested that hill.

My face pinched, and I cried out, scrabbling my grip on his shoulders, and hips moving back and forth to draw out the pressure of his fingers. My own got tangled in the long silkiness of his hair, but he didn't seem to care about that, either. As I fell, he kissed and licked his way down to my neck. "Fucking beautiful." He spoke into my skin, and my chest heaved as I tried to get a hold on my breathing.

N-Number Twelve.

His shoulders, corded with a surprising amount of lean muscle, were my anchors as I floated back down. Río didn't pull back from giving wet kisses to my throat until I'd gotten my body under more control.

When he did, I heard fabric shuffling and the metallic *zsst* of a zipper before I was lifted into the air. My mind was still a bit mushy, and my limbs twitched with aftershocks.

Río settled me into his lap and tucked my head beneath his chin, and post-orgasm, the gesture made me feel a weird mixture of comfort and cornered. Was I so pathetic that he felt that he had to do this? Did he feel bad for me or something?

I started to move off of him, but his arms just tightened around me. "You're not going anywhere." He pulled back and looked down at me. His hair brushed against the side of my face, some of the strands tangling with mine. Río flicked his thumb on my bottom lip, and the pop of it slapping back against my teeth made him chuckle. "You're going to sit here with me, and then I'm going to take you home."

His commands had been loosening my defensiveness, but the last directive made me still all over again. We'd gotten off together, but that was maybe pushing it a bit too far. At least more than my now fuzzily sober mind could handle. Before I could protest, though, he smirked and flicked my lip again. "Not to mine, Princess. Do you need a ride or do you have friends here to take you home?"

I blinked a few times, letting his words sink in, and whispered, "Uh." My voice was raspy, and I cleared my throat like a nervous loser, but his smirk still stayed in place. "Um, a ride would be nice."

"Cool. We'll go in a minute." He gave me a final peck and relaxed us both back in the armchair. I leaned into the hollow of his throat and closed my eyes.

He circled the curve of my bare knee while another finger ran up and down my full sleeve. "You ever ridden on a motorcycle before?"

CHAPTER EIGHT

RAMONA

Río swaggered around the side of the house and held my hand in a loose grip as we made our way to a haphazard collection of cars and a few motorcycles parked out back. There were a few people smoking and drinking out here, and they all gave lazy waves or head nods that Río returned. They didn't eye me with him like it was strange that he was leading someone around that they didn't know, and I wasn't sure how to take that. I barely knew him, and I very much didn't want to be the blushing virgin that attached themself to the first person they'd shared an orgasm with. At the same time, though, I really didn't want whatever sizzling connection between us to fizzle when the sun came up.

His hair swished on his back, and his boots crunched on the gravel. I'd been so preoccupied with taking in the shifting of his muscles beneath his clothes and the way the light from the back porch of the house swam against the inky color of his hair that I stumbled into him when he brought us to a stop.

I flinched, starting to pull myself away, but he curled his hand around my lower back, keeping me nuzzled next to him. "You ain't gotta be so skittish, Princess." There it was again—that southern drawl that came out sometimes when he spoke. It was uncommon enough in this region that it stood out, and I found myself burningly curious to know where he was from.

Then his assurance sank into my mind, and I scoffed, albeit weakly. "I'm not skittish."

His lips pulled into a wide, knowing grin, and the metal in his face shined brightly against his skin. His thick, black brows and sharp nose were strong lines that contrasted so much with the softness of his smudged eyeliner and long lashes. Not to mention those kissable fucking lips. I'd never thought of lips in that way, but finding out that they were just as soft as I'd imagined after seeing him for the first time was as exciting as it was a little unnerving.

"Sure." He bopped me on my nose and turned to the bike in front of us. He dropped the arm around my waist, and I immediately missed the warmth. The anchoring.

Río's motorcycle was a sleek black, and the helmet he plucked off of the leather seat was the same color. He handed it over to me. "You weren't worried someone would steal this?"

I pulled my hair behind my shoulders and lifted the helmet above my head. Río watched me pull it on and fiddled with it, making sure it was on properly. He shrugged his broad shoulders. "I'd find anyone who did." The words sent a shiver down my spine. Río seemed cool and nonchalant most of the time, but there was something underneath his words that made me pity anyone that crossed him. Shifters, generally, weren't people you wanted on their bad side, and I had a feeling Río wasn't any different.

He sat on the seat and pressed on the ignition. The bike roared to life, a deep rumbling purr, and he patted the stretch of leather behind him.

"Not scared of a little ride, are you, Princess?" The words were a little muffled with my ears in the helmet, but the teasing in his tone was abundantly clear.

I rolled my eyes. "That's a stupid nickname. Especially since you know my real name, now," I grumbled while I hitched my leg over the seat and settled behind him. My skirt was pulled high with the position, but it wasn't like I could do anything about it. And he'd already had his fingers up under it anyway.

Río snagged a hair tie from around his wrist and tied his hair back in a messy bun. The shaved hair above his nape and behind his ears was a shadow of black against his skin. He let his hands fall to his lap and twisted around to smirk at me. "I'd have to disagree. You've had that pretty nose in the air every time I've seen you, Ramona."

Out of his mouth, my name sounded rough and smooth at the same time. It was doing weird things to my chest, so I just grunted to acknowledge that I'd heard him.

He plucked my left hand off of my thigh and placed it against his stomach. My heartbeat picked up, and I tried like hell to get it to slow, but to no avail. He brought my right hand to his front, and I swallowed at the touch of the hard planes of his stomach. How this was more nerve-wracking than having his cock in my mouth, I didn't know. Was being dick-drunk actually a thing? It must've been.

"Make sure you lean with me as I take turns. If you don't, it could throw us. And if you need me to slow down, tap twice on my hip, all right?"

I nodded and belatedly gave him a verbal reply. "Yeah."

"Now, where am I goin'?" I fumbled in the back pocket of my skirt and pulled my phone out. One-handed, I pulled up my brother's address on Google Maps and showed him the directions. Río ran his eyes over the screen and nodded back at me once he was done reading.

"Hold on." I put my phone back in my pocket just before Río revved the engine and pulled us out of the makeshift parking area. My grip on him tightened, but I wasn't scared, necessarily. He guided us smoothly onto the deserted streets.

It was past one in the morning, now, and though the party we'd left was still going in full swing, Antler Pointe as a whole was dead. The summer night air whipped past us, fluttering both of our hair as we left downtown. On the long, quiet road out to where my brother lived, the motorcycle was a pleasant, growling vibration against my legs, and I felt stronger with my arms around Río.

Just like he directed me, I leaned with him as we made turns, but it wasn't hard with the way my body sank into his. He didn't wear any cologne, and even with the air coursing past us, his clean smell of chile and clove filled my nose. The fabric of his t-shirt was thin and soft to the touch, but I held back the urge to move my fingers against the ridges of his muscles like I wanted to.

Soon, we were crunching on the gravel road of my brother's private drive, and Río slowed the bike while we went between the trees. My brother's cabin came into view, and the glowing of the porch lights had my throat constricting. O and Sylvie had never left them on, as far as I knew, so it must've been because of me.

Río pulled up next to Orion's car, and steadied us by planting his feet on the ground. I released the hold my own boots had on the passenger pegs of his bike, but untangling my arms around him took longer.

I studied the patch of skin between his shirt collar and his hairline, wondering what I should say. Would it be weird to give him my phone number? He didn't seem like the kind of guy who fiddled with social media, and it wasn't like I was super active on there, anyway, but I really didn't want this to be a one and done.

Before I could settle on what to say, the front door of the cabin opened, and my heart sped up for reasons other than before. My brother stepped out of the house, clad in only his pajama pants, and marched down the steps. Orion's tattoos swirled up and around his pale arm, spreading to his chest and ending just above a large pink scar just near his ribs. Río's tattoos, on the other hand, were harsh, striking artwork that marked him nearly everywhere.

My brother's stare was icy, appraising, and it was weird how much it reminded me of Mom's. I'd rarely seen the look on him before, but based on the times that I had, I knew what it meant. This wasn't my gentle brother, but Pack Leader Orion.

Río cut the engine of his bike, and I fumbled the helmet off of my head. Orion came to a stop a few paces from us and stood with arms crossed. Shit, I didn't think he'd be awake. Or at least, I didn't think he'd bother to come outside while I got dropped off.

"Hey, O." I barely succeeded in keeping my tone light, hoping to deescalate the tension pinging back and forth between my brother and the shifter I'd attached myself to, at least for the night. Río's body wasn't loose and relaxed like it'd been at the house and on the ride over here. His back was straight, and the muscles tensed against my front. By the similar strain in Orion's jaw, I briefly worried how I would pull the two shifters apart if it came to that.

"Get in the house, Mona." Orion's voice wasn't the dry monotone it was most of the time with me, which was not fucking good.

I started to scramble off of the motorcycle, but Río's hand on my knee made me hesitate. "What are you, her dad?" His defiant tone made Orion's light green eyes flash in the low light, and I groaned in exasperation as Dahlia's little head poked out around the frame of the door. Even with her bonnet on, fuzzy red ringlets always managed to escape. Sylvie's satin-wrapped head popped up above hers but with the same curious tilt. Great. Just perfect.

"No," Orion shot back at him then turned to me. "Ramona, you had Sylvie worried when you didn't answer her texts. Get in the house."

I heaved a long sigh. As much as I wanted to do my own thing tonight, I did feel bad for worrying my sister-in-law.

Río looked at me over his shoulder and raised a brow. "You gonna be okay, Princess? I can take you somewhere else if you want."

I winced at the warning growl Orion gave and shook my head. I swung my leg around and stood beside the motorcycle. My hands straightened my skirt and smoothed the long sleeve shirt I wore. "I'm good. Thanks for the ride." Wisps of his hair floated around his sharp cheekbones, and I really wanted to twine my fingers around the soft waves. Now I was worrying that I'd never get the chance.

Río didn't seem annoyed by my brother's territorial display, though. He grasped my waist, brushing the sliver of bare skin above my skirt, and pulled me closer. I shuffled as close to him as I could, and he lifted his chin expectantly. Without thought, I lowered and was met with a soft kiss on my cheek. In my ear, he whispered, "See you around." It wasn't a question, which made me deflate a bit, but he pressed another kiss on the shell of my ear.

When we pulled away from each other, Río looked back at my brother and his family in the doorway. With a wry smirk, he winked over O's shoulder. "Hey, pipsqueak." Orion's answering growl would've raised anyone's hackles, but Río just snickered, put his helmet on, and started up his bike.

Without another glance at me, he backed out and left, gravel dust flying up in his wake. I watched him go, disappearing into the darkness within the woods, and the rumbling of his bike loud in the stillness of the night.

"We're going to talk about this in the morning."

I shot my brother a narrow-eyed look, but he just returned it, unimpressed. "You're not my parent. *God*, did you have to act like such an asshole?"

Orion's brow scrunched and he let loose a gust of air through his nose. "You go to a party on your own, with people you don't know, ignore my mate's texts to see if you're all right, then turn up smelling like a *cat*."

Heat blazed on my cheeks, and I let out a frustrated noise. Fuck shifter noses. And fuck territorial Wolves. I stomped closer to my brother and glared at him. "I'm a goddamned adult, and I don't need you scaring off the people I meet. It's none of your business."

Orion looked at me, not backing down. "Any shifter on pack land *is* my business. Especially any shifter that associates with my sister. *Especially* any shifter that knows my daughter. Care to explain that, Mona?"

I threw up my hands. "He's at the skatepark sometimes, okay? Fuck, I thought you weren't with this *'get off my land'* bullshit."

He huffed. "I'm not."

I gave a dry cackle. "Oh, *sure*. Whatever, I'm going to bed." Without giving Orion a chance to volley something back, I swerved around him and bounced up the wooden steps and onto the porch.

Sylvie backed away to give me room and offered a reassuring smile. I patted Dahlia's head and mumbled an apology to them both as I quickly took off my boots and lined them up by the door. I felt three sets of eyes on me as I retreated into the guest room but couldn't be bothered to explain myself any more.

CHAPTER NINE

RÍO

Being a manager fucking sucked.

Truthfully, it'd been one of the first jobs I applied to when I blew into town, and on each application, only a small portion of my information was accurate. Including food service experience. It wasn't like I would be able to write down my actual work experience without getting arrested by authorities, human and otherwise. Or, I shuddered to my core, my family would catch up to me.

It wasn't really all that hard, I'd found. Vinny's was a pretty well-oiled machine, the menu simple, and the mixture of townie and student employees were far more chill than other... associates I'd dealt with in the past.

But when some perfect storm of food poisoning, no-call/no-shows, and summer vacations hit, I was the one it fell back on. When Robby had started looking pale and slightly green, I'd sent him home despite his protests. We hadn't been busy by any means, but there was a large gap between manning a closing shift with one other person and doing it in your own. I'd never be frightened by a human, but wow, people got fucking *difficult* when it came to their food. Combine that with having to make the food and take the orders *and* shut everything down on my own, I was ready to get the fuck out of here.

One of the last things on my checklist was to take the trash out, and the final task had my skin buzzing with the knowledge that I'd be free soon. The skatepark would still be hopping, alive with people out, and I could already feel the vibration of my wheels rolling on the concrete. Metal and sweat and fucking air. They were all waiting for me.

And maybe a certain honey-eyed girl.

While I lifted the trash bags into my hands and nudged my hip at the door to get it to swing open, I replayed the feeling of her mouth on mine for the thousandth time. How the hot suction of her pretty lips almost did me in. Christ, how she saw Alex kneeling for me, and instead of turning that little nose up and running out of the room, she'd just sunk down beside him.

The first trash bag flew into the dumpster with a heavy, plastic thud, and my back shivered with the memory of Ramona clinging onto me while I touched her. How she'd done it again while I took her home. One was with my fingers swirling between her legs while the other was while I handled us on my bike, but both were her giving me her trust. She handed her body over to me so easily and beautifully, just the barest flash of it in my mind's eye had my heart picking up and my cock plumping in my jeans.

I flung the last two bags over and into the dumpster, the noise more muffled now. What I wouldn't give to brush my teeth over Ramona's soft skin again. For her to let me peel back all that she'd slathered over herself to try and hide what those gorgeously haunted eyes screamed anyway. Would she be able to do the same thing to me? Flay me open and leave tears streaming down my cheeks and my fangs coming out?

My chest started a weird pulling at the thought, and I yanked the hair tie from the top of my head. I breathed a sigh, trying to get my futile desires for Ramona to clear as the tension on my scalp released. My hair fell across my back in a comfortable, swishing weight. I wiped my hands off on my jeans.

Nah—my heart twinged, but I pressed on with the reality check—any long-term *thing* couldn't happen.

I locked up quickly, whistling the newest song the band was working on, and climbed onto the back of my bike. Night creatures chittered, barely audible beneath the engine rumble and the whistling of humid wind as I made the ten-minute trip to the park. There were no screaming cicadas within the symphony of sound, which kept me from truly sinking into the comfort, but the heat seeped into my skin, burying in my pores. Dios ayúdame if I ended up sticking around through the winter.

I pushed that awful thought away at the sight of the white fluorescent lights and illuminated concrete. The chain-link fence surrounding the skate park just outside of town was a transparent shadow that kept the place in its own sort of bubble.

After parking amongst the five or so cars and settling my helmet on the seat, I was already pulling my board from the straps that secured it to my backpack by the time I made my way inside. Someone was playing Arch Enemy on a bluetooth speaker, and the sound of boards kicking off into the air and slamming back down helped the rest of my tension from work bleed away.

I dropped my stuff near a free stretch of fence and rolled to the bowl. Some kids were already taking turns dropping in, and once I had an opening, I let myself tip down the steep incline and glide into its depths.

Time slipped away, my worries crumbled and fell, and it was just me and the board. I spent some time grinding one of the rails, laughing along with the companionable hollers when I landed a kick flip.

People came and went, and a little while after I discarded my shirt on top of my backpack, Tyler showed with his board and waved me over.

He pulled two Tecates out of his backpack that he'd dropped next to mine. I accepted the one he thrust toward me and popped the can open. The cold, hoppy taste slid comfortably against the loose calm I was already feeling. Goosebumps prickled my heated skin that'd become a little damp from me working my body with no break since I'd gotten here.

Tyler's sharp elbowing at my side had my eyes flying open, not sure when I'd closed them, and his babyface filled my field of vision. He was scrubbed clean from work, probably, and it always weirded me out to see him without his usual get up. To make him look less soft. Older.

"You left with her the other night, right?" His eyes cut somewhere over my shoulder, and like a fucking Pavlovian bell, my body heated from the inside like a rolling fire. My tongue licked droplets of beer off my lips, testing, hoping, that some lingering taste of Ramona was still there. The bar in my tongue clicked against my teeth in a gesture that I would never fucking admit was nerves.

Annoyed with myself and excitement shooting all the way down to the ends of my fingers and toes, I didn't even bother acting nonchalant. What would be the point?

I turned, and, sure enough, Ramona was sitting on one of the concrete ledges that'd been waxed and grinded on thousands of times over.

She was in a delicious pair of denim shorts and a white sweatshirt that made her light brown skin look even deeper. A long, black plait sprouted from the back of her scalp, fell down her neck, and bounced softly against her chest while she laced up her hot pink skates.

"Yeah. I gave her a ride back home." My voice was steadier than I felt, watching the meditative way Ramona secured her laces and lifted her over-ear headphones into position like she always did.

Tyler said something else, but I was drinking in the sight of those long, brown legs straightening as she stood and began to roll over to the flat area that wasn't much a favorite for everyone else here. At first, I thought she hadn't noticed me, very brazenly, staring at her as she rolled around. She circled her shoulders, rolled one-footed while shaking out each leg, and when she'd apparently warmed up enough, she pulled her phone from her back pocket. After tapping on the screen a few times, she cut those honey eyes to me as she stuffed her phone back in her jeans.

I grinned and swept my stare down to the quad wheels under her feet and back up to her face. Now that she was back in front of me, no longer a crystalized version in my memory, I felt my usual bravado slip into place. I made no mistake in my perusal of her body. The cute little furrow between her brows just before she twirled and began skating in rhythmic loops and bounces made my mouth water. What an intriguing minx she was.

"So, did you hit it? Is that why you didn't come back after you left with her?" Tyler's voice filtered back into my awareness while I watched Ramona dance to whatever music was playing from her headphones. If I'd really been concentrating, I'd have probably been able to discern what it was, but the forms of her arms and legs making fluid shapes out of the song she listened to, and Tyler's presence pressing against my side, were stealing all of my attention.

It took me about ten seconds longer to process his question than it normally would've, but when I did, I didn't even bother keeping the venom out of my words. "Why the fuck does it matter?"

I looked back at him, but he was just drinking his beer and watching Ramona, interest clear in his stare. Just to make it worse, he answered with eyes still glued on her, "I mean, I usually prefer dick, but she's hot as fuck."

I had to breathe through the possessive wrath that crashed into me and almost took him out at the same time. My hand crumpled the aluminum of my half-empty beer, and moisture spurted around my fingertips where my claws had sprung out to sink into the can. "Shit," I muttered and willed the razor-sharp points to retract.

This wasn't me—I didn't dream up ways I could murder one

of the few friends I'd made in town just because he expressed interest in the same piece of ass I couldn't go more then five minutes without thinking about. Sex was fun, and combine that with my commitment to put down roots a total of nowhere, there was no room for certain stuck-up girls with wolf shifter blood and the most enticing scent I'd ever encountered.

I plugged the opening on the top of the can with my thumb and turned it sideways so I could shotgun the rest of the beer through the holes I'd made. No use wasting a good Tecate when it was so hard to find in this town.

The fizzy cold shot down my throat, cooling off the instinct to shift and maul the shit out of Tyler's face and throat. It didn't, however, douse the flare of possessiveness and desire I felt while I watched Ramona wind and spin on her toes, arms outstretched and braid swaying. Her black lashes fluttered against her cheekbones, and it reminded me of how prettily she'd held me in her mouth and tasted. Choked.

After I'd downed the whole thing and crushed the can the rest of the way, I shoved the empty into Tyler's chest and caught his surprised startle. "Don't touch her." I knew that I was being an asshole to the first person that'd been nice to me when I moved to town, but as I started rolling over to Ramona, I couldn't make myself care. I wasn't a stupid dog that had trouble sharing, but the thought of Ramona leaning in and trusting someone else made me want to roar.

The closer I got, the more I recognized the music sound coming from her headphones. It was a deep, groovy sound that just emphasized the buttery way she moved and bopped on her skates.

On my board, I circled her imaginary dance floor while she did some intricate repetitive crossing pattern with her feet. Her gaze rested on a fixed point on the ground in front of her, but every few seconds, she'd look up at me with a wary expression and flick her eyes back to the ground again. As I made another revolution around her, I sniffed the air, but there was no fear.

"Working on something new?" I asked, letting my board screech as I pivoted to keep circling her. She was chewing on her lip, continuing the pattern over and over. It lacked the fluidity of her other movements, and every so often, she'd lose the rhythm, pause, and start over.

After a few seconds of her flying through the movement, she lost pace again. This time, though, she huffed and made a quick spin with a jarring stop, as if it was its own gesture of irritation. "I was."

A warm tug pulled at the middle of my chest, and I brought myself to a stop, facing her. Ramona managed to cock a hip, thigh muscle flexing with the movement, and her eyes were challenging.

"Am I bothering you, Princess?"

She flicked her braid over her shoulder and tugged at the cuffs of her sleeves. Like she'd done when she walked in on me and Alex.

She lifted her chin, just a little bit. "No. What's up, Río?" *Damn.*

I stepped off my board and crossed the few steps to her. Ramona didn't look away as I approached, but she did that tugging at her sweatshirt again.

Her shifter blood called to mine, made it hum, but where the specific note of Wolf usually just made me irritable, the hint of it on her was smoother. Twisting with the half-there human scent that was lighter. She was a mixture of soft and wild, sweet and sour, other and alike. I leaned into her ear, letting the strands of my hair be the only part that brushed her heated skin. "I like it when you say my name, rich girl."

Ramona's answering shiver was fucking delicious. So much so that I shoved my hands into my pockets to keep from pulling her close to me so that I could drag her somewhere dark and lick the sweat that was running down the sides of her face and neck.

She didn't move to touch me either, but she also didn't roll away. Desire was wafting off of her like thick trails of steam, and I fought to keep myself on the edge. So that I could stay trapped in it.

"Well, I don't like it when you call me 'rich girl'." Her voice was steadier than I expected, and when I pulled back to see her face, her honey eyes were narrowed in defiance. My lips pulled up, and the corners of hers twitched in answer before she wiped her face flat.

Again, I leaned forward, but this time, Ramona gave the barest tilt with her expression still nonexistent. Our mouths were a quarter breath from touching. "But that's what you are, Ramona. A pretty rich girl who looks even prettier on her knees."

She sucked in a hitching breath, and my half-hard cock went fully stiff at the challenge I felt rumbling within her like the rearing of a wave before it crested and crashed into you. "And you're an arrogant fuckboy. Isn't it about time to go home and lick your own asshole? Or whatever cats do."

I felt like I was going to punch out of my fucking jeans. Before I could catch myself, my hands were around her waist and pulling until there was absolutely no space between our fronts anymore. I gave into the urge that'd been tugging at me since I'd rolled over to her and dragged the flat of my tongue up the side of her face.

Ramona stopped breathing all together and clung to my bare shoulders, fingers scrambling in the same way she had when I'd made her come. The memory of it was engraved in my mind and my body. My chest rumbled with a purr that would've surprised me had I not already been all-in with this girl. It was like I was in quicksand or some shit. "I'd rather taste that little pussy of yours, Ramona."

She stilled. For a split second. Tiny. But when she moved her hands with a forced smoothness, it was as if someone had shoved my head into a bucket of cold water. My body was slower to calm, but the coolness was closing in. My grip on her waist softened. I chastely kissed the edge of where I'd licked. "Or I could have you on the back of my bike again."

A gust of tension left her body. "Uh. Sure."

I smacked another kiss, barely there and gentle. "Can I give you my number, Ramona?"

"Um, yeah, that's fine." She paused, but when I didn't release her, she just fumbled her hand into the back pocket of her shorts and produced her phone. After opening up her contacts, she held it out to me, silently asking me to put in my number.

Instead, I bent again to whisper in her ear. "Put it in for me, Princess."

She shivered, even though I knew she was damn-near over-heating in that sweatshirt. With shaky fingers, Ramona typed in the number I recited slowly for her. She spelled out my name into the contact last, and her thumb on the 'save' button felt final. A voice in the back of my mind, laced with warning, tried to stop me from what was already done. Because she was far from a piece of ass or some tasty souvenir to remember this town by.

Shit, shit, shit. "Text me," I said with a finality that I knew I desperately needed.

I felt Ramona's stumble when I turned to grab my board and march over to get my stuff. Out of the corner of my eye, I made sure she wasn't going to fall, and when her body slowly began to bob and sway again, I focused my attention on shoving my shirt into my backpack and strapping my board to it. Tyler was over by the bowl, talking with whoever, which was good. I didn't know what I would've done if he'd still been gawking at Ramona. Probably not something smart.

It was absolutely not fleeing when I shoved on my helmet, got on the back of my bike, and started her up. It totally wasn't running away when I felt Ramona's eyes on me but didn't meet them. My body was still antsy, vibrating with the release of skating and wound right the fuck back up with my princess in front—

No. She's not 'my' anything, I growled into the air coursing past me as I rode home. This town and this life was just another stop. Temporary. Sure, I could use her to pass the time, go back and forth and explore both of our bodies together until time was up.

And watch those honey eyes darken and truly close off when I packed up my shit and moved on to the next place.

Maybe she wouldn't care, I turned down my street and tried to reason with myself. Antler Pointe's historic downtown was small compared to other cities I'd been to, but when I'd been passing through those weeks ago, it'd been unknown to me and those from my past, had a skatepark, and a large enough forest to get lost in when I needed it.

My apartment wasn't anything fancy, but it had large windows and a loft so that I could sleep high up. After the less than ten-minute ride from the park—what with literally no traffic due to the small town streets being completely dead at this point —I was pulling up to the souvenir shop I lived above and went around the corner. There was a small parking lot for employees and those of us that lived in the units above this block's shops, and I snagged one of two spots left.

I sucked in a deep breath that did nothing to calm the conflict in my head. Everything in me wanted to bolt back down the street to the park. To catch Ramona before she went home.

To that Pack Leader she lived with.

"Fuck," I muttered and climbed off my bike. I'd forgotten about *that* fucking detail. Packs were annoying, insular groups, and in my experience, their leaders were the worst of them all. Territorial on a whole, irritating level, baring their fangs and touting claim to land that should belong to everyone. Once I'd set my sights on this town and learned that there was a Wolf pack, I reasoned that I wouldn't be here long enough to ruffle their fur. If I'd been a Wolf, that would've probably been a different story.

But I'd gotten a taste of the sister of the Pack Leader. When he'd stormed out of the house, I could immediately scent the familial bond between them.

The competitive part of me, the fuckboy, as Ramona had called me, wanted to pull her into a tree, right there on her brother's land, and fuck her until she screamed. To give us both something to claim on Wolf land.

I was lost in the fantasy of that as I started toward the little alleyway where the door leading upstairs was. What it'd be like to sink into Ramona and drag my claws across her side as I held us pinned and steady, way up high. She'd make that groaning and screeching noise of hers, wrapping her legs around me with terrified pleasure.

"Ayo, cousin." As soon as I rounded the corner, the familiar voice echoed softly in the darkness, and I stopped in my tracks.

Benny pushed off of the brick wall he'd been leaning against, and a mixture of fear and brain-splitting rage crashed inside of me. This couldn't be fucking happening. Not today, not here, not now.

He walked closer toward me, bringing himself and his black, perfectly tailored suit into the light. I never understood why my father insisted his employees dress the way they did, other than the fact that he was infuriatingly old fashioned. About a lot of things.

But Benny was low-level, a hanger-on that was tolerated because he did whatever bullshit job was thrown at him. "You're not my cousin." I forced my spine still and faked a rigidity to disguise my muscles already descending into that slinking place.

He shrugged and tried to stand taller at the same time. Now that we were just six feet or so from each other. I wasn't short, but he had a good few inches on me and at least fifty pounds. His suit fabric shifted softly as he put his hands in his pockets, but I saw the sleekness of a gun tucked in a holster underneath his jacket.

"We were basically raised that way. You never used to have a problem with me calling you that before."

I couldn't help but laugh. "I think you've got the history confused. But it doesn't matter. What do you want?" How had this happened? How in eight years had I finally been discovered?

His dark hair was slicked back with some gel that made it look shiny under the yellow-toned security lights. Benny gave me an unimpressed once-over, undoubtedly taking in my ripped jeans, helmet tucked under my bare arm, and windswept hair. But being underestimated by anyone from my father's life was to be expected. They'd always treated me that way. Maybe that was why I let my guard down. Put down more roots here than I had anywhere else. Madre de Dios, I'd even fucking joined a band.

"I was sent to scout out this area, and wouldn't ya know it? I caught scrawny little Río's scent while walking to grab some dinner? Followed it back here and figured I'd wait to see what happened. You caused quite the stir when you slunk off into the night, cousin."

He was going to have to stop calling me that. Although, he wasn't going to be speaking for much longer, so I guessed it didn't matter.

"So," he continued, inching closer to me, "now that I've laid eyes on you, how about we head back and smooth over this whole thing? Your old man will be relieved to have you back."

I fought the bile trying to rise in my throat and the phantom lashes, the torture that'd reached almost every inch of my skin. "Didn't you hear? I don't have a father. He's dead to me, and I should've stayed dead to him. Trying to offer me up so he'll throw some promotion at you is fucking pathetic, Benny."

The easy demeanor cracked, frustration crumpled his face, and he put a hand on his gun like that would do anything. "Name's not Benny, and you know that, you piece of shit. I'm letting them know I've found you, and then we're gonna go back to Georgia."

Quick as if it hadn't been there, my fear was snuffed out. What *Benny* just let slip was that he was here alone. And that he hadn't told anyone of this personal mission to follow my scent and ambush me. I'd tried so much to be like Mamá, to kill all parts of me that were like Dad and my sisters, but the darkness that spilled over me like ink running over my soul was like putting on a favorite, worn jacket. It fit perfectly and was an armor I'd been kidding myself into thinking I'd shed forever.

Apparently, the fear I'd shoved off of myself and over a cliff fell right onto Benny. He tried to hide it, but the wisp of it in the air made my mouth water. What this idiot cabrón, as Mamá would have called him, and others like him always seemed to fucking forget was that I'd been given the same treatment as my sisters. Just because I wasn't a sociopathic bitch, or untethered more than not, didn't mean that I was any less dangerous.

"Well, *Benjamin*. Seems like your shifter blood was good for something. But I'm not coming with you." The thin trail of who I liked to think I really was silently apologized to Ramona for what I'd said.

It did land the mark that I wanted it to, though, because Benny pulled his gun and lunged toward me. Probably to try and get his arms around me and put the gun to my temple.

At this point, it was just insulting. But flashes of that time with my father were a low soundtrack as I twisted, dropping my helmet, and pounced. Dark rooms, blows to the head, punishing lacerations that left me bloody and malnourished and hollow when I did anything that was deemed incorrect. I wasn't going back. I *wasn't*.

I clung onto his back, letting my claws sink through his suit and into his flesh, and used my weight to twist us back into the darkness of the alley. I heard the gun clatter to his feet, and it thankfully didn't go off. There weren't any security cameras back here, as far as I knew, but I'd have to check back afterward to confirm.

He grunted and gasped in pain and surprise, and we both hit the ground, with him first and me still on his back. Benny tried to throw me off, and that sick part of me was disappointed with how little of a challenge this was. If he'd been smart enough to call in my location to someone with half a brain, they would've discouraged this half-cocked plan that wasn't a plan at all. He bucked and hissed beneath me, shouting curses and trying to get the upper hand.

It was messy but oh so satisfying as I released my fangs and clamped them over the base of his skull and the top of his spine. Teeth crashing through tissue and bone and blood. I tightened my jaw that'd grown wider with my fangs and severed his spinal cord.

Blood smeared on my face, tasting delicious on my tongue, and his last twitches and garbles just made me hold on tighter.

I killed Benny in the alley behind my apartment, and I didn't feel an ounce of remorse. Or, much of anything aside from inconvenience and the trails of adrenaline.

As much as I hated it, my father's training continued to drive me as I listened for any concerned neighbors that may have heard our struggle. When there were none, I lifted his limp, heavy body into a fireman's carry and went up the two flights of stairs to my unit.

On autopilot, I unlocked my door and dropped him gently to the ground. After running back to the alley to grab my stuff and his gun and confirm that there were indeed no cameras that could've captured the whole bloody encounter, I went home to deal with the body.

I kept the lights off as I stripped the suit from Benny's body to properly dispose of later. His limbs flopped lifelessly as I moved him around, and once everything of his was in garbage bags by the door, I unbuttoned my jeans and kicked off my Vans.

A ding from my phone reverberated against the robotic calm. With a bloody and dirty thumb, I swiped open my screen.

UNKNOWN

Hey, this is Ramona. Wanted you to have my number, too.

I blinked at my phone, reading the message over and over until who Ramona was sunk in, and the roots of her in my mind grew even more. Honey, acid, winter cold, soft skin, haunted.

A burning sigh forced its way from my lungs and through my nose. I clicked off my screen and threw my phone onto the couch.

Naked and tired, I closed my eyes and shifted, letting the magic woven through my body take over and rearrange. My muscles and bones contorted, and my psyche rode the current, bobbing with the change. Never fighting it but not getting lost to it either.

When it was over, my front paws thumped to the ground, and I was still Río. The most important parts of him, anyway. A roaring hunger that I'd been ignoring since I left work had curved and shifted to one that was more than content with the body I was dragging up to the lofted area near my bed instead of craving something like a burger.

The rest of my evening was spent making my way through Benny. Filling my belly with the meat and bones I pulled from his body. My Jaguar wasn't fond of the taste of intestines, but my rational mind pushed us through. There couldn't be anything left of him, and eating everything was killing more than a few birds with one stone.

So, I crunched and tore, tail swishing, while I looked out of the large windows that let in the ghostly glow of the moon.

CHAPTER TEN

RAMONA

I checked my phone again before shoving it back in my pocket. No text back from Río, no matter how many times I looked.

The sun was brutal overhead, air like a convection oven with the slight breeze wafting from the lake. I dug my fingers back into the earth, pulling another sweet potato from the damp soil that filled the raised bed. With a little more force than necessary, I threw it into the basket I kept beside me and continued down the row.

"How's the book coming, Sylv?" Josie drawled in between ear-splitting slurps from her straw. It made me cringe, but I didn't say anything. Just kept focusing on the coolness of the dirt and smooth ridges of the vegetables I was harvesting. On what O would decide to make with them. And certainly not on my infuriatingly silent phone.

Sylvie sighed. "It's fine. I'm taking some time away from it a little. My brain always rejects something about being firmly in the middle of drafting."

"Does the main character die at the end in this one, too?"

Sylvie snorted. "Wouldn't you like to know." After a moment, she called over to me from where the two of them were lounging on the back porch, "Are you still doing okay, Ramona? You really don't have to harvest those right now. They'd be fine for at least a few days more."

I dropped another one into the basket, creating a sea of dirty orange and yellow leaves. I twisted to look over my shoulder at them, and strands of my hair stuck to my sweating neck. "I'm good." Sylvie and Josie were lying out in bikinis underneath a large umbrella. They both glistened with a layer of sweat, and I eyed their scant clothing with envy. The denim shorts I was wearing were borrowed from Sylvie, as the only two pairs I'd brought were both in the wash. Even with their scandalously short length, I was dripping.

But being out here amidst Sylvie and Josie's jovial chatter and with my attention on the garden was far better than being alone with my thoughts pressing against the slivers of hope that felt shaky and paper clipped together.

"Well, come up here and take a break at least. You're gonna pass out with that sweatshirt on." I wiped at my forehead with the back of my wrist, but I still felt the grit of soil leave a gross smear on my skin.

My instinct was to snap back at Sylvie's friend, but the sweating pitcher of lemonade that sat on the table beside them started calling to me.

I clapped my hands over the garden bed, trying to clean them off as much as I could. My legs had already deepened in color a full shade or two, and my muscles felt both tight and stretchy as I stood. The wooden boards of the back porch were hot under my bare feet, and I wiped my palms off even more on my shorts before pouring a glass of lemonade for myself. While I drank and the two witches continued to talk, I checked my phone again. Nothing.

"You should get a text from whoever you're waiting on in..." Josie lifted her sunglasses to squint at the bright sky. After a moment, she lowered them and reclined back in her seat. "Like half an hour maybe?" That was fucking creepy. For many reasons.

I was pretty used to Sylvie's brand of witchiness, which mostly had to do with her garden. Or when she sometimes took walks with me in the forest, and she'd caress and whisper to the fungi she'd encounter like they were dear pets. Which, yeah, had weirded me out the first time I'd watched her do it.

But there was something psyche-chilling about being able to see the future so clearly. And being so comfortable to just blurt stuff like that.

When I remained silent, Sylvie sat up and swept her stare down and up my body, lingering on my wrists. She'd asked me a few more times if I wanted to talk to her about 'it', but she didn't press when I refused each opening. What the fuck was I supposed to tell her that wouldn't invoke a look of pity? Of serious, pointed questions of whether I was okay?

And more terrifying—she would feel obligated to tell my brother. Which I was *never* going to be ready for.

Sylvie opened her mouth, and I braced myself, finally having to confront what I'd been so set on avoiding. "This wouldn't have anything to do with that Jaguar, would it?"

My mind floundered, shorting out for a moment after being built up to shut down or maybe start an argument with her.

"Jaguar?" Now Josie was sitting up, Kool-Aid red buzzcut bright against her tanning skin. Her swimsuit was in the same color. "I didn't know there was such a thing." She lightly smacked Sylvie on the arm. "What more have you been keeping from me?"

I shot a look to my sister-in-law. "Shouldn't you not tell people that?"

Instead of hitting me back, her face got a little redder, even though the rest of her remained relaxed. "She'd know if she ever met him. Witch, remember?"

A sardonic snort shot through my nose before I took another gulp of lemonade. It was true—Sylvie and I both knew immediately what he was when we first ran into him at Vinny's.

Aside from the distinct scent, he moved with controlled, rolling movements that barely passed for human, in my opinion. Especially when he was on stage or leaping into the air on his board.

"Okay, this may seem like a dumb question," Josie piped up while she picked under her fingernails, "but when you have sex with a shifter, do you ever do it when they're like… not in human form? Is that bestiality?"

My throat spasmed, and deep, stinging coughs wracked my body. The lemonade was like acid as I tried to get a control on my breathing. When I looked over at Sylvie who looked calm and contemplative, I had to mentally swipe away the gross things that came to mind.

"What?" Josie glanced between us with lips turned down in a pout.

Sylvie shrugged. "Not sure what other people do, but I wouldn't think of having sex while half-shifted as bestiality." I started choking again. "Why?"

Now it was Josie's turn to go almost as red as her hair. She directed her attention back to her nails. "Just wondering."

"Can we *please* not allude to what you and my brother get up to? I already kind of hear it. I don't want even more details."

But Sylvie's attention was still on Josie, curiosity and knowing swimming on her face with furrowed brow and pursed lips. What conclusion she was coming to, I had no idea, but before I could say anything else, tires crunching on gravel sounded from around the house and up the road.

Again, I brought my phone out and checked the time. The hours seemed to have slipped by while we were out here, even though it was hot as fuck. It was one of the days Orion's classes ended earlier, but he typically stayed in his office doing work until it was time to pick up Dahlia, and Ollie if he wasn't at home with Sylvie, from school.

Sylvie and I glanced at each other in question while two sets of doors thumped closed, and I caught my brother's scent. With it was one I was familiar with, and the quietly distressed voice was as soft and deep as I'd remembered.

They bypassed the house all together and proceeded around the side and over to us. My brother was dressed in his work clothes that weren't a far stretch from what he wore in his free time. The simple, gray long-sleeve and dark jeans made another round of sweat run down my face and neck, but he only seemed lightly flushed by the heat. At least for now.

The Wolf with him had loose hair down to their waist, sharp eyes that were emphasized by long, delicate lashes. A thin, golden headband glinted in the sun, and the billowing purple blouse they wore caught in the summer breeze.

As they got closer, I saw the lines pinching their expression into one of worry that made them even more interesting to look at.

"Hey, Juno," Sylvie called pleasantly, but her brows were turned up in concern, noticing the look on their face as well. I'd been around my brother's best friend a handful of times in the past, but they'd always seemed in good spirits and calm. Now, though, they were only able to muster a weak smile in our direction before plopping down at the iron porch table.

They undid the top buttons of their shirt before leaning back and running a weary hand from their brow to scalp.

My brother sank down into the lounge chair with Sylvie, and she automatically settled between his thighs. Sweaty and all, Sylvie leaned back into Orion's embrace, and he closed his arms around her waist.

A few ducks in the lake quacked and splashed in the water amidst the weird silence that'd fallen over all of us. I shifted where I stood, unsure of my place here. No one called me out or eyed me like I didn't belong, but I also had no idea what the hell was happening. Josie's face was crumpled in frustration as she looked between Juno's chest and their face, and it was she who finally broke the silence. "What's going on?"

Juno pinched the bridge of their nose. "Family stuff. I need to fly out as soon as possible, and Orion offered to drop me off."

"Oh," Josie frowned, "are... do you need anything?"

My brother's friend gave a dry chuckle that, even to me, seemed very uncharacteristic. They pinched the front of their shirt and jostled the fabric, hair waving as they fanned themself. "For my family to actually tell me what the hell is going on. Apart from that, it's fine." They craned their neck to look over in her direction, and their face noticeably softened. "But thank you."

As if she couldn't sport any more red, Josie looked down nervously at her toes. "Are you sure?"

Sylvie and Orion seemed to communicate something to each other with just a glance, and right as I was making a mental note to ask my sister-in-law about it later, my phone dinged with an incoming text, cutting through the thick air like a bell. Or a gunshot.

I turned away from the three of them on the porch, trying to give myself space in case I was about to be royally disappointed.

Facing the lake, I opened my phone to find what I'd been waiting all night and morning for. Which, really, wasn't much time at all. But seeing his name on my screen released the band that'd been pulling my chest tighter and tighter. It was like I could finally take a deep breath after only panting for so long.

RÍO

Hey, Princess.

And then I was sent into another round of anxiety—this time instead of a low, rolling discontent, it was tinny and sharp. His response was an acknowledgement but also nothing. And I couldn't respond right away. Could I? Oh, god, had I accidentally turned my read receipts on at some point without knowing?

As my mind spiraled, three dots appeared on his side of the exchange, and I almost started choking again. My lower back was pouring sweat, but I was shivering at the same time.

RÍO

What're you doing later today?

"Oh, shit," I whispered to myself. What was I supposed to say? 'Nothing'? 'Let me suck your dick again'? I had half a mind to turn back to Josie to ask her what I should respond with, but when I snuck a glance back at the four adults on the porch, they were talking very seriously about something that obviously didn't have anything to do with me.

Bitch, you're an adult, too. Get it together. I forced myself to take a long inhale, clench all my muscles and jaw, hold, and then release.

Without allowing myself more time to think, I typed out a quick response.

ME

Depends. What are you doing?

Río obviously had no qualms with immediate text-backs, because he shot off another response almost as soon as I texted mine.

RÍO

Thinking about skating after work again. You gonna be there?

ME

I can be

RÍO

See you at 11

Just like that? Was it that easy? It couldn't be. What—whatever this thing with Río was or could be, I felt far from having earned it. And yeah, I'd seen him multiple times at the skatepark, but they were always unplanned.

Was this a *date*?

Something about his last text felt like a goodbye, so I couldn't think of anything else to write. I sank to the ground beside my basket of sweet potatoes, fiddling with the cuffs of my sweatshirt. The edge of one of my fingers nudged its way beneath the fabric, almost to see if the raised, bumpy skin had disappeared.

Of course, it was still there. It was like a cruel fucking joke that the quick healing I inherited from my mother didn't extend to these wounds that would sound the alarm of anyone I encountered. They were a bookmark that constantly called back to the lowest I'd ever felt. Well, actually, not the lowest. I shoved my hands back into the soil as whispers of the pure relief I felt the moment I took blade to flesh ran down the back of my neck.

I breathed through the longing that followed, focusing on the simple task in front of me. I thought of my brother and sister-in-law behind me, along with my niece and nephew. Now, they were the thin threads that kept me tethered here. I nodded to myself, drops of sweat falling off my nose and edge of my chin. Yes, seeing Dahlia and Ollie grow up. I wouldn't have that if I gave into it. Hurting all of them would be the consequence of me making that final decision.

Was it fucked up that when I woke up in my bathtub, in water on its way from deep pink to just red to match the bits that'd landed on the tile, that I hadn't thought about them at all? All I felt as I weakly climbed into an Uber with towels wrapped around my bleeding arms underneath my jacket was disappointment that I was still here.

Fucking typical that I'd survived the attempt but was unable to erase the physical reminder.

If I hadn't been weakened by the blood loss, I would've never thought going to the hospital to get stitches would be a good idea. Because after they treated the wounds, I'd blinked and found myself being moved to an inpatient facility.

We watched some good movies there, at least.

I reached my hand back in the dirt, searching but finding no more sweet potatoes that were ready to be pulled. What the fuck was I supposed to do for nearly eight hours?

"Hey, do you want me to pick up the kids?" I twisted around

to find everyone standing. Josie was pulling on her t-shirt and shorts that she'd had in a crumpled pile on the floor.

Sylvie was leaned into Orion's front and looked over his shoulder to answer me. "If you want, but you don't have to. Josie's actually offered to take Juno to the airport instead. So, Orion and I were just going to go."

I waved a hand. "Nah, I'm just going to take a quick shower, and then I'll go. I'll take them to get ice cream on the way back."

"Are you sure you'll be able to handle them both on your own?" Orion asked.

Instead of bristling and getting defensive at his dry question and expression, though, I thought it over as I stretched back to standing. Any time I'd been in charge of them alone, it was either at the house or for drives to and from school. "I think so. But if it's looking like I can't, I'll just come straight back here."

My brother nodded, face still blank. "Okay. Text us or call Sylvie if you need help." For some reason, my brother's readily given trust in me to keep his children safe made a sudden flood of tears threaten to fall. I blinked them away as I brought myself and my basket back to the porch.

I stretched it forward. "Sounds good. Think you can make something with these?"

He gave them an appraising glance while Josie and Sylvie exchanged parting words. "I'm sure I can. They look good."

It was stupid, because I wasn't the one who planted them, nor was I the one with any magical abilities that aided in the vegetables being large and hearty, but I felt a swell of pride all the same.

"All right, thank you, friend, for your help. Can I get my things out of your car?" Juno looked a bit more relaxed now, the lines of tension on their face seemed a bit smoother. But there was a weird tingly tension between them and Josie, even with her offering to help them out.

"Sure." Orion started to pull away from Sylvie, giving her a whisper that was too low for me to hear and a lingering squeeze on her ass before following Juno back toward the front of the house.

With just the two of us on the porch together, Sylvie ran a hand through my spoils, humming in approval.

"Do you ever get jealous?" Sylvie's quirked brow asked me what I was talking about, and I honestly didn't even know why I'd blurted the question. When I'd dated Matt, it was a shallow, high school relationship, sure, but the sting of finding out he was cheating on me with a girl he claimed as 'just a friend' had left me feeling angry and paranoid. Even now, the thought of Río with someone else, when we weren't even anything at this point, made me want to fume.

In it now, I jutted my chin toward the direction my brother, Juno, and Josie had headed. I didn't think Orion would ever cheat on Sylvie, but that wasn't the point. It was the proximity. The knowledge that they'd had a past.

Sylvie's easy shrug was of a woman who was nothing but secure in her relationship. "No. They'd been just friends for a while before I came along. I trust Orion completely. And it's hard to explain, but being mates, even the thought of going outside of that doesn't happen. For the two of us, anyway."

I thought about the dozens of people I knew my mother and father had cheated with during their marriage. And the many more that I probably wasn't aware of. "You truly believe that?"

She nodded, thankfully not seeming offended at my curiosity. "Yes."

"Okay, but what would you do if the impossible happened? Don't you ever get worried? However irrational that may be?"

The look she gave me, a dangerous curl of her lips, was far from the kind smile I was used to seeing on her face. My sister-in-law was obviously a strong person, and the magic I'd seen her wield had always been to connect with nature. Or entertain her children. But the darkness behind her eyes made me feel scared and strangely more connected to her than before. "No. I don't worry about it. But, if the impossible happened, goddess help anyone in my way."

And just like that, the darkness cleared like fast moving clouds, and her expression brightened to match the clear sky above. She started to gather the pitcher of lemonade and glasses to bring back inside, and I tried to make sure I hadn't imagined the flash of viciousness I'd seen in my sister-in-law.

What the fuck else could she do, and more importantly, could she teach me?

Before I could ask, Sylvie started to head back inside. "Thanks again for offering to get the babies. Don't feel obligated to take them to get ice cream—two kids can be hard to wrangle, even if they're in the best of moods."

I followed her, shower and another opportunity to be occupied and not alone with my thoughts on my mind. "I think I'll be fine. If it's too much, I'll just head home."

We walked into the house that felt like a freezer compared to outside, and the buckets of sweat on my skin began to do that gross, salty cooling thing. Yeah, a good scrub was definitely needed.

"M'kay. Either way, make sure to text us when you're on your way back."

The request made me pause, but when I saw her mischievous smirk, I gagged. Yeah, I'd figured they'd want time alone, but I didn't need a reminder as to why.

Sylvie's giggles rang throughout the cabin while I retreated into the bathroom. Yeah, just eight more hours to kill, and I would be fine.

CHAPTER ELEVEN

RAMONA

I hoisted my skates over my shoulder, wheels bumping against my back, and shut my brother's car door. The summer evening air was cooler than this morning, but I felt just as hot as before.

When I'd pulled up, Río's motorcycle was nowhere to be seen, so I'd thought I'd have to wait for him. But once I scanned the skate park, gray concrete illuminated by the overhead lights, I immediately homed in on him rolling in lazy, relaxed movements. He threw a few jumps in here and there, but it looked more of a warming up than anything.

I'd sat in the car, watching him and freaking out about how I was going to approach. What I was going to say.

But then he looked over his shoulder, straight at me as if he'd known I'd been there all along, and raised both brows expectantly. Because he probably had known the minute I drove up, by sound or scent alone.

Now, I was making my way over and forcing myself to take deeper breaths. This was just hanging out. Skating was something that relaxed me, and it obviously did the same for him. Nothing to worry about. At all.

Yeah.

I couldn't keep my free hand from making sure my freshly washed denim shorts were sitting just right. The new long-sleeved bra top I'd finally bought was in that moisture-wicking, workout fabric. Hopefully that with the short length would stop me from turning into a gross, stinky blob. But time would tell.

As I crossed the threshold from parking lot to skate park, Río rolled toward me, black eyes alight with something like excitement.

To see me.

My face got really hot, and I stopped at a length of fence with a bench and dropped my skates to the ground.

Río's board scraped the concrete as he came to a stop a few feet from me. He was wearing a red band t-shirt this time, and the bottom hem had obviously been taken to with a pair of scissors. It left an inch or two of his belly exposed, and his black jeans sat low on his hips.

"Like what you see, Princess?"

I hadn't realized I'd completely stopped putting on my skates and been staring. Even though I knew I was blushing, I narrowed my eyes at him. "You wish."

Río crouched so that he could look me in the eye, and it made the back of my neck bristle. I didn't think I had issues with eye contact like my brother, but... maybe I did. Río's unflinching stare was making me squirm.

"Yeah, I do." He replied simply, cocky smirk still painted across his face. Río ran a hand through his shiny hair that was hanging in languid waves around his face and down his back. "You hungry?"

I frowned and swiveled to look around. I'd just gotten here. Did he already want to leave?

He must've seen my confusion, because he chuckled and offered, "I brought a pizza from work."

"Oh." I took stock of my empty stomach. I'd been too hopped up with nerves to eat the roasted chicken and vegetables my brother made for dinner, and as if it was being called to outright, my stomach gave a hearty growl that even a human would be able to hear.

Río looked smug as hell and darted away without a word. I watched him go toward his stuff, and sure enough, he returned with a white pizza box, the smell of cheese and pepperoni almost a cloud around him.

He sat down next to me on the bench, bare arm brushing my clothed one, and opened the box.

"Extra pepperoni?" I asked with brows raised.

Río shrugged and offered nothing else, but the heat wouldn't leave my face. When was the last time I'd been to Vinny's? Certainly not since the first night I showed up in Antler Pointe. Did he remember, or was it just a coincidence?

I took a slice that was still pretty warm and started eating. Grease immediately coated my fingers and lips, but it was fucking good, and I soon knocked back my first slice and two more while we sat in silence. Apparently, the long day in the sun and wrangling two pups from school to ice cream to home drained my energy more than I'd thought.

Licking the sauce and oil off of my fingers, I finally looked back at Río beside me. The silence had been so nice, just watching the other skaters zoom back and forth, that I hadn't thought to speak. Instead of looking annoyed or antsy, though, he was staring right back. The fluorescent lights reflected off of his facial piercings, and his sea of tattoos were even bolder in this light.

Río still wasn't saying anything, just continuing to face me with an intense expression that held no hint of his usual cockiness. "Um... are you not going to eat?"

His eyes darted to somewhere lower on my face. "Nah. Too full."

I blinked. "Oh. Well, I think I'm done for now. Thank you for the food." I straightened and began wiping my hands on my shorts and dusting off remnants of pizza crust.

Río closed the pizza box without looking at it and set it beside himself on the bench. He planted his legs on either side of the metal seat and faced me. "You're welcome, Princess."

I frowned. "I don't know why you insist on that nickname. It's stupid."

He raised a brow and leaned closer to me. I froze in anticipation, feeling his warm breath fan over my face. It smelled faintly fruity like gum or candy.

Río raised a finger and ran it in the air just beside my jawline. He didn't touch me, but the heat from his almost-touch did. "You're pretty like a princess."

My frown stayed firmly put in place. In fact, it was even deeper. "I'm pretty. That's not very original. And if that's the case, I'd rather be a queen." Río seemed mesmerized by the action of tracing the air around my face, now doing the same with my cheek and temple, and he followed the shapes he was drawing with his eyes. It was weirdly entrancing, watching him watch me.

While he moved over the curve of my ear and down my neck, he huffed a laugh. "Ah, but princesses have more fun." His gaze flew to mine as if it'd never left. "Don't you want to have fun with me, Ramona?"

My lashes fluttered, worrying what the right thing to say was. What did he mean by 'fun'? Like skating 'fun'? Or sex 'fun'?

Well, with those two options, it was far simpler to say, "Yeah."

The hand he'd been running along the lines of my skin shot down and landed on the bench with a reverberating thump that I felt on the backs of my thighs and all the way up my spine. Río lowered even further and allowed the tip of his nose to trace the upper curve of my cheek.

It would have been a simple, almost innocent gesture if it'd come from anyone else. But something about this jaguar shifter had my skin feeling electrified the moment he touched me.

Almost worse now that I was stone-cold sober with nothing to dull the way my body reacted to him.

I gasped when his tongue darted out, licking at the corner of my lips. And I didn't mean to, but when he did it again, the tip of mine was already out to meet him.

Río's arms immediately wrapped around me, and I found my legs draped over his thighs, front nearly plastered to his. For the first time since the night of the party, Río kissed me properly. Fully.

My arms wound around his neck as I let him take full control of the kiss, of me. His tongue piercing was a hard, tantalizing pressure that contrasted deliciously with the softness of him. Our lips moved against each other, and our breaths were heavy through our noses as we gave into the tension between us.

Far away, whistles rang out in the summer evening air, but, like our first real encounter, I was fully content to be his and not worry about the rest. People could see us, and I wouldn't give a damn. Being in his arms felt too good.

Río was the first to pull away, and I was already addicted to him, because my mouth chased his, not wanting to let go. He put a firm hand on the back of my head, holding me steady so that he could separate our faces, and my body reacted almost instantly and leaned into the silent command to stay.

Thankfully, he only left an inch or so between us, restraint still tight around me. Already missing being as close as we could possibly be, I scooted my hips forward, nearly straddling him now, and felt the warm pressure of his dick beneath my thigh. It was hard and warm and trapped within the confines of his jeans.

"Fuck." Río murmured quietly, more to himself than me, but I nodded back all the same. If he was thinking that this was intense —intoxicating—then I was in full agreement.

The currents of lust were still running through me, and with the cologne of his warm spice scent twining all around me, I couldn't keep my hips from rolling against him again. It wasn't my fault, okay?

He cursed again, flexing his own so that there was more contact between us. He directed my head in for another hard kiss that I moaned embarrassingly into.

But, just as our tongues began swirling around each other in earnest again, Río broke away to pant in my ear. "You keep this shit up, and I'm taking you back to my truck to lay you down and fuck you until you scream."

The tone of his voice was far from teasing, but it wasn't flat either. The same word came to mind when I'd asked Sylvie about what she'd do if my brother ever cheated on her.

Vicious.

My body reacted completely differently to this side of Río, the one that'd been directed at Alex when they walked in on us at the party. Now, though, it curled around my neck, threatening and ensuring my safety at the same time. Was it fucked up that it didn't scare me in the slightest?

No, what made me pause was the thought of having to tell him that it was my first time. That I'd throw a bucket of cold, rank water on both of us by admitting that piece of humiliating truth and make him regret taking up with me all together or think he had to go easy on me.

When he'd looked down at me while I swallowed his dick, reducing this cocky male to a series of writhes and pants, I'd felt caressed and powerful. Like nothing could touch me while I stayed wrapped up in that bliss.

Río seemed like he'd be the type to not want to take the time. And really, I didn't blame him. Any sort of fun with me beyond this came with too much baggage. I couldn't even get naked with him, for god's sake.

"Where'd you go?" he whispered in my ear while scratching the blunt tips of his fingernails on my scalp. I had a fleeting thought that I wished it was his claws instead.

My own fingers were tangled in his hair, but he didn't seem to mind. I risked meeting his eyes, finding the black soft, gooier, and not the hard onyx they'd been before. Disappointment and self-loathing made my stomach dip. "Nowhere."

Río planted a closed-lipped kiss on the side of my mouth before nuzzling against my ear. "You don't want me to?"

I scrambled at the idea of him pulling away from me completely. "I-I do. Just—"

"Not right now?" I bit hard into my lower lip and nodded. His face was hard and soft against mine, and his scratching sent a shiver down my back. "That's fine, Princess."

"I'm sorry," I blurted, tears collecting and making my vision go blurry.

Río somehow pulled me even closer, but the urgency of our lust was gone. Because of my stupid hangups. How was letting him fuck me any different from sucking him off? It was all sex.

"Shh. Don't be. I can get carried away sometimes."

Somehow, my face had found home in the crook of his neck, and he was allowing it like I wasn't some random girl he wanted to fuck. It was pathetic, how my body moved to this embrace without my permission. But I couldn't bring myself to give up the comfort, either. "No. I like it—that you want me like that."

"Mm, is that right?" He started placing tiny little kisses into my hair. I nodded. "You like that I can't stop thinking about the way you clenched around my fingers when I made you come? Or imagining how it'll feel when you milk my cock dry while I tell you how pretty and perfect you are?"

Was that moaning noise coming from me? My hips were making small movements against his again, my arms clinging to him.

"Watch it, Princess. You keep doing that, I'm not going to be able to pump the breaks, and I'll have the both of us coming right here in front of everyone."

What I meant to come out as sharp was more of a whine. "Well stop saying shit like that."

Río chuckled, and I felt it down to my bones. Low and smooth. "Hm. Maybe next time, then." He straightened, and I was automatically angry at the air between us. He brought a thumb to smooth the skin of my lip. "Don't look at me like that."

"Like what?" I bit back.

"Like you're mad I'm not spreading you open right here."

My eyes gave a dramatic and lengthy roll. "You're so full of it."

Río threw his head back and barked a laugh. "Lucky for you, I like a little brattiness. Keep it up, and I might let you tie me up and see how hard you can get *me* to scream." My jaw dropped, which only made him laugh harder. He gently pulled away, and I was so stunned by his words and the renewed wave of desire they incited, I let him stand and walk toward his board.

He picked it up and came back over to me, hair tousled and half-hard dick obvious. His gait and expression was back to that easy, cocky confidence, but it took me awhile to move past images of his wrists bound to a bed with pleasured tears in his eyes.

Well, didn't know I'd be fucking into that.

Río grinned down at me, as if he knew exactly what I was thinking. Instead of teasing, he jutted a chin toward my skates that'd been left abandoned on the concrete beside the bench. "Ready to skate?"

No, I wanted to say. But the world around us was filtering back in, and with it, was my more rational mind. Maybe it was good that he'd stopped us. Though I'd obviously proven to myself that I didn't have as many reservations as I thought I did, my reaction to going further right now wasn't just nothing.

I agreed, and Río stayed close by while I laced my roller skates as quickly as I could. Once they were on, I made my way over to him, tracing circles like I always did. Except, this time, after I grabbed my headphones and turned on my music, we were lost in our own worlds but never far from one another. Like orbiting planets, I worked on my toe-spins while he pulled kickflips and shove-its, lost in his own movements. When he went over to the bowl, dropping in and revolving in its depths, I practiced turning my hips out, bending my legs so that my feet formed a straight line and the placement of my weight let me wind delicate curves around the bowl.

Río and I exchanged glances that felt comfortable and intimate. No need to talk, just content that the other was there, within reach.

The hours bled into each other, the passage of time marked only by the people that arrived or left. All the while, Río and I didn't really speak with anyone else aside from quick greetings or head nods of acknowledgement.

The skate spot technically had a closing hour, but since it was considered a public park and the lights stayed on at all hours of the night, many ignored the signs that told us to get out at midnight. The cops rarely came by here to enforce it, so when I opened my eyes after losing myself to the music I danced to, I was surprised to find the park empty aside from Río and me. The last skaters were heading to their cars or walking down the road, to go home and sleep or continue hanging out elsewhere.

When I turned over my shoulder, Río was already standing, watching me. He had one foot on the tail of his board, angling it up in the air. He'd removed his shirt earlier in our skate session, and the thin sheen of sweat made the vibrant colors and deep blacks of his tattoos glisten. The trio of graceful cranes before a bright, orange sun took up most of his right side and contrasted sharply with the macabre skulls on the back of each of his hands. There was little space on his upper body that wasn't covered in art, and I had the urge to run my fingers over each piece.

Feeling a bit more comfortable with him now, I rolled over to Río, my braid sticking to the side of my neck from the hours of sweat I'd worked up. With the added height of my wheels, Río was only about two inches taller than me. I stopped, close enough to see the tiny black hairs that'd begun to sprout on his cheeks since his last shave, and I gave into the prickling urge in my fingertips.

Río's hair was up in a messy bun, but the hairs that'd fallen free tickled the back of my hand as I traced the bold dahlia flower on the side of his neck. The petals were sharp and drawn with thick, black lines, but all together, they conveyed a gentle grace.

I swept my touch down to his chest, tracing the flapping wings of three cranes, two smaller than the third that seemed to be leading the flight they'd taken. My fingernail just barely scraped a path around his pierced nipple as I mapped the other tattoos that were expertly drawn on his flesh.

"Ramona." His voice held the beginning rumbles of a purr, and I rested the pad of my finger on the blade of a dagger along his ribcage. I tilted my head to look up at his face, eyes winding up past the silver studs beneath his lips and the rings punched through his nose.

Río rested his hands on my hips, and when he dipped in to kiss me, it was a soft press of lips. My palm flattened against his chest, feeling his heart beat and his lungs swell. Number Twelve, it turned out, wasn't just sex, or the pleasure he coaxed out of me. *No*, I amended my list. *It's this, too.* We pulled back for air, resting the sides of our noses against each other. I breathed him in, let the feel of his body ground me.

Then, I felt his hold on me clench. Not painfully, but the bubble around us shifted. Río biting at his lip caused it to bump against mine. I held my breath, heart beating faster as he kept me close.

"I'm not staying here."

My lashes fluttered wildly, mind trying to catch up to what he was saying. Even though we were too close to be able to focus on much of anything, I looked into his black eyes, trying to decipher what path his mind had taken.

Here, I noticed the almost-invisible ring of contact lenses around his irises, but that curious detail was in the background as I realized what he was trying to convey with that one sentence.

That he wouldn't be staying in town. That he would be leaving at some point.

That he liked me. That he wanted to keep me close while he was here but not close enough to be here long-term.

I swallowed the conflicted lump in my throat. While my stay in Antler Pointe had no definite end, I could easily be leaving, too. He was warning me that whatever this was, it was finite.

I reached up to hold his jaw with both of my hands, nodding with small, jerky movements, and brought our lips together again. I'd never expected anything lasting. Not this shaky peace I'd been feeling, not the care of my brother or his family. Not my life.

Knowing that Río and I had an approaching deadline was okay. It had to be.

CHAPTER TWELVE

RÍO

The rest of the band began to pack up their shit, but I felt myself hesitating. It wasn't unusual for me to hang back after practice when we were at Tyler's, but it was mostly so we could shoot the shit and talk about non-human things. Today, there were more serious thoughts in my mind that were itching for an audience. Or just—a third party to bear witness and help me make sense of them.

But I couldn't tell him *everything*.

I put my Iceman in its case, raised a hand to Brody and Jess as they started the process of loading their respective cars.

Tyler's house was huge and outside of town—the perfect place to set up all our gear and play as loudly as we wanted. When I'd first come here for practice and took in the sleek, modern home with black walls and gleaming floors, I'd been struck with how much it looked like my father's. Where I'd lived out my imprisonment with staff at my beck and call that would also look the other way because they were just as likely to be killed as I was to be beaten.

But, the closer I looked, Ty's home was also different. Not as many walls of windows, as he truly liked the darkness, the modest-sized kitchen in contrast with the sprawling rooms and grounds. A room specifically dedicated to our practices that was set up with pretty much everything we needed.

I'd been fiddling with the edge of a leather sofa that was pushed up along one of the walls of the practice room, but Tyler's scratchy voice interrupted my anxious fiddling. "Are you leaving or staying?"

He wasn't dressed in either of his personas tonight. No eyeliner or metal band frontman getup. No pressed suit and styled hair. Just a baggy t-shirt and cargo pants. "Thought I'd fuck around here in the lap of luxury for a bit."

"Whatever, dude," he flicked his eyes toward the door, "got a bite coming over in a few, but you can stay."

Brody and Jess came back, all laughs and casual chatter, picked up the last of their stuff, and said goodbye. The front door closing behind them vibrated beneath my feet, though to them, it was probably just a soft thud.

"They actually know what they're coming over for?" I raised a brow at him, teasing. Mostly.

He evidently took my words as a more serious accusation. His fangs descended. "I have some common decency. And the bagged shit gets old. What did you wanna talk about, because you've got that look on your face." He waved a hand at me, as if my inner turmoil was distasteful.

I cocked my head and examined him a little more closely. I'd known vampires before, sure, but I could never call one of them a friend. And, though I'd never, ever say the words out loud, Ty was—my best friend. "Do vamps feel differently than we do? Like not as intensely or something?"

He returned my question with an exasperated glare and waved me behind him. I followed him up the hallway to the living room that was comprised of a sunken space decorated with leather couches, a thick glass coffee table, and a pristine fireplace. The windows to the left overlooked the manicured lawn that led to the forest beyond.

"We feel things differently like two humans feel things differently. It depends on the person, asshole."

"Yeah." I plopped down on the couch and put my socked feet up on the glass in front of us. At least, until a rage-filled glare from Ty made me drop them. "But don't all the years and killing just… numb it all?"

He sat cross-legged, elbows resting on his thighs, and looked at me like I was completely and utterly full of shit. "And you've never killed anyone?" When I betrayed panic, wide-eyed before I got my features to settle, he tsked and pulled open a drawer hidden in the table. Tyler retrieved a small box and began to use its contents to pack and roll a blunt. "I can smell the death on you."

I swallowed, fought to deny it or give some bullshit excuse, but the years reflected in my best friend's eyes were truly well beyond his appearance. Nah, I wouldn't bullshit him. It was probably what made me gravitate toward him in the first place. It wasn't like he was the only non-human or only vampire in town.

Once the blunt was tightly rolled, he struck an honest-to-goodness match and lit up. His first drag was long, but when it was over, he sat back against the couch cushions, slouching further than he normally would.

When he offered it to me, I shrugged and put it to my lips. Instead of the weak human shit, the first taste of it made me shudder with anticipation. Recognition. I took a pull, drawing the smoke into my lungs, let it swirl and seep into my blood.

On my exhale, a cloud rushed from my mouth toward the ceiling, as did a round of coughs that let the drug seep in even further. "G-good shit," I managed and passed it back. It'd been years since I touched the supernatural-grade stuff, after relying on it for so many years to help me get through to the next day. But after striking out on my own, trying to find it was too much of a risk, and the human-grade shit made my throat raw without any of the benefits.

This, though, I could already feel taking effect. I leaned back into the leather beside Tyler, both of us looking at nothing in particular. Just breathing, smoking.

Through the smoky haze trailing around the room, I imagined Ramona's face. The way her blank facade would twitch and crumble if I tickled her just right with my words or my touch. The way my Jaguar would rumble and long to pounce on her. To truly claim her, drag her beside me while I kept running.

"So, what did you really want to talk about?" Ty's knowing question broke me out of my daydreaming, but I was already way too high to actually startle.

He passed me the blunt, now halfway gone, and I took another hit, trying to draw my words. What was I here to talk about? "I might…"

"See the Wolf girl as more than a convenient fuck?" His short black hair shuffled against the leather behind him as he turned to look at me. I did the same and took in his already-reddening eyes.

I tried my best to glare at him through the smoke while I coughed, but it'd pale in comparison to anything Ramona would manage. And then that got me thinking about the cute pout she'd get when I said something stupid. The irritation that I could so easily turn to desire with a whisper in her ear or a tender nip at her neck. What would it be like when I finally got to taste her and sink into that—

"Ugh, if you're gonna pop a boner and some heart eyes just *thinking* about her, you're absolutely further gone than you think."

I looked down at my lap, and, sure enough, my half-hard dick was evident through my jeans. Something about that made me laugh, but it came out more of a wheezing cough. And then *that* made me cough for real.

Tyler slapped my back a few times while taking the last draw from the blunt until it was a spent roach that he tossed in the ashtray on the table. "But—" I tried and sputtered "—what do I *do* about her?"

"Whadoya mean 'what do I do?' It *can't* be that different for you shifters. You spend time together, you fuck, you die, happy-ish-ever-after."

"Happyish? I can't just be happy?"

He snorted. "Not in my experience."

My brain was too muddled to hang onto that enough to respond with something, my thoughts already drifting to the murky future that I didn't even see clearly for myself. We'd met up more and more at the skate spot, me and Ramona, and each time, it felt... easy. Peaceful like hot coffee while watching the sunrise on a chilly morning. Normally, I got my dick wet and moved on to the next hole and next town.

Yeah, her tight throat was a fucking dream, but I'd only had it *once*. Besides that, a few stolen moments we could snag at the spot when we were arriving or leaving. Like yesterday, when I'd walked her to her car after skating for hours in the humid night. She'd parked near my truck, so we took a detour. Those that were still skating were far away, but that didn't stop me from sitting her in the passenger seat and pressing my hand between her legs until she came. To my surprise, she'd squeezed and moved her palm back and forth on my crotch until I was coming with her, in my jeans like a horny teenager. It was hot and frantic and sticky, the confines of our clothes only adding to it, and I had to tug at my pants now to relieve the pressure that was growing just from thinking about it.

The doorbell rang, melodic and lingering, and Tyler stood smoothly. "You already made it clear that I'm never fucking you, and *I* don't get fucked. So if you're gonna keep doing that shit, you need to go to the bathroom and take care of yourself or leave." On the way to the door, he mumbled, "Fucking stinking up my house," and I couldn't help huffing a laugh while contin-uing to adjust myself.

While Ty met his supper at the door, I started on rolling another blunt for us. I was in a pleasant, soupy place after the first, and there was no way in hell I was gonna be able to drive home. Luckily, he had at least two spare bedrooms and these comfy-ass couches to crash on.

If I thought he was gonna take his meal with linebacker shoulders and fiery red hair elsewhere, I was mistaken. They plopped down on one of the other couches in the living space, and my hands stilled as I tried to identify the guy that I could've sworn I'd met before. Max? Matthew? Adrian? Whatever.

"Hey, Río." Welp. He knew my name, apparently. "You joining us?"

I frowned as I struck a match and lit the end of the tightly rolled blunt. Even with my loose fingers, it was more neatly rolled than Ty's had been. Still had it.

Before I could respond, Tyler cut in *again*. He ran his hands through the guy's hair. "Take off your shirt," he directed at the redhead. "And no, he's got a *girlfriend*." The teasing in his voice and annoyance on his face made for a weird combination where I didn't know what to get defensive over. That 'girlfriend' felt exciting but also wrong? Or that he somehow saw being attached to another as lesser? Which didn't fucking help the conflict I was already experiencing.

"I came here for advice, shithead. Not to just get high and talked down to."

Max-Matthew-Adrian tossed his shirt onto the floor and kept his hands obediently in his lap. I could pick out a series of bite mark-shaped scars on his neck, which explained the familiarity he exuded with Tyler touching him. "How boring. Hope she's not a *total* snooze," he added but grinned.

My instincts were still on alert amidst the drugs, because I felt my fangs emerge as I growled and leaned toward him for insulting her.

The guy blanched, going even paler than he already was, and pressed against the back of his seat. I stayed glaring, waiting for him to fucking say something else, but Tyler sliced through the tension with an amused chuckle. He tapped his finger along the guy's neck that was straining with fear. "Watch it, Finn. Best not get between an animal and his mate." To me and my own shocked face, he gave a sideways glance. "Just be with her. Quit fucking worrying about what it means because you already *know* what it means." And without preamble, his fangs dropped and sank into Finn's neck.

The guy's yelp of surprise soon turned to moans, and I didn't miss the tenting of both of their pants while Tyler drank greedily, thin trails of blood escaping his lips and running down Finn's bare chest. The lust filling the room was more stifling than the smoke in my lungs.

Shoving to my feet, I held the blunt between my lips as I marched toward the kitchen and then further until I was out of the back door. The sun was only a faint orange sliver amongst the tree line, now, and the illuminated pool cast an aquamarine glow that filled my vision.

"Fuck this," I said at nothing and everything. "She's not—" but I couldn't finish the sentence. My throat spasmed with something other than a cough. Angrily, I shoved off my clothes and took one last hit from the blunt. I was no fucking closer to understanding this thing between Ramona and I that I really didn't need to *become* a thing in the first place.

She was... good. Underneath or perhaps *because* of the hard exterior and gooey inside, she was better than me, and I couldn't afford a distraction like her to make me slip up further than I already had.

Because when were they going to come looking for Benny? Or was he low-level enough to have his disappearance be only a minor inconvenience to them? What—what would she say, how would she look at me, if she knew all the things I had done? What danger being with me would actually bring.

A blissful groan from inside reached my ears, and I crouched, stubbing out the blunt on the concrete lip of the pool. Great. Now

I'd gone from relaxed to fucking anxious and in no better place than how I'd started.

I launched into the water, hoping it'd help calm my thoughts again or take away some of these burdens, at least for a little while. But as I let the water envelop me, the weightless feeling only reminded me of how I felt with her.

CHAPTER THIRTEEN

RAMONA

I waited in the front of the witch house, as I'd started calling it after hearing a few members of the pack refer to Sylvie's grandmother's home as such. We'd gotten out early on this Saturday morning, so the heat hadn't fully awoken yet. Though I'd normally slept in as much as I could, my brother and his family were early risers, and my internal clock was already adjusting to the shift in schedule.

I took an icy gulp of the iced coffee in my hand. At least, I was almost adjusted. Enough to sneak a sunrise cigarette while Sylvie and Orion started on the babies' routines.

My mom had smoked all my life, my dad occasionally, and my brother had until quitting around the time he met Sylvie. The cancer sticks had only the briefest of appeals, but when I'd had those two weeks of crawling my way back from the edge, they'd become a part of my outdoor time ritual.

I was tapering off of them, but this morning had been one where I'd indulged. Río and I had hung out a few times since he'd told me he wouldn't be staying in Antler Pointe. There was nothing to make of that information but meet it with steady resignation. Expectations would only end up hurting me.

And after being so numb to almost everything, my emotions felt raw and pink, like newborn babies that would throw meltdowns at the slightest provocation, leaving me scrambling and quick to tears myself.

Weird analogy, but it feels right.

An old, economical sedan turned onto the short driveway, and I saw my friend stuffed into the driver's seat and grinning at me. I waved and returned his sunny smile as he unfolded himself out of the car that looked way too small for him.

Delaney wore a pink t-shirt and hunter green shorts that matched the headband he used to hold back his golden hair. He jogged up to me, arms rising like he wanted to give me a hug, before pausing. I sighed and initiated the hug myself. And, instead of the quick gesture, he squeezed me tightly and even rocked a little bit before letting me go. My chest fluttered, but the color of it was different. Río made me feel… crimson. With passion and desire and something deeper that threatened to blow everything up.

With Delaney, it was almost the color of his shirt. Sweet and fun and comforting. His orange and vanilla smelled lively today, and I felt my body work to react to and reflect his enthusiastic nature. "I hope I'm not too late! I don't have any gardening experience, so I was a little unsure what to wear, and I'm still a little unfamiliar with this town, so I got turned around, but it's so nice to see you!" His deep voice jumped with his energetic words, and I would've struggled more to follow if I hadn't been accustomed to my niece and nephew's similar sort of prattling by now.

"No specific time. Just wanted to beat the heat as much as possible. And you look fine." I started toward the side of the house and around the back, and Delaney followed. His scent was popping with citrusy excitement, and for a second, I worried that I wouldn't have enough energy to keep up with him.

The garden was like a meticulously planned jungle, and I

sensed Delaney's surge of surprise and delight as he took in what I'd already grown used to seeing. The large section of colorful flowers and blooms with neat pathways for better access when tending. The multiple areas for vegetables that were another variety of greens and pops of color. A few benches sat amongst everything, and I set my half-finished coffee on the iron seat before starting on the tour.

"Sylvie and her coven sister Josie enhance the garden as much as they can, so it takes care of itself a lot more than a normal one would. But we still have a lot of tending and harvesting to do with the vegetables and herbs. And since they keep it going through all seasons, it's a year-round thing." I kept us on the path-ways, pointing out and identifying everything I could remember and gave a little description of how I'd been instructed to care for them. "And, apparently, it's okay that these to turn red instead of just staying green."

I turned back to Delaney's large form behind me, catching a strange thread of unease, and he was rubbing at his cheek with wary eyes casting around. I was about to ask him what was the matter, but his Adam's apple bobbed with a swallow before he answered my unspoken question. "I don't think I'll be able to remember all of this."

My lips turned down. "Oh, that's okay. No one's saying you have to. Sylvie is inside with the babies for a sec, but I usually just do what she tells me. That's the only reason I know all this."

He dropped his hands to his front and fiddled with the draw-string tie of his shorts. "You're really smart."

"Uh… thanks? How about we just wait for her to get out here and give us our tasks for the day. Do you have any questions?"

Delaney looked around and rubbed the side of his face again. "Is… is your brother gonna be here too?"

"Huh?" It wasn't his question that took me off guard, but the reddening of his cheeks and the uncertain way he asked it. I took a sniff of the air, and I tried not to wrinkle my nose at the telltale boiled egg smell of fear and… the remnants of bubblegum. Like an old crush. "Uh… no. He's working on some stuff at home." Oh, god, he used to have a crush on Orion? While part of that made me want to gag, I worried that it wasn't such a good idea that he was here. Hell, even in the pack at all. Though I could tell it was an old crush, his skittishness now made a little more sense.

"Good," he said under his breath but then seemed to realize that he'd said it out loud, eyes widening in horror. "Oh, no—I mean. I just—"

My face twisted, feeling wholly awkward now. "Look… I know he can be aloof, but he really isn't scary. If that's what you're worried about. And, he's also happily mated to Sylvie, so…"

Delaney's eyes were blank, his brows furrowed, and we stood in silence as he worked to make sense of what I was trying to imply without outright saying it. Eventually, he blinked, blushed harder, and looked horrified. "Oh, no no no no, I would *never*. Please believe me. I really like Sylvie." His hands clutched together beneath his chin, and tears threatened to shed.

I felt like an asshole. "God, please don't cry. I wasn't—" fuck. "I shouldn't have. Like spied on your feelings or whatever. Um, it's okay."

He rubbed the heel of a palm on one of his eyes, as if that would stop the tears from escaping. "What do you mean spying? I don't get it?"

Now I was rubbing at my eyes. When Orion had pointed out that it could be done, I'd had lots of practice over the years, identifying and cataloguing the complex notes that lay underneath the more obvious scents people gave off. I couldn't even remember how the conversation first started, but I'd learned that day that my brother had used and honed the skill to understand and navigate social situations that otherwise made little sense to him. With a mother who rarely spoke what she was actually feeling, and most people obscured their emotions so much that it was commonplace, I'd gotten pretty good at it, too.

"Ah, shifter nose? Like, underneath your scent I could tell that my brother makes you afraid. And…" I tried to soften my words, something I wasn't used to doing around adults. "That you used to have a crush on him."

Delaney's face fell, looking devastated, but before I could rush to apologize even more, he started pleading again. "Please don't tell him or Sylvie. I swear, I stopped as soon as I realized he had a mate. I just always saw him when he was dropping off at the school, and he was the first shifter I'd come that close to since moving here, and his Leader scent, but I *swear*, as soon as I knew about Sylvie, it went away. Please don't be mad."

Oh good god, I was not equipped for this. I should've kept my big mouth shut, and now he was really crying. I raised my hands, hesitating for a second, before laying them on his arms that were hard with muscle but soft to the touch. "Hey, hey, Delaney it's okay. Let's just—let's just start over, okay? I'm sorry. That I said all that. We're glad you're here and invited you for a reason. Okay?"

He sniffed, but his wide and red eyes on me made him look heartbreakingly young. "You mean that you'll still be my friend?"

"A-absolutely."

"And you won't tell your brother? Or Sylvie? *Please.*"

"Won't tell me what?" Sylvie padded into the garden on bare feet with both her children in her arms. Dahlia and Sylvie looked worried, Ollie curious.

More embarrassment wafted off Delaney, so I squeezed his forearms in what I hoped was reassurance. "Just that Delaney's a little nervous about his first time helping out."

Sylvie's long look let me know that she knew it was bullshit, but she thankfully didn't push. "Oh, well that's okay." She walked closer. "I'll show you what to do, but you're also welcome to just sit and chat if you'd like."

I dropped my hold on my friend, and he swatted away the last remaining tear before it could fall. He cleared his throat. "No, I want to help. Thank you for inviting me. And being so nice to me."

My sister-in-law's gaze softened and she relented to both of her kids' squirming. "Oh, honey, no need. As Ramona already told you, I'll put you to work if you give me the chance. You might not want to thank me once we're done for the day." Sylvie let her daughter and son down, and instead of taking off to run amongst the plants, Dahlia took Ollie's hand in hers and marched toward Delaney.

She almost had to stare straight up to look at his face. Ollie wobbled a little bit but was able to stay upright. "Mr. Delaney, do you wanna water the flowers with us?"

He blinked down at her, face clearing and relaxing. He crouched until he was still quite a bit taller than my niece but much closer to her height. "You gotta show me what to do, but I'd love to."

Dahlia gave a serious nod, looking scarily like my brother. "We'll teach you." Sylvie chuckled and stood back while her daughter started doling out demands, waving Delaney and Ollie behind her as they went to retrieve the watering cans to get to work. She instructed Delaney to take the bigger one while she and Ollie shared a smaller, child-sized one.

I watched them for a while, Delaney seeming much more at ease with conversing with Dahlia and Ollie. Guilt still wrapped around my throat for making him upset, but the big guy looked to be able to bounce back pretty quickly. His smile was back as he watered and smelled the different blooms. All three laughed when their watering sent up a flurry of butterflies and bumble bees that flew around them.

"He's had a difficult go of it."

"What do you mean?" I'd heard her approach but didn't bother turning.

"Not sure what it is, but it'd be hard to ignore. Sadness and trauma aren't as easy to hide as some would think." Her statement held a silent echo, one that made me feel too vulnerable. Seen. Or was I reading too much into it? Was that what Sylvie saw when she looked at me?

"Well, he seems good right now." I waved in the direction of

Delaney, mouth pursed in concentration while he carefully watered a cluster of orchids that, amazingly, bloomed delicate and proud amidst everything else. "And if he gets more used to—*what the fuck!*" I'd turned to my sister-in-law but now had to stop myself from smacking her arm and running into the house.

Petunia, at least I assumed it was the same spider, had been slowly crawling up Sylvie's bare arm but stilled at my outburst.

Sylvie took a step back from me, too, looking afraid and concerned until she followed my gaze to the spider now resuming her ascent to perch on the curve of Sylvie's shoulder. Petunia sat beside my brother's mating mark, just like, sunbathing or some shit, and I tried to stop from progressing to full hyperventilation.

She sent her eyes skyward. "Dude, you've got to get over it."

"Are y'all all right?" Delaney ran over with the kids behind him.

"Tooney!" Ollie screamed and waved his little hands toward the giant fucking dinosaur of an insect.

Dahlia tugged on Delaney's shirt, ushering him to crouch again, and when he obeyed, she whispered in his ear, "Auntie Mona is scared of spiders."

"Damn right—Petunia is huge!" I pointed at her, and when did I start thinking of the thing as a 'her' and referring to her by name?

Dahlia said some other things to Delaney, but I was far too focused and horrified when Sylvie took Petunia in her hand and transferred her to Ollie's eager little palms. The little boy *put the spider on his head* and took off, wandering around the pathways while babbling in excited baby talk.

My stomach churned and my skin crawled with a hundred imaginary bugs. "I think I'm gonna be sick."

"Pssh, you don't have to be so dramatic."

Delaney and Dahlia giggled, and I realized that they were looking at *me* as they did it. I shot my palms toward Ollie, running and laughing in high-pitched joy. "Come *on*. That's insane. Am I the only one rooted in any sort of reality?"

Dahlia's new best friend, apparently, stood, body trembling with suppressed laughter. "It's okay to be afraid sometimes."

I narrowed my eyes but cut it out when I saw Delaney's joy start to crumble in the face of my sharp expression. Before I could apologize again, my phone dinged in my back pocket, and I didn't have a thought in my mind aside from hoping that it was who I thought it was.

RÍO

Morning, Princess. Wanna hang later?

"Is that your boyfriend, Auntie Mona?" My niece nearly screamed her question, and my fingers fumbled, dropping my phone into a raised garden bed.

Her open, curious stare had me choking back my instinct to shoot something back at her. I took a deep breath as I picked my phone up and dusted the soil off of it, reminding myself that my four year old niece was not going to try to use whatever Río and I were against me. "He's not my boyfriend."

When I straightened, they were all looking at me, and disbelief, amusement, and confusion were swirling violently around us. Ugh. "Are you sure?" Dahlia asked, obviously not able to read between the lines.

Sylvie swooped in, placing a hand on my niece's shoulder and beginning to steer her in another direction. "I don't think she is, sweetheart. But that's okay."

I opened my mouth, closed it, and looked frantically at Delaney who barely knew me but witnessed this humiliating ten minutes. My face was hot, and I tugged at my sleeves, not knowing whether to prepare for questions, shoot while he was hesitating, or just flee in another direction and ignore it all.

"What do you think we should do next?" He asked instead.

"Uh…" I started to stuff my phone back in my pocket, but remembering I hadn't responded to Río had me bringing it back out and firing off my response before tucking it away again.

ME

Sure. Whenever's good.

"Let's go get the pruning shears and see what needs clipping, I guess."

Delaney gave me a determined nod and followed me toward the little shed that held all of the tools. While I pulled out all we needed and handed it to him, he accepted everything with concentration and nods when I named each thing. When we started back toward Sylvie who was holding an outstretched hand over a growing cluster of mint, Delaney whispered, "I'm a good listener if you ever wanna talk. And thank you for being my friend."

My eyes itched, and I mumbled something back, too stunned and affected by his simple yet powerful words.

CHAPTER FOURTEEN

RÍO

I smiled down at my phone, despite being splattered with marinara sauce and being at the tail end of my opening shift. My freakout at Tyler's had been quickly forgotten when I'd woken up the next morning, sprawled in jaguar form in the woods beside his house. I'd prowled lazily back to my shit at the pool and pulled my phone from my jeans pocket, only to squint when the screen was just a blur. At some point, I'd plucked out my contacts to shift—it was a literal pain when I'd forget and leave them in—and had to rely on my previous visits and sense of smell to lead me to my backpack still left in the practice room. By some miracle, I had a spare pair of glasses shoved in the front pocket.

Able to see clearly, I'd checked my phone to find a few texts from Ramona, and I'd returned them so that by the time I drove home, we'd had plans to meet up after I got off work.

Which was right about now.

ME

> Come on in. Might convince the manager to give you free breadsticks

The little bell on the door sounded, and my heart actually picked up, maybe even fluttered.

"I'm out," I called to Vanessa and Rob who were manning the kitchen and returned with noises of acknowledgment.

There was a small bathroom for employees connected to the office, and I stopped in there to change into the spare shirt I'd brought with me and washed my hands and face. There'd be no getting rid of the pizza smell until I was able to shower, but hopefully it wouldn't bother her too much.

When I emerged into the dining area, bag slung over my shoulder, I took a moment to drink in Ramona while her back was turned. It was just a second before she turned around, but it was just enough for my eyes to sweep over her long, bare legs that were a delicious, glowing brown. Her usual sweatshirt obscured the shape of her torso and arms, but her ass was round and tight beneath the skimpy denim shorts. I wanted to squeeze the strong but giving globes in my hands, but that wasn't what made my jaw drop.

Her hair wasn't in its usual braid. It was… down and cast in bounding ringlets that flowed like a lion's mane. Glints of orange and red flared from the light streaming through the windows and lit up the sea of her black curls. It called back to the night I'd learned her name, to when she'd gotten on her knees for me. But seeing her this way in broad daylight, was… more.

I didn't turn away from my staring, even when her expression went from nervous to irritated to uncertain. "Uh… is this a bad time?"

Most of our time together was spent rolling around the skatepark, but I'd had another idea for today. "Course not. I'm the one who told you when to get here, anyway." I stepped closer, keeping our eyes locked, and indeed wrapped my arms around her waist to settle my hands on the upper curve of her ass.

I dropped a kiss onto her lips and felt her surprise before she pressed into it. My nose buried in the crown of her hair, inhaling the concentrated grapefruit scent that had me high in a lighter, more sustainable way than any drug I'd ever had.

"So…" She tightened and relaxed her hands on my shoulders. "What did you want to do? You said to leave my skates at the house."

The wary confusion in her tone made me give a reassuring chuckle into her scalp. "You down to go see a movie?"

She flinched back completely, now, and her honey gaze was more vulnerable than usual. "That… that sounds like a date."

I swallowed and grinned. "Whatever you wanna call it. You like scary movies?"

At first, she frowned. "They're—" but something flitted across her features and made her stand straighter, though the change was lightening fast "—of course." The smile she gave was the most pleasant she'd ever given me, no venom to brighten it. Before I could parse out what exactly gave me pause about the shift in her expression, she gave a tender pass up and down my shoulders. "Did you want to go now?"

With another kiss to her head, I nodded and grabbed her hand to lead her to my truck. Ramona kept her hand soft in my grip, trailing readily behind me.

"All right, what kind of snacks do you want? Have you eaten today?" We stood in the concession stand line that was quickly moving forward. I kept a possessive hand on Ramona's ass, squeezing at my leisure, and she didn't even balk at my display. On the drive to the movie theatre, she'd asked me about my day at work, spoken gently about her morning with her family, and even talked about the *weather*.

The person behind the register called for the next customer, and I pushed further, snaking my hand into her back pocket and keeping my hand full of her cheek.

Nothing.

We stepped up, with her standing behind me by a half step, and she looked up at me expectantly while I was watching her with eyes narrowed. "Río? What do you want to eat?"

"What do *you* want?"

She didn't even look at the menu, just kept that sweet and polite smile on her face. "Whatever you want. I'm not picky." My gut twisted, constricted, even as her shoulders relaxed, just a fraction, when I ordered a large popcorn and two Cokes.

I couldn't keep hold of her ass while I carried my soda and our popcorn, and I almost dropped both when she held onto my bicep, letting me guide her to our theatre and seats. Naturally, I picked something in the way back and promptly put my arm around her shoulders as we settled.

Another staggering current of her scent hit me, intoxicating me with fantasies of what I wanted to do to her in the dark and nearly empty room.

While the previews rolled, I paid them no mind and let those desires creep in. She'd called this a date, and while I'd been too chicken to confirm that for her, I *had* wanted to make this—more than just skatepark hookups.

I pulled back a mass of her curls to get access to her neck, where I planted a kiss. Her body stilled, her breathing stumbled, and I prepared for her strike. Or a little grumbling before she melted between my fingers.

What I got instead was a little mewl and immediate craning into my touch. My body rejoiced while my mind tried hard to figure out why this didn't feel right.

In her ear, I whispered between nibbles, "You don't care about seeing the previews, Princess?"

Her hand, soft and smooth, lightly grasped my jaw, just holding it to her, and I braced myself for her to push me away. She would push me away, call me a fuckboy, then pull me back in with a fight before succumbing to me.

But, no, instead she just held me there, made more of those quiet, high-pitched whines. Ominous music began to blare through the speakers, encasing us in the impending horror atmosphere, but I was too preoccupied, and too confused, to let myself be swayed.

I pulled away, and Ramona let me. I tried to see her through the darkness, read the emotion in her eyes that were awash with the blue-tinted light coming from the screen. I planted my nose in her temple, taking a draw through my nose, but all I could identify was desire. That should've been fine, that should've been all the permission I needed to feel her up and make her come in this public place.

Instead, I planted one last peck on her hairline and settled back into my seat.

There was a moment of tension between us, where we both were confused at what the hell had happened, but I was too busy trying to make myself focus on the movie with her still stiff in my arms.

Eventually, we relaxed into our seats, munched on popcorn and drank our drinks. At the first jump scare, Ramona didn't react, just continued to stare forward. The next, though, she hid her eyes in my shoulder. When a character was murdered in the most brutal fashion, a gnarly strike to the neck with a makeshift weapon that sprayed blood everywhere, she didn't curl into me until they'd pretty much hit the ground.

When the movie ended, the final girl driving away as credits rolled, I was a weird mixture of pissed and fucking *confused*. As we left, I threw out the mostly-full bucket of popcorn that we'd both barely touched, and marched us toward the exit.

The sun was on its way down, adding to my disorientation because it was flying high and bright when we'd arrived. Ramona clasped my hand, and it just pissed me off even more—alone, it *shouldn't* have made me angry.

When she walked up to the passenger side of my truck, she stood, looking and… waiting for me to open the *door?*

I slammed my hand on the window beside her head, making her startle, her brow to wrinkle. Now, with the light of the sun, I watched her honey eyes turn from hard to soft to glazed over, and I slammed my other hand, caging her in.

"I want you on your fucking knees. Suck me off. Now."

Something flared, a flicker of fire before she softened it *again,* and I stared back in horror when she gave me that little smile and started to slide down the body of the truck. To do what I demanded.

I smacked my hand beside her head, startling her to stop. I'd parked further away from other people as a habit, but I was too angry to care if someone saw. Fooling around with Ramona with the risk of people seeing was fun, but something we shared together. This… meek, agreeable act wasn't fun. Finn's words last night, when I'd been insulted at the mere implication Ramona was a *snooze,* ripped another growl from my chest.

My brow connected with hers, and I could feel her pulse skyrocketing, the thumps of it vibrating the air between us. "I don't do that fake shit, rich girl."

She gasped, and a few moments of crackling silence coursed between us. "W-what are you talking about?"

"Don't fucking play stupid with me. You've been acting weird all day. Like I want some weak little thing to agree with everything I say or do. I don't know what's gotten into you, but if you're gonna keep it up, I'm taking you back right now."

"I don't—"

"*Bullshit.*" I sneered. "Like I want some empty-headed rich girl. If you don't want me to go drop you off, get on your knees, suck me down that tight throat of yours until you fucking choke— because now you've pissed me off—or start fucking acting right."

Ramona jerked her head away from mine, and when our gazes collided, my gut swooped. "Stop."

I raised a brow, body craning around her even more. "Stop

what, rich girl? Trying to get off? Wanting to fuck your throat until you gag? The way you acted tonight tells me that's all you're good for."

I watched my crude words pummel into her and the resulting hardening. Her amber eyes turning to beautiful, glinting gems instead of the digestible murk they'd been since we'd left Vinny's.

She shoved at my chest so hard that I stumbled back a few steps, trying to keep my ground and not fall on my ass. Her fists clenched at her side, hair wild and fluttering in the slight breeze coursing around us. "You talk to me like that again, and I'll kick your fucking ass!"

My laugh was mean, too loud and sharp, and I took two steps back toward her. I could hear the blood pumping through her heart, the echo of it in her chest. Her outraged panting whistled in and out of her lungs. The fluttering of her lashes as she blinked.

The scent of her lust as it spiked.

"I'll make you a deal, Princess." I let loose the claw on my finger as I pointed it at her. Another step, and she let me graze it against the ticking muscle on her jaw, all the way down to the pulsing on the side of her neck. "You act right, and I'll only say that stuff when you wanna hear it."

"You're an ass, and no one talks to me like that." The venom in her words had tilted, swirled.

I let mine twine around hers, react and spin. "Wrong. I do, and you *like* that I do. You need to fight back so that when you finally drop to your knees and open your mouth, it's even sweeter."

Her nostrils flared, and a car honked in the distance, followed by some shouts. A few birds squawked past us, flitting from one of the sparse trees in the lot to another. But my attention was on her, nearly on my toes with anticipation for what she'd do next.

She had my own breath catching, my grin ticking higher when her hands shot out again, but instead of hitting me, they went to my waist. And in a flurry, she had my belt undone and was unzipping my fly. "You're an un-evolved child. I'm surprised no one's ever put you in your fucking place." My palm returned to the warm glass of my truck, hips canting into Ramona's touch as she flipped my steel-hard dick out of my boxers. She teased the barbell hooked through the slit, and I groaned.

"Who said no one has before?"

She scoffed and collected on her thumb some of the precum that was already sliding down the crown of my cockhead. Ramona shoved it in my mouth, and I sucked the salt from her fingertip. Underneath my own flavor on her skin, I caught remnants of popcorn butter and whatever lotion she'd put on, probably after she'd showered this morning. My thoughts flashed to what that would look like, Ramona's slender curves twisting and bending under shower spray, and another spurt of precum dripped down my cock.

My princess withdrew her thumb, and I groaned again at the sight of her spitting into her palm. She somehow glared at me tenderly and started the hottest fucking handjob I'd ever received. She didn't tease me into it, just let her hand fly.

I buried my face in her hair, let it swallow my moans and babbling. "Fuck, Princess, just like that, shit you're so fucking—"

Her other hand reached in and tentatively caressed my balls, making me nearly choke. Taking my reaction for the encouragement that it was, she gently rolled them. "God, Ramona, wanna be in that pussy s-so fucking bad." I could smell it, her getting wet for me, and my release was creeping closer and closer down my spine.

"Yeah?" Her voice had gone all husky. "You do?"

I nodded like an idiot, strands of her hair tickling my nose. "Want it so bad, wanna have you screaming on my cock." She jerked her hand faster while she teased my balls. "Shit, I'm gonna come."

"Well, come then."

The words were so simple and all I needed. My claw tightened against her neck, threatening to draw blood but never breaking the skin, and my vision short-circuited. Cum spurted from my dick, and I thought I heard her moan along with me while it made a mess of her hand and trailed down her wrist.

She lazily pumped, milking until she pulled it all out of me.

A shuffling had both of our heads whipping to the side, and meeting the shocked looks from a middle-aged looking couple that were standing stupid, probably having seen the whole exchange. I threw my head back and laughed while Ramona dropped my softening dick and wiped her hand on my t-shirt.

The couple eventually snapped out of it and fled toward the movie theatre, like they were afraid we'd start up again. Which, I turned back to Ramona, wasn't really a bad idea.

She clutched the neckline of my shirt and pulled me down for a hard kiss that ended with her shoving me away from her again. "Put your dick away," she grumbled and opened the passenger door behind her. She climbed into the seat and slammed the door in my face.

Ramona faced forward, arms crossed, but even the metal and glass between us didn't hide the desire pumping through her with every beat of her heart. I stuffed my half-hard dick back in my pants like she'd told me to and walked around the front of my truck.

After settling in the driver's seat and starting her up, I backed out of the parking spot and turned up the newest song we'd been working on. Ty called it 'Blessed Be', and it filled the thick silence between Ramona and me.

She twisted against the old leather seat, but before I could think about it, my hand was on top of her thigh. I looked both directions before turning onto the main road.

"Are we going back to your place?" she asked with uncertainty showing clearly through her nonchalance.

My fingers tightened on her bare skin that was warm and smooth to the touch. "We can."

I felt her eyes on the side of my face as I kept my eyes on the road. Up until now, she'd acted skittish when I'd made it known that I wanted to fuck her. And I didn't want her to feel beholden to something she'd said in the heat of the moment. Even with my cock hard again in my jeans at the thought of being inside of her.

"Do *you* want to?"

A low chuckle left me. "Princess, if you let me, I'd be fucking you right now in the back seat. But we can go back to mine and just hang out if you'd prefer that." She was sexy as hell, but I'd be able to behave. Now that I'd made it clear that I didn't want her to play any bullshit act with me, I was more than happy to just... be around her.

She took a deep inhale, pushing the air out through her nose, and another sweet taste of her desire filtered through my system. "Do you have condoms?"

My grip tightened on the wheel, but a loud grumble escaped from my throat anyway. "Yeah."

She laid her hand on top of mine on her leg. "Good."

CHAPTER FIFTEEN

RAMONA

Río closed the door, sealing us in his apartment. Alone.

The sounds of his neighbors were faint and in the background, so he no doubt picked up on my heart pounding within my chest. Because I could hear his, too.

Río stepped up to me, gaze intent and hot. His chile and clove was richer, affecting my body more than it had any right to. I'd never had this response to the lust of another, even when I *had* been in a relationship. Normally, the connection I needed with someone kept me far from getting to this place, and even when I'd managed it with my high school boyfriend, something still kept me from doing what I was absolutely about to do, now.

Río crowded even closer and tucked a lock of curls behind my ear. I'd been told before that my hair, when I could get it to behave, was pretty. But he seemed to be fascinated by it. "I like the smell of you in my apartment, Princess."

And I jumped him. My lips slammed onto his, and my legs wrapped around his waist. Río growled, and the sharpness of his claws just on the other side of my shorts had me wiggling and moaning against him. Though I closed the distance between us,

Río took charge of the kiss, despite me pressing against him, trying to communicate with my tongue that I just wanted him to fuck my mouth already.

Instead, Río walked us further into the fairly spacious room that was a combination of kitchen and living area. He sat us on a couch, slow and controlled when I felt like I wanted to just pull him under my skin, to live there always.

Jesus.

He broke the lock of our lips to kiss down my neck and start sucking, as if he already knew that it would send me into high, trembling mewls and shifting on his lap. His hands continued to squeeze my ass and keep me pressed to him. "Fuck, baby," he groaned into my neck, "you're so—*fuck*." He almost sounded frustrated.

Which made two of us. My body was aching for him in a way that I'd never felt with anyone before. To have him inside of me. We'd made each other come multiple times at this point, but it was like the base, animalistic part of me was done waiting to be *taken*. "Plea—want you."

"Yeah, baby? What do you want me to do?" He moved his hands up my sides and between our bodies, finding my nipples that were almost too sensitive against the fabric of my bra and sweatshirt. Río used his thumbs, still sucking hickeys on my neck, to flick and rub the sensitive points.

I whined, hands buried in his hair and rubbing over his cock that was hard between my legs. "Need you inside of me. *Now*."

He pulled back, and through my haze, I saw him staring with half-lidded eyes and lips parted. The scent of our desire swelled even higher, staring at each other, and my skin felt almost too hot for comfort. He palmed my hips and tugged on the belt loops of my shorts. "Then take these off for me, baby. I'll give you what you need."

Wouldn't say that I scrambled off of his lap to take off my shorts and panties, but it was quick work to unbutton, unzip, and shove everything off from the waist down. I couldn't even be bothered to make a show for him or even think about slowing down to do so.

And by the way he reached in his back pocket before unfastening his own jeans, he was just as hungry for me, too. He fished out a condom from his wallet and pulled his cock out.

The light in the apartment was low, but I could perfectly see it, long and thicker than I would've guessed. My mouth watered, remembering what it tasted like and how that piercing felt against my tongue. Río pumped his fist, causing precum to bead and start running down the shaft.

It was ridiculous what this shifter was doing to me, but while he turned his attention to opening the condom wrapper, I swiped my finger through the trail of precum before popping it in my mouth. I sucked the salty bitterness off of my skin, watching Río as he rolled the condom on. What would it be like to have him bare inside of me? The thought of it made me squirm impatiently, letting out another pathetic noise.

"Get the fuck over here, Princess," he ordered, and, for once, I didn't object.

We were both breathing harshly, fighting the urge to completely tear into each other, but—

I wanted it, *I did*, but what if it hurt? Or I wasn't good at it, or —I tried to shake the thoughts away, but the closer I got to finally having him, the panic set in. Any sexiness I'd mustered in my mind as Río kissed me was gone in an instant as I hovered over his lap. His hands held my hips firmly, yet even with his claws poking into my skin, there was a lightness, like a gentle caress on the edges.

My hair was a mass around both of our heads, and I knew that he could hear my heart rate jackrabbiting in my chest. My fingers clenched tighter on his shoulders, in time with my breaths as I tried to fight off tears.

"I've never done this before," I blurted, and half of the weight on my chest disappeared. My eyes had slammed shut at some point. And if I just continued to not breathe, maybe the despair wouldn't come back twofold like I was so accustomed to.

It took a moment, after I realized I wasn't going to combust from sheer embarrassment, for me to calm and tune back into the room. To the couch that Río and I sat on.

I opened my right eye first, focusing in on his nose because that seemed like the easiest thing. When he still wasn't pulling away or trying to push me off, I forced open my left eye and took in the bottom half of his face. The light streaming in from the apartment windows was more than enough for me to see a muscle ticking along the angle of his jaw. Gaze jerking upward, I was immediately sucked in to those black eyes. Although, now, there was a yellowing at the edges, more than I'd seen before.

A steel grip took my chin, though I was close enough to his face anyway. Río sat up straighter, taking me with him, and if I hadn't caught the thick scent of a fresh wave of arousal, I would've thought he was upset with me, his gaze was so intense.

"If you don't want to do this, Ramona, tell me now."

I didn't answer. My mind was particularly aware of the tension in my thigh muscles, but I didn't relax onto his lap or get off altogether. Wanting this wasn't the issue. If I hadn't, I wouldn't have came over in the first place. Certainly wouldn't have taken off my shorts.

Río's eyes didn't flinch from mine for a second, probably taking in more than I even knew myself. But that was okay. I just needed someone to hold it for a while. For him to know and to continue to see me.

His lips were on mine, tongue taking over my mouth and forcing past the hesitation. My short fingernails dug further into his skin, but his claiming was good. Necessary.

When Río parted our mouths, claws still prickling on my face, he spoke in a low voice that was halfway a snarl. "You say that shit to me again, and I don't know if I'll be able to keep it gentle."

My knees scooted even further apart, and I reached down to steady his cock at the base. Río's chest heaved, and when the tip met the warmth of my skin, his lips parted to reveal the deadly tips of his fangs.

Even with the condom on, the hard press of his piercing added an element of friction I'd never felt with the things I'd bought and tried on myself. I gasped as I slid down, stretching over the hot press of him. My head tucked into the side of his face, afraid that he'd see the nerves and pleasure and strain rushing back and forth within me.

I bit hard at my bottom lip when it felt like I couldn't take any more. The real thing was so different from cold silicone, and what would he say when I admitted that it was too much? Would he call off everything and pull out? Would he say 'fuck it' and make it hurt? My chest rose and fell in blustery pants as I tried to take another inch and was met with an answering burn.

"You feel so good, Ramona. My beautiful princess, relax for me, okay?" His breath tickled the curve of my neck.

I released my fingers from his shoulders and twined my arms around him instead. Hiding or clinging or both, but the tumbling roll of his voice brought a soothing warmth that cascaded from my ear down my spine.

"That's it, relax and open up for me." Another whimper trailed out from my parted lips and curled around his loose hair. I forced a deep breath, to take in Río's scent and do as he said. That's all I *had* to do.

He slid further in, continuing to give me reassurances and commands. I focused my mind on his words, on the purr that was starting to rumble through both of us, until my hips lowered the last inch and met his. "Fuck," I breathed and pulled away from my hiding spot to look between us.

Sure enough, Río was all of the way inside, my body full. I clenched around him and moaned at the fullness that responded. The burning was nearly gone now, and left in its wake was the exhale of *finally*.

Río threw his head back and cursed. "*Mierda*. Do that again." It hadn't been conscious, but I was able to will my walls to tighten around him again, and we both groaned from either side of the pleasure we were sharing together.

As if my body knew just what to do, and maybe it did, I pressed up on my knees, rising just enough for air to kiss the backs of my thighs, and sank back down. The movement made the piercing and girth of him known, forcing a longer, louder noise from my lungs.

His palms and claws remained on my hips, exerting enough pressure to remind me of their presence but allowing for the rhythm to be set by me. Noises of slick friction rang out between us as I went from tentative movements to full-on riding him.

The sharp, sweet physicality of it blanketed my mind in desire and lust to get to the top. My eyelids pressed together, and I tightened my fist in his hair while I rose and plummeted over and over.

Río placed wet kisses and licks while he growled underneath me, affected by this just as much as I was. I chased it, racing toward the crest that he was pushing into me with every thrust of his hips. The pain of his claws just deepened everything, and when I felt them break my skin, I cursed in joy.

"Just like that, Princess, fuck yourself on my cock. You take it so well." He added more force behind his movements, pulling me down harder and thrusting upward in a way that was tearing me apart. Someone was chanting in hoarse screams for *more, harder, more,* and it took me too long to realize that it was me.

Río obliged, shoving my release closer and closer, and when he added a spit-slicked thumb to press between my legs, fireworks danced behind my eyes.

While every muscle tensed and I lost all semblance of self, Río pounded into me, running up to meet me in ecstasy. He let loose a scratchy shout that was more growl than anything, and I could feel his cock lock and fire inside of me, filling the condom while we fell together.

The smell of my blood soothed me instead of sending me into a spiral of familiar self-loathing, and I accepted the clawed thumb that he forced between my lips. Mind hazy and loopy, I licked myself off of his finger, teasing the sharp edges that'd been so gentle with the softest parts of me.

Fluttering my lids open while he traced the plush flesh of my lip, I adjusted to the brighter darkness of the room. Immediately, I homed in on the set of pale yellow eyes hooded by black lashes. His pupils and irises were just as black, but what had been the whites of human eyes before were now a glowing pastel color.

I hadn't seen Río's shifter form yet, and I wondered if the half-shift of his eyes matched the color of his fur. Would the spots be the exact same color as his hair?

He placed a tender kiss on the point of my chin. "Let me go trash the condom," he commanded, and I nodded silently, lifting slowly and letting his softening dick slide out of me. I fought down the bits of embarrassment that tried to trickle in as I shuffled off of his lap and unwrapped my arms from around him.

Río stood and slipped the condom off of himself while heading toward the kitchen. The apartment was small—I could see all corners of it from where I sat—but it felt so much like him. Clothes were tossed haphazardly, but only in the area of the loft where I'd caught sight of a large mattress with a low bed frame. A stack of books rested on the beaten up coffee table in front of me.

Before I could start examining what Río elected to read in his downtime, his lean hips filled my line of vision. His jeans were still unbuttoned, and the red fabric of his boxer briefs matched the color of a small bleeding heart beside the V leading to his crotch.

Río gripped my jaw and forced my neck to crane up towards him. I went willingly. His lids were lowered more than usual, and I wondered what he'd look like truly sleepy. Río was either intense or cocky and cracking jokes, but I imagined that he was different when he was alone and at his most vulnerable.

"How was that for a first time, Princess?"

He was being so casual about it. I didn't give a shit about my *virginity*, or lack thereof now, but the fact that he was acknowledging it made heat rise to my cheeks. "Do you even have to ask?" Though I didn't doubt him, I'd always had in the back of my mind that my first time would be a throwaway. Something that would probably be mediocre at best. An obstacle to get to the truly good stuff.

Leave it to this asshole to have me skip that awkward phase altogether. I came so hard that I was pretty sure I stopped breathing there for a while.

Río sank to his knees, just like that, and pushed my thighs apart. Insecurity flashed quick, and I tried to push them back together. But he didn't let me. He took the back of my knees and pulled them toward himself, slouching me down into the couch.

"Nah. If I believed in God, I would say I'm pretty sure you saw Her up close and personal just now."

He hooked my legs on his shoulders, eyes between my thighs where he'd just been. I squirmed under his gaze. Being inside of me was different than this. I wasn't even sure what to be insecure *about*, but when he wiggled a clawless thumb between my labia, I sucked in a sharp breath. "Shut up."

He ignored me, pressing down on my clit. My toes curled in the air, and I bit down on my lip to not give him the satisfaction of the moan that threatened to slip out.

"Are you hurting?" He replaced his finger with a delicate flicker of his tongue that had my head dropping back on the couch cushions. I lost the very short battle to stifle my reaction to him, and a whine shook out. "Hm?"

He didn't go further, and I looked down in frustration. Río's hair was cascading around his shoulders and down his back, like the rolls of ocean waves. He cocked a brow, waiting.

"Um." I had to think for a second to remember his question and took stock of my body. There was a dull throbbing that I'd been completely ignoring. "Not really. A little sore, maybe." I was surely blushing, now, but he didn't make fun of me for it.

He directed his attention back to between my legs. "You're bleeding a little." For a second, I panicked that my period had started or something, but I remembered that some blood after was possible.

"Sorry," I mumbled.

Río took the moment to give a long, slow drag with his tongue, ending with quick circles that had my body electrified. My back arched, weight mostly resting on my elbows.

"Don't apologize," he said with a hard twinge.

He didn't give me time to respond, going back to eating me out for the first time in my life. Again, it wasn't the unsatisfactory fumbling I'd expected to receive at some point in high school or at a frat party or something. Though I'd never tell him, I was glad that circumstances and my own disinterest in most people had led me into taking Río's cock and his tongue as my first experiences with someone else. He certainly knew how to use them, and the flash of jealousy was quickly erased as another wave made me curse.

If bouncing on Río's dick ripped me apart, having him go down on me was melting me and putting my body back together. My mind, though, was even more messed up. How was I going to give him up when he left?

Río groaned, continuing with his expert movements, and a new sound had me cracking my eyes open. With a little tilt of my head, I saw his arm jerking and fist flying over his hard dick. My mouth dropped open, watching him jerk himself off while his face was buried between my thighs.

He looked up at me with those yellow and black eyes and speared his tongue into me, thrusting and swirling. Wetness dripped down on to the couch, but it didn't even register as my hips moved in time with his tongue.

It didn't take much longer for my pleasure to break, and I threw back my head again and screamed to the high ceiling. My thighs tightened and shook on his face, but Río didn't seem to mind.

When my breathing slowed enough for me to relax and open my eyes, it was to the sight of him pressing little kisses on the inside of my legs. The scent of cum filled my nose, and I sat up on my hands. At the same time, Río released my feet to rest on the floor and pulled his shirt off. If I weren't still trembling with after-shocks, I would've melted all over again with his naked torso and tattoo-covered skin in front of me.

He used his shirt to wipe off his hand, then the floor beneath us. Satisfied that he'd gotten it all, Río dropped the t-shirt and climbed onto the couch beside me. His hands snaked around my thighs and back, sitting me on his lap. He kissed the side of my neck, and I clung to him with a scoff. "You're developing a bad habit of manhandling me."

His chuckle was deep and lingering, which just made my frown grow as I leaned into the press of his lips. "But Princess," *kiss*, "I know," *kiss*, "that you like it," *kiss*.

I sputtered, wanting to reject the notion but knowing my movements and scent would show me a liar. "That's irrelevant."

"Is it? Just say the word, and I won't touch you anymore." When I froze and didn't say anything, he laughed again and gave the side of my hip a light spank. A bone-rumbling purr rolled out of him. "You *like* it when I touch you."

His hands were painting lazy circles over my back and on my still-naked lower half. My own rested lightly beside his heart. It was a steady, content beat. "No shit." Like, though, was too weak of a word. My stomach flipped as a tiny voice in my mind spoke the truth. That I *was* the pathetic virgin because I was already in love with him. How embarrassing. "I wouldn't be here if I didn't."

Río's touch paused and resumed almost immediately. The side of my face itched with his stare boring holes into my skin, but I was becoming used to it. If he was going to say something, he would.

It was odd, the lack of a record playing in the background. I'd gotten so used to the ever-present noise in such a short period of time, but the silence between Río and I wasn't uncomfortable. With the way my body relaxed into him, it was what I needed.

We sat for a while, my head tucked into the curve of his neck, our breaths and heartbeats syncing, and sleep was coming over me like a warm blanket. I tried to fight it, but comfortable darkness closed in. And with Río beneath me, I let it in.

A deep, quiet serenity, like peering into the mouth of a familiar forest, startled me awake. But my body felt too languid, too good, to move more than a sleepy shuffling.

My fists tightened against the unfamiliar sheets, accidentally pulling at my own hair in the process. As I stretched my legs beneath the covers, my toes bumped against bare skin dusted with hair—a leg and the knot of an ankle. A light brushing sound filled my ears, as did the breath of the body beside me.

I cracked my eyes open and was met with faint, yellow light amidst the darkness that filled the rest of the room. With more purposeful blinks, further stretching of my limbs, the image of Río, bent over a large book, solidified.

He surely knew that I was awake, but I was content to take him in as my conscious mind finished percolating. The side of his face that was closest to me was cast in shadow, emphasizing the slight but strong curve along the bridge of his nose. The tender bow of his lips.

His long, black waves were plopped on top of his head in a messy bun, and his chest was bare. Admittedly distracted by the detailed artwork on his skin and the fluid peaks and valleys of his muscles, it took me some time to notice that he was... wearing glasses.

Not just that, but his eyes were moving quickly over the book while he swept a pencil back and forth on an ivory page.

"You okay, Princess?" he asked without looking away from what he was sketching. His voice wasn't bogged down with sleep, so I guessed that he'd been awake for a while. Maybe he hadn't gone to sleep at all.

My mouth tasted stale, and there was a low ache where he'd fucked me earlier, but it was more than manageable. I propped up on an elbow, testing the water before peering at what he was drawing. When he didn't recoil or turn the sketchbook away from me, I risked it.

He was using a black pencil, holding it at a slant to shade the delicate silk of a chrysalis, full with the changing insect inside. I watched as he took finer, darker strokes that looked like some sort of pattern that ran on the wing curled within.

"Danaus plexippus, or the monarch butterfly," he informed before I could ask. The image he'd drawn was in startling detail and took up the whole page. Like the sort of illustrations in my high school textbooks.

I had to try a few times to get words to form, but it was at least another minute or so before I was able to mutter, "It's beautiful."

Río reached beside him, where I couldn't see, and came back to the page with a white eraser that he used to swipe away a few pencil strokes. He set back to sketching, emphasizing the transparent nature of the butterfly's cocoon. "Thanks." The corner of his mouth gave a little tilt, but it was me that blushed.

"Uh… do you draw a lot?"

"Yep, always have. Did most of my tattoos, too."

"Holy shit—" my words came out louder than I'd intended, and I scrambled to whisper "—you did all of these?"

Río used a finger to quickly push his glasses a few centimeters back up the bridge of his nose and immediately went back to his work. He shrugged. "Yeah. The ones I could reach, I did myself. The other shit, like on my back and stuff, I just designed then had someone else tattoo them."

I hummed, entranced by Río's tattoos once again and the way he was stroking his pencil against the page. The detailed crane feathers along his torso and the dragon scales along his spine took on a whole new weight.

The light streaming in from the windows was faint but more than enough for me to take in his studio apartment. Now, though, we were in the lofted area that contained his bed. The sheets and pillows smelled briefly of laundry detergent, but much more prominent was the wild, peppery scent that was Río's.

A few more minutes passed, wherein I fiddled with the end of my braid and watched Río finish his butterfly illustration. With the final shadows that brought out the highlights that curved around the figure, he wrote in a neat and elegant script, *D. Plexippus, pupal stage*. Below that, a quick jotting of the date.

Satisfied, Río closed his sketchbook, which I now recognized from the coffee table stack downstairs, and turned to me. He brought a finger, the side of which had smudges from his artwork, to caress the height of my cheekbone. A watery depiction of my face reflected in his large, clear lenses, but there was no mistaking that he was looking right into my eyes.

"Are you okay? Physically, mentally, all that shit."

I frowned. "Why wouldn't I be?"

He shrugged and settled onto an elbow to mimic my posture, then resumed his barely-there tracing of my face. "A lot of people don't care about their first time, but I wanted to make sure that I at least did right by you. I guess."

The backs of my eyes prickled, a lump forming in my throat at his soft words, the crease between his brows that was so far from the quick jokes and jabs we so often exchanged.

I pushed myself up on to my hand, ready to scramble out of the bed. This was exactly what I didn't want—him feeling like I was some charity case or pathetic virgin or, or—

"Hey, hey. Cut that out." Río's command was soft but harder at the end, and he moved too quickly for me to block the arm that shot out and pulled me toward him. I melted while shoving at his shoulders as he flipped me onto my back, head hitting the pillow to release a rush of my scent mixed with his. Just that turned my physical protest into a curling of my fingers into his skin.

Río bent his head and bumped his nose against my top lip, once, then twice, before pulling back. "If we're gonna fuck, you're gonna have to be able to talk about this stuff. Got it?"

My chest rose and fell in large, expanding breaths, brushing against his bare skin. The back of my neck was beginning to heat with his demand and the bunched up hood of my sweatshirt beneath it. Why did we have to talk about it? Couldn't we just— do it? It'd felt so good to be out of my head, to only concentrate on the sensations between us.

"Ramona? It's either that or nothing. And I think you like my dick too much." That got an incredulous, choked noise out of me, which just made him smirk like the asshole that he was.

Instead of taking my mouth, commanding with his tongue, Río pressed his lips to mine with the sweetest weight. With a tenderness that threatened tears and left me giving an embarrassing mewl when he pulled away to speak. "So. What'll it be?"

I bit the inside of my cheek, wanting to fight him but finding it harder and harder to remember what I was protesting. "Fine."

He kissed me again, this time with a slow heat that I felt in my chest. Only to have it spread down my belly, to my legs, and down my arms to the fingers that were now buried in his hair. The edges of his glasses bumped my cheeks, a cold line of metal and glass that was so different than the hot slide of his tongue against mine. I teased the barbell pierced through his tongue and earned myself a groan and the pressure of his hips against mine, rolling.

Before I could get my legs wrapped around him, he stopped again. "You didn't answer my question."

I huffed and let go of him, running my palms over my face that was certainly giving away my arousal and embarrassment all at once. Muffled beneath my hands, I snarked, "What the fuck do you think? I feel good, and I like your dick, okay?"

What was once an expectant smirk turned into a full on, shit-eating grin, and I wanted to punch him in the face. "Yeah? What about my tongue?"

"You are so arrogant—*yes*. I loved them both. Great experience, ten out of ten. Are you happy now?"

He rewarded my stupid vulnerability with a dragging of his tongue from the corner of my jaw to the crest of my temple.

Frankly, it should have been gross, but the scratchy flesh and hard jewelry and *purr* really felt like a gift. In my ear, he whispered, "Was that so hard? I'm not a mind reader—I want to know how you feel."

I rolled my eyes, though he couldn't see them. "Whatever. Are we done talking now?"

"Aren't you going to ask me what I thought of being in that sweet pussy for the first time?"

"Oh my god, you don't stop, do you? I had no idea fuckboys did this much pillow talk. Fine, please, do tell."

A dark chuckle coming from him wracked both of our bodies as he continued to hold me close. "Why, thank you for asking." Río took the flesh of my earlobe between his front teeth, nipped, and followed the sting of his bite with open-mouthed kisses. When he spoke, it was with a deep rumble that had my breath catching. "I had to stop myself from tearing you apart. You were so fucking tight and *perfect*. Knowing I was the first one inside of you almost had me flipping you over and pinning you down." Another bite and kiss on my ear. "And you taste better than candy."

I was back to clinging to him, arms circling his shoulders while he kissed down my neck. When he settled in the valley between my throat and shoulder, instead of giving me the bite that my illogical instincts were screaming for, he latched onto my skin, licking and sucking out my soul.

My muscles tensed, anchoring him to me while he planted hickey after hickey, and I whined through my nose and tried to breathe.

A muffled growl rang beneath our pleasured panting and the sound of our bodies shifting against the fabric of his sheets. When Río pulled away for a third time, I actually groaned at the loss and flash of frustration. Somehow while I'd been asleep, my underwear found its way back on me—I was *not* going to think too closely about him dressing me before carrying me to his bed—and was now in the process of becoming completely soaked through.

"Wanna get food, Princess?"

"Right now?" I squeaked, and my stomach gave another hearty growl.

The kiss Río gave me was a quick peck, and I exhaled, defeat calming my racing heart. "Yeah, lemme get you some food. I *am* the one who made you work up an appetite by tearing that ass up."

I groaned from everything but pleasure, making him laugh at his own ridiculous ways. "What time is it anyway?"

"'Bout ten, last time I checked." He sat up, thighs spreading my hips, and I grumbled at how much I missed his body against mine. His glasses were adorably fogged and slowly clearing to reveal his black eyes full with amusement.

"Fine. And I'm ordering the most expensive thing."

He laughed loudly and stepped off the low mattress, standing and giving me a full fucking show of his golden brown skin decorated with artwork that I now knew was of his own hand. His muscles were the sort that came from activity and his shifter heritage, not some purposeful workout regimen. His thighs and calves looked hard to the touch, his biceps and pecs well-defined without being bulky. I wasn't small by any means, and I already knew that he was able to throw me around as if I weighed nothing. In fact, he did it right then, bending at the waist to lift me gently to my feet.

A good bit of his hair had now fallen out of his bun and was fanning around his face and neck. With a light smack on my ass, he turned to a low dresser and fished out a pair of jeans. "I'd expect nothing else from my favorite rich girl. Let's get you a good, greasy burger."

CHAPTER SIXTEEN

RÍO

Ah, ah, ah, getting into a bit of a bind, aren't you, Yoyo?

I knew that there was a dopey smile on my face, but I couldn't get it to flatten. Nor could I completely ignore the familiar voice in my mind that steered me from trouble and dark places.

I took a pull from my straw, gulping down the Coke to chase away the saltiness of my fries. I squeezed my arm, pulling Ramona even closer to me. The lights inside the fast food restaurant were way too fucking bright for this time of night, so we were sitting at one of the tables outside instead. Cars stopped and started in the drive thru line, break lights painting Ramona and I with a ghostly wash of red.

"So, what was with the airhead act earlier, Princess?" I crunched on a fry and watched her face go sharp, but the little wrinkle between her brow showed her contemplating my question. Don't get me wrong, submission in a... partner was exciting as fuck. Not that every shifter liked it, but my natural instincts lent very easily to *pindowntakefuck*. Didn't mean that I wanted her to give in to me in that way, though.

I took another slurp of my Coke to give her time. See if she was gonna keep up this end of the deal to be honest with me. At least when it came to how we acted with each other. Not like I could promise total honestly about my past.

Ramona avoided my eyes, looking at the line of cars before us. "I... I don't." She made a little growl of frustration and clenched her eyes. "You said the movie was a date."

I tried to loosen the moment. "Didn't say it was explicitly. But go ahead." And, yeah, I was a bit of a hypocritical asshole.

Ramona munched on a handful of fries like they'd offended her personally. "I don't know how to act on a date, okay?" She shrugged, but her lashes fluttered with nervousness as she continued to avoid my gaze. "Thought that's what you'd want. That's what I've observed men like, anyway."

As sad and fucked up as that was, her words made me smile because, in a roundabout way, she'd let it slip that she wanted to please me. "Is that what your Pack Leader brother expects of his mate?"

She pursed her soft lips for a second, enough to distract me with the thought of them on mine again. "No. But. Sylvie isn't... like me. She's sweet and caring. I've been called a bitch enough to know that I don't come off well sometimes. Guess I get that from my mom. And—" she sighed and picked her burger back up "—she's different when my dad's around."

"Hm, okay, I get it now, Princess." She'd initially grumbled about me sitting on the same bench as her instead of across or adjacent, but when I put my arm around her shoulders, she cuddled up to me so that our sides molded together. It was gross to eat so close to someone, she'd said, but now she was munching and slurping just fine. A small purr started involuntarily in my chest, and I let it be, offering her the reassurance of how I felt. Seemed like I couldn't *stop* offering her things. "I hope you know now that I don't want you to be any way but yourself. Prickly and all." She grumbled but didn't pull away, and I took that as her agreement that I was right.

"Hey," she took another bite of french fry and tilted her head up to face me, "what's with the glasses?" For emphasis, she tapped the corner of the frames I'd had since I was fifteen.

I set my drink back down on the table and furrowed my brows at her. "Who knew you were so nosy, Princess." She didn't take the bait or back off, and maybe I hadn't expected her to.

Give me credit for stalling. I rubbed my nose, jostling the frames a little while I relieved the pressure there. Mostly, I wore the contact lenses, only taking them out when I was turning in for the night in my human form. As soon as I'd tucked Ramona into my bed—because that's apparently what I did now—I'd taken them out to give my eyes a break and gotten under the covers with her. Blame the fear of night terrors for my sitting up twenty minutes later with my sketchbook. Certainly not the churning in my chest and stomach that brought on a torrent of questions about what the hell I was doing.

I sighed, but it really wasn't a hardship to give her more. "I got injured as a kid. Fucked up my eyesight." Her lips turned down in understanding, but the pity was missing, just like I'd hoped. *That* would surely crop up if I told her how I'd gotten hurt. Who'd ordered it and who'd carried it out. My back itched and my chest constricted until I took a deep breath, forcing them both to clear.

Ramona continued studying me with those honey eyes, and I had the dumbass thought that I would explain anything to her if she asked. "Even when you shift?"

Now, Yoyo, you never reveal your weak—"Yeah."

She took a slurp of her Sprite, mapping the shape of my glasses with her eyes. "Is that hard?"

I shrugged, nudging her head at the same time and earning myself a beautiful scowl. "Got used to it." It was disorienting and depressing as fuck when it'd first happened. When the rest of my body healed but it felt like I'd almost lost a limb. Shifters already had heightened senses, and to have my sight damaged enough to be weaker than the average human's was a fucking ego hit, too.

But, I learned to manage, other senses got worked harder to

compensate. "I like the glasses. Makes you look cute." My head jerked back at Ramona's deadpan assessment. Well, there was that, too.

"Cute?" She nodded, and I shook my head. "Gotta say, Princess, ever since I started getting tatted and pierced, nobody but my mom ever calls me cute."

She rolled her eyes and picked up the last half of her burger. "Just accept the damn compliment." A grin stretched across my face, only to grow as I watched Ramona take a giant bite, nearly finishing her double cheeseburger altogether. Her cheeks were adorably round as she began to chew, but when I grabbed her jaw, she gave surprised and indignant mumbles before and after I planted a kiss on her puckered lips.

I licked a little ketchup off the corner of her mouth, letting the flavor swirl around my tongue while I waited for Ramona to furiously swallow. She stared daggers at me. "That's so gross."

I leaned in for another kiss, and as much game as she liked to talk, she melted for me almost immediately. Sure, some shifters could be persnickety, but I was not one of 'em. I gladly licked my way into Ramona's mouth, fighting with and forcing her tongue into submission while tasting the meal she'd been eating. Savory and salty and sour from her soda but sweet in the way she yielded to me. Her hands crumpled the fabric of my t-shirt, similar to the way she'd clung to me when I slid into her for the first time.

Her first time. I still couldn't believe that.

What more did I need to see or experience with her to know that I was in deep, deep shit? Because every moment I spent with her was trying to convince me that she was mine.

A car honked its horn at us, making her jump in my arms, and I flipped them off while kissing and licking down her cheek and the side of her neck.

"Get a room!" the asshole shouted from their rolled-down window.

I had to remind myself to take a breath, otherwise I'd be crashing through their window, claws and fangs drawn. I was fully intending to curse the motherfucker out—really, they were stuck with cars in front of and behind them, so it was stupid to pick a fight in the parking lot. But Ramona beat me to it and leaned viciously over the table.

"Why don't you go fuck yourself you piece of shit? Sit and wait for your food and shut the fuck *up*." She didn't yell, but her words rang with a cold promise to retaliate.

The guy sputtered, surprised at her reaction, but the drive-thru line moved, saving him from having to say anything. I, on the other hand, was now trying to keep myself from blurting something really *really* stupid like, 'be my mate.'

Instead, I watched in awe as she smoothed her features, erasing them with an expertise that was at the same time arousing and unsettling. If I didn't clock the flush on the tops of her cheeks, I could've almost forgotten she'd said anything.

Ramona angled her body toward me again. "What?"

She pulled at her sleeves yet again, a tick that revealed the limit of her collected facade. We'd both kept our shirts on earlier, so I hadn't thought anything of it, but for all the times I'd appreciated those mile-long legs, I'd never seen her arms bare.

I ran a finger along her forearm and catalogued the flinch she tried to stifle while I did it. Interesting.

Her shoulders wilted a bit, like fearful acceptance of what was coming, and I swallowed the question that was bubbling in my mind. In its place, I scooted closer until she was where she belonged, plastered against me, and asked, "You wanna wait for that fucker to pull around and watch me kick the shit out of him for you?"

She chuckled through an exhale, releasing the hesitance that'd been creeping up and straightening her spine. Rolling her eyes, she took another slurp of her soda. "You'd commit assault for a girl you barely know? Assuming you win the fight in the first place."

How was it that I wasn't deflated in the least when she insulted me? I leaned into her ear, brushing the shell with my lips.

"Don't let the glasses fool you, Princess. If I barely know you, you barely know me and the things I've done. If you want, I could crack open his skull, sever his spine, and gift you his brain before you finish that Sprite of yours." I feathered a kiss to punctuate my threat. I'd done worse for far less, and maybe it was better she realized a taste of who she'd let inside her. Even if she thought it was a joke.

Going along with this whole theme of surprises, though, was the shudder and *lust* pouring off of her. It was one of the easiest things to identify with scent, and Ramona's was like the richness of grapefruit that'd been reduced to a syrup I wanted to lap up completely.

I kept her pinned to me, let the heat between us fog up my glasses. "You like that? You smell like you want me inside of you again, Princess." My fingers snaked their way between her legs that were slightly parted. I didn't press on her clit, where I could already sense her heart beating, but high enough on her inner thigh to make her squirm. Her cheek brushed mine, pressing into it while she shifted in her seat to make my hand connect to where she wanted. "You like to spit a lot of insults, but I know you're already a slut for me. Aren't you."

She retracted, leaning her face away from mine but not enough to relieve the pressure of my fingers. Those honey eyes tried so hard to fake like they were freezing me out, but I knew her game, now. "If I'm a slut, then you're a stupid fuckboy—"

My teeth sinking into her lip stopped her short on a yelp, and I licked away the sting and taste of blood I'd caused. "You can do better than that, Princess. The way you cling to me when I'm fucking you is evidence enough that you're *my* slut."

A slender but strong touch wrapped around the base of my throat and forced me back, putting breathing room between us. Enough for me to take in the frazzled widening of her pupils, the irritated sneer of her swollen lips. "Fuck you." The words were lacking heat or ice, and I smiled. Ramona swallowed, lashes fluttering before she whispered, almost tenderly, "What's your favorite color?"

Like a record scratch, a hidden flavor of a lollypop, she switched so fast on me to reveal an almost… shyness.

When I was a boy, my mother used to discourage me from my tendency to maintain unflinching eye contact, saying that it was rude, that it made people uncomfortable. That it reminded her of my sister.

Sure, we both wanted to know, to see inside past all the bullshit, but where Mara wanted to twist and distort it to eviscerate, I wanted to understand. To learn. And what I'd learned so far about my princess was that she was a symphony of dichotomies. Willing to rip a stranger's head off for shouting out a window, turned on by the prospect of me killing said stranger, but timidly sweet when I had my arms around her. She'd beg me to fuck her harder but look back at me now with the liquid gold stare and ask me one of the most innocent questions I'd probably been asked in my entire life.

"Red. Yours?"

Her tongue swiped against the last bit of blood that welled where I'd bitten her. "Black."

Minutes passed between us, the muted bumping of people's car speakers vibrating against the relaxing air around us. It wasn't churning with sexual tension anymore, my hand on her thigh a still point of contact that now felt softer and more intimate. Hers on my throat flattened into a caress at the top of my chest where that string pulling me toward her was wound even tighter.

"You spending the night with me, Ramona?"

An adorable little wrinkle formed between her eyes that dropped to that space between us, and I gave her time, watching her mind work and turn over my question that I didn't want to admit to either of us was a request.

If she said no, that'd be fine. We'd throw away our trash, and I'd give her a ride home on my bike so that I could feel her arms wrapped around me. And then I'd go home alone, sleep in my bed alone and have the space to remember why this couldn't fucking work. I was on the run, would be for the rest of my life that was barely one to begin with.

As much as I relished the idea of bringing her into my darkness, just for a little bit, I already liked her too much to do it.

"Okay," she said, firmly, and I cursed myself while I smiled and led her back to my apartment.

CHAPTER SEVENTEEN

RAMONA

"Um." My voice came out raspy, and I took a gulp of the water Río had set on the coffee table beside the eggs and bagel he made for me. "Thank you for all this."

He came over with his own plate, plopping down on the stretch of floor between the table and couch. "Lose your voice there, Princess?" I almost shot something back, but the way he took a giant bite of his bagel sandwich, looking up at me with messy hair and his glasses on with nothing but cheer and affection, had the barb softening on my tongue.

After we got back to his place last night, Río set us up in his bed with a laptop propped on the mattress with us. We settled on a stupid comedy sketch show that was easy to watch, and before I knew it, I was waking up, head on his bare chest, to the morning light streaming through the windows.

The cute Jaguar that was now lounging at my feet was a far cry from the one that I found myself on all fours for, moaning hoarsely into a pillow while he thrust slow and deep.

Río and I ate in silence, watching downtown Antler Pointe awaken for a lazy and hot Saturday. I could already taste the rising temperature and humidity, making me even more aware of my need to shower and change. Río had offered for me to bathe here, that I could borrow clothes of his to tide me over till I got home.

But I'd declined, not wanting to open myself up for questions or to catch a glimpse of my scars in the mirror and pop my own bubble of happiness. I'd nearly succeeded in ignoring the friction between my sleeves and the raised, bumpy skin, until I saw his curiosity while he traced the exact length of the trail I'd taken my knife that day.

He hadn't asked, so I hadn't said anything about it.

"I've got a double shift today, so I gotta drop you off on my way in." My thoughts broke and dissipated, ushering in disappointment. But of course, he had work. He'd spent all afternoon and evening with me yesterday, cooking for me this morning.

I nodded, trying to swallow the greedy urge to ask about when I'd see him again. The last thing I wanted to be was his needy… something. Friend with benefits? Lover?

We continued through our breakfast, and the companionable meal and subsequent clearing of the dishes felt more intimate than when he'd dug his claws into my hips. He didn't have a dishwasher, so I washed our plates and the pan he cooked the eggs in while he got ready for work. He disappeared into the small bathroom, but all I heard was his toothbrush swishing and the faucet going. While I dried the dishes I washed, he emerged, sans glasses, with his hair brushed to a smooth, wavy sheen.

No shower.

I clenched my eyes shut while he bounced up to the loft and got the rest of his stuff for his shift. Sometimes I could almost convince myself that I was all the way human. There was no animal form to tap into or blame for the way I felt with my scent still sitting heavily on his skin. Did other women feel this way? When the person they slept with kept the remnants of them for the rest of the day?

Mom had never appeared possessive over Dad, at least, not in that way. As the provider for our house, as a catch, sure. But I was positive it wasn't my human half that wanted to tote him around with me, to flaunt him and our scent to all. To bare my teeth at anyone that looked at him too long.

And I didn't have any fangs, so I'd look like a fucking idiot while I did it.

"You thinking about something really hard, there." Río palmed my hip, twisted, and pulled me into his chest. I'd been drying the same plate far longer than it needed, but with him in front of me, I easily dropped it to the counter with a clatter. The dish towel followed.

"Mm." I could clearly see the edges of his contact lenses, and it made me wonder how severely he'd been hurt to cause such an extensive and long-lasting injury. What right, though, did I have to ask about it when I hadn't been exactly forthcoming about much of anything about myself?

If I did, would it be meaningless since he had no intention of making this anything lasting, anyway?

A kiss right between my eyes halted the familiar, somber path. "Thank you for doing the dishes. You ready to go, Princess?"

I frowned but felt myself relax. "If you get to call me that, why don't I have a nickname for you?"

He flipped my expression, reflecting back to me how I truly felt when I was with him, underneath all the bullshit that threatened it. "Whatcha got in mind? Daddy?"

Now I was downright scowling. "Fuck no." His chuckles rumbled and shook the both of us. "Maybe you don't deserve one, after all."

"Well, keep thinking. Maybe you'll convince me to work for it." At some point, his hands had snaked down to grab my ass, resting as if they belonged there. Maybe they did, at least temporarily.

I reached up and pet the top of his head. "Hmph. *Maybe* if you're a good boy, I'll give you a treat." My lips trembled as I tried to hide my smile, but the way his fingers clenched on me and the speed with which his smirk dropped then reappeared was confusing. At least until I picked up on the quick, lingering flash of his lust spiking. *Interesting.*

"Ha ha," he said dryly. "Let's hit it." He swatted my ass and grabbed his keys, leading both of us out of the door.

We didn't speak as he fit his helmet on my head, nor did he ask for directions to the cabin, remembering the way from the first time he'd brought me. Was that only a few weeks ago? Only a small part of me had believed I would be arriving on my brother's land on the back of his bike again. No way in hell had I thought I'd be doing it after spending the night with him.

Luckily for us, though both Sylvie's and O's cars were here, there was no one out front. Río kept his bike rumbling while I climbed off and removed his helmet. I blinked a few times and cleared the flyaway hair from my vision.

Río sat with his feet planted on the ground, gazing at me and continuing to stare even after I caught him. "You gonna text me later?" The casual way he said it was so at odds with the intensity that poured off him in waves. That promised repeats of our time together and the way he'd taken me. His question was a request and a demand and a confirmation all in one. How the fuck was this real.

"Perhaps." I couldn't help myself. I really couldn't.

And I really should've known that he wouldn't give two shits about snapping my body to his and fucking my mouth with his tongue, forcing moans out of me that were all too eager in the first place. Fuck, I was a slut for him.

My tongue was happy to let him stay in control of the kiss, and when I grazed the unmistakably sharp edge of a *fang,* I whined, clinging to him like I needed our mouths pressed together to survive.

Could I take him to my room really quick? Or would it be better to go a ways into the forest and just let him press me up against a tree? Río was squeezing my ass cheeks again, and my body felt like it was further electrified by the vibration of the motorcycle still idling. I bet if I straddled it while still kissing him, it wouldn't take long for the pleasure to bust and for us to both come after all.

I started pushing at his chest, working on hitching my leg up and over his lap on the leather seat, needing him, needing it—

"Ramona." I stilled.

Our lips parted with a mutual smack, and I was relieved to see that Río looked about as much a wreck as I felt. He was so rarely flushed, but there was no hiding the redness on his face, and his fast breathing parted his mouth enough for me to see the tips of four ivory-colored fangs.

"Ugh, please don't make me have to physically pull you apart." The exasperated voice sounded even closer, and I realized that I'd been leaning back into Río for more. And he looked prepared to do the same.

Tearing my eyes from the black holes of safety felt a little like I was dying. Or slicing off a piece of me, but not in the way that'd usually settle my emotional storm.

But I did it, trying to focus in on my sister-in-law who held a basket overflowing with wild mushrooms. Her feet were bare, and her hair was in her usual topknot.

"I'm glad you're having fun and all, but I have to draw the line at fucking out in the open in the front yard."

My face flamed, words escaped me. What did it mean that I was more embarrassed about not feeling badly at all?

That snarky, dark chuckle just made it worse, forcing an actual shiver down my spine. "Sorry. Didn't see you there."

She looked Río up and down, and I didn't fucking like it. For a flash, I envisioned stomping over and plucking her eyes from her skull.

"Even if I weren't here, it's pretty dumb to try to fuck the Pack Leader's sister in front of his house without at least introducing yourself. There's also the common decency thing, since, you know, kids live here."

"Oh, god," I groaned. Yeah, the crazed lust was completely

simmered down now. What had I been thinking? Was this normal? Was everyone else just walking around wanting to mount and ride the person they were sleeping with whenever and wherever? I'd gone my whole life barely being attracted to anyone, and when I was, it required time and getting to know them to even truly feel it. But whatever spark I felt when I first saw Río had drawn me to him far more quickly than anyone else. And now that he'd opened me up to true desire? When would the flood settle?

"Not really one to care about pack dynamics. Sorry to disappoint, witch." I smacked his chest, and he coughed as if it'd actually done something.

"She has a name, you ass. Sorry, Sylvie." Low in his ear, I spat, "You're never getting that fucking treat at this rate. Now, be good." Unlike most people, I truly cared about what my sister-in-law thought of me. Maybe even more than my brother.

Instead of volleying something back, Río cleared his throat and inclined his head towards her. "My apologies."

I smacked him again, though it was weak this time. "Don't overdo it." He didn't even try to hide the deep roll of his eyes.

"Whatever. I'll see you later, Princess." He chucked the edge of my chin, and I stepped back, letting him back out of the drive and head to his shift at Vinny's.

Sylvie stepped up beside me, but I refused to look at her. The damp earthiness of the spoils from her morning walk grounded me when it felt like a piece of me was driving away, too. This was all so dumb.

"Your brother was wondering where you were this morning, but I can understand why you didn't check in."

"Sorry. For acting stupid. I don't really know what's happening with me, to be honest."

I felt her studying the side of my face, and her knowing hum made me brace for witchy impact. A ray of sunshine lit up our backs, but I felt rooted in place, waiting for her to share what she so obviously had deduced.

"What?" I asked when the anticipation got the better of me.

The basket shifted against her clothes as she shrugged. "Too soon to tell for sure. Now, go shower and then come and help me wash and sort these."

She left me to breeze back into the cabin, and like the coward I was, I waited until she'd gone inside to follow her command.

***

My brother had indeed been looking for me, and after I showered and helped Sylvie wash the dirt and debris from her wild mushrooms, Orion scooped me up to run errands. If I was still a little sleepy following my night with Río, I didn't mention it, all too happy to be moving and doing.

Though we had a personal chef and my mother's assistant that ran most of the household errands back at my parents' house, when I *was* dragged into going out and about with Mom, it involved a lot of interrogatory lunches and sitting in luxury stores while she tried on clothes and shoes. So much so that I often hid in my room until she gave up, and when I'd discovered that my peers elected to do the teen version of that, I stopped trying with them, too.

Orion's idea of ticking things off of his to-do list consisted of picking up enough books on hold at the library to fill a large tote bag, making a Pack Leader house call for an elder that needed his patio railing repaired, and grabbing groceries for the next few days.

Any extraneous words were nonexistent but so was any lick of tension. In my brother's kind of silence, I could exhale, and in my mother's I felt suffocated. While we wove in between aisles at the grocery store, we both wore our headphones, in our own worlds and utilizing silent gestures to communicate back and forth. A tug on his shirt sleeve, and he'd follow me to the crackers I liked. Just a jerk of his chin, and I'd know to meet him by the baby stuff.

And after we returned, hauling it all into the house and organizing until everything was in its rightful place, I blinked back my surprise when he offered me a beer and to help him with his newest woodworking project.

Sometime after my niece was born, Orion added a good sized shed he outfitted as a workshop, though I'd never found myself in here before. If Sylvie had her grandmother's house as a place for solitude, my brother had this place that was outfitted with neatly organized tools, sealants, paints, and a large, sturdy table.

One thing it didn't have, though, was air conditioning. A large industrial fan blasted and kept the air moving, though it was far from cool.

At two different ends of a crib, my brother and I worked sandpaper in the delicate grooves of the spindles to prepare for staining. Which, apparently, would help it attain the color requested by the pack member who'd commissioned this particular project of refinishing their childhood crib for their own pup on the way.

Instead of a record player, my brother had a large bluetooth speaker on one of the tool shelves, and I mouthed along to 'Grandma's Hands' while trying to get the smoothness Orion had instructed me to achieve.

The work was simple, soothing, and I let my mind narrow to that one task while scraping away the roughness of the wood. The tightness in my chest with Río away from me wasn't nearly as immediate, and the numb gray that was a constant companion was now almost forgotten.

Even when Dahlia and Ollie came stumbling up to the entrance of the workshop, their usually excited babbling was quieted to cute little mumbles. A cool new bug, they announced from where they stood with Dahlia cradling the creature in her palms. Orion paused his task to examine what they'd brought and watched with a smile and with love in his eyes when they ran off toward Sylvie who still sat amongst their toys and snacks near the lake.

But it all was part of the rhythm. More notes played with the sweltering summer song that was a meditation as much as my time with Río was a lifeline.

After finishing one wall of spindles, I set down my sandpaper and took a quenching pull from the tallboy can of citrusy beer that I'd found to be far more palatable than the overly hoppy stuff Orion enjoyed.

I took out my phone to find another few messages from Río who'd been responding to me throughout the day. I frowned at the name he'd given himself in my phone last night, but resolved to keep it for a little while.

SEX GOD

I guess I'd have to go with Michoacán.

ME

Why there?

SEX GOD

Dunno. It's warm. My mom's from there. You?

I thought for a moment, uncertainty striking me as I tried to think of any place that I truly enjoyed being. But, how could I when my mind followed me everywhere?

ME

Not sure. I haven't really been to too many places.

I waited for him to have some quip about me being rich, being able to go anywhere I wanted to. Which wasn't a lie. I'd been to Japan, taken months-long trips to Europe and its most luxurious cities, able to see and experience everything that my or my parents' hearts desired.

To be truly present, though? To see everything with clear heart and mind? No, *I* hadn't really been there.

"Mona." I stilled and set my phone down to find Orion glancing toward me while he started on the first spindle of the next side we had to do.

"Hm?" I took the easy way out and lifted my beer to my lips. To partially hide my face and do something with my hands.

He didn't meet my eyes, but by their general direction of my forehead, I knew that he was looking at me and trying to figure out what to say. All our conversations today had been about the tasks at hand. I'd really been hoping that my brother's idea of quality time truly didn't include pointed conversations, but... maybe it did. "How are you doing? Are you enjoying your time here with us?"

He sounded sincere, but it raised my nonexistent hackles, and I narrowed my eyes at him. "Did Sylvie put you up to this? I'm good, O."

Orion huffed and shook his head. He continued sanding, no longer looking weirdly formal and uncomfortable. "She did tell me that I didn't spend enough time checking in on you." Leave it to my brother to keep it a buck.

"Sylvie's nosy," I groused and picked up my little rectangle of sandpaper. My wrists and fingers were tender and on their way to aching, and sweat poured down the sides of my neck.

But the work with my brother was nice. As long as he didn't meddle in my emotions, a plane of existence that neither of us were comfortable with. I already spent enough time with Sylvie and her intuitiveness.

"She's empathetic and cares about you. About all of us. And she's far more comfortable discussing these things than I am." He glanced up, briefly locking eyes with me. "You didn't answer my question."

I gulped. "I'm good, O. Thank you for letting me stay here. Really." My words were slow but, to my surprise, sincere. This was leaps and bounds better than the half-life I'd been living. School, work, home—dry and alone, rife with self-loathing and exhaustion.

I couldn't even get fucked up. Best believe I'd tried—to be self-destructive with my peers who drowned themselves with weed and coke and alcohol. Harder stuff sometimes. But wouldn't you fucking know it, I was practically immune to that too. At least, enough so that truly becoming inebriated would be wildly expensive and suspicious. And I'd never truly wanted it enough to seek out the supernatural channels, though I was sure they existed. Humans couldn't be the only ones to get high, right?

I wondered if Río knew. With a mother that seemed to loathe her Wolf, I'd been waiting for him to take the lead on bringing up anything shifter-related.

He hadn't of course. He hadn't even let me see what his Jaguar looked like.

"How… how long did you wait to show Sylvie your shift?" I forced my voice to be light, casual, and by Orion's quirked brow, the question took him off guard. Good.

He wiped at his forehead with the back of his hand. "Ah, well." His gaze unfocused, and his cheeks reddened, as did the tops of his ears. Catching himself, his white brows lowered over his eyes as he studied me. "Why?"

My lips twitched, fighting at making my brother blush, but I truly did want to know the answer. Río and I were two leaves, blown from different trees and flipping through the air, buffeted by gusts of wind until we crashed and twirled into each other. Pretty soon another gust would pull us apart, and I was determined to discover every surface and bend and edge that I could before that happened.

I'd been lost in my thoughts, trying to find an explanation that wouldn't give too much away, but Orion beat me to it. His voice deepened, and a new presence started filling the workshop. "I have no judgement, but there is no sense denying the shifter's scent that clings to you."

I bit the inside of my cheek but said nothing. He was right, and I didn't need the influence of his Leader scent to stop me from dismissing it.

Whatever connection Río and I had forged in this short amount of time wasn't something I wanted to deny or skirt around. Not when I didn't have to, anyway.

My phone dinged with a text. "Is that him? You've been texting away all day."

Defensiveness surged up my throat, something to throw the conversation back on him. A tease, and accusation, but nothing made the true leap into being spoken.

"What do you know about him, then?"

Internally, I flailed for an answer. So many things small or intangible. His name, the color of his bedsheets. The way he smelled of mischief and delight when he looked at me sometimes. "Enough."

I expected a fight, or a stabbing remark, aimed to shake my foundation or shame me for my actions, but Orion just sighed and nodded. "All right. But if he's going to come by here, I need to have a conversation with him."

That got me sputtering. "Wha—*no* you don't."

He moved the sandpaper more furiously over a spindle, wood dust falling like rain. "I know that you're grown, but you're living in my home, and he's already been here. Twice. Not to mention that Sylvie and Dahlia know him. As the Leader of this land, if he continues to see you, he's my responsibility."

"No, no he's not." I huffed. "This isn't. That. We're not like you and Sylvie. He's just passing through town. Nothing but having fun." *Don't you want to have fun with me, Ramona?* Yes, yes I did, and I wasn't going to ruin it by trying to turn it into something that it wasn't.

Orion winced, shook his head, and remained silent, not pressing the issue further. And when he continued to work, bopping his head to the music and essentially paying me no mind, I released my held breath in a rush. He truly wasn't going to—

"A month, I believe. I was scared what Sylvie would see if she truly saw me. What it would change." I kept my eyes on my hands, moving quickly over the wall of the crib but hanging on his words. I'd witnessed glimpses of the love and intimacy between my brother and Sylvie but had never heard him speak of anything like this. After a moment, he pressed on, "But, it was a concern only founded in my fear and insecurity. She's been understanding and wonderful from the beginning. And having her know both parts of me is one of the best gifts she's ever given me."

That was… my eyes prickled, my chest tightening as I glanced at my phone, now resting facedown on the table.

We worked for a while more, reaching all the spindles and the legs of the crib until there was nothing left to sand. My back ached a bit from the work, but I could see how these projects were satisfying to him. How he could lose himself in it.

I stretched my legs and twisted my back left and right. When I picked up my phone, Río's texts filled the screen.

> **SEX GOD**
>
> This job is somehow the most stressful one I've ever had. Just got yelled at by an old lady.
>
> Favorite movie? For research.
>
> What's your stance on nudes? Happy to receive or supply ;)

If he'd been in front of me, I would've chewed him out, but behind my screen, I snickered.

> **ME**
>
> You're an ass. And I'd rather experience all of that in person.

My brother cleared his throat, and I clutched my phone to my chest, as if he could somehow see what I was talking about. But he was busy retrieving the selected stain for this project and the needed brushes for application. "I'm not teaching any courses this summer. They've got some summer programs at the Montessori school, so Dahlia and Ollie will still go, just not as much." I nodded, though he wasn't facing me. He coughed again and settled everything on the work table. "And… I'll be pulling back from most of my classes in the fall semester."

I straightened, the hitching tone of his voice making me take notice. "Um, okay…"

He swallowed, face scrunched as he worked out what to say. "I've been… having a difficult time. Doing everything."

I froze, and my stomach dropped. The dry, sure note of my brother's voice was gone. Instead it was raspy and uncertain. The glass edge of his jaw was clenched beneath the short stubble of his beard, and his fingers tapped and knocked against the thick slab of the table.

"Are… you okay?"

Orion exhaled and set the wood stain between us, a brush for me to use before me. His nod was a quick twitch. "Yes. I think this will help." He gestured to the crib and the rest of the shed around us. "Since I've gotten back to carpentry, I've taken on commissions from the pack and humans in this town. Teaching and taking care of the pack has been… a lot."

That made sense. I picked up the brush and twisted it, trying to work out something helpful to say. I knew that my brother had his own challenges, but since I'd been old enough to recognize it, he'd already found ways to navigate and cope. To embrace what made him different to the point that it wasn't something I thought much about anymore.

But I also knew that he was most comfortable by himself or with his mate and children. Between leading classes every day and a whole group of people *outside* of his family, I was overwhelmed just thinking about it.

I'd no clue that he was struggling to the point of having to pull back from his job, though.

"Uh… is it…" I chewed at my lip and forced the words out. If he asked me, I would follow through. "Do you need me to go? I don't want to put too much on your plate."

Orion had started tapping the handle of his own brush on the table, watching the jumping with unseeing eyes. At my question, though, the rhythm stuttered, fell. "No." He dipped the brush in the can of stain and started applying it in steady strokes to one of the legs of the crib. "Sylvie suggested the idea, and I talked it over with Chris. They both suggested I adjust to the idea by telling a few people."

"Chris?" I asked as I dipped my own brush in the stain.

"An elder member of the pack. It's not like I can talk to a human therapist about these things. I trust his wisdom enough, though. And Sylvie noticed before I did."

We descended into silence again, spreading an even coat that turned the light wood to a darker, richer color. It wasn't like I had a… preference or something. In regard to Sylvie's or Orion's schedule. She worked from home, so we ended up spending the most time together, but if he was home more, I was content to leave him his space or help him like I had today.

After finishing the two legs and wall on my side, an uncomfortable twist of my stomach flung my gaze back to my brother. He was making progress far faster than I, already halfway through the second wall of spindles and railing. "Why are you telling me this," I demanded.

He said nothing. Didn't even look up at me, but he didn't have to.

We weren't the type of siblings to talk about this shit, and, and, if I hadn't caved to *Sylvie*'s prodding about my feelings, I *certainly* wasn't going to fall to some crafty strategy they'd concocted behind my back. The wooden handle of the paintbrush snapped between my fingers.

No, there was no way I was going to talk about it with them. I'd never judge my brother for getting the help he needed or pulling back where he could, but it didn't mean he was allowed to… back me into a corner so that I'd have to see the worry or pity or—

"I just needed to say it out loud." He nodded to himself, as if he couldn't hear or scent the panic of my heartbeat or panting. "And I knew you wouldn't think less of me for it. Thank you."

Eyes wide, I sniffed repeatedly, tasting the air surrounding us. True to his word, his scent rang with the steady calm of gratitude, like the magenta sunset end of summertime.

He didn't push me to talk, didn't ask questions or request for me to spill my guts in return, even as I kept pausing my brush-strokes to warily glance his way. The scars beneath my sleeves itched, but we finished the wood staining without me having to reveal them or the darkness that led to their creation.

After we put everything away and closed up the shed, to return to once the stain was dry, Orion and I walked side-by-side to the cabin under the sky that was a deep tangerine. The small, too-soft voice in my head wondered if remaining silent was such a good thing.

CHAPTER EIGHTEEN

RAMONA

The heavy clouds overhead provided enough cover so that Dahlia and I weren't completely baking while we finished yet another revolution around the skate park. The flat surfaces, anyway.

We'd graduated to me being able to have my skates on as I led her around and around and picked her up when she fell. The sturdy trooper that she was, no tears or chin-wobbles came with the wipe-outs. Just me helping her dust off, and we went again. Instead of my headphones, I kept my phone, speaker up, tucked into my back pocket so that we could glide to the same beat. I'd even bought myself a helmet, knee, and elbow pads so that she'd feel less self-conscious being the only one with safety gear on.

"Atta go, pipsqueak!" I smirked as I kept my hand steady so that Dahlia could cling to it. Río entered the park, grin wide and hair tied up into a long, swinging ponytail. My body started turning towards him, which happened to veer Dahlia and me straight toward a rail. I corrected our path before we could collide with it, though she was almost short enough to skate right on underneath.

Río jogged towards us with his board at his side, and I softly reminded Dahlia of how to use her toe-stop to slow herself down. I'd long since taken mine out, so I set my right foot perpendicular to and behind my left, dragging it until we met him in the middle.

Without a lick of shame, Río palmed the back of my sweaty neck and smacked a kiss to my lips. For Dahlia, he bent down and led her through their handshake that I still wasn't allowed to learn. She wrinkled her nose up at him once they were done. "You kiss as much as Mommy and Daddy." Which, you know, made very reasonably sputter and grasp for something to retort with.

Río was as cool as ever, standing and pressing another to my brow for good measure. This time, he ended it with a ridiculous smacking sound that had Dahlia and me both chuckling. "What's wrong with kissin'?"

She was doing her best to stay standing still, wheels moving back and forth in place. "It's weird," she said with a grin and arms stretched wide for balance.

"Huh. It is kinda weird when you think about it," I said and was given a somehow brighter smile in return by both she and Río.

The three of us skated around for a while as the sky above continued to churn but refused to give rain. The resulting breeze and my insistence on multiple water breaks kept us from getting dehydrated. At one point, my niece and I sat on a ledge, feet swinging, while Río jumped a stack of concrete steps and practiced his grinds on a rail. We clapped each time he landed and hollered with every flip of his board that he threw.

After another round of Río's showboating sent Dahlia into a fit of squealing laughter, I pulled out my phone to check the time. I responded to Delaney's text, confirming our next coffee hang, and stuffed the phone back in my pocket. "All right, Dolly, time to go."

And the whining started. From what I'd glimpsed at their school, this was a normal thing almost five-year-olds did, so I fought to gently stand my ground. She wasn't actually that hungry, she said as I floated us back toward our stuff. She wasn't ready to go and everyone else was staying, so it wasn't fair, she cried.

And she turned her pouts and wide eyes at me, wielding them like a well-honed weapon, and I nearly caved. With a deep breath, I firmed my stance. "Dahlia, it's time to go so you can have a bath and eat dinner. I promised your mommy and daddy that we'd leave at this time, and I told you the time before we got here. Remember?"

That got no retort, just more pouting and her holding still while I unlaced her skates and helped her out of her knee and elbow pads. She was able to get her helmet off herself, and I had to stifle a snicker at the very prominent helmet-hair she was now sporting.

Well, I took mine off, I guess that made two of us. While our braids were frizzy from the increased humidity today, the hair on our scalps was packed down tight.

"Hey, Princess." I turned and immediately rolled my eyes at the amusement clear on Río's face while he looked at my hair.

"*What*, Río."

He remained unperturbed and pressed on, "We got rehearsal at Ty's later tonight. Wanna come over and listen?"

I crossed my arms and kept my face impassive while my stomach fluttered at the prospect of spending more time with him. Meeting his other friends. "Uhm, maybe. What time?"

Warm, strong hands eclipsed my hips and pulled me into an even warmer chest. "Aw, don't be like that." Río's teeth lightly teased my ear. "I know you wanna come over and see me play. Then maybe *we* can play. How's that sound?" He stole a lick and kiss on the outer curve of my ear before I swatted him away, blushing. Río laughed and danced away.

"Fine. When?"

"Any time after eight is good. I'll text you the address." I didn't voice my disappointment that he hadn't offered to pick me up on his bike, just gave a tight nod.

"Sweet. See y'all later." I let him pull me in for a lingering kiss that held the tease of tongue before hustling myself and Dahlia out toward the car.

That night, I pulled Sylvie's car up the long, paved driveway that snaked between some trees and a pristine lawn. Very much not what I envisioned Tyler's home would be, but sure enough, when I arrived at a black, modern house, his challenger that I recognized from the skate spot was parked out front. Along with Río's truck and a few other cars I didn't recognize.

My fingers curled around the strap of my backpack, and I forced myself out of the car with it in tow. Río had suggested that I bring a swimsuit. That Tyler had a pool, and we might as well make use of it.

On the way here, I'd run out to the nearest Target, hastily bought a suit, and pulled the tags off of it with my teeth. Because... I wanted to do this with him. To be able to get in as easily as everyone else, and feel Río's arms wrapped around me while we floated in the deep end.

Couldn't do that with a hoodie on, though. Still hadn't figured that part out yet by the time I was knocking on the large front door.

Before I could come to a conclusion, it opened wide.

Río had showered since the skate park, wet hair pulled back in a bun. His sleeveless band tee displayed his toned arms that were as equally covered in tattoos as the rest of him.

Just like at the skate spot, he took charge of our reunion, pulling me in. I stumbled over the threshold as our lips met, and somehow, the door closed behind me as I sank into Río's lips and tongue. I tickled the tip of mine over the barbell stuck through his, eliciting a moan that I gave back in kind. My backpack dropped with a shudder, and I wrapped my arms around his neck.

My back pressed against the door, but that just allowed him to trap me against him. Something that I was *not* going to admit to him that I was all for.

But, how was I supposed to react when he pulled our hips together, demanding I take notice of how much he wanted me? I swept my thumbs against the shaved section of hair at the nape of his neck, feeling the soft and prickly hair and the twin thudding of our hearts.

"There's a guest room down the hall." Río planted himself at my neck, sucking and nibbling in a way that went straight between my legs. I was already nodding before he finished the sentence with his voice rough and low. Now that I'd experienced what it was like with him, the need I felt was ramped up even higher. I *wanted.*

We'd had sex a few times since the first time at his house, and we'd had more conversations. Río had gotten tested, sending me the results this morning. I absolutely hated thinking about him with anyone besides me, but it was comforting to know that he'd been safe nonetheless.

I confirmed for him that I'd gotten an IUD when my mom caught my high school boyfriend sexting me and that it was still good for another two years. It'd been an exciting few hours, when our childish friendship and budding relationship resulted in the first stirrings of arousal I'd ever felt in my life. Go figure that I realized I was demisexual right before finding out he was cheating on me, which halted anything physical between us. And then years passed with no one else. Until now.

"Keep it in your pants, and come back to practice." A familiar grumble had me stumbling and throwing panicked eyes over Río's shoulder. Sure enough, Tyler stood in the hall, arms crossed and looking as unimpressed as anyone in the world, even as Río ignored him completely and continued to kiss and lick at my throat.

I slapped at his back and gasped as he gave a harder nip of his teeth in response. "Río, knock it off." But instead of authoritative, my command ended on an embarrassing whimper when he gave a frustrated and hot roll of his hips before stepping away.

"You didn't see me cockblocking you and your little snack last time I was here, did you?" I was used to his words being laced with humor, half-serious more often than not. But the heat of his anger was like sweltering peppers with no reprieve.

Tyler continued to remain unmoved. He waved a bored hand. "No, but we weren't at the end of figuring out a new song, so, chop chop." He even added an impatient clap while looking between the two of us.

"You keep fucking looking at her, and see what happens. Come on, Princess." Río took my hand and dragged me down a dark and pristine hallway. He made sure to knock into Tyler's shoulder that really only met the middle of his bicep, but the vampire was like an immovable pillar.

Tyler whispered so that only we could hear him, "I don't know who trained you, but this is the only fucking pass you get." Then, more to himself, "Fucking animal instincts."

My legs were long, but it took some effort to keep up with Río's hasty, irritated strides, as we wound through the modern and masculinely-decorated home. Blacks, dark wood, and sleek metal surfaces filled the space, but it somehow felt warm at the same time. Candles, either lit or not, were found everywhere, as well as large, boldly colored landscape paintings that lined the hallway.

Low, steady strums of a bass guitar grew louder as we neared our destination, and I straightened my spine and tried my best to brace myself to formally meet Río's band members. Aside from Tyler, anyway. Who I wasn't too sure liked me in the first place.

Tendrils of weed and vape smoke curled out of the doorway before we'd even made it inside, and once I was pulled into the practice room, I quickly took in the full band setup, a black leather couch, and deep maroon color on the walls. Flyers from their band, Concrete Executioners, lined the walls, as well as a few vintage flyers from bands like Black Sabbath.

I blinked past the overflow of scents that assaulted my nose—substances, people, emotions, it was all a lot to parse through and send to the back of my mind.

"Hey Río's Girl." The one on the bass kept strumming but gave me a small smile of acknowledgement.

"Hey—"

"She has a name, Brody, and you know it." He'd spoken about me to his friends?

"Don't mind him, Ramona. I'm Jess." She waved a drumstick at me from her perch behind the drum kit. Her mullet was dyed a hot pink that matched her brows.

"Uh, hey. Nice to meet you guys." I nodded at both of them, trying to add some life to my tone that didn't include nervousness.

Then, I turned my head, to introduce myself to the other person sitting instead of standing with an instrument, and I actually had to keep myself from growling by clenching my teeth so hard that they creaked in my mouth.

Alex, the one who'd been sucking Río's cock the night we started this thing, was sitting perched with legs crossed and their hair in two space buns. Their cropped shirt highlighted their lithe frame, and their denim cutoff shorts were similar to mine.

Pretty. They were very pretty, and I wanted to kill them. Why the fuck were they here, did Río *want* them here, did they still have their sights set on him, why the fuck were they smiling at me—

"All right, let's get back to it so we can get out of here at a reasonable fucking hour." Tyler picked a notepad off of the coffee table beside the couch, and joined Brody and Jess.

Río pulled me close by the waist. "Sit for a bit, Princess. Let me know if you need somethin'." He kissed me on the temple and swatted my ass on his way back to his purple guitar.

I grunted, secretly pleased that his display showed everyone, especially Alex, that he was *mine*, but pissed because there was nowhere else to sit but on the same sofa as someone who knew what Río's dick tasted like. Maybe even knew what it felt like to have him inside of them.

I sank down onto the soft leather, right on the edge of the seat, and put my bag at my feet. The band began going back and forth, discussing the best way to craft the bridge of their newest song, what chords to use, and some other musical terms that I knew nothing about. I fiddled with my sleeve cuffs, wishing now that I'd stuck with the piano lessons Mom had forced me into for a while, if only so that I could understand the jargon that was now flying through the room. *You've got nice, long and elegant fingers, Ramona. Perfect for a piano player.* When I'd refused to go after the fifth lesson and requested to have dance lessons instead, I promptly quit once she realized I had potential and convinced my father to put me in boxing instead. Luckily, my mom could never really say no when he made a decision.

"Hey, I'm Alex." They angled their body to me and even scooted closer.

At risk of succumbing to the territorial urges that were screaming to pounce and pull their throat out for breathing in the same room as Río, I scooted a few inches away and kept my eyes on the one I was actually here for. "I know."

"All right, let's go back to the second verse and lead into what we've got," Tyler decided, and everyone fell in step. Río settled his guitar across his chest and picked up a pick. When he met my eyes, though, he tilted his head as if to ask me what was wrong.

The reassuring smile and weak wave I sent his way only had him narrowing his eyes, but he didn't call me out or march over. The room filled with ear-splitting music and Tyler's growls and screams, to the point that I'd wished I'd brought my headphones or even a set of earplugs. It was loud enough for the three humans here, but I didn't know how Tyler and Río did it. It was almost too overwhelming to sit still with everything going on around me, not to mention the disquieting thoughts of killing the person next to me. I'd never taken a life, but the way I kept imagining it, testing my resolve to the point that I had to invoke therapeutic breathing, should have been worrisome. Maybe it would've been if I weren't so on the edge.

Feelings are fucking overrated, I grumbled to myself. At least, until I refocused on Río's strumming fingers. The way they flew effortlessly over the strings and the focused peace on his face. His thick, straight brows were just slightly furrowed, his head nodding with the beat, and his mouth pursing and moving along to what he was playing. When he caught me looking at him, the warmth that took over his cold eyes, and that *wink*.

Okay, no, maybe some feelings aren't overrated.

The band worked for another two hours, and I kept all my attention on Río. The stifling scents and sounds were a dull throb in the background while I watched him play and create and joke. He sent me looks throughout their practice that ranged from cocky to sweet to heated.

After running through their new song all the way through, recording it this time, Jess stood from her stool and initiated a round of high-fives. "That's it—time to celebrate!" Brody called, and Jess sent up a resounding shout in agreement.

Even Tyler's mouth went a tick above a flat line, and he let Río jostle his shoulder. Apparently the moment of tension between them before was forgotten.

Río skipped over to me and crouched to my level. "You good to stay for a little pool party?"

My stomach clenched like there was a boulder in it, even as I tried to convince myself that pool party didn't mean I had to take off my sweatshirt. That my swimsuit could remain forgotten in the depths of my backpack.

At the risk of my voice trembling, I jerked a nod and let him stare into my eyes as he so often did. Río tilted his head again and brought a thumb to sweep across my cheek. "You sure? Did you bring a swimsuit?" I nodded again, hoping that he'd take that as an answer to both questions when it really wasn't.

I glanced to the rest of the room, where the other band members and Alex were chatting and putting away their stuff. Their skin looked so smooth, unblemished and perfect, and I hated them. Myself.

"Hey, hey, where'd you go?" Río's touch moved to my jaw, and I let him turn me to face him. He followed where I'd been looking, and realization swept his features. When he refocused on me, he wasn't mocking like I'd been fearing. "Ah."

Well, that was fucking *worse*.

He pulled on my arms, ushering to my feet, and without another word to me or glance at his friends, he guided us through Tyler's house. I kept my mouth slammed shut and chewed the inside of my cheek. Really, it was his fault for bringing me here, knowing that his, his, ex-*something* was going to be present. Or, did he not care enough about my feelings to even think about it?

Río selected a room that was a few doors down a hallway I hadn't yet seen, far enough away from the others that they were an ignorable buzzing in my mind.

There was a neatly made, king-sized bed dressed in a black comforter and white pillows. The dark wooden floor and deep maroon walls were brightened by white candles on the night tables, as well as a large, erotic sketch that hung behind the bed. A stretch of windows looked on the side of the house and the darkening night. The grass was manicured and a sharp contrast against the wild forest on the other side of the lawn. It was the same forest that housed my brother's land, the same that neighbored the witch house, and there was something grounding about its depths.

"Are you going to be a big girl and use your words, Ramona?"

I whirled around, no longer using the sight outside as my excuse to not look at him. Still, my mouth stayed stubbornly closed, but my fists were balled up at my sides. He just had to do that. Goad me while—while looking and smelling and being like that. It was bullshit. Frustrating.

Scary.

He stepped up to me, taking advantage of the four or five inches he had on me to stare down. He didn't touch me, despite how close our chests were, and it made me even angrier. "I'm not pulling it out of you. So tell me, or stay stewing. Your choice."

Despite my breaths accelerating, my shoulders rising and falling faster and faster, he still denied me the comfort of his skin on mine. My body felt like it was on fire with the need for his care, for his touch, and it just infuriated me further. What the fuck was happening to me, and what the *fuck* was he doing to me?

"You knew they'd be here." My words, that he'd so lovingly demanded, were a venomous hiss. If I'd had any magic like Sylvie, the force of it would've struck Alex, all the way on the other side of the house, dead.

Río continued to trap me with his black eyes, face and body unmoving. "Who."

"You fucking know who. Do you still want to fuck Alex?" I barely held myself from spitting on the floor after saying their name. No matter that they were nice and had done nothing to me except know Río first and have some unknown range of sexual experiences with him.

Something that should be all mine, a growling thought roared in my mind, making red halo around my vision. The only thing saving both of them was that there'd never been a whiff of Alex on Río since the party. Just me.

As if he could sense how close I was to breaking, Río crossed the churning chasm widening between us and took my face in his hands. But he didn't lick my face or kiss me. His hold was almost too tight when he brought our faces so close together that our noses touched. "The only one I want to fuck is you, Ramona."

The words simultaneously hit me straight through the heart while batting uselessly against the stone walls I'd erected around myself. How could he just want me? "Why." He was confident and without a care in the world, despite what he'd certainly been through if his damaged eyesight was any indication. And I was me. Broken and floating uncertainly. Not a pretty and charming person like Alex, or cheerful like his friends Brody or Jess. Or even Tyler, with his dark, unshakable personality.

Sharp teeth snapped my bottom lip between them, drawing blood and a gasp from my blustering lungs. He let me bleed.

"Because you're mine, Princess." My stomach flipped, and my heart thundered.

His. It was too good, too much of what I'd been longing for but too afraid to speak. And how dare he fucking say that when he wasn't even going to keep me.

Instead of melting in his arms and begging him to fuck me until I had no energy to object or fight anything he said, I took my hands and shoved.

Río's hold on me was ripped away, and the loss of contact made tears rise and spill onto my cheeks. I swiped at the wet trails with the backs of my wrists, but the reminder of my hoodie, the cuffs scraping on my skin and soaking up my tears, just made me scream.

A hoarse, wet shout that only served to build my frustration. "You don't fucking know me! I'm not nice. I'm not polite or sweet. Or *pretty.* Not like the people you apparently like. And. This is temporary, so how can I even be yours?" I was close to hyperventilating, or maybe even already there.

"Princess—"

"*Stop.*" I was done, so, so done with pretending that I was able to do this, but he kept calling me that name. Like I was something precious to be played with and treated with pleasure and care. Not broken and barely patched together with the pathetic list of mundane things to cling to.

Before I could think it through, I was tugging at the hem of my hoodie, fighting with it to pull it over my head. My braid got caught, but I kept on until I slid it the rest of the way, off of my arms. I threw it to the floor, bare torso now covered only with a plain, gray bralette. "There." I held my scarred arms out for him, shoving them in his line of sight as the damning evidence. "You wanna go out there and swim with your friends now? Let pretty and perfect Alex see that I'm no competition? Don't fucking tell me that shit!" I screamed the last bit, crying again while his stare was glued to what I showed him. Not my eyes, where he wouldn't truly see what was wrong with me. What I'd not told anyone since I was discharged from the inpatient program.

My chest heaved, my arms quivering but remaining outstretched toward Río.

Whose face was hard and serious in a way I'd never seen before. His angular jaw was clenched so tightly that I could see the muscles straining under the tension. He didn't even seem to breathe as he stood and watched. And when he stepped back toward me, his chest still didn't move.

He dropped to his knees, still silent, as if any more noise would scare me away.

In horror or awe, sweat trickled down my temple, and my eyes widened sharply as he cradled the backs of my forearms. He lowered his head, examining the long, raised line that was the ugly reminder of what I'd done. Sloppy and frantic to end it all.

And then his eyes flicked upward, veiled by long, black lashes that did nothing to obscure his intense gaze. Or the way my soul pulled toward him.

Río opened his mouth, and I braced for what was to come. Pity, empty words.

But, no. None of that. None of the words I expected, and in their place, unfurled the long, flat pink of his tongue. Half-shifted, it wasn't the smooth and soft of his human form but the rough version that was designed to scrape the meat off of the bones of his prey.

Never breaking eye contact with me, Río bent his head the last few inches. I gasped again as he began dragging that gentle and scratchy tongue up the length of my scar, tasting it.

I was frozen while I watched him do it twice more before

switching to my other arm and delivering the same treatment, communicating far more than I could handle.

I yelped in surprise when he dropped my arms and took my hips instead, giving a sharp tug until he was pressed against my front, nuzzling into my sternum. His purr, another… gift, vibrated my skin and filled the room. What could I do but hold him to me and let my bare arms and torso touch someone for the first time in years?

Río pressed kisses on my skin, rubbing my sides with passes of his callused fingers, until he stood, running his front against mine the whole way. He let me take the bottom of his shirt and helped me pull it off of him until it was a heap of fabric beside my discarded hoodie.

The first caress of his warm skin against mine left me whimpering, and not even the deep kiss he pulled me into stopped it. Río took over my mouth, licking into it and dominating my tongue with his rough one. His arms were like life-giving vises, keeping me close and giving no chance for escape or fleeing. The sensation of his shoulders against my scars was tender and new, and more warm tears fell down my face.

Río broke our kiss to lap up the salty liquid from my cheeks, swallowing my emotions with a hungry growl.

Before I could start the rest of our undressing or beg him to do it, cold air smacked my front and forced my eyes open. Río took my wrist, pulling me toward the sliding glass door of the room that was hidden amongst the windows. After opening us to the hot summer night, he marched us outside, tops bare. Need and confusion pulsed within my brain, but I wasn't stupid enough to object or stop us.

No, I let him pull me into the dark stretch of Antler Pointe forest that embraced Tyler's property until the house and the laughter of his friends was a flicker in the distance.

We were barefoot, and we crunched over the dirt and tree roots until he slowed us to a stop. I let Río circle the base of my throat with his other hand and push me back toward god knew what. His eyes were yellowing, and his lips were parted enough to reveal his fangs.

A gust of air punched out of my lungs when my bare back met the hard and surprisingly smooth bark of a tree. Río inclined his head, as if expecting an answer, and I nodded. Yes, I would stay put.

Though he let go of me, I still felt his warmth on my wrist and neck and remained exactly where he left me. My heart pounded in my chest, a pressure that knocked against my ribs as I watched Río's back while he rubbed his fingers quickly at his eyes and flung his hands toward the ground, as if flinging something away. He removed his jeans and boxer briefs and discarded them carelessly on the ground before tuning back to meet my eyes once again.

And it started.

An audible hum started deep in my chest, behind where Río had nuzzled into me, and intensified with the swirling that held him as the epicenter. Part of me wanted to object when his eyes shut, and his neck arched back, letting the change take over.

His skin rippled with the rearranging of his muscles and bones, the sound that accompanied it almost grotesque. Like thick, resounding thumping that was muffled by his blood and skin... that was darkening.

Río's legs bent at angles that looked odd. His thighs widened at the same time his fingers and toes did to become the shape of paws. He dropped to the ground, catching himself despite trembling. I was entranced as his chest broadened and took on the distinct and impossibly large feline shape.

Not a full member of my brother's pack, I'd not yet been to the pack runs, so the only shifts I'd witnessed were my mother's and brother's. Sights that were a very rare occurrence.

The wild beauty of Río's more than stole my breath, and I let the grounding presence of the tree behind me hold me still. While I watched his long, wavy hair shrivel and disappear at the same time fur sprouted all over his body. Río's facial features slid and rearranged until they were that of a strong and vicious Jaguar.

A black Jaguar.

Because where I'd expected tan and white fur dotted with black spots, there was instead a dark absence of color. Until, shift complete, he shook himself, all the way down to the end of his long tail, and opened his yellow and black eyes.

CHAPTER NINETEEN

RÍO

I shot a gust of air through my nose and shook my shifted body. My eyes blinked quickly, adjusting to the blurry sight of the forest now that my contacts were gone. The forest was alive with scents and sounds of the animals that lived here. Rodents scurried between and beneath tree trunks. The predators that stalked them flew above. I could feel the batting of their wings against my skin.

But most of all, I stalked forward, I sensed her. Honey eyes.

She stayed where I'd put her and watched while I shifted. I took another draw of the air to taste and exhaled my purr. She didn't stink of fear, anymore.

The closer I got, the easier it was to see her, staring with an arm out. My purr shook my chest as she pet between my ears. My tail swished on the ground, and I went further. I still couldn't see her clearly, even this close, but I didn't need my eyesight. The working of her hands through my fur was more than enough of a guide. Her cold grapefruit scent, I would never lose.

"Río." Her whisper filled my ears and took over my mind. A little scratchy from her crying. I didn't want her to cry.

I snuffled into her arm while she moved her hands down the back of my neck. The skin was bumpy but soft because it was her.

She was mine, sweet and sour, and my purr turned to a new sound. One I'd never made before that felt more than right. A raspy bark that wasn't loud to call out. It was quiet, just for her. Even still, she jumped, and the signal I was giving her traded for a wheezy hiss.

"Are you… *laughing* at me?" The hiss got louder, and I bobbed my head like I would in human form.

My honey eyes liked to bite when I laughed at her like this, but tonight, she crouched and pressed her lips just above my nose. Even when I snuffled, she didn't pull back, just kissed me again. "You're magnificent, Río."

I craned my face into hers, swished my tail along the forest floor. Compliments were nice, especially from her. My human and jaguar forms had received so much to the contrary.

"Do you want to go for a walk?" she whispered right in my ear, and a shiver traveled down my spine in pleasure. I liked having her close to me.

She stood but kept a hand against the back of my neck. Even though the wood was a dark blur, the symphony of scents and sounds made up for it. Honey eyes, my Ramona, and I walked quietly over the forest floor. Neither of us led, just let our bodies drift where they wanted. Together.

After a little while, she began to talk in hushed tones. A number, a list that she recited of random things. Coffee, nicknames. The last two, she mumbled as if she didn't want me to hear. But I did.

"Number Eleven. Princess. Number Twelve. Jaguar."

I chuffed, pleased that whatever the list was, those last two were about me. Showed that I mattered to her.

We continued on, walking a makeshift loop that followed no defined trail. We hopped over fallen trees, progressing in the heated night that delighted my animal half. To have my female with me, touching me.

And when we ended up back where we started, we both stopped without having to communicate it to each other.

Ramona bent before me, not quite fully crouching due to my height, but close. And I almost knocked her over with how hard I pressed into her. Like always, I licked up the side of her face, letting the barbs on my tongue taste her.

Desire curled in my belly, deepening my purr, and in complete accord, my human form pushed forth, taking some of the reins. Half-shifting from jaguar to human was weirder than the other way around. But it felt good in a different way to feel the air on my skin with no fur present. My claws still dug into the earth, but my long, human fingers replaced the stubbier, tougher paws.

My contacts were lying somewhere around here, so Ramona was still a blur of browns and black, but even then, I knew her smile.

"Your ears are so cute." She barely held back her giggle, and I answered it with a teasing snarl that was still all animal.

Instead of scaring her though, it just made her gasp and clutch my shoulders, now smooth and broader than before. I knew the smell of lust, and hers was as clear as day, twining and merging with mine. I'd never before felt this high and peace with someone else.

"You get turned on watching me shift, Princess?" My voice was a harsh grumble, still adjusting to the change, and my dick was heavy between my legs and pointing towards her as if we were in full agreement on what we wanted.

I ran my tongue up her cheek again, loving the way she trembled and held back the moan that begged to slip out. She caressed my shoulders, down to my biceps where there were still patches of fur-covered skin. "I almost didn't notice your spots before," she whispered. Technically, they were called rosettes, but she was right. From a distance, my fur appeared a wash of black, but up close, the large spots were actually black while the rest of me was slightly lighter.

"That wasn't the question I asked you." I took her earlobe

between my teeth, careful not to sink in too far. And my efforts paid off in the form of a full body shiver that skated down her body. She was mine. Mine, mine, mine.

I brought us both to our feet while keeping her close. "Yes."

I slammed my mouth onto hers, felt her sigh on my face. She tangled her fingers in my wild hair, and I relished in scraping my claws down her bare back. Well—I sliced through the fabric of her bra—now it was bare. And she didn't even bat an eye. Just shrugged out of the straps and returned her hands to me, where they fucking belonged.

Mine trailed to her front, where my hard cock was already pressing against her and painting her skin with lines of precum. I helped it along with the tips of my claws, causing streaks of wet goosebumps as I made tiny thrusts with my hips.

And when she gasped at my pinching of her nipples, I had to hold myself back from digging the razor points of my claws into her flesh. Like hell would I add to her scars, physically or emotionally. I wanted to be the one to help her heal.

She arched her head back, letting her whimper out and into the perfect night. I wanted every living thing remotely near us to witness this, and she was so good to give me what I craved.

Her breasts were smaller and round, and I tore my lips away from hers to close them around the perfect little handful on the left. She keened, straining on her tiptoes and clamping the back of my head to keep me from escaping.

My sweet and sour princess who let me be the first one inside of her. "Am I the first one to suck on these, Princess?" I spoke before flickering my tongue over the hard nub like it was her clit. By the way her mewls and groans turned to screams and a string of yeses, it felt about the same. "Such a good little slut. You saved these for me, and you're gonna keep it that way. Right?"

"*Río*, yeah, ye—*shit*." Ramona's words were lost again when I switched to the other nipple while pinching the slippery one. My hips were humping helplessly, trying to catch her thigh for any sort of friction while the scent of her arousal was close to driving me insane. Holy fuck, she was going to come like this. I could feel it in the hummingbird beating of her heart and the trembling of her frame.

I kept going, tasting her skin that was sweeter than any candy, and I had to pull on every ounce of strength to keep myself from busting when her release finally slammed into her and threatened to bowl me over, too. Her knees buckled at the same time her arms tightened around me, another flood of syrupy grapefruit washed over us.

But my princess wasn't done. The opposite, actually, but that was just fine because I was so hard that it hurt.

I released her tit with a wet pop and looked up toward her. The hand I'd used to pluck and pinch snaked to her waist and undid her shorts before pushing them and her panties out of the way. I shoved a finger between her legs, immediately becoming drenched. I was careful with my claw but kept it out as I tapped softly against her clit, and I felt the pulses of the lingering orgasm. She tried to squirm, but I kept on, helping her through the over-stimulation and right toward another one.

"Did you get the results I sent you this morning?" It was getting harder and harder to ignore the need to fuck her, but I also needed to hear from her that she was okay with it. I never fucked raw, but it wasn't like there were any condoms out here for me to roll on.

And I wanted to sink into her without a barrier between us. Watch and feel my cum drip out of her and down her legs. Shit, I forced myself to exhale, even the thought of that almost made me come.

It took her a second to respond, but the desire never wavered, and her body was still helplessly clinging to mine. "Mhm."

I'd played it safe with everyone else I'd been with, but I got tested anyway, knowing that I wouldn't be able to resist asking how she felt about it. "You good with that? Me fucking and coming in you raw."

My body and mind both froze in anticipation, waiting for the slightest tell that the idea made her uncomfortable, but Ramona surprised me by holding me even more tightly and undulating her hips more frantically over my finger. "Yeah, yeah, do it."

God, I groaned, my relief was almost painful. "Get on my back," I ordered while I was already ushering her behind me and grabbing at her thighs. She scrambled into position, and I tasted the air, sniffing and sensing the pulsing presence of the trees around us. The deep resonant groan of a sturdy, ancient maple tree guided me to the wide trunk.

"W-wait, Río what are you doing?" Ramona still sounded a little dazed, but there was a clear thread that held a bit of trepidation.

I grinned to myself since she couldn't see my face from clinging to me like a backpack. "Been wanting to fuck you in a tree for a while. Hold on tight, spider monkey."

This time she actually smacked my shoulder blade while tightening her legs around my waist. "This isn't fucking *Twi*—" she gasped when I jumped and started up the maple. Careful to not scrape my hard cock too much on the rough bark, I used my claws and muscles to climb us steadily toward the branches above.

My attention was divided between our ascent and making sure Ramona was secure on me. I'd been climbing trees in human and jaguar form pretty much all my life, but by her half-excited and half-fearful panting, I could guess that she wasn't as acquainted with tree climbs. I couldn't say I'd ever done it for this purpose, even though I'd fantasized about it plenty.

I felt my way along the trunk and the first branches we encountered. I wanted to be high, to feel the breeze around us, but not so high as to fill her with so much fear to spoil the moment. I sniffed and caressed a particular branch that felt good. It was wide enough for us, and when I cleared it and felt for the nearest branch above, I was satisfied to find that there was enough room above it for me to stand.

While I was confident in my abilities and for my Jaguar to keep me steady, Ramona clearly wasn't. When my feet settled on the selected branch, I shifted her around to my front, balancing on the tree with no hands.

She was a little scared, but my princess was so good and didn't squirm. She let me maneuver and position us until her bare back pressed against the safety the tree provided. Ramona relaxed a little at that, and I held her asscheeks and nibbled at her neck. "Look at that, Princess. Want me to fuck you so bad that you're willing to do this for me."

Her heart was still hammering against my chest, and I smirked into her throat, taking her flesh between my sharp teeth and leaving even more little bruises.

"Shut up. If you drop me, I'll fucking kill you." But the threat was a moan. She wiggled her hips a little until my dick nudged against the hot and slick haven that only she could provide.

"I won't ever let you fall, baby. You still sure you want me bare?" My hips thrust again, slipping against her skin, just outside of where I wanted to be more than life itself.

Ramona kissed my temple and scratched her nails against my scalp in a tender way that made me actually whimper. "Yeah, baby. Fuck me."

If I weren't so experienced with balancing in precarious situations, my legs might've actually given out at the pet name and the command. Or when I held her steady and sank home in one long, tight and wet plunge. I bottomed out, balls slapping softly against her ass, and I couldn't keep my claws from digging into her skin. Or pulling back and slamming into her again. Harder than I ever had with her.

She clamped around me, in all ways, and a wild—feral— hunger took over. To take my mate and impale her on me while soaking up her trust and craving. I held her against the tree trunk and fucked hard and fast while she screamed. But those were for me, too, so I sealed my lips over hers in something way too harsh for a kiss. Our tongues and teeth tangled, and when she lapped at my fangs, I tried to let up so as to not hurt her. But she didn't let me go, fucking my mouth even harder until the deep, delicious flavor of her blood flooded my tastebuds.

I drilled into her harder, swallowing all she was giving me and let her take from me too. I cut my own tongue on my teeth and let our flavors mix. Blood dripped from our joined mouths, and her juices overflowed between us.

It was coming, the burst of pleasure that I'd been seeking out since she pulled up to Tyler's house hours ago. But something else too, some invisible string that'd gone taut in recognition since the second I sensed her that night at Vinny's. The punishing rhythm of our fucking stuttered, grew, and our kiss just became a gasping, licking mess as we fought to breathe. My damaged vision was darkening around me, narrowing with my impending orgasm. "Come, baby. Need you to come before I do."

Taking a cue from what I'd learned about my princess earlier, I transferred one of my hands from her ass to her right nipple between us and pinched while I fucked her so hard that I felt like I'd reach her heart.

Not five seconds later, she tightened around me and stopped breathing. I gave an approving growl at her screeching in pleasure as I gave just a few more unsteady thrusts into tight bliss. I bore our bodies into the trunk and my feet and claws into the branch, making sure I kept my promise while my mind scrambled. My cock shot out ropes and ropes of cum that filled her and rained down, dropping onto the wood beneath us.

We both groaned through it, the sweet, sweet mess that we made. "Shit." I settled into her throat again, now that it was safe, and waited to get a handle on myself. Getting my dick wet in a tree had seemed like the perfect hint of danger and a way to satisfy both parts of me.

This was something fucking else, though. I'd half expected Ramona to refuse, but she'd truly been everything I could've asked for. Her showing me what it was that put that haunted note in her eyes and opening up past her anger was its own gift. And there was no giving it back. No, I showed her my Jaguar and took her into my safe place because she was never not going to be mine. Not after this.

"Question," she sighed. "You can't see shit right now, can you?"

She surprised a chuckle out of me, and I shifted my hips, more than happy to get acquainted with my new home inside of her. "Pretty much."

Ramona sighed again and pet the back of my head, eliciting a rolling purr from me. "And I'm the idiot that let you fuck me forty feet in the air."

"Cause you trust me. And like my dick."

She hummed but didn't deny it. "So, how are we getting back down? And back to Tyler's without everyone noticing."

My eyesight was truly shit, but my hearing was more than razor sharp. I paused for a second and caught the drunken laughter coming from the direction of Tyler's pool area. Jess half-heartedly asked where we'd gone but got interrupted by Brody who called for another round of shots.

"We go back down the way we came. All you gotta do is keep holding tight. They're all drinking by the pool, so we can sneak back into that room."

She nodded, and I very reluctantly slid out of her. More of my cum fell onto the branch, by my feet, and I growled again in satisfaction. I held her against the tree while I turned and pressed my back to her front, making sure her legs stayed wrapped around me. I'd never had any sort of breeding kink, but there was something about coming in her that soothed the deepest parts of me. The only way I could claim her any further would be to give her a mating bite.

"Don't get dizzy," I warned before starting us on climbing back down, heads pointed toward the ground.

CHAPTER TWENTY

CATALINA

I glanced at my watch and fought not to grind my teeth. "They're almost late."

There was nothing I hated more than tardiness. Second was dealing with overgrown puppies who thought they were sneaky. Dealing with one pack back home was e-fucking-nough.

Our soldiers guarded the entrance to the warehouse, silent in their black suits and not attempting to respond to me. Which was just as well. Any wrong answer might resort in their blood streaking the concrete floor.

A metal door creaked open, letting in the orange-tinted light of late morning, and we all stiffened. Weapons trained on the figure slipping through the side entrance, but I kept my own piece holstered within my blazer jacket. The stiletto knife stayed hidden in my boot.

A lumbering figure rounded a set of shelving, hips shimmying and leather shoes purposefully clacking toward me. "Desculpe pelo atraso." I was used to that booming voice by now, as well as the wide grin and eyes. Wired headphones blared music loud enough for me to hear the Mariah Carey song very clearly.

I tsked. "You're not late, but they're about to be. Of all the packs to give us trouble and be so disrespectful. This little town was supposed to be a *break*."

Xo's head tilted back and forth in contemplation, teeth clacking against a sucker between two pursed lips. "S'not all bad, mana." a pause and some obnoxious slurping revealed a bright red tongue. "This is about to be fun. *And*," the baritone flipped in a singsong rhythm that spelled trouble, "I've got a surprise for you."

I sighed. "Not too much fun, mana." Xo's manic laugh, deep and rumbly, grated on my ears. If this got out of hand, it'd be *me* cleaning up the mess. At least it wouldn't be me getting *dirty*. No, my suit would stay clean whilst Xo's—barely stretched over bulging muscles—all too often ended up drenched in blood and whatever else.

We continued to wait as I tried to not keep glancing at my watch and count down the minutes. Almost waiting for the moment I could deem the Wolves tardy and kick this whole thing up a notch. It'd serve this Leader fucking right.

Xo was prattling on about the journey, the mess down South that we were still fucking cleaning up, when a clear voice called, "They're coming in!"

I straightened and clenched my teeth. Right on time.

This leader had balls—had to at least give him that. He strolled in the warehouse with four other Wolves, nonchalant as anything. And every single one of them was dressed down in jeans, which made me even more irritated. They all stood proud and unbothered, the Leader's white face blank and revealing nothing.

Xo laughed in anticipation, and I followed the uneasy glances the lesser Wolves gave at the unprovoked noise.

Instead of shooting Xo a silencing glare, I tried to catch the Leader's eyes, but he kept them sweeping around the warehouse that wouldn't be empty for too much longer.

"Thank you for coming." I broke the silence to only be met with a curt nod of acknowledgement in return. When he finally met my eyes, the Leader raised his brows, as if—as if *he* was commanding *me* to get on with it.

How fucking arrogant. "We brought you here so that you could further understand what we're proposing." I waved a hand to gesture at the large space around us. "Leave to conduct our business on your land and move our products as needed. No more, no less."

The Leader crossed his arms, but the gesture lacked the usual chest-puffing that so many usually did. At least until they remembered Xo's hulking form at my side.

"Demanding."

"Huh?" Xo asked around the cherry red sucker.

The Leader clarified, "You're demanding that we do this. Not proposing. There is no benefit to us or our territory, yet we are the ones that stand to face the consequences."

I kept my face neutral while I imagined how my penthouse bedroom would look with a Wolf-skin rug. With a small smile, I countered, "Our more… human-facing business will add revenue to this town's economy, as well as providing employment and benefits to all who may work with us. This side of our affairs, should you agree, will never need to affect you at all."

The Wolves behind him stood tall, committed to their roles as backup and muscle, just as Xo was to me. They obviously deferred to him, so I didn't spare them a second glance as their Leader thought this over. Though I could appreciate it, I was unaffected by the dense smell of Pack Leader that wafted off of him, rolling with wild power.

"And just what will you be moving through here? Will you not eventually demand that we not only allow this venture but directly support it with our labor and protection, as you've done to the River Fall Pack in Georgia?" His voice remained dry, blank, and he pressed on, "Or overrun our community with drugs, ripping our pack apart from the inside out with chaos? To the point that the humans nearly catch wind? I'd assume that this outcome isn't solely reserved for what used to be the Howl's Fury Pack."

Cold. It settled so easily. "Unfortunate outliers. And any additional involvement on you or your pack members' parts is entirely your choice. Any and all would be compensated significantly—"

"At the cost of honor and lives. My refusal stands. Was this all?" He took another glance around and looked at me expectantly.

Was this all? No, I was wishing I could rip open his stomach and make him watch me decorate our new space with his entrails. Which would be a mercy compared to what would happen when I reported back.

I crossed my arms, let the shifting of my jacket reveal the twin Glocks that I much preferred to use than my own claws or fangs. "That is all, Leader Orion."

One of the Wolves' eyes flickered, showing their uncertainty, before they schooled their expression once again. That aside, for a pack, they were surprisingly stoic.

"Oh, one more thing!" Xo gleefully added and ran to one of our soldiers.

I watched the Wolves, bracing for what was coming, and tracked the wariness with which they watched, what they assumed, my right hand skipping with his hands behind his back.

"Don't forget this!" Xo's smile was sunny, bright, and a beat of confusion coursed through the little group at the meaty thud before them.

One of them screamed. Another turned green, another began trembling. The last took one look at the severed head and shot their eyes to the ceiling, tears falling.

The Leader, though, tilted his head for a beat and then crouched. He sniffed the air, gave a long exhale, and took the head in his steady hands. And when he straightened, he stood tall with what was left of the sandy-blond Wolf they'd sent to spy on us.

"You and your brother have made your point. We won't forget this." Though his eye contact had been fleeting during our brief parley, it was unflinching, now. A decade or so ago, I may have been moved by the steely determination in the hard edge of his jaw, but he knew as well as I that if they attempted to retaliate now, they'd never leave here alive. While all of us would. I had also been doing this long enough to know that Wolves were far too proud to take something like this lying down.

Xo and that damned katana had probably just started a war.

The Leader turned around with the felled Wolf's head held close and led his pack members back out the way they came. Our soldiers watched with disinterested attention, having seen far worse displays than this, and returned to their rounds once the pack had officially left.

I pulled my phone from my back pocket and put it on camera mode to check my makeup. I set to reapplying my lipgloss. "You said that you had a surprise for me, Xo?"

"Hmm?"

I rolled my eyes at my reflection and pursed and puckered my lips to make sure the tinted sheen was to my liking. "Sua mente é um lugar podre."

"Vai se fuder, Cata." But Xo's grousing only lasted long enough for a maniacal grin to spread. "Guess whose scent I picked up on after I caught that little weasel."

I put my phone and lipgloss back in my pockets and crossed my arms. Xo kept nodding, waiting for me to guess, but I really wasn't in the mood. We stared at each other, the only sounds being the music still blaring from Xo's headphones, the shifting of our soldiers near the perimeter, and the buzzing of the fluorescent lights above.

Tone dry as the Sahara, I gave in. "You finally found Benny?" The little shithead had gone and disappeared on us when I'd given him the most simplest of tasks that wasn't even really that necessary. If Pai hadn't been on our asses about it, I would've been perfectly fine to let him just fuck off or rot wherever he was.

Xo's eyes sparkled, and two giant hands interlocked to tuck

under a dimpled chin with a dreamy shine in black eyes that matched mine. "*Better*. Nosso irmãozinho querido."

PART TWO

CHAPTER TWENTY-ONE

RÍO

Someone pounded on the door, jolting me awake. I blinked up at the ceiling and reached for the bedside table where I could've sworn I put my spare glasses. With my propensity to have unplanned shifts to release the tension that would build from being in my human form too long, I'd learned to carry them with me pretty much everywhere I went. After a few seconds and more irritating knocking, I managed to snag the frames and put them on without jostling Ramona too much.

She was stirring a little from the noise but hadn't fully woken up yet. I was going to kill Brody for disturbing her.

Carefully, I slid out from under her and settled the covers over her chest and arms. After taking a second to make sure she was covered and still asleep, I silently stomped to the door.

When I flung it open, just enough so that he could see the scowl on my face, I noticed the amused grin on his. He was still wearing yesterday's jeans but was missing his shirt. "We were gonna order somethin' to eat." He tried to crane his head to see inside the room, and I had to hold back my snarl. Brody was as human as they came, so I just crossed my arms and blocked his snooping with my body.

So, he turned his attention to me and trailed his gaze down my naked form. He whistled. "Did that hurt?" He pointed to my dick that was still half hard from sleeping with Ramona beside me.

I rolled my eyes. The piercing had been a spontaneous decision during one of my stints as a tattoo apprentice at a shop out west. "No. What are you getting?"

He mentioned one of the breakfast places in town that wasn't too far. Lord knew we weren't gonna find any food in Tyler's kitchen. How did Brody and Jess make sense of that?

"Hold on." I closed the door in his face and turned back to the bed. I sat on the edge and caressed the side of Ramona's face. Her brow was adorably furrowed, her full lips pouting, and I kissed the side of her mouth before doing the same to the top of her cheek. I pulled back to see her face smooth and a precious and sleepy smile spread. My heart jumped.

"Princess," I whispered gently in her ear and licked at her delicate skin. She squirmed like it tickled, and I did it again until she turned over.

Half-asleep, now, she rolled onto her back and puckered her lips for a kiss. As much fun I had with her prickly side, I loved this one too. I met her lips with mine but kept it fairly chaste. Even when she brought her hands to my neck and kicked her legs, trying to find my hips and hold me to her. "Ramona," I spoke into her lips, "are you hungry?"

"Uh-uh," she mumbled, but that was not what I wanted.

I separated us, in the little cave that my loose hair provided where it was just me and her. Brody tapping his foot impatiently on the other side of the door didn't matter. "Baby, what do you want to eat."

Ramona huffed, coming back to her usual self, and I smiled affectionately. I swiped her lip with my thumb. "Whatever. I'm not picky. What are you making?"

"Not making. Brody and Jess are ordering from the diner on

Fourth Street. You ever been there?" She shook her head. "They got the usual. Pancakes, waffles, bacon."

She rubbed at her eye and scrunched her face in such a cute way. "Uh, just get me whatever you get. And iced coffee."

I kissed the tip of her nose. "All right."

I left her on the bed and went back to the door. Brody looked less chipper now, but whatever. "Two orders of chicken and waffles, bacon extra crispy, scrambled eggs with cheese. Two large iced coffees. Extra syrup on the side."

Brody's eyes were wide, but he pulled out his phone and started tapping away, adding our breakfast to their order. "Jesus, you both gonna eat all that?"

"Damn right. I tired her ass out. Gotta feed my lady."

I grinned at Brody when Ramona's indignant shout flared behind me. "Don't fucking tell people that!"

I glanced at her over my shoulder, gut lurching at the sight of her sitting up and swaddled in the sheets. "But it's true. I'm sure they all heard you screaming my name last night." After coming back from outside, we'd returned to the guest room and used the connected bathroom to shower before tumbling into the bed. For hours, we alternated between talking and fucking any which way we could. Her riding me, me hitting it from the back, with our tongues. During our breaks, she told me a little about growing up in a rich family with less than affectionate parents, and I reminisced about the good years. When I'd spend my time on my aunt's land and playing in the woods. How I taught myself how to draw and play the guitar.

"Well, if they heard me, then they heard you too," Ramona grumbled.

Brody shook his head and gave a final tap on his screen before putting his phone back in his pocket. "Unfortunately. Went to take a piss in the middle of the night," he jutted a thumb up the hall where there was a half bath, "and was forced to hear it." He made a stupid come face and tried to mimic my voice, "Yeah, Princess, take that dick." I socked him on the shoulder which just made him laugh harder. "Food'll be here in thirty." He turned and started up the hallway, and I slammed the door.

"You do sound like that," Ramona snickered but yelped when I pounced on the bed and yanked the sheet off of her.

It was later in the morning, now, and with the bright light from the windows and my glasses correcting my vision, I greedily drank up the view of Ramona's naked body. I yanked on her legs until she slid back down on the mattress. Her chest rose and fell quickly, jiggling her tits. My dick was all the way hard, now, and I thrust it lazily against her stomach. The black barbell pierced through the crown of my cock clacked against the silver one stuck through her bellybutton. It sent a zip of pleasure straight up my length, and I did it again and again.

"You too sore from last night, Princess?" Well, if I was remembering correctly, our final round had to have been just a few hours ago, when the sun was making its way back up the horizon. But time had also blended together as we lost ourselves in each other.

I eyed the red and purple bruises along her neck and around her nipples that hadn't lightened quite yet. She was gonna walk out of this room with them visible for my friends to see.

Before she answered, I went a bit lower, nudging myself right against her clit. She scrabbled her heels over the bed, whimpering with her teeth sunk into her bottom lip. "Huh? You gonna let me come in you again?" She nodded, her black and curly hair frizzy and magnificently escaping the confines of her braid.

I used my hold on her thighs to raise her hips. She was still slick from all we'd done earlier, wet with herself and my cum, and I threw my head back. "God, Princess, I'm never gonna get tired of this." I drew my hips back and sank in slowly, deeply.

It didn't take long for her to come, especially when I lightly pinched her clit while we fucked. The cat had long been out of the bag, so she just clenched her eyes and let her loud cry of ecstasy out.

The tightening of her walls around me and the sight of her neck flushing and covered with my teethmarks were my undoing.

My face screwed up, absolutely *not* in the way Brody had mocked, and I spilled into her. I was honestly surprised my balls had anything left after the marathon we'd run together, but sure enough, I filled her up again.

I pulled back and watched, entranced, as my cum leaked out and started to pool beneath her. Fuck, I was already addicted. Did this count as a breeding kink?

Ramona relaxed back onto the bed, now sighing in content. The corners of her mouth tilted upward again, and I answered with a swipe of my tongue along her arm. She still smiled, but a wrinkle between her brows formed as she watched me.

Another thing we did talk about a little bit was how she'd given herself these. Based on how she spoke about her life before moving in with her brother, I wasn't exactly surprised.

Now wasn't the time to get truly sappy and tell her that I was thanking every deity and the universe that it hadn't worked. That I was at the point of needing her. So, I let my tongue speak for itself and adored our mingled scents and the taste of her skin.

Eventually, her expression settled, and I switched to the other arm. Let her know that I loved them both because they showed how much she'd overcome.

I ended one swipe with a light flicker, getting what I was looking for in the form of a giggle. The little noise startled her, so I did it again. And again.

"*Stop*, that tickles." Her belly shook, and I did it once more before settling her hands at my waist. Like the brat she was, she moved to grab at my ass instead, squeezing in the same way I liked to do to her.

"As much as I would love another round, we should probably get up so we can eat soon."

"What is it with you and making sure I eat," she said more to herself, watching as she pet up my sides and ribs. I was used to the sight of my tattoos by now, so that I barely noticed them, but she seemed to be cataloguing every corner, every curve of my art on my skin.

I shrugged. "Gotta take care of you," I answered honestly. It wasn't like I could even imagine doing anything different. She didn't have an answer for that one, but she also didn't argue with me. For my princess, that counted as a win. "Come on, let's throw some clothes on." I hopped out of the bed and started searching the floor for our clothes. Her hoodie was near the door to the bathroom, my shirt had been almost kicked under the bed.

After doing a sweep of the floor, I groaned.

"What?" she asked while pulling her sweatshirt over her head.

"Half our shit is still in the woods." Apparently she hadn't realized it either because her groan echoed mine. "Be right back," I mumbled and marched to the sliding glass door. Not like there were any neighbors to look out for. I ran across Ty's yard, butt ass naked, and went into the trees. A wolf whistle rang across the grass, my ears telling me it was Jess who saw me sprinting toward the woods.

I let my nose guide me to our clothes, and I ran back to the guest room under the bright sun.

When I handed Ramona her shorts and panties, she took them with nose wrinkled in disgust before shaking them out. She opted not to put on the underwear and stepped into the skimpy denim. I did the same with my jeans and tucked myself in, sans boxers, before zipping and buttoning up.

With quick splashes of water on our faces and taking full advantage of the extra toothbrushes under the sink, we emerged hand in hand.

I guided Ramona to the pool where everyone was again congregated. Jess was lounging beside the deep end in a one-piece swimsuit while Tyler looked only slightly pissed beside her and under a parasol. Brody was bobbing along in the shallower end of the pool with Alex who must've spent the night, too.

I glanced down at Ramona as we padded to a lounge chair on the other side of Tyler. They didn't stop their conversation, but every eye followed us as I sat and pulled Ramona between my legs. We settled back into the wooden seat, and I didn't have to look at her face to know she was shooting me a dirty look. I kissed her cheek.

"You done with your all night fuck fest? My house isn't a rent-by-the-hour motel, you know." Tyler groused without any venom. He just took one look at us and rolled his eyes like we were dumb kids. Which, maybe we were to him. I'd never asked how old he was. Certainly older than he looked, which was younger than my twenty-six.

"Nah? Then who did I give my money to?" I snarked.

There was a round of good-natured laughter, and Jess started filling us in on what we missed. Brody getting wasted, doing stupid flips and only belly-flopping a few times. Some of Jess's friends already listening to the new song we finished and giving positive remarks.

"It does sound really good," Alex piped up, and Ramona stiffened in my arms. He gave a nice but weak smile our way, probably all too aware why she was being cold towards him.

My glasses nudged against the side of her face, and I whispered low, "Be nice, baby."

She whipped her head around, knocking into my glasses, which just made her scowl deepen. "Not possible."

I pulled against her stomach even more, trailed my nose against the edge of her hairline. "Yes, it is. He didn't do anything wrong, and I already told you. The only one I want is you. That's the truth. Or do I need to fuck you in front of everyone to get it through your stubborn head?"

She sucked in a breath and hissed, "You wouldn't." Was that lust I smelled?

I grinned evilly into her skin and rocked us from side to side. "I would. Gotta teach you how to act right."

"No, please don't do that," Tyler grumbled, the only one privy to our hushed conversation. The rest of them turned even more curious glances our way, though Alex was trying not to look too long.

I laughed and spoke loud enough for the rest of them to hear.

"Y'all would be so lucky." As much as public sex thrilled me, none of these shitheads deserved to see my princess naked. That was for us to share. If she asked me to though…

I grabbed her jaw and planted a deep kiss on her lips, and she didn't resist even a little bit. More of Jess's whistles coursed around us, and I smiled into Ramona while I continued to dance us in our seat. Was this happiness? How could I make sure that we woke up together every morning and went to bed beside each other every night?

"Food's here!" Brody hollered and slapped his wet feet across the concrete poolside, opting to go around the house instead of through it. When he came back with arms weighed down by food bags and drink carriers, we all gave a round of applause. Besides Tyler, at least, who just took his extra large coffee and started loading it down with sugar packets. When I was twelve, freshly scooped up and training with my sisters, I once asked a vamp that worked for my father if they puked when they ate food. Apparently, vampires didn't, but it all tasted like shit. Liquids and strong flavors were more palatable, and I wagered that Tyler excused himself out of eating by stating he wasn't a breakfast person.

Ramona and I separated just enough to sit with our to-go platters in our laps, the iced coffee cups sat on the small table between us and Tyler.

Just like I thought, she immediately shoveled down her food, and after watching her awhile in appreciation, I started on my matching meal. It was hot as shit out, but this kind of weather never bothered me none. My Jaguar loved the heat, and I'd grown up in the South. How I'd lasted this long this far up north was beyond me.

After about ten minutes, Ramona and I finished our meals, just before Brody who scarfed down his pancakes and eggs a minute or so after us. Alex and Jess ate much more slowly, talking and laughing in between bites while Tyler just sipped and chipped in here and there. He was a little like Ramona in that way. He'd scowl and sneer, but he never *really* kicked us out. Always opened up his fancy house for us to practice. I wondered if he was… lonely.

The six of us stayed outside for a few hours, talking about a bunch of nothing, but the company more than made up for it. After we threw our trash out, Ramona and I switched to sitting on the edge of the pool with our feet in the water. Her cute little toes were painted the same shade as my Iceman, and even though it was probably a coincidence, I decided to take it that she thought of me as much as I thought of her.

"So, what's your story, Río's Girl?" Brody had returned to swimming in the water, and he turned the conversation to zero right in on Ramona. She'd been fairly at ease beside me, splashing the blue water. Instead of trying to splash Alex who was treading a few feet away.

But I could tell that she wasn't one to enjoy an entire group's attention. She cleared her throat. "What do you mean?"

Brody shrugged. "Dunno. Did you grow up here? Didn't remember seeing you around."

"Oh. No, I moved here back in May to stay with my brother and his family. I grew up in New York."

He whistled like he was impressed. "City girl, all right. Who's your brother? Maybe I know him."

Ramona picked at the frayed edge of her shorts, so I moved my leg just a little to nudge her toes with mine. My nails were painted black, and our feet looked good together.

She wiggled her toes against mine. "Orion Gealach. He's a professor at the college. His m-wife is Sylvie Williams."

"Huh, weird last name you guys have." I flung a splash of water at him for being rude.

But Ramona didn't shoot back. "That's his. Mine is Wells." When she'd first told me her last name when I'd asked, I'd experimented with funny nicknames for her in my contacts. Welly Belly stuck for a little bit. At least, until she saw it in my phone and demanded I change it. She'd still grumbled when I reset it to 'Princess' but didn't outright protest.

Jess flipped up her sunglasses and leaned forward to squint at Ramona. "Wait, that name sounds familiar. Are you famous or something?"

That got my princess stiffening. She glanced at me, just for a split second as if she was going to ask for reinforcements, but then she blanked out her face and arched a brow at Jess. "No." What was going on?

"No, no," Jess waved her sunglasses at her, "*you* aren't famous, but is your dad Sean Wells by chance? My dad and I watch football every Sunday," she rolled her eyes like it was a stupid tradition, "and you look like his kid."

"Fuck," Ramona mumbled before sending an almost apologetic smile my way. She turned back to Jess. "You got me." I took her in, my princess who I'd sussed out as a rich kid from the moment I saw her. I didn't watch sports at all, but my uncle had kept it on every weekend before he died when I was ten. Back then, Sean Wells played for the Giants, if I wasn't mistaken.

Jess laughed like she'd discovered some great secret. "Holy shit, I gotta tell my old man about this. You know, your dad's his favorite commentator to this day. Wait—could you get us tickets?"

"How presumptuous of you, Jessica." Tyler drawled, but it didn't deter her. She was looking at Ramona with hope and excitement lighting up her face.

I rubbed a hand on Ramona's back, willing the tension in her spine to ease. Obviously, she didn't want to talk about her family, but Jess was a weirdly avid football fan. Soccer was a better sport, in my opinion, but the two of us had already gotten into it enough about it.

"Uh, we're not really… close. Sorry."

"Oh," Jess deflated, "well that's okay." I tightened my mouth and caught her eye before cutting mine to Ramona and back. Jess blinked a few moments, not understanding what I was trying to indicate until at least ten awkward seconds had passed. "Are you coming to our next show?"

Ramona exhaled and leaned a little into my side. I grabbed her waist and scooted myself the rest of the way. My Jaguar tossed and turned with the need to purr, but I couldn't exactly do that here, so I settled for scenting her all over. Running my face up the side of hers, sniffing in her hair. It was a fucking shame I had to go to work soon because I could already feel myself ramping up for more rounds with my princess. And just alone time, listening to her talk and taking care of her.

"Damn, man, let the girl breathe. You're like a damn cat." Brody shouted before losing himself in a round of deep belly laughs.

I shot him the finger and gave Ramona's face a hearty lick for good measure. The humans groaned in disgust, but Ty's dark chuckle made me grin with the inside joke.

The rest of the hour passed far too quickly, and how I ended up being the only one who had to work that day, I didn't know. It was fucking unfair, but I had to tear Ramona and I away from the hang that looked like it was going to continue for hours more. She'd started adding to the conversation by the end, and I felt like a jerk for taking her away. But when I declared that I had to head to Vinny's, she said her goodbyes and followed me inside to grab our stuff and back out to the driveway.

I was already cutting it too close to run to my place and drop off my guitar, so I opted to keep it at Ty's. No way in hell was I leaving her in my truck.

Ramona opened the door of her brother's black SUV and turned to face me. I palmed her ass and pulled until our hips connected. Fuck, how swas I supposed to get through the next eight hours without her? Especially after the night we had.

She had her fists balled and rested against my chest, but her fingers were nervous as she pulled at the fabric of my t-shirt. "I'm... um, sorry I didn't tell you. About my family."

I squeezed her cheeks and kissed her hairline. "Aw, don't

worry about it. I knew you were a princess from the first time I laid eyes on you. Makes a lot more sense now."

Her expression didn't settle like I'd hoped it would. She kept on picking at my shirt. "And. I." She breathed out, back in, then out, as if that was going to calm the galloping in her chest. My own heart rate quickened in sympathy, and I worried for a second what she was about to tell me. "I… really—like you. Río."

My cheeks pulled back to show every one of my teeth, and I even flashed her my upper fangs for good measure. "Yeah, baby? How much?"

Ramona stared at my mouth, and it wasn't just hunger that flitted across her face. It was something akin to adoration, and my smile softened. "A lot," she whispered then clamped her mouth shut. Her brown cheeks deepened with a fierce blush, and she glared as if daring me to say something smart.

But I didn't. I took her chin in hand and kissed her. With no tongue, just soft movement of my lips that she returned just as sweetly. "I lo—like you a lot, too. Princess, I think I'm gonna have to keep you."

She gasped, but whether it was because she caught my slip up or because she was surprised by my declaration, I didn't know. By the widening of her eyes, I was starting to panic that it was the former. "Okay," she whispered.

I cleared my throat. "I gotta go, but I'll text you. Wanna come over to mine later?"

Ramona nodded, and I kissed her again before giving one last lick at her temple. With my friends, she'd acted begrudged or resigned with my grooming. But now, when we were alone, she preened and sighed. "All right, baby. Be good."

It was hard to get my body to cooperate, but I managed to step away and let Ramona slide into the driver's seat. She didn't try to hold her eye roll. "Yeah, yeah. See you later." Once she was buckled in, I closed the door for her and headed to my own truck. I waited for her to back out, turn the car around, and head up the drive. Pantera blasted through the old speakers while I followed her out. She turned to head further out of town, while I went the opposite way with a wave. Ramona smirked and waved back before going in the direction of her brother's cabin.

"Fuck, fuck, fuck," I chanted. Now that I was by myself where she couldn't see, I had the freedom to freak the fuck out. I was so whipped that I'd almost admitted to her that I loved her.

The whole way to Vinny's, I tried to convince myself that I was still fuck drunk or having a damn heat stroke. But I knew none of that was true as I parked in front of the small pizza place. We were two months into this… thing between us, and if I had any sense, I'd declare it too fast.

I walked into the restaurant and straight back to the manager's office to drop off my backpack and clock in. Van, the other manager who had opened today, gave me a nod that I absently returned, thoughts still churning. All right, if I loved her, and it was looking a hell of a lot like I did, then I was really going to keep her. Which led me to ruminate on broaching the topic of leaving town with Ramona. I was a sitting duck, but I wasn't going to go without her.

My mind whirled with… hope. Plans of where we'd go. I could take her to Michoacán, show her the city for a while before letting her pick the next place. We'd have to find temporary jobs to sustain the constant travels, but I also had a hefty nest egg if we wanted to just sight see for a few weeks. Or years.

Years.

Literal butterflies, like the last sketch I'd drawn, fluttered in my belly as I checked the cooler temps and turned the ingredients that needed it. What if—what if she wanted to be my mate, too?

A la mierda. I had to grip the prep counter to calm myself and keep the mating roar from coming out. Now that I'd done it once, my Jaguar didn't want to stop calling out to her. Again and again and again until she answered. When I'd done it the first time last night, I *felt* the answering buzz under her skin.

The chime on the front door sounded, and my thoughts were still a haze of animalistic desire as I let go and went to take the order. Dealing with customers never failed in turning me all the way off.

Unfortunately, as soon as I pushed open the door that led from the kitchen to the register, I knew that I had truly fucked up. I'd thought almost confessing my love for Ramona was bad?

No, this was so, so much worse.

"Oi, maninho." The tiny female grinned wide at me. I'd been so wrong. My doom was already here.

CHAPTER TWENTY-TWO

RÍO

I needed to run. I should run, right?

Mara's eyes and grin widened, as if she was daring me to do it. Madre de dios, how had I been so fucking stupid? As soon as Ramona had dropped to her knees for me, I should've thrown her kicking and screaming on the back of my bike and hightailed us both straight to Mexico.

"So, how you been, Yoyo?" My tiny big sister drummed her fingers on the front counter, and I swept my gaze around and widened my senses. Thank the universe for small mercies, Catalina wasn't here.

Mara was still smiling, turning my own black eyes back at me, and I had to shove all thoughts of Ramona to the back of my mind. How was I going to protect her from my family if they were already here?

"Fine. What do you want." Shrugging into my old training, the version of myself that hid all feeling, felt like putting on wet clothes. It molded to me, sticking uncomfortably, but was also familiar.

She pouted and flipped her short, wavy hair. After eight years, she'd chopped it to a bob that ended just below her ears. Her bangs were short enough to show a sliver of her forehead and thick, black brows. Like the perfect soldier, she wore a sleeveless vest and black slacks to make up her own kind of suit. And— Jesus fucking Christ, she had her katana slung on her back. Was she here to use that on me?

"I missed you." She kept the pout on her round lips, but her eyes danced with mirth.

I put my hands in my pockets. "You saw me. Say what you really want, or leave me alone."

Mara tsked, and I already knew more bullshit was coming before she swiped her hand so quickly that a human wouldn't have been able to track it. The to-go cups, straws, and napkins all set beside the register crashed to the floor.

She didn't even look down at the mess she made. Just kept watching me. At least the smile was back. If Mara was smiling like that, I'd learned that I was likely to make it out of the exchange unscathed. If she looked angry, a fight was surely going to come. But if she grinned with her eyes faraway and blank, there would be a massacre.

"Candy?" She offered a sucker she'd produced from her pocket. I shook my head, and she popped it into her mouth. "Is that the thanks I get for helping you escape, baby brother?"

I didn't flinch. Couldn't give her any ammunition. Yeah, she'd been the one to jostle me awake that night, told me to pack my shit, and occupied our father's soldiers on my side of the compound so that I could ride off on my bike and finally leave. A few weeks prior, she'd discovered my nest egg when it was just a tiny thing. An account in a different name that my father had no access to that I was using to help Mamá and quietly growing to fund my escape.

Until Mara had found out about it. I'd thought I was dead for sure, but she wasn't Catalina. Mara had hissed at me to stop giving our mother money, because if she was able to discover it, it was only a manner of time before he used it against the both of us.

I held no illusions that my father was truly done with Mamá. But I'd rather go back to being an enforcer alongside Mara than give her up. I'd be a good little Serafim soldier until the day I died if that meant keeping Mamá and Javier safe.

Cata, Mara, and Pai didn't know about him, though.

So, I'd left and heeded Mara's warning. To save myself and keep my real family hidden and safe.

"Buena suerte, hermanito. No seas pendejo." Mara didn't hug me, but a rare tinge of emotion shone in her bottomless stare. If I had to guess, as I shoved on my helmet and started up my bike, it was fear and resignation. We weren't friends, exactly, but she'd been the one to patch me up when my wounds were too extensive to do myself. She was the one who taught me how to beat someone for just enough information while keeping them alive to get or deliver the message. Her long hair fluttered in the soupy Georgia air while this side of the compound was dark. I stopped myself from asking how she was going to explain my absence. She could tell Pai that she killed me, for all I cared. It'd be better that way.

Those had been the last words she'd spoken to me, but this was not the caring version of my sister that'd snuck me extra flan after I cried the first night away from Mamá. Or the one that watched over me after the worst beating I'd fared—the one that took most of my eyesight.

She gestured to the glasses now with a slender finger. "You still wearing those stupid things?"

I stepped closer, skirting around the counter so that no barriers stood between us. I couldn't show that I was afraid, but I also couldn't give her too much to spark her interest. Just boring old weak Río working a dead-end job. Nothing worth reporting back to our father about.

"Not all of us are virtually indestructible."

Mara crossed her arms and scoffed, but the action wasn't anywhere as cute as when Ramona did the same thing. "Well, if I'd known it'd leave you looking like a fucking *nerd* for the rest of your life, I would've just kept it at the broken legs."

How I had survived living in a house with her was beyond me. And Mara was the *sensitive* one. "Whatever. What did you come here for?"

"¿Sabes donde está Benny?" She tilted her head, watching and waiting for me to slip up. It wasn't phrased as if she actually gave a shit where our *very* distant cousin was.

And I already knew how this went. "Lo maté."

Mara shrugged, unsurprised by the news but also unsurprised that I'd admitted to it. It's not like he'd been well-liked. "Boring. Well, I'll leave you to your poverty." She took a disdainful sniff and looked around as if the sight of the register and old booths sickened her. Just as randomly, my sister spun on her heel and walked toward the door.

I forced my breaths to stay calm, to watch her put a hand on the door and leave.

She froze, and my heart plummeted all the way to my asshole. The afternoon rays lit her up, casting blues and reds through her hair. If I wasn't stained with the same darkness that filled her, I would've said she looked angelic. Mara snapped her fingers as if she *just* remembered something important. "Oh, and I'll meet you at your place for a beer when you're done with this shithole for the day. Then you can talk to me about your mate."

RAMONA

My brother was smoking again.

Sylvie rubbed his back, mouth pursed, while I occupied the kids as best as I could. Dahlia had already told him that what he was doing was unhealthy, and I had to apologize to both him and Sylvie for having the pack hidden in the guest room. In my defense, I thought that O had been so far past his addiction that he wouldn't be tempted.

But, in regard to the Wolf pack, shit had totally hit the fan.

They couldn't say too much with the kids around, but those people Orion met with had apparently retaliated violently. Sylvie had done her best to pantomime a literal beheading, and I'd thought she'd been joking before my brother solemnly confirmed.

I took a drag of my own cigarette and watched Ollie and Dahlia play in the little blow-up pool set up beside the garden. Sylvie rolled her eyes at me as I exhaled, but I just gave a helpless shrug. I'd been feeling happily anxious about the progression of my and Río's relationship, but I didn't want O to smoke alone.

Good god, the way he'd *smelled* when I left Tyler's house. He tried to cover it up, by agreeing that he liked me, too. Which had been embarrassing as hell—how old were we, twelve? But the rich scent from him that'd embraced me at the same time his hands did… it was almost how my brother smelled when he was holding Sylvie.

From Río, it wasn't as solidified, signaling a newer feeling, but it was fucking *there*. I took another drag and exhale from my cigarette. Could he smell the matching emotion that wafted off of me when I was around him?

"Mo ghrá, I don't want you to watch me. I know that you don't like when I do this." Orion lit up another smoke to replace the one he'd just finished.

And Sylvie went on, caressing him and giving him support. "I don't, but you need me more than I dislike the cigarettes, baby. How can we help?"

Ollie let loose a happy little screech while he splashed the water around him. Dahlia joined in, and it was at least endearing to see some joy. I watched them while I sat on the edge of the porch, between the two conversations. Originally, Orion had come out here to smoke alone, but the kids had insisted on a pool party outside with their daddy, and it turned into all of us out here.

"You can't. They delivered the… rest of him by the time we got back from the meeting. I had to notify Jasper's parents."

I remembered the Wolf who'd gotten off of some kind of punishment during my first pack meeting who'd also stepped up to scout for the pack to get any extra info on the Serafim Group. It was looking like they weren't going to take my brother's refusal for an acceptable answer.

"I'm so sorry, baby." Sylvie kissed my brother's cheek, despite him dangling the cigarette out of the side of his mouth while he stared unseeingly at the lake before us. How would I comfort Río if we were in their place? While I wasn't *heartless*, I definitely wasn't sweet like Sylvie. Whether maternal instincts were inherited or reared, I didn't have a chance in hell.

Princess, I think I'm gonna have to keep you. He was so damn snarky, but I believed him. There was no lying with emotional scents, and even now, I felt my chest want to hum with the particular note that went along with his Jaguar's roar. There was a second there, when he held us both in that tree and worked on fucking me to oblivion, that I'd thought he was going to bite me. Like, really, *really* bite me.

I must've been losing it, because I wanted it. For the tie between Río and I to be complete.

"Mona." Orion's voice reverberated with *Leader*, and my body snatched to attention of its own accord. "I need to meet your... Jaguar."

"Why?"

He ashed his cigarette in the handmade ceramic tray on the patio table. "Because, you reek of him. I will not demand he become pack, but I also need to know him since he'll be sticking around."

I squinted, sensing that there was something he wasn't telling me, but if there was anyone that could escape the little trick I'd learned over the years, it was the one who'd taught me. Under the heavy scent of Leader, Orion mostly buzzed with stress that was like muggy air after a hot rainstorm. "He... I don't know whether he'll be staying here."

"Bullshit."

Hot anger flared within my chest, and I actually snarled. It was nowhere near as intimidating as a real shifter would have been able to do. The sound wasn't human, though. "You're not my Leader. You can't order me around."

My brother's green eyes flashed, glowing around the edges, and his growl forced my eyes to lower, my shoulders to hunch. *Goddammit*, I swallowed the whine that almost slipped out, too.

Distantly, I noticed Sylvie get up from her seat and swipe up the babies from the pool before retreating inside. Leaving me and my brother to have it out.

"You are not yet Antler Pointe Pack, but you are still *my* pack. You intend to mate him, fine. But I will speak with him, too."

I nearly choked. *"What the hell are you talking about*? I'm not…" But the words died on my tongue because it would be a fucking lie. My intense, half-shifter brain was fully on board with the idea of becoming his mate.

O stubbed out his spent cig but didn't pick a new one out of *my* stash. The last nicotine-filled exhale made him look like a dragon as the smoke flowed out of his nose. "Invite him for dinner. Beers. A two-minute conversation, whatever. He *will* be here, or I'll go to him myself."

With that, my brother stood and went back into the cabin, leaving me to simmer down on my own and try to figure out what the fuck to do.

Before I could really stop myself, I pulled out my phone and pressed call beneath Río's contact photo. It was a shot of him, tongue sticking out as he rolled past me on his board. I'd been scrolling through my playlist when he'd started rolling toward me, and I'd been lucky to immortalize his silliness in high definition.

The fireflies were out again, their yellow-green lights catching in the dying sunset. I hollowed my cheeks as I took the last draw from my own smoke and stubbed it out on the wood beneath me. Yeah, leave a burn mark for my asshole of a brother to deal with later.

I thought for a second that he wouldn't pick up, but Río

answered on the fourth ring, just before it went to voicemail. "Princess? What's up?"

My lips turned down as I exhaled the smoke, not in nearly as cool of a way as my brother had. Usually Río sounded happy whenever he talked to me, but he sounded preoccupied. Almost irritated.

"Is this a bad time?"

"What? No. What did you need, babe?"

The term of endearment helped me soften, but I still didn't like the way he sounded. It was so unlike him. Or maybe I still really didn't know him at all. I pinched the bridge of my nose. "Stupid fight with my brother. Are you too busy?"

"For you? Never."

I waited, but he didn't say anything else. "Uh… so can I come over?"

"Um—yeah. Yeah, absolutely. Whenever's fine."

"Are you sure?"

"One hundred percent. See ya in a few, sweet cheeks." And the call disconnected. For a while, I stared at my blank phone screen, chewing on my lip. He sounded weird, but I *had* asked if he was certain.

Cursing, I stood and went to dump the ashtray and cigarette butts. Unsure of where the ashtray lived when my brother wasn't relapsing, I set it back on the patio table before going to pack my overnight bag. Like hell was I staying here to be ordered around any more.

Even though my brother and I were quarreling at the moment, Sylvie offered up her car when I said I was going to Río's for the night. Orion had been giving the babies a bath, and I didn't give any of my typical protests when she assured me that I was more than fine to spend another night away.

I parked next to Río's truck, stomach flitting with anticipation.

That is, until I started up the steps that led to his apartment and took in the unmistakable female scent that led right up to his door.

Before I could parse through the different notes of it, Río flung open the door without me so much as knocking. His eyes seemed heavy, as if he'd suddenly become exhausted. His hair was in a messy nest atop his head.

"Hey, good lookin'. I missed you." Río tried for his hallmark grin, but it was tight until it faltered to a weak smirk.

I made no secret of my sniffing of the air. His neighbors' scents were faint, Río's chiles and clove was strongest. But there was another. Like his, but it slipped and shifted, trying to escape me, as if it was the ghost of what a scent would be. Not a shifter, not a human or vampire—not *anything* I'd smelled before.

"Who did you have over here?" I shoved past him into his house, following the trail that led to the living area but went no further. My bag fell off my arm and onto the wooden floor with a thud as I continued to sniff around the couch. It was just so *odd*.

He sighed, and it sounded of a weariness I hadn't heard from him before. Just when I was thinking I knew him, I was being hit with all of these uncertainties. "My sister surprised me."

My nose stayed scrunched. He had mentioned that he had two older sisters that he'd gone no-contact with. But, again, there were a lot of blanks and missing information when it came to Río and his family. "That's... nice?"

He snorted and ran a hand over his face. "You haven't met her. It was far from nice."

"Oh." I dropped onto the couch. Shit, I just barged in and hardly even acknowledged how exhausted and down he looked. "Should I go?"

Río lowered his brow, as if he was really trying to decide whether I should stay or not, and my heart started to crack. "Nah. We can order some dinner? Watch a movie?" He inhaled and tried to give me another smile, succeeding a little more than last time.

"Yeah. That's good. We can lay down and have a picnic in

bed?" That usually made me feel better, anyway. Maybe he'd like it, too?

"Tryna get in my pants, baby?" He chuckled, but I decided that I didn't like it.

I went over to him, trying my best to put my comforting hat on and raised on my toes while bracing my hands on his chest. He still smelled like me, and that was really all I needed. I kissed his cheek. "Or we could just eat and watch something where we don't have to think."

When I pulled back, Río looked pained, face pinched, but he didn't back away. He grabbed my hands and planted small, light kisses on my knuckles. "Yeah," his voice was thick, "thanks, Princess."

I kissed the tip of his nose like he always did me. "I—no problem. Thanks for letting me come over."

His smirk in return was easier, and we went back and forth about what we wanted to eat, eventually settling on sushi. Despite my disbelief that this town had any worth trying. Río pulled up the menu of a place two blocks over, but when I suggested we just walk over and pick it up, he said he wasn't really up for walking anywhere.

His resistance struck me as a little odd, but I didn't question it, and once the food was delivered, we set up our dumplings and trays of sushi while resuming the comedy sketch show that we were quickly making our way through. By now, we had favorite episodes that we alluded to with each other, and I'd now learned that, though he was quick to joke and laugh in real life, Río was a hard critic when it came to TV and movies. This show, though, he said, was one of the best he'd seen so far.

I left him in the loft while I dumped our empty trays and containers in his kitchen trash. While I walked barefoot over the old wooden floors, I turned over again and again the words that'd been on the tip of my tongue.

He'd done so well with my freakout last night, helping me

take more steps in my healing that I didn't even fully comprehend yet. I wanted to do the same for him when I didn't need my scenting to know something was wrong.

By the time I got back on the bed, Río was leaned against the headboard, and he wordlessly opened his arms while his attention was still on the screen. The mattress dipped as I answered his call and settled between his legs. Drawing strength from his steady arms around me, I took a deep breath and opened my mouth.

"Río."

"Huh?" He grunted and kissed the top of my head. He swept his fingertips on the fabric covering my inner arm, reminding me again of how much he'd already helped me. I wanted to do that for him, too.

Leaning up, I grasped the hem of my hoodie and pulled it over my head. My braid flopped against my chest, and I tossed the shed fabric over the side of the bed. Río's arms returned around my middle, claws absently fiddling with the edge of my bra but not attempting to take it off.

Another breath. "Do you wanna talk about it? Your sister." I was no good at this type of shit. This was the first… relationship I'd ever had, as an adult anyway. He was the first person I'd been this intimate with and the first of the people in my life to know what I'd done. His kind acceptance meant more than a lot to me. It was everything.

Río sighed. "There's not a lot I can say. She and my other sister had been influenced by our father long before I came to live with them. Before that, they'd only visit."

"Was it—" I hesitated but decided to press on "—bad?"

"Like abusive?" I hadn't wanted to use the word when he hadn't, but I nodded. Río's sharp, black claw played with the silver barbell through my bellybutton. "Yeah," he uttered quietly. "S'how I lost a good chunk of my eyesight. The other scars and bruises healed, so I made sure to tattoo over where each one had been. Was depressed all the time. Finally got the hell out right before I turned eighteen."

I stiffened, and the flood of tears was so sudden, I couldn't stop them from spilling down my face. Again, the art on his skin took on new meaning. This time, it was somber and almost too much for my heart to take. "I'm so sorry, baby." Río was so darkly bright, I couldn't imagine someone being that cruel to him. His own family, no less. If I weren't feeling so devastated for him, I'd want to crack his family's skulls.

"Don't cry, Princess." Río caressed the line of my jaw and moved my head so that I couldn't hide. His sharp fingertips prickled against my skin, and I leaned into the touch.

I let my tears flow and bit the inside of my cheek. "I hate that they hurt you."

He chuffed, and a small smirk, a ghost of his usual sardonic expression, shifted his lips. Río planted a gentle kiss on my mine. "Thank you, baby." He blinked a few times, worry creasing his forehead and moving in the air around us. I held his gaze while he figured out what to say, and I hoped like hell it wasn't something to push me away.

"They're the reason I move around so much."

My heart started to pound at the memory of him being up front with me that day at the skatepark. That he'd eventually be leaving. Did his sister appearing mean that we were already at the end? More tears fell down my face, trailing into my mouth with salty dread. "Are you... going away?" Goddammit, my lip was trembling, but I needed to know.

Río's Adam's apple bobbed, and he took my arm, turning the scar up towards him. He bent to kiss it, and I already knew I wasn't going to like what came next.

"So, there's this Wolf girl with mile-long legs who's kinda thrown a wrench in my plans to get the fuck out of dodge."

The pivot of conversation almost had me getting pissed before he could finish the rest of his sentence. His black eyes were tender as they looked down at me through his glasses lenses. The light from the lamp reflected against the glass, and I saw the barest hint of golden specs in the depths of his irises. "Oh."

"My family is complete shit and dangerous. It's selfish of me, but I really want to keep being with you, Ramona."

I gasped, and my heart racing in alarm turned to fluttering out of excitement. Hope. "I want to stay with you, Río."

His jaw tightened and so did his arms around me. Squeezing and maybe a little uncertain that I was speaking the truth. "And when I have to move again?"

Could I promise this now? My stay in Antler Pointe wasn't a vacation, but I also had the luxury to not worry about work or school while I was living in my brother's cabin. Not that I'd thought the rest would last forever, I also hadn't really thought through what I'd do afterwards. Other than the fact that there was no way I was going back to NYU or my parents'.

But with this Jaguar? Making a new future with him, spending our evenings just like this, taking rides on the back of his motorcycle? "I'd go with you."

Río's entire face went blank for a moment, and I worried that he was having a medical event or something, but then it turned thunderous. His body crowded around me, and he leaned down until we were nose-to-nose. His glasses slid down, almost bumping my face, but I couldn't even chuckle at the cuteness of it. "Don't fucking lie to me, Princess. That's a shitty thing to do." Four large fangs flashed at me as he spoke, outraged at what he perceived as an empty promise. I'd have to teach him how to read emotions, because if he could, he would know that I was telling the truth.

I pulled back my top lip, snarling right back at him with no heat. "I'm not lying. Take me with you."

He froze again, with the two of us baring our teeth at each other, until—until his face crumpled. His fangs didn't go away, but his eyes weren't flashing with anger anymore. He pulled me into a smashing kiss that I accepted with my whole heart. Soft, wispy hair of his tickled my face, and his claws pressed into my bare skin. But the only urgency was to settle into this. That the next time he had to run, he didn't have to be alone.

Río's chest vibrated with a purr, and my own hummed in kind.

CHAPTER TWENTY-THREE

RAMONA

Splinters of bark from the dead tree flew with each blow, but the tape on my hands protected my knuckles enough.

Alone in the forest, I used the sturdy trunk as a punching bag since my brother didn't have one, and I needed something sturdier.

I kept my phone on vibrate, so at least, the notifications of my mother's texts didn't interrupt the music blaring in my ears. I aimed another combo at the imaginary opponent, this time throwing it southpaw just because. The unfamiliar stance felt weird, but it focused my thoughts on that, instead of Mom's threats that'd started bright and early today.

MOMSTER

Ramona Marie Wells. When did you stop sharing your location? We already know that you dropped out. Where the fuck are you.

You ungrateful child, answer your damn phone.

Your father is worried sick. Unless you want him contacting the police to find you, answer. The damn. Phone.

Even with my headphones on, I could feel the vibrations of my phone beneath my bare feet. It sat on top of my shed hoodie, and another two texts from Mom left me throwing jabs in quick succession, fighting with what to do. If she knew that I was at O's, she'd blow up all of this. My peace with my brother's family and what was growing between Río and I.

When I finally pulled back from the tree, chest heaving and breaths ragged, I'd gouged a crater into the side of it and felt no better than I had when I came out here. The pastel blue above had deepened slightly with the passing hours, and I went back to my stuff. If I kept on, the dead maple would collapse all together.

Ignoring the screen full of messages from my mother—and none from my father—I went to my string of messages with Río. Instead of the text I expected, there was a voice message.

I set it to play while I rolled out my shoulders and started a quick round of stretches. "Hey, Princess. Just wanted to say that I missed ya. Work is bullshit right now, and I wanted to hear your voice. Don't make that face—you've got the prettiest little bit of raspiness that hits my ears just right. I know you got babysitting duty tonight, so I guess it'll just help me miss you more. Whadoyou wanna do tomorrow? I'm *thinkin'* you, me, some good takeout at the skate spot, then back to mine where you can smother me with that pretty little pussy. Just a thought. Anyway, see ya sweet cheeks."

The incredulous laugh that flew out of my mouth, along with the blush creeping up my neck and face, was a welcome distraction. And a relief that he seemed back to his normal self. Seeing my Jaguar haunted by the memories of his family and his sister's visit didn't even piss me off. It just made me so sad for him and embarrassingly emotional. At least with anger, I could do something.

I snatched up my hoodie, shook it out, and pulled it over my sweaty body. If I knew I'd be able to return to the cabin and make a beeline for the shower without anyone seeing me, I would've stayed in just the sports bra and shorts.

After thinking over my response to Río and walking back toward the cabin, I started my own audio message. "First, skating and food sounds good. Although, I'll be choosing what we eat, because that sushi was mediocre at best. Second, I don't know about my voice, but… I like yours too. Third, you're absolutely ridiculous, but if it'll get you to shut up for once, I'll sit on your face all night." That last part made more heat flame on my face, but I hit send before I decided to rerecord it. A night away from him wasn't great, but I had an afternoon in the witch house gardens with Sylvie and Delaney later, as well as the movie I was gonna watch with Dahlia and Ollie already decided on.

The sight of the cabin emerged as I walked out of the forest, knuckles still a little red as I unraveled the tape. My brother was sitting on the porch in one of the black rocking chairs, book in hand as he talked softly with Ollie who sat in his lap. They were reading a large board book, and when I got closer, they both looked up with small smiles of greeting.

My brother and I both nodded at each other as I passed into the house, and I waved at Sylvie as I walked into the kitchen for a glass of water. The record player was going, music louder than usual to account for the sink running. Dahlia sat in a chair from the dining room, boosted with books and cushions so that the back of her head could dangle over the sink. Sylvie was answering the random questions my niece fired off in her toddler curiosity as she rinsed out the shampoo from my niece's hair and began to detangle her curls with a wide tooth comb.

Dahlia gave me a happy little wave, neck craned back at an angle but padded with a towel to keep her away from the hard counter edge. I waved back and went off for my shower, almost forgetting why I'd even needed to run out into the forest in the first place.

I paced the living room, clutching my phone tightly as another string of texts came through. Luckily, the babies were in bed now, but not having the excuse to ignore this part of my life made me feel like I was suffocating. Orion and Sylvie would be gone until the early hours of the morning, if past pack runs were any indication. So, I was stuck.

Now, the babies had been read to and were sound asleep, so there was no more ignoring the slew of texts that were from someone I *definitely* didn't want to talk to. My phone went off again, though this time, the notification wasn't the simple bell of a text but the ringing of a call. I checked the screen and felt like I was going to throw up. A video call.

Frozen, I watched my father FaceTime me, but I couldn't bring myself to do anything—to accept or reject the call. *Shit, shit, shit,* and just to jam the knife in further, a text from Mom came through and hung like a banner announcing my execution.

MOMSTER

You answer your father. Now.

Cornered.

Really, I knew that I'd eventually have to face my parents. That, though I'd been transferring money from the accounts they managed to ones solely in my name since I was in high school, they'd eventually find out that I wasn't living business-as-usual in my apartment near campus. That they'd discover I'd withdrawn from school, packed my shit, and left.

What did it say about me that it took them months? This was probably the first time Dad had even inquired about me at all.

It was like smoothing fuzzy felt over my senses, over my mind, as I walked to the room I'd claimed as mine and opened my laptop. Sure enough, another incoming FaceTime from Dad rang on the screen, and this time, my finger moved woodenly to accept.

I wasn't surprised when I was met with my mother seated at

the kitchen island. Her white-blonde hair was tied back in a pony-tail, which made her icy blue eyes pull even sharper. For some reason, mine focused in on the shiny white cabinets and counter-tops behind her. The green tile backsplash only adding to the coldness. Even across miles and two screens, I could tell that the house was silent, as it always was. No constant crooning from a record player, no warm brown from wooden walls. Any home-made meals were made by whichever chef Mom had hired. I thought the current one was Yusef, but I could've been wrong.

"Well, I see you're hiding out with your brother."

The disappointment and venom were almost sharp enough to open up the scars on my arm. But the fuzziness was my buffer, tried and true, for as long as I could remember. That day before I left for Antler Pointe, it'd worn down, but maybe it was still enough. To at least last through this. I missed Río.

"I wanted to visit."

Mom narrowed her eyes, and her lips pinched. "You decided to drop out, leave your apartment—which we're still paying for, by the way—and essentially go missing to go *visit* your brother? How ungrateful and stupid can you be, Ramona?" Her words got hissy at the end, her voice low and cheeks flushing with an angry pink.

When my father entered the room and sat beside her, it was like a strip of my barrier fell away. I shifted in my seat on the floor beside the guest bed, balancing the laptop on my knees. "Ra Ra, what's going on?" I bit the inside of my cheek, hard enough to taste blood. Dad was dressed in his typical casual attire, today's being a black Nike sweatshirt and joggers. All my life, it seemed, I saw him in some variation of this or the suits he wore while commentating on television. There was practically no in-between.

But Casual Dad was the one who took me to the skating rink and for ice cream that first time. Now, he looked at me with mild concern bunching his black brows. His expertly cut low fade was a black shadow against his deep brown skin. I could practically smell the cologne he always wore.

"Hey, Dad. I'm at O and Sylvie's. Helping with the kids."

He looked even more confused. "Did they ask you to do that?" My brother and father had never really had much of a relationship. There wasn't animosity, just a distant respect. After he'd gotten married to Sylvie and they had the kids, the dynamic hadn't shifted at all.

"No," I swallowed, "I asked if I could visit." Dad looked toward Mom, whose face had melted into one of demure concern. She placed a gentle hand on his shoulder and waited for him to speak again.

Dad's frown deepened. "You really had us worried, kiddo. We had to pull some strings to find out what was going on—why haven't you been answering your phone?"

Because I was a glutton for punishment, I allowed the fuzziness to shift and blurted, "You called me?"

He looked perplexed for a moment. For that brief time, I imagined it was because he was wondering how he'd gone so long without checking in on me. But when he turned his eyes to my mom beside him, I knew that the thought hadn't even occurred to him. She cut in, voice ten times softer as she glanced at my dad. "It's all right, honey. I was just scared and didn't know what to do. Your father saved the day and was able to pull some strings with the school to find out you'd withdrawn."

Dad nodded and turned my own eyes back at me. "Why in the world would you do that? All that work just down the toilet, and for what? I know we spoil you, Ra Ra, but this is unacceptable."

I fought to keep my face blank, and when my mom spoke up, it was the voice of the good submissive wife. She sighed. "Don't get worked up, Sean. Do you want a drink or something to eat?"

Dad grunted in answer and watched Mom get up and start moving about the kitchen. He relaxed back in his seat and rested an arm on the marble island surface. "You got anything to say for yourself?"

I was losing the battle. He was treating me like I'd had a tantrum and ran up his credit cards. Hot tears collected just at the edges of my lashes, and I batted them away with the heel of my hand before they could fall.

"Well? When are you gonna stop this foolishness?"

"Whenever I feel like it," I spat back with anger that was taking over my frustration.

That, at least, my father picked up on. I was wearing Río's sweatshirt, and the sleeves were more than long enough to cover my scars. Even before, when they were shorter nicks to just release the tension in my mind, he'd never noticed. At least, at the time, I chalked it up to my fast healing erasing all of the evidence by the next day.

But this time I'd fucking tried to kill myself. In the moment, I'd barely even thought about my parents, just the relief I was feeling at the fact that everything was nearly over.

Now, though, I felt that suffocating block climbing up my chest and into my throat. My chest was so tight I could hardly breathe.

Dad's eyes widened then narrowed. "I don't know who you think you're talking to, but I'm not one of your little friends. Lord knows I thought you'd grow out of this shit by now." My fingers were itching, the back of my mind already trying to plan how to get to the nearest sharp object. Just to take the edge off a little.

Mom popped up on the screen, putting a sandwich and a can of coke in front of my father. Some of her harshness seeped through as she spoke. "You apologize to your father, right now."

Instead of a response, I gave a dry laugh. At this point, I didn't think even showing them my scars would have them believing that what I was experiencing was real. What did I have to be depressed about, anyway? I'd never wanted for anything. All that I needed was provided for me, and even with their anger, my parents never threatened to cut me off.

"You need to get your shit together. There is no damn reason for you to be acting like this. Are you even thinking about your future? How much work we've put into helping you succeed in this world? I didn't work my ass off for you to think you can just lay up spending my money forever." It wasn't worth it to reveal to them that I'd had a part-time job on campus since the third week of freshman year. That I'd juggled working in the campus library and my classes, all while feeling like I was walking through a sludgy dream.

Just as the plan solidified, to go into the kitchen and bring back one of the kitchen knives to my room, my eyes landed on Ollie's toy chest that rested in the corner. It was still open from when I'd been in the middle of straightening up the house after bedtime and been interrupted by the slew of texts from my mom.

A wet sob choked up my throat. I'd been about to hurt myself in Ollie's room. With one of my brother's knives that he used to make meals for us, something that made him feel at peace.

Dad's expression loosened, but his voice still had a harsh edge. "We'll give you some time to think about your actions. At least we know you're safe at Orion's. But best believe that if you don't come to your senses, we're dragging your ass back here."

Mom sat back down next to him, and when their eyes met, she nodded and leaned into him. "You know what's best, Sean. And I agree. We'll keep checking in."

Dad gave a final nod, and they may have said more, but it was all muffled, distant. I snapped my laptop closed, and as I climbed under the covers enclosed in a circle of more blankets, I held my face into one of the pillows while I tried to cry as quietly as possible. My body shook with rage and despair and longing for my Jaguar, and that's how I fell asleep. Tear-soaked pillow sticking to my cheeks while I fought to still keep one ear open to make sure the babies were sleeping soundly.

CHAPTER TWENTY-FOUR

RÍO

Four days. Just over half a week, and I was too close to ripping someone's face to shreds. I pulled my phone from my pocket, simultaneously checking the time and to see if I had any messages. There were two texts from Tyler, asking if I'd be cool changing the time of our next rehearsal, and it'd only been ten minutes since I'd last looked at my phone.

I pulled up the conversation between Ramona and I, and though she'd responded to everything I'd sent, she was off. Four days since we'd last seen each other. Since I'd gotten to hold her in my arms and feel her body writhe with mine. Or see the way she would grumble and huff before I coaxed a small grin out of her.

I'd opened Vinny's again today, and I luckily didn't have to close. But there was still another hour before my shift was done, and my skin was crawling with the need to go to my mate. I scrolled through our last conversation, and instead of the short, bantering words, they were perfunctory, one-word responses.

Was she free?

LIMÓN 7

No.

Did she want to skate?

LIMÓN 7

No, sorry.

Was she okay?

LIMÓN 7

Yeah.

"Shit," I muttered as I finished typing out next week's shift schedule in the tiny office near the kitchen. I also had a fucking migraine. It was Mara—finding me and trying to wedge her way back in my life. To *catch up*, she kept saying, but I didn't believe a word she said. Or her promises not to report back to our sister or father about where I was. I had a splitting headache trying to decide what to do.

Something was wrong with Ramona, but she made me swear not to say anything about the scars on her arms, about what she'd tried to do. And, yeah, at the time, my desire to care for her eclipsed all else. It made me agree to her demands while we lay together in Tyler's guest room. And, like I'd said that night—who would I even tell?

Did her family not even know? Or care?

I threw my phone on the cluttered desk and hit print with enough force to make the desktop mouse creak in protest. The two college students working today laughed loudly at some stupid shit they'd been talking about, and the sound of it made red flash at the edges of my vision. This was all so fucking stupid. I knew what it was like to be pulled down into the depths of my mind. Even Mara's small, crazy hand that petted me when the coast was clear wasn't enough sometimes.

I snatched the paper schedule from the printer and stomped out of the office. I ripped off last week's and stabbed the new schedule to the cork board. We had a virtual calendar, too, but it was some weird tradition to keep a paper one up for people to look at and start shit when it was slow.

The rest of my shift dragged on in a way that was dangerous for everyone around me. The kids working caught on real fast that now was not the time to whine or even try to pull me into their goofing off. I did an inventory of the walk-in, cleaned the bathrooms, and swept the dining area. Anything to keep my hands busy, and that was even precarious.

When the time finally ticked to six, I tossed my apron in the bin marked for laundry and high-tailed it the fuck out of there. With my work t-shirt on and the smell of pizza still clinging, I climbed onto my bike. I shoved my helmet on, jostling my glasses that I'd fucking forgot I had on in the first place.

"Fuck," I cursed but kept going. There was no way I was going in the opposite direction of checking on Ramona to change and put in my contacts.

She'd never invited me into her brother's place, but I still remembered the way. The sun blazed down on me, warming my already overheating skin and threatening to get in my eyes. But I pushed on, weaving in and out of traffic and gunning it down the quiet road that led out to the Pack Leader's land.

Even the smell of it raised the hairs on the back of my neck. Technically, all of the forest was their territory, but as I drove through the trees and sent gravel flying, I sensed the claim of the land. What did it feel like for my princess, being around those that quite literally belonged here, while she didn't?

I pulled up next to two sensible SUV's that screamed 'we have kids' and killed the engine. My glasses got tangled in my hair and helmet while I fought it off.

From where I was, I could hear voices inside, and a quick stretch of my senses catalogued the two adults, two pups, and the female that was mine.

Did I know what the fuck I was doing? No. What would happen when the time came to get my head out of my ass and move us to the next town? No fucking clue. But I knew for certain that Ramona was mine. The unmistakable bond rooted in my chest was evidence enough.

I flew up the front steps. The door was unlocked, but I didn't get but a foot and half into the cabin before a hand grabbed the front of my shirt. Claws cut through the fabric and stabbed my skin while the thick scent of Wolf Leader was its own punch to the face.

Ramona's brother was just an inch away, fangs drawn and half-shifted face twisted in fury. "What the fuck do you think you're doing?" he roared.

My own claws extended, and I took hold of the front of his sweatshirt. He was taller than me by an inch or two, but I wasn't afraid. If anything, he should've been.

While his deepened voice was filled with hot anger, mine was ice-cold. I pulled him closer. "Get out of my way."

To his credit, the Leader didn't back down. The air around us continued to churn, two shifter males protective of what was theirs. If I were in my right mind, I'd agree that a random shifter barging into my house where my mate and children were would've been met with the same treatment. Well, actually, no, they'd already be lying on their stomach with blood pooling beneath them.

But even with my instincts taking the front seat, I knew that Ramona would never forgive me if I killed her brother or hurt him in any way. Fuck, would it make this easier, though.

"*Río*? What the fuck!" A set of hands forced their way between us and pushed. The cold that'd been filling my veins began retreating with her touch and scent filling me up instead. Honey eyes that blazed like the sun above met mine at the same time she smacked a heavy slap on my chest.

I immediately let go of the Wolf and pulled Ramona to me, plastering her body to mine so that I could feel the pressure of her and that she could feel mine.

"What's wrong, Princess?" I didn't have time to be embarrassed by the crack in my voice as I ran my face against hers. Her body had been stiff when I'd circled my arms around her, but she couldn't resist me for long. I cradled her head, and purred when she leaned into my palms.

Her lips were still pinched, probably with irritation at me, but I caught sight of the dark circles beneath her eyes and the frizzy halo of hair that swayed with my breaths. An aroma of staleness surrounded her, like she'd been sitting in the same place for a long time without doing much. I couldn't fucking take it.

I licked from the height of her cheekbone to the top of her hairline, and the sound of my rough tongue scraping her skin made my purr intensify. Dark, fuzzy despair clung to her, but underneath was the sweet and sour.

She placed her hands on my chest and gently pushed, despite her craning her neck as she continued to accept my grooming. One more swipe of my tongue, and I pulled back, but only enough so that she could look at me. Like hell was I going to let her go.

A V-shaped wrinkle formed between her brows as she took me in. "There's nothing wrong."

My arms tightened around her. "I told you that I don't do that fake shit. Don't fucking lie to me," I begged.

A set of growling sounded from behind her, but I wasn't tearing my eyes away from my mate. And the shift in her expression, like a crack that exposed the slivers of exhaustion and sadness beneath.

She did her best to wipe it away, to erase all emotion from her face, but the vacancy was even more telling. Anger surged back through me like a tornado that'd dropped down, and I set my sights on her brother behind me. "You've been here with her all this time and let her go on like this?"

The Wolf was still half-shifted with claws and fangs at the ready, but instead of continuing to go after me, he was staring down at Ramona with a look of frustrated confusion. And that just pissed me off even more. "Huh? I know dogs are stupid, but I expected more from her fucking family."

That got him going, and when he met my challenging stare over Ramona's head, I was itching for it. Warring growls erupted from both of us, but before I could drop my hold on Ramona to shift, she shot a hand out to block her brother as he tried to advance. Her bare forearm connected with his chest, and he reached up to pull it away.

When he did, though, his head snapped down to look where his fingers circled around her skin. I saw the moment Ramona realized what was happening, and pure panic flared in her eyes. She must've heard her brother and me fighting and rushed out here, completely forgetting to throw on something to cover her arms.

With my hold still on her, I felt Ramona try to pull her arm away from her brother, heard her panting breaths as she struggled while he didn't let go.

And then he surprised the hell out of me. I'd been prepared to throw her on the back of my bike to avoid any retaliation or beat him in front of his mate and children if he tried to cut her down for it. But the Wolf Leader ran his eyes over the puckered skin that showed where she'd been. That she'd once marched right up to death, begging to be taken away, and instead had been returned against her will.

Her brother lowered his head, despite the warning growls I gave and the choked protests from Ramona, and sniffed along the length of her scar.

The Leader gave a tortured whine as he cradled Ramona's arm with both hands, claws now gone, and when he finally looked back up at her, his eyes were shimmery with tears.

"Mona?" It was barely above a whisper, but I could hear the sadness and regret in it. The worry. And by her shaking, Ramona could too.

Instead of answering him, she shoved me away with more strength than I'd thought she had, and this time, when she pulled at her arm in her brother's grasp, he relented. Ramona ran back into the house, moving past the witch that stood in the doorway who must've been watching the whole exchange, baby Wolf in her arms with wide, curious eyes.

Ramona's brother and I watched her go. Her footsteps thundered as she ran further away from us, and we both flinched when the slamming of a door seemed to make the whole house tremble.

The witch went to her mate, reaching out with her free hand, and caressed the side of his face. His eyes were still stuck on the direction Ramona had headed, but his shoulders visibly relaxed as he accepted his mate's comforting. "It'll be okay, baby. I'll go talk to her."

"Nah, I'm checking on her. You both obviously haven't cared enough," I spat and started inside.

A flash and sting on my cheek threw my head to the side and actually made me stumble. I caught myself before I fully crashed into the wooden rocking chair behind me, but it was fucking close. My glasses nearly went flying, and I righted them while collecting myself. I hated how vulnerable the action made me feel.

Another slap stung my skin so badly that I felt like I'd been flayed. "How fucking dare you."

I managed to glare down at the witch, and I blamed my own surprise at the surge of power I could almost see around her when a fucking freight train in the form of a right hook made my head spin and my body drop.

My glasses were on the floor somewhere, but I didn't need them to make out the Wolf, witch, and pup looming over me. The Leader's fists were at his sides, ready to go again.

"I'm going to talk to her, and if you say any more slick shit, I'll make you beg for my mate to rip out your throat." Even with the baby on her hip, the intensity of the dense, electric power around her made my retort shrivel and die on my tongue. I'd been around scary people nearly all my life, not to mention murderous females who I had watched do some sick stuff.

The look in her eyes was one I'd seen from my sisters enough times. I didn't say a word while she marched inside.

The air on the porch began to thin, giving room for breath and rational thought. I managed to gather myself as smoothly as possible to my feet. I couldn't help but grumble, cleaning my glasses on my shirt to give my hands something to do. My legs kept itching with the need to see to Ramona while my skin was still stinging from the witch's slap and the Leader's blow. "How the fuck are you not afraid of her? She could muzzle you in your sleep, easy. Or worse."

I put my glasses back on, and the Pack Leader's face became less fuzzy. Instead of protective rage, he'd settled on irritated and blank. He did answer me, though. "I don't cross her."

"Ha. I guess that's one way to stay on a witch's good side."

The Leader grunted, eyes roving over me and nostrils flaring. I knew when I was being sized up. Normally, I'd let the silence lie and fill the space to create a sense of discomfort I could use to my advantage. Though I'd had a tough time learning how to do it when I was younger, the tactic got beat into me like everything else.

Now, though, I needed something other than the sound of our breaths and the music playing inside to drown out the voices of Ramona speaking with her sister-in-law. "Look. I'm just here to check on her. I could tell something was wrong."

He crossed his arms. "I should kill you for trespassing."

"Well, I'd prefer it if you didn't. So would your sister."

"Are you sure about that?"

Don't be a smartass, don't be a smartass, don't be a smartass. "Yeah, one-hundred percent sure. And," I sighed, opening my pride up for the ego hit, "I'm sorry for barging in." In my head, I told the Wolf to count himself lucky because apologies from me were few and far between. Even I could see, though, that retracting my claws would get me to my goal faster than keeping them out and swiping.

Though, if this went south, I wasn't opposed to it.

The Leader grunted again, and it sounded so much like Ramona, my heart skipped a beat. His eerie green eyes were nothing like the gooey warmth of hers, but the warning was said with just that amount of dry venom I'd learned to expect from her. How was it that I was already missing her when she was just a few rooms away? "Don't let it happen again. The only reason you're still breathing is because of my sister's apparent bond to you."

The voices speaking in hushed tones inside tried to pull my attention, but I forced myself to stay here. To give Ramona a moment before I pulled her back to me. "You didn't know… about her depression, then."

The downward tilt of the corners of his lips was the only shift in his expression. "Not that it'd gotten that bad. No confirmation until now." His words were spoken with a halted rhythm, as if it was painful for him to admit.

I opened my mouth to volley something back, probably something to get me punched again, but a little head peeked around the doorway and gazed up at us both with unafraid curiosity. While I'd never seen the other pup before, I was familiar enough with Ramona's niece, and she gave me a happy wave before going over to her father.

He scooped her up into his arms and gave her a kiss on the top of her head. Dahlia twisted to reach out an expectant fist, and I jumped up to meet it. She'd done a good job of memorizing the silly handshake I'd taught her at the skate spot, giving the final dap with a delighted giggle.

"Nice one, pipsqueak." I chuckled.

The Leader's transparent brow quirked, and when the two of them looked at me, it felt like being held under two sets of laser beams. Dahlia at least looked excited to see me, even if she must've heard me brawling with her father. "Daddy, look," she pointed at my neck, "he's got a drawing of my flower." Her speech was high pitched, the words running together, but I was able to follow what she was saying without strain.

Ramona's brother gave the tattoos on my neck and arms a cursory glance. "I see that, darlin'."

"Are you done fighting?"

I couldn't tell whether it was innocent naiveté that left her unshaken by what'd occurred between me and her parents not five minutes earlier, or if she'd already grown accustomed to shifters and witches going at it.

Instead of responding, I looked to the Leader to answer her question. It took him a moment, a few of them, actually, but he drew some sort of conclusion and gave a soft nod to his daughter and then a tighter one to me. "Wait out here. If she wants to talk to you, she will."

The door closed behind them with a decided click. The lack of a lock turning felt like extra salt in the wound that was still throbbing on my face, and I stood for a few moments before I slumped into the rocker behind me. My Jaguar wanted to rip the fucking door off its hinges and cut down everyone that kept me from my mate, but I breathed through the urge.

There was no way I was leaving without speaking to Ramona, even if I felt nauseous for essentially showing my belly to people I didn't give a shit about.

CHAPTER TWENTY-FIVE

RAMONA

I was so mad, so past the point of screaming that heavy teardrops fell down my cheeks, testament to my shortcomings. For succumbing to the depression or not finishing the job, I couldn't tell.

"Ramona, please look at me," Sylvie's voice was gentle, like a healing embrace, but I didn't want it. Didn't deserve it. They already had so much going on, and it wasn't like them knowing would change anything. I was still alive, and as upset as I was... I couldn't do it.

I dragged my eyes upward, meeting Sylvie's dark ones, the color of the soil I'd grown so used to working, and knew that I wanted to live. That this hurt so much because there was no way out but through. Not anymore.

Her arms dragged me into her chest, holding steady against my resistance until I went limp, sobbing. Snot running, throat-cracking sobs that made my ribs hurt.

And, as if she knew what I needed, she refrained from using her powers to calm me. It would've completely stopped my outburst. But instead, she let me stay raw and bleeding until there was nothing left coming out of my eyes. My body shivered and shook, but there was no other noise left to give.

She pulled back first, and I accepted her light touch on my face, smoothing my tears before trailing down to my arms. I was just so tired, I couldn't even muster a flinch when she trailed her thumbs up and down the puckered skin. They were tipped in razor-sharp, cherry red nails, but so, so gentle that they coaxed a sigh out of me.

When I drummed up the courage to meet her stare again, I found it already on my face. And her smile was cooling and warm and bright all at the same time. My lower lip wobbled, but my eyes remained dry.

"I'm so glad you're here, Ramona." Sylvie's voice was quenching sunshine, and I pulled my legs closer into myself, feeling her words soaking in. "And I'm so happy to call you my sister."

I gasped. She'd never said these sorts of things to me, but I'd never been receptive to them, had I? Through the fuzzy overlay I kept on my mind or the forcefield that was prepared to darken and shoot back tenfold anything sent my way, her assurances never would have felt like this. Like they were almost… true.

"I-I'm… sorry," I croaked. My voice was already raw from my crying, though. How long she held me in her arms, I had no idea. But what I said was the truth. I was sorry for so many things— bringing more stress to her and my brother, disrupting their calm routine, being prepared to leave them forever.

Most of all, that.

Sylvie kept caressing my scars, like they were unblemished and presentable. She didn't say it was okay, but she shook her head. "I know that speaking like this is difficult. So I'll keep it brief. You are so, so loved, Ramona. Especially by me, the babies, and your brother." Her features twisted up. "And by that Jaguar of yours."

I surprised myself, letting loose a desperate chuckle. "Yeah. Maybe."

She dragged a light touch down the very center of both of my scars, unafraid of what they meant. "Oh, I don't know. Your brother and I knew from the very beginning. But regardless," she added pressure, gently emphasizing, "you are at home here. You belong here. And whether you stay living with us or not, you are one of us. Always. I hope you know that."

My brow crinkled, trying so hard not to immediately write off what she was saying to me. Did I feel like I belonged? The cabin at once felt like my home and not. The room I stayed in would eventually go back to being Ollie's, where he would grow up instead of being sequestered into his little play pen in the corner while Sylvie comforted me. He played there, now, entertaining himself and happy to have his mother within sight.

But the gardens, the kitchen here where I helped my brother, even his work shed, all felt like a piece of me. And when I spent time with each of them, Sylvie as we talked and joked, my brother as we worked in connected silence, and my niece and nephew as we played, there was no need to hide.

I nodded, slowly. "I… know that. Now."

Sylvie slid her hands down to mine, lacing our fingers together and squeezing. I squeezed back. "Good. And…" she hedged, but I kept still, kept squeezing. "If you'd like to talk about this, you have me, and I know that—" I felt the tremble in her touch until she steeled herself "—that your brother has some experience in feeling the way you have. And if you want someone impartial, we'll help you find them, too."

I sucked my lip into my mouth, pulling at it with my teeth. O had been stressed lately, and reasonably so, but I'd no idea that… that he'd been as depressed as Sylvie was alluding to. "Guess it runs in the family," I tried at humor, but it was hollow.

She took it in stride anyway. A little tinkling laugh that also held a related twinge of sadness. "Maybe so. He had to figure out how to lean on us, too. Me. Chris. Juno, even with them and Josie still away helping their family. *You.*"

"Me?"

"Yes. He's always loved you, Ramona. And he loves having you here. Despite enjoying his solitude, Orion has always craved family. To have you here means it's complete." When I stared dumbly at her, struck stupid by her words, her laugh was lighter now, almost teasing. "Have you not realized? You two have your own language where you don't even need to speak. It's kinda creepy to watch, actually."

I glared. "Says the one who wanders barefoot in the forest at night."

Sylvie grinned, flashing her teeth and crinkling her eyes. "All the better to make my blood sacrifices."

"… You don't actually do that, right?" When she gave a nonchalant shrug, I let my question fly, "Can I see?"

She threw her head back, laughing in a musical lilt, and I found myself snickering, too. Yeah, totally joking. It was doing a good job in making me feel a little steadier.

Sylvie leaned forward, and I sat still as she pressed a kiss to my forehead. She still wasn't giving me calm through her magic, just her words and presence, and her scent was filled with the sweet, pure love that smelled like warm pastries and so often coursed between Dahlia and Ollie.

Because… because I was her sister.

"Now, what do you need?" What *did* I need? Was it different from what I wanted? "Because I can hear your brother pacing while he tries to keep Dahlia occupied. And your Jaguar's still sitting on the porch. Just say the word, and I'll get rid of everyone. I'll even make myself scarce."

I sniffed. Fuck, I'd not been thinking about Río and the mess he'd caused with O. Or how the onslaught of worry coming from my brother had made me want to crumple. "Uh… I'll apologize to O before I handle Río. I'm sorry again that he went off." Yeah, when I gathered myself a bit more, I was going to let him fucking have it.

And if that didn't fill my stomach with excited little bubbles.

"All right, honey." Sylvie stood and helped me up. "I'll keep the babies occupied so you and Orion can talk a sec. Let me know if you need me to intervene with your Jaguar, too. Though, his skin's still probably stinging, so maybe he'll show some respect."

I groaned. "Oh, god, Sylvie what did you do?"

She shrugged as she went to Ollie and picked him up. He stayed clinging onto a teething toy, fighting through the discomfort of a few new teeth that had been cutting through his gums as of late. "Taught him not to even think about insulting *my* mate." She opened the door and called over her shoulder, "Make sure he knows that next time he tries, he won't be walking away from it."

And then she was gone, meeting Dahlia's questions with more assurances, this time telling her that I was fine and that I just needed to talk to the grown-ups. No, she couldn't go skating with me and Río right now.

The shiver at her ominous threat had just reached my toes when my brother's broad shoulders filled the doorway. Purplish bags hung heavy below his eyes, which weren't meeting mine but stayed on my arms that I was just managing to not hide behind my back. Sylvie said that he would understand.

We stood in silence, in letting our creepy way of communicating, as Sylvie so lovingly put it, flow. I shifted my forearms, took a deep breath, and presented them to him. Let him see.

Even when a tear, and then another, trailed into his beard, wetting the white hair, he didn't look away. He nodded, his fingers on both hands flicked and twitched, and my body somehow tapped into my reserves and let a pair of silent tears run down the sides of my face, too.

I'm sorry. I won't hide from you anymore.

I'm so sorry, I love you.

We met in the middle, me and my brother, and his arms crushed me to him. His heart was beating frantically, and I wrapped my scarred arms around his waist. We trembled and breathed and swayed, and his hard kisses into my hair helped me stand more firmly. His heavy pats on my back made me feel stronger.

And when we pulled away at the same time, O held my shoulders, and managed to meet my eyes. I nodded, lips shaking again but back straight. The pastry scent was taking over the room, now, never having fully dispersed from my conversation with Sylvie, and I again fought to accept it. To let it flow over the walls I'd constructed around myself and cast me in the sweet glow.

You belong here. You are strong.

Thank you.

O pursed his lips, but when he opened his mouth a moment later, it was a scratchy and reverberating whisper. "I—I love you, Mona. Anything I can do for you. There's no hesitation."

"Even if it's to talk? About feelings?" My lips twitched in half-jest, but my stomach flipped with real nerves for what his answer would be.

He didn't waver. Orion gave a steady, sure nod. "Even to talk about feelings. I'm getting better at it, and I would do anything for you."

And when an aftershock in the form of a hitching sob wracked my chest, Orion just pulled me into him again, where it was warm and safe, and I whined pitifully. Like a puppy that was finally being soothed.

"I didn't even kill your mate." O said dryly, and my whining cries turned to laughs once more.

"He's not."

Orion grunted, and I felt the vibration of it against my cheek. "I may miss some things, but I'm not stupid, Mona. I can tell that he makes you happy." I sighed, resigning myself to just accept his assertion. Not to mention that it made the non-human part of me grumble in delight. "I'd say be careful, but I know you can take him."

That got me giving big, rolling laughs. Especially because he sounded one-hundred percent serious. "Not sure if I'm much of a match for shifter strength, big bro. But he wouldn't hurt me."

He grunted again and slowly dropped his arms. "You're as

strong as any of us. And I've been to a few of your old matches. You can knock him out as easily as I could."

I shook my head, still snickering at the visual of me doing just that.

Orion and I left the guest room to find Sylvie on the floor, reading with Ollie and Dahlia. O nodded at me while I went toward the front door, but I paused when Dahlia darted toward me. She crashed into my leg, giving me a tight hug and a few pats before running back to her parents and brother. The gesture was so fast, I barely had time to pet the top of her frizzy little head, but it was enough to give me the strength to face Río.

The heat instantly wrapped around me as I stepped outside, but for once, I didn't feel like I was burning up. Instead, the wind that shook the leaves and branches of the forest swept against my arms that were many shades paler than my legs and face. It felt... nice.

Wood creaked, and I turned to Río who was now standing.

One side of his face was both red and purpling with a bruise, and my mind pulled in two very separate directions. On top, most evident of all, was the desire for his sort of comfort that was a deep, life-giving red. Under that, was irritation at him showing up here and starting a fight with my family.

He wasn't tender like Sylvie or stoic like Orion. Río's hair was wild and so were his black eyes, hidden behind his glasses. And he didn't wait, just grasped my face and slammed his lips to mine.

As fiercely as he held me, the kiss was gentle in comparison, and when his tongue requested entrance, I opened for him without hesitation. Río's chest rumbled as he claimed my mouth, and... and mine did too as I let him have me.

And then he abruptly broke our contact to snatch my arm up and drag his rough tongue along my scar. It tickled, but not in a way that made me want to giggle. In a way that made my core flip. He looked up at me from under his thick, black lashes and did it again. And again when I whimpered and held his hand more tightly onto me.

Río kissed my arm over and over, leaving no inch of my damaged skin untouched, and he did the same to my other arm. "Tell me what to do for you, Princess. Anything." The promise was so different from the one my brother gave. In that moment, I knew that they'd both kill for me. But the way Río was looking at me was like… was like he was saying he'd die for me, too. That he'd tear the world apart for me.

"I'm still pissed at you."

He groaned and passed his tongue over my arm again. "I'm sorry, Princess. For making a scene here." He looked up again, black eyes wide. I watched his throat bob with his swallow, saw the regret painted on his face.

"Did you apologize?" O hadn't said whether they'd spoken at all while Sylvie was comforting me, but I'd be damned if they continued on the wrong foot. Lord knew that my mother wasn't going to approve of any of this, and by extension, my father. Orion and Sylvie were the family that'd taken me in. Seeing me like Río saw me. I *needed* for them all to get along.

He gazed down at me, worriedly, arms still holding me close. "Yes. But I'll do it again. Over and over if you need. Are we good?"

It was almost funny. Seeing him like this, all uncertain when it was usually me who felt that way. More than that, it was refreshing. I scratched my blunt nails on his chest. "We're good."

"Thank fuck." He kissed me again and licked the side of my face, from jaw to hairline. "I missed you, baby. Please don't disappear on me like that again," he mumbled and into my hair, holding and swaying us. His glasses were certainly getting smudged with the oil I'd halfheartedly put in my hair this morning, but I didn't have the heart to tell him to stop.

The days since my FaceTime with my parents had blended together in a string of isolated haze. I barricaded myself in the room, eating in bed amongst the mounds of blankets and extra pillows I'd found, but even that didn't provide the comfort it usually did. Number Two had been specifically dedicated to the ritual, but it'd done little for me while I responded to Río with the bare minimum and tried to ignore the worried looks from my brother and sister-in-law. I just couldn't handle them seeing me like this.

But maybe there was another way. They'd now seen the full extent of everything, but instead of dismissing or raging, they met me with compassion. Just how my Jaguar did, the first one who'd known. He didn't deserve for me to treat him as I had.

"I'm sorry. I... my parents called me, and it just—" I took a deep breath to calm a sobbing aftershock after it wracked my chest. "It really set me back."

Río kept rubbing my back and arms, skin passing over my scars just like the rest of me. "I gotcha, Princess. How can I help?"

I separated our heads just enough to see his face. To ponder the question of what I needed from him and find the courage in the expanse of his stare. The scent of love pouring off of him was better than any soft blanket could be. I glanced to my left, where his sleek, black motorcycle was parked crookedly beside Sylvie's car.

"Can we go for a ride? And... and maybe go back to your place?"

Río's grin wasn't teasing or cocky. Just relieved and tender, and I gave him a small one in answer. "You know, Ramona, I love it when you bite at me, but I think I love your smile even more."

I scowled, and he chuckled, deep and pleased. "Shut up." I tried and lost the fight to keep my smile from retuning.

He grabbed my hand and walked us down the front steps. He picked up his helmet and started situating it on my head. "Feel okay?" I nodded, and we climbed on the back of his bike. Just like the night I learned his name, Río pulled a hair elastic off his wrist and tied his hair back for the ride. The nape of his neck was shaved, and with a familiarity I felt with no one else, I clamped my left arm around his waist and ran a finger over the prickly hair beneath his bun. Río started the bike, sending pleasant grumbles and vibrations against my thighs, and plucked my hand off his neck. He kissed my palm before settling it atop my other hand.

And then we were off.

The sun had a few hours left to give, burning with summer heat, but on Río's bike while he rode through the trees and onto the main road that led to town, it only made the wind feel cooler. The two enhanced one another as they whipped past us, and I relished the hot licks of sunshine and soft sighs of breeze on my bare arms. I didn't dare move them from their place around my Jaguar, where I could feel his lungs filling in excited gulps and his heart beat steadily.

I'd never given motorcycles much thought, and my joy might not extend as far as wanting to take the handlebars myself, but riding with Río made me feel free. Like walking with him in the forest when he showed me his other self.

And just like that night, time passed without a care, and when we pulled up to Río's apartment, the sky had gone from blue to a pretty, light pink. The wispy clouds had taken on a orangish tint, and I watched the skulls on the back of Río's hands as he parked beside his truck and pressed the ignition button to turn off the bike. He extended the kickstand and guided me to my feet.

With his help, the helmet came off next, leaving sweaty little curls clinging to my brow. Río kissed them. "All right, baby, whatcha wanna eat?" He tickled my stomach, as if emphasizing its empty state, and I swatted at his hands.

His laugh rang throughout the stairwell, and he was still chuckling while we went inside.

CHAPTER TWENTY-SIX

RAMONA

The three of us sat on the concrete, legs outstretched. The oversized t-shirt I wore was almost longer than my shorts, the sleeves extending to my elbows. After making the very conscious decision to not hide my arms today, I'd arrived at the skate spot and nearly ran home to change. But a half hour skating on my own and then a few with Río and Tyler, had me almost forgetting about the scars.

Río took a large swig of beer, and I had to fight to keep my attention from locking onto his Adam's apple bobbing as he swallowed. I tore my eyes away and leaned forward to look at both him and Tyler. "You mean you guys have never…?"

The vampire smirked while Río choked on the last bit of Tecate going down his throat. I clapped him on the back a few times while his breathing evened out. He swiped the back of his hand across his lips, and I brushed a lock of his hair over his shoulder. "Fuck no. I would never let this sadist *anywhere* near my asshole."

A relieved chuckle bubbled out of my mouth the same time Tyler slapped Río's shoulder with the palm of his hand. "That's racist, dude. I'm dead, not evil."

Río cocked a brow while rolling his eyes. "Yeah, but you told me once that you want a *pet*. And one that'll like it when you make it hurt." I snuggled into Río's side, and much to my satisfaction, he slung his arm around my shoulders.

I'd crossed paths with vampires here and there, but I didn't think I'd ever seen one blush. Though they were technically dead, if you meant that their human lives had ended, their resurrected hearts still beat, their stolen blood still flowed. And as above-it-all as Tyler appeared to be most of the time, he evidently had a softer side that was able to be embarrassed. "Doesn't mean I want to *actually* hurt them," he gritted through his teeth.

Call my curiosity piqued. "Is it like a control thing?"

Tyler blushed harder, really highlighting his boyish features. "Uh—"

"Oh, completely," Río supplied.

"I don't know how you don't want to kill him most of the time," Tyler mumbled.

I grinned conspiratorially. "Who says that I don't?"

Río whirled around, switching almost instantly from betrayal to scheming to amusement. He slanted his lips over mine, taking my face in unflinching grip, and I immediately opened up for his prodding tongue. My heart rate rocketed, my belly swooping in anticipation. These few weeks filled with Río made Numbers Eleven and Twelve on my list. Fun and pleasure and contentment.

Also, desire. Something I'd felt so rarely was now a steady coursing whenever he was near, either physically or simply in my thoughts. Within that was lust, sure, but to have his jokes and care was even more fulfilling.

But you wouldn't know that from the little whimpers sparking from my throat as he owned my mouth, only touching my face and lips but taking over everything. Never did I imagine I'd willingly relinquish it all for someone like this. But the past two weeks had been... good. After the nightmare of my parents' confrontation, I'd grown even closer to my people in Antler Pointe. And myself.

Río kissed his way to my ear and gave it a tease with the tip of his tongue. "Keep talking, Princess. I like showing everyone how much of a slut you become for me."

I twisted my head, bringing us brow-to-brow, and glared. That only pushed him to snicker and plant a kiss to the tip of my nose. More heat rose to my cheeks, but I was too focused on cooling down so as to not give him the fucking satisfaction. He leaned back, still holding me close.

There wasn't nearly enough self-consciousness in my chest when I remembered that Tyler was just on the other side of Río. The dark eyeliner smudged around his eyes only made the widened pupils more prominent. He looked between the two of us and sucked his teeth with a pensive look on his face.

The flash of his finely-tipped fangs sparked enough curiosity for me to grab onto. "Is it true that those have venom in them?" I pointedly looked toward his mouth so that he'd know what I was talking about.

Tyler raised an unimpressed brow but still answered. "Yeah."

"And does it hurt? The bite?"

Río nudged me. "You looking to get bit by someone else?" A few shades of his usual taunting were gone, but it truly had been innocent curiosity. And he'd never made to truly bite me with *his* fangs. Despite him coming close multiple times now, and each time, my dormant Wolf begged for it. He already called me his, and I craved his fangs piercing my neck. No matter that it'd only been two months or that I was still healing—I'd probably be doing that all my life. At least, that was the conclusion that Vera, an elder in the pack, and I had come to.

When I returned to the cabin after a few days at Río's, I decided to take Sylvie up on her offer to find me someone to talk to. It wasn't like I was completely against therapy, but, like Orion had concluded, a human who had no knowledge of what it meant to be Wolf wasn't a good fit, either.

Vera was younger than what I would consider an 'elder', just shy of fifty if I had to guess. But she didn't bullshit, calling me out in a way that was familiar. I pulled my phone out to check the time and saw that it was just a few more minutes before I was due at Vera's house to talk again.

Though I knew he naturally preferred the hours after sundown, Tyler seemed to be in an okay mood today, even throwing a few dry jokes at me while he hung out with Río and I. Now that I'd been around him more, I realized that he didn't *dislike* me—he was that way with everyone, save for his friends, with whom he was slightly more animated. And I'd never been able to sit down with a vampire before, let alone one who seemed willing to answer any sort of questions. All the vampires that I'd seen here and there were far too intimidating to just go up to and request they divulge all their secrets.

Tyler ignored Río's heated question, and he instead responded to me. "From what I've been told and what I remember from before, the bite is slightly painful, but the nature of the venom chases it with enough pleasure so that it doesn't matter."

"Huh." I took a sip from Río's beer. "And how old are you, anyway?"

"Sixty-five last December."

Río gave a long whistle and clapped a hand between Tyler's narrow shoulders. "Coolest old man I ever met." In his defense, he didn't look a day over twenty-one, and I suspected that without the eyeliner, ripped jeans, and t-shirt, he'd look even younger.

"Remind me why I'm hanging out with animals again?" Río returned the insult by ruffling the top of Tyler's head to make his short, messy strands even messier.

"Hey, I can't shift, so leave me out of it."

He swatted Río's hands away and scoffed. "Doesn't matter. You still smell like dog, but I guess you're both not as bad, comparatively."

A group of kids shot past us on their boards, excited chattering and whoops forcing us to halt our conversation until they passed and headed toward the bowl. The sun was working on setting, now, and more and more people were entering the park now that the day's heat had fully broken.

Once any human ears were far enough away, I ventured, "Compared to what?"

Tyler's darkly delicate features pinched as his eyes narrowed. "Lots of things. True shifters, Fae, humans. At least the last two usually have their wits about them. Some of the time."

I wracked my brain, trying to remember if I'd ever heard of true shifters before and come up blank. Fae, I'd had some idea about, especially since apparently Sylvie had a grandfather with horns or something. He was a nice guy when I met him at her and O's wedding, but what that meant as far as her powers, I had no idea.

But, "*True* shifters?" What made them different?

Tyler looked at me like I was stupid but relented with more information. "Can change their form to mimic any living crea-ture…? Have you really not heard of 'em?"

I shook my head and felt a bit like Dahlia when I tried explaining to her something like why ice floated even though it was technically water. "No, but that sounds… cool."

Río snorted and lifted his beer to his lips. He paused before downing the rest and crushing the can in his hand. Tyler chuck-led. "Sure, until it drives them crazy."

"Not always." Río dropped his arm around me to recline back on his hands. He studied the skaters that dropped in and jumped out of the bowl.

"Not always," Tyler agreed, "but think about it. Changing to different forms all the time? Maybe enough to forget what your real body is? I've heard of some shifters, Wolves and shit, that stay shifted more often than not. But that's a consistent other form, like a tether. But to not even have yourself as an anchor?" He shook his head and crushed the rest of his beer.

That… yeah, when he put it that way, it didn't sound so

appealing. A waft of unease twined in my nose, like burnt toast, and I rested my hand on Río's thigh.

He blinked a few times then smiled over at me. Whatever he'd been thinking about, probably what it would be like to not have his Jaguar to lean on, cleared just as quickly as it'd come on. He tapped my nose and laughed when I scowled. "Leave it to this geezer to be a walking encyclopedia, huh?"

Tyler didn't have a retort to that one, aside from a scathing glance and pointedly facing forward, ignoring the teasing smirk on Río's face.

We sat and people watched for a minute, cheered for a few kids that worked up the courage to drop in and jump out the other side of the bowl until my alarm went off, and I had to tear myself away for the Antler Pointe Pack version of therapy.

Río had picked me up from the cabin, so he was the one to drop me off at Vera's. The sky once again threatened rain, filling the air with a humid pressure that'd been teasing us all week. Maybe by the time I left her house today, it'd finally rain.

When we pulled up to Vera's driveway, she was sitting on the porch already, book and pencil in her lap. I hopped off of Río's bike and pulled off the helmet that he'd surprised me with last week. It was black to match his, and I tucked it under my arm as I tried to smooth down my hair and stop the blush rising on my face.

I hadn't given Vera too many details about Río—only that I had someone in my life and that it was new. By the pops of curiosity and amusement coming from her direction, she was certainly going to ask me about him.

Río left his bike running but climbed off to walk me to the edge of her yard. It was a modest-sized brick home with pretty hydrangeas out front that her mate, Lauren, cared for.

"All right, Princess. Be good." I rolled my eyes and leaned into the kiss he planted on my lips. He twirled a finger around a loose curl that fell across my shoulder and lightly pulled before letting it spring back in place. "I'll pick you up in a few hours?"

"Yeah."

Vera cleared her throat, now not paying her puzzle book any mind. Río gave her a head nod of acknowledgement, but I heard the feline grumble he tried to hide. "Never thought I'd voluntarily be around this many Wolves," he mumbled before giving me a final, deep kiss that pressed our bodies together. "I'll miss you, baby."

At times like these, my learned response, to clam up and ignore the endearments or actively brush them off, would have been easy to fall back on. But I was working on a new way.

Over his lips, I whispered, "Miss you, too."

Río blinked a moment, then pantomimed cleaning out his ears, so I shoved him in the chest. His deep laughs rolled through us, and he gave one last nip at my ear. "Oh, I'm gonna eat you up later. Now get goin'." He swatted my ass and got back on his bike.

No amount of glare I gave broke the cheeky expression on his face. He even waggled his tongue and winked before shoving his helmet back on and watching me walk up to meet Vera. My face felt like it was on fire, but I still watched him shoot off back up the street once I was safely on the porch. What an ass.

"Your mate's a Lion?" Her purple-tipped pixie cut curled lightly around her ears and the back of her neck, and she was the only person I knew who *might* have had enough tattoos to rival Río's. Hers, though, were a collection of classic American style that were faded and comforting to look at.

While Wolves could be any gender, any color and size, if I had to envision a female Wolf, I would certainly pick Vera out of a line up over my mother.

"He's a Jaguar, actually." I tucked my hair behind my ears before shrugging out of the jacket Río insisted I wear when I rode with him. That'd been the companion gift to my helmet, even if *he* hardly wore outer gear himself. When I righted myself, Vera was still staring at me, with that knowing smirk she gave me on the first day I came here. I'd been… barely pleasant. "What?"

She shrugged and stood, meeting me eye-to-eye. With a hand,

sure and solid from her work as a tattoo artist, she ushered me inside her home that was becoming more familiar. I was here nearly every day, adding to my rotation through other peoples' houses that I was slowly putting my stamp on. Each had their own versions of lived-in chaos, but Vera and Lauren's was by far the most eclectic.

Each room was painted a different, bright color, or contained a sprawling mural, and the coffee table Vera led us to was so splattered in paint, I wondered if it had started that way as a design choice, or if it'd been a casualty that they decided to display.

The color gradient puzzle we'd been working on since the first day my brother dropped me off like sullen child at school was only a quarter of the way finished, and our mess sprawled the entire surface of the table. When he'd told me that he approached Vera specifically, as he'd thought we'd get along well, I'd been more than a bit skeptical as her mate's soft-spoken and flowery introductions led us through the house.

When I'd first seen Vera, sitting on the floor as she was now, she'd demanded I help her with the puzzle. Naturally, I'd glanced at my brother, communicating the need to cut and run.

His flat eye roll retorted, *Don't be ridiculous. I know you well enough to not steer you wrong.*

My dramatic huff and glare had spoken for itself.

Turned out, though, it was easier to speak about my emotions when my hands were occupied, and the almost mindless task of selecting a piece and trying to find where it fit was something that sifted through the darker thoughts until they more readily became a blip in the back of my mind.

"All right," Vera drawled as she sat cross-legged and unceremoniously picked up where she'd left off on her side of the table. I put my helmet and jacket down beside me and did the same. Now that we'd long made it through the corner and edge pieces, the rest was very slow moving, but by the whole bookshelf dedicated to an array of puzzles and my own years of unprocessed issues, we had more than enough to work through. "You were saying about your mom."

I tsked. "Now you sound like a therapist." The piece I tried was the right shade for the top of the puzzle, but the solid purple hue gave no other clue as to where it might go.

She took a piece that matched the tips of her hair and found a fit near the corner closest to me. "I'm sure you don't need a therapist to tell you that for most of us, our mothers are our introduction to the world. And for you, your introduction to your Wolf, as well. If she denies hers, it's no wonder that yours is largely unknown to you."

Vera had taken one look at me after Orion left on my first day and smiled, pointing at my chest, *'Your Wolf is just as surly as you are. You'll do fine here.'*

"Well, if she'd show herself, it'd be a little easier," I groused and tried for another fit but to no avail.

Sock-softened footsteps rounded a corner and headed toward us, sound of ice tinkling making my mouth water. Lauren wore a pair of AirPods, as she always did when I came over, and gave us a nod while she deposited two glasses of Thai iced tea on the floor beside us. It was always perfect, not too sweet, and apparently a family recipe Vera's mom had taught her. I took mine up with a "thank you" while Vera caught Lauren's deep-toned wrist and planted a kiss while never taking her eyes off of the puzzle.

The chocolate and berries aroma in their home was even deeper than O's and Sylvie's—*decades* of love that was woven through their scents. To the point that I couldn't imagine one without the other.

Yesterday, I'd finally told Río about my little trick that I'd learned from Orion, and the confusion then delight that coursed through him when I further explained left me stumbling over my words.

"Aight, what am I feeling now?" he tested me, and I took a long inhale. Dry air like a hot day, the first sip of lemonade, and spiced chocolate and berries.

With a wry smirk, I listed them out. "You're really hungry and excited. I'd guess because of the new riff you figured out earlier today. And… happy. Content that I'm here."

He absolutely beamed at me, bringing my head into his chest while we lay in his bed, and kissed my eyelids. "You coulda cheated on that first one since my stomach growled five minutes ago, but well done, baby. Didn't fuckin' know it could be done, but leave it to you to figure something like this out. I'm proud of you."

"Just because you don't have the magic to let her take over doesn't mean that she's not with you. Always. *My* mother is like you, but she was raised just as her siblings. To acknowledge and honor *all* parts of her. I wonder how differently you'd feel if you were given that same opportunity."

"Probably still fucking depressed."

Vera hummed and picked another piece from the open box. "Are you depressed? Right now."

"According to my two week grippy sock stay and the Major Depressive Disorder diagnosis, I'm going to go with, yes."

"Not what I said. I asked if you were depressed right now. Not whether you had depression."

I frowned and took a final sip from my iced tea before setting it down. I flicked away a drop of condensation that'd dripped on to the puzzle. Was I depressed right now? The episode with my parents calling came to mind, but—since then, no. From gardening, to skating, to hanging out with Delaney, the clouds hadn't quite cleared all the way, but the pale blue sky was there, too.

"Don't you think I haven't been by myself enough to give a true answer, though?"

"You've *got* to get out of that mentality, kid. You do know that Wolves are pack-oriented, right? You think we decide to form these groups for shits and giggles? We *crave* not only companionship but community, too. Did you ever have that before you moved here?"

I hated it when she did this. Pointing out all the obvious holes in my ship that'd caused it to inevitably sink.

"Thought not. Your mom is probably subsisting off of pure force of will at this point. But that's not your burden to bear. Shit way of getting here, but moving to Antler Pointe was probably the best thing you could've done for yourself."

What I didn't hate was how she never skirted around what I'd done. "I guess."

"You guess." Her brow rose while she tapped a jagged-looking piece against her chin. "So if you'd've kept living life as you were, you guess that everything would be totally fine? If say… Ana had stumbled across your Lion instead of you, you suppose that would've been okay?"

My lip curled, and I grunted threateningly at images of Río being curled around the serious looking blonde I'd seen at pack meetings and working at the library. "He's a Jaguar, and no, okay?"

"Ah, your Wolf doesn't like that one bit, does she?"

"I… really like him." I blushed.

She tapped the corner of a piece on the table, searching for where it might go. "And are you going to mate him?" I almost spat out my iced tea. "What?"

"Shouldn't you not encourage I do that? Aren't I… not healthy enough for that?"

She tested the piece in a few places before settling on the right one and sitting back to look at me. "As long as you do it for the right reasons, who cares? Only you will know if you're following your shifter instincts or running from your problem. It's not for me to say. You may be half human, but I sense your Wolf. Do you feel her pull toward this Jaguar?"

Her words hit me square in my chest, where I'd been feeling the tug toward Río since I first saw him at Vinny's.

She nodded through my silence. "From what I know of you so far, and from our Leader, your Wolf side has been stifled. Though some choose to live the human way, when it comes to companions, our minds and spirits are naturally a bit different." Vera looked up toward the kitchen, and her expression brightened like the sun breaking through the clouds. I followed her gaze through the doorway and landed on her mate, Lauren, who was washing dishes. "When your Wolf knows, she knows."

Ugh, I frowned as a headache started pinching behind my eyes. "I didn't come here for relationship advice."

"No, just to stop wanting to off yourself. So far, we're succeeding. Yay." The corners of my lips twitched, and when I snuck a glance across the unfinished puzzle, hers were doing the same. I'd already told her about my list, though I was still trying to find a time to hit her with the fact that she was lucky Number Thirteen. Through these weeks, I more so brought out my running tally as a reason to pause when moments like this hit, but it was still a comforting resource when I needed.

Vera laid off of pressing me about the whole *mating* issue, and we wandered between further discussing my mother and the intricacies of pack dynamics that I'd never learned as a child.

I got lost in the conversation and our puzzle—so much so that when Río called me, I took a step back and found that we'd only just gotten the gradient barely halfway complete.

"I'm starting to think that we're not good at these."

When I put the phone up to my ear, trying to find the home for the piece still in my hand, I could hear his voice through the walls of the house and on the other end of the call. "You ready to go to mine, Princess?"

"Yeah, be one second." I put the barely-purple piece in one slot, changed my mind, and guessed at the next one that turned out to be a fit.

Taking that as my cue to go, I unfolded my legs and tapped the table in goodbye. Vera was still working on her last puzzle piece for our session, so her mumbled goodbye wasn't surprising in the least.

Going back out the way I came, I felt that familiar stir when I was on the precipice of meeting Río's black gaze again, having his arms around me again. And sure enough, when I stepped out of the house, his face lit up like the bottle rockets I'd once watched him light at the skatepark with childish glee.

The air was still thick with the hints of a summer storm, but with Río's mouth on mine, I didn't even need the relief of a good rain. My helmet clunked against his back when I threw my arms around his shoulders in an embrace, his hands palming my ass and pulling me flush toward him. He nipped at my lip, teasing me with those sharp teeth. "Let's hit it, baby."

CHAPTER TWENTY-SEVEN

RAMONA

Ollie happily clung to the oversized long-sleeve shirt I'd put on this evening for the pack meeting, and Sylvie worked on carefully carrying the key lime pies she'd made for everyone. My brother crouched behind Dahlia, trying to calm her high-pitched concerns.

"Daddy, you gotta fix it!"

I slung the backpack they brought with them that had all the kid-type stuff while O unraveled one of the twists he'd put in my niece's hair before we left the house. He used his tawny claws to comb through the large twist that Dahlia had somehow destroyed on the ten minute ride to Vera's house. "I'm fixing it, darlin'." He tied off the end with a hair tie and the green hair bobble that matched her overalls and complemented her red hair. "There." He kissed her cheek, and the impending meltdown cleared as fast as it'd come on.

O held his hands at his sides, fingers moving restlessly while Dahlia clung to his pant leg. Though he was surprisingly good at doing Dahlia's hair, the sensation of hair product on his hands, I knew, made his skin crawl. When we stepped inside Vera's house, he promptly headed toward the bathroom to wash his hands, and I took the babies with me through the house and out into the backyard.

It wasn't as extravagant as Tina's, or as expansive as Orion and Sylvie's, but it was curated with personality and care. More hydrangea bushes bordered the small, fenced-in property, and delicate wind chimes and stain glass hangings decorated the porch. Enough seats had been set out around a fire pit that I hadn't seen before in my sessions here, and a few other members were already setting up.

There was a little pond in the corner, and as soon as they saw it, both Ollie and Dahlia squealed to join the other Wolf pup that was peering into the water. With her hand in mine, I took them both over there and left the setting up to the actual adults.

I sat cross-legged and monitored the kids' marveling and splashing at the water, like they weren't used to living with an actual lake in their backyard. A pup whose name I couldn't remember babbled and waved their arms excitedly, ramping up the playtime to ear-splitting levels. I tried my best to shush and focus their energy on being quiet for the little fish that darted anxiously under the surface, but it was only halfway successful.

While I kept them occupied, more members arrived, but the atmosphere was noticeably more somber, like the last meeting I'd gone to. This was the second meeting since the Wolf named Jasper had been killed by the Serafim Group. The pack members paid special attention to the murdered Wolf's parents, and even I mustered small, encouraging smiles whenever they glanced my way.

As the time for the meeting drew nearer, I caught the cream-sicle scent of my friend before he made his way onto the porch, and my shoulders perked up while his surprisingly quiet gait headed straight toward me.

"Hey, Ramona!" His blond hair was damp and looked more brown today. The t-shirt, shorts, and converse were all color coordinated, and he didn't hesitate to plop down cross-legged beside me.

I accepted his request of outstretched arms, our side hug quick but warm. "Mr. Delaney!" Dahlia screamed, to which Delaney chuckled and waved. Ollie and the other pup grinned gummy smiles and happily returned to taking Dahlia's lead in their play around the pond.

"What's up with you?" I asked, itching at my sleeves but keeping them pulled down. My mind kept warring between the safe yet stifled sense I got while wearing them.

Before I'd… tried to kill myself, I largely felt comfortable in my own skin. Especially in the summer time, I wore tank tops like a uniform. Back when I competed, shorts and sports bras were the norm.

And, I thought tentatively, *maybe I can get back to that*. Now that my Jaguar and closest family knew, it didn't seem so impossible. The last time I'd seen Delaney, shortly after I started coming over here to Vera's, I purposely pushed my sleeves to my elbows during one of me and my friend's regular coffee excursions. He was the sweet spot of familiar enough to where I felt I could be a smidge more vulnerable, but also new to my life enough that I wasn't frozen in terror at the idea of him rejecting me.

Just as I'd predicted—other than him just not noticing, which would have been fine, too—he eyed them for a stilted moment, and I tracked the subsequent comprehension that swept his features. I was kinda used to him being very easily reduced to tears, now, so when his eyes shimmered, and he grabbed my hands, I was prepared for that, too. He'd held them for nearly the whole time we sat together, but the benefit to him knowing was far greater than the apprehension I'd trembled with beforehand. Number Eight was no longer a hug from a stranger but the support from a true friend.

Now, Delaney sighed a fulfilled noise, brown eyes sparkling. "I'm good! My grades this past semester were good, and I'm excited to start the next one in a few weeks. I think having such a nicer pack to lean on has helped. Working for Lauren has been so amazing. Remind me to thank Sylvie and Leader for connecting us again!" He'd needed a summer job with his scholarship stipends only depositing during the school year. Luckily, Lauren needed barista help at the coffee shop she owned downtown.

Now, the scent of coffee beans also trailed along with him, but it was a homey smell. I snickered a little. "Not so afraid of him now, I hope?"

Delaney shook his head, still smiling sweetly. "No! You were right, he's not scary! I'll admit, I was shakin' in my boots when he wanted to ask me about my old pack, but he said it was really helpful information, and he got me a job!"

Dahlia proved to have the ears of a true Wolf pup, because she interrupted her directing of her baby pup followers to giggle over at us. "Daddy's not scary!"

We both chuckled at that, and I didn't miss the flush on Delaney's face from being called out by a toddler. I nudged his arm with my elbow. "So, what's this about your other pack?" He'd alluded to it a little bit. But nothing more than it becoming a really bad situation. "Where are they?"

"Were." He chewed on the edge of a fingernail. "I was born near Huntsville, but stuff with Howl's Fury got really," he glanced toward the kids and lowered his voice, "scary. I don't like to think about it, but your brother said what I'd told him was really helpful. Bad memories."

"Shit," I muttered in sympathy. He looked truly afraid even saying that much, so I couldn't imagine what he'd witnessed to cause such a reaction. "Well, I'm glad you're here, then."

That quick, his face changed to a beaming grin, and he gave me another side hug. "Me too!"

We chatted a little more until the meeting started with the general updates around the fire pit. Harrison, the adolescent pup that always seemed in a cheery mood, volunteered to watch the pups as they wandered about the yard, so I was able to pay full attention to O and the elders leading the meeting.

They still didn't have any concrete news about the fucking shifter mafia trying to move in, but I also knew how much my brother was agonizing over it. He hid his emotions fairly well, but I knew him and knew how to track the nuance of his scent. I'd never seen him this stressed in all my life.

But, as Leader, he kept his posture and appearance strong while being honest about the danger we all faced with a promise to lead us to the best of his ability. He'd increased sweeps of the land perimeter, directing none of us to travel alone for the time being. The Mountain's Peak pack to the north had agreed to lend assistance whenever we needed, and he and the elders were continuing to meet and discuss ways to covertly attack the Serafim Group. They'd already gotten their business licenses rejected and were working on taking the bureaucratic way to kick them out of town, though I could tell that some were itching for blood. When a few members asked about staging an all-out attack, O calmly stated his reasonings, wary of the size of their retaliation should we avenge Jasper in such a way.

The elders and most of the pack backed him up with head nods and relaxing back in their seats, but the whole thing had everyone on edge. Even me. It wasn't like there was too much I could do, but I would help as much as I could. And if that meant making other areas of my brother's life easier, I'd continue trying my damnedest.

An hour and a half later, the formal part of the meeting came to an end, and one or two Wolves hung back to speak more privately with Orion. Sylvie made her rounds as his mate, with Dahlia and Ollie now hanging onto her. Bugs buzzed around the lights set around Vera and Lauren's yard, the smoke of the fire trailed up toward the black sky that was churning with collecting storm clouds. A few pack members were gathering stuff, feeling the rain coming on, but I wasn't super concerned.

I checked my phone, expecting a text from Río but seeing none so far. I fought back the anxiety since we'd already planned for me to spend the night after the pack meeting and sent a quick heads up that I'd be leaving for his apartment soon.

"All right, I'm 'bout to head out. I'll see you later," I said to Delaney who'd just finished a round of small talk with the mate of one of the Wolves.

He glanced toward my brother and sister-in-law. "Do you need a ride?"

I shrugged. "Nah, I was gonna grab my stuff from O's car and walk. I'm going to…" I took a breath and remembered that last time I was there, he'd given me a key to his apartment, for god's sake. "My boyfriend's house."

Delaney sputtered and did a little dance of excitement. I'd mentioned I was seeing someone, but this was the first time I'd called him anything specific. Even though the label didn't feel whole enough. "I'll drive you!"

"Oh, ah, no, it's—"

"Please, let me do this for you! You heard Leader—I can't let you go alone!" He gasped. "And do you think your boyfriend can introduce me to someone?"

"Um, well, I can as—"

"Even if he can't! I can't let you *walk* when it's about to downpour, and I know you don't wanna wait around for Leader and Sylvie. But anyone worth *your* time must have some friends that'd be worth *my* time, right? Ugh, what I wouldn't give for a nice boy for once."

I got swept up in the airy flurry that was my giant friend—Oh, god, was he my best friend? Besides Río and Sylvie, it was looking like, yes—and let him lead me to the cars. I got my overnight bag out of Orion's car, returned his keys to him with a grunt of thanks, and let Delaney drive me away from Vera's.

His little car was probably about two decades old, but it was clean with only a few random things making it slightly messy. A few drawings that looked to be from his students at the school, his hat from the coffee shop, a hot pink keychain.

I directed him to Río's apartment, and when the sky opened

up and dumped buckets on Antler Pointe, I was grateful that he'd offered to drive. Not that I wouldn't have been fine on my walk, even in the dark, but it was definitely preferable to arriving completely soaked.

"Thanks for convincing me to take the ride." I unbuckled and gathered my bag in my hands.

Delaney smiled and nodded toward the building. "I'll watch you go up to make sure you get in there okay."

I nodded and braced myself for the run to Río's apartment. From here, the rain made it too difficult to scent whether he was inside or not, but my heart picked up speed in anticipation. My family and friend were... safe, but I was really starting to view anywhere with him as home.

RÍO

I easily lifted the garbage bags from inside and pushed my way out of the back door. While I went to the dumpster, the heavy door cracked against the can of tomatoes that propped it open, but it wasn't the loud noise that had my hackles raising.

Mierda. I tossed the trash into the dumpster and called out into the night. "What do you want, Mara."

My sister rounded the darkened corner of the building like she wasn't just spying on me not a minute before. Her pinstripe vest and pants looked pressed and impeccable, so unlike the rumpled and ripped clothes I wore. Today had been another double shift, and more callouts had caused me to work register and back of house all damn day. These were my last duties, and I just wanted to go home to my princess. Good thing I'd given her a key, cause no telling what bullshit my sister would spit today. Was she finally here to kill me? Or worse—drag me back to our father?

She pouted and did a dramatic turn around, as if there was something to see back here beside the old brick facade of Vinny's and the dumpster. The very top of the black dragon tattooed on her back was visible and a perfect match for mine.

I wanted to shake the sixteen-year-old me who'd spent that year trying to accept and truly settle into life with my father and sisters. One thing Mara and Cata could never talk shit about was my art, and when we got high one night off our own supply, they'd convinced me to make some sort of design for the three of us to get together.

Drawing my own interpretation of Kukulkan, the Mayan winged serpent deity, had seemed like a cool idea at the time, and my sisters, in the haze of enhanced marijuana, thought the sketches looked 'badass'. Reading and drawing and drugs had been my escape in those days, when time to climb and explore had been scarce, and I'd been fixated on indigenous mythology from our mother's homeland at the time.

I still wasn't sure they knew the significance of the artwork, but it was a nod to our mother that they couldn't reject. The enchanted ink that outlasted our healing abilities made sure of that.

"I can't just wanna see you again, Yoyo?"

"No. I'm busy, if you haven't noticed. And I have nothing to say to you, so if you're not here to kill me or take me back, I'd appreciate it if these ambushes stopped."

She cackled into the air, slight frame shaking without any consideration of how much she could fuck up what little life I'd scraped together for myself. "If this is an ambush, maybe you need to be reminded of what it's like to be hunted."

"*¡Ya párale!* All of you tortured me for *years*. I got out, and I'm *done*, Mara. I thought you understood that."

Her laughter died as suddenly as it'd come on, and she stared into my eyes with no expression at all. I smelled the coming drops of rain a few minutes before they started hitting the top of my head, dotting my work shirt. Mara's short, black waves twitched with the warm breeze that cycled around us, and my muscles reacted automatically to this side of her. How she'd looked before she became what truly haunted my nightmares. As a boy, I used to think of this version of her as Xiomara. My father's most valuable and secret weapon.

Mara, who I'd once happily had in my blunt rotation, would disappear whenever the change took over. Hell, I didn't even know if she truly realized how terrifying it was. Even though she'd eventually become Mara again and take care of me after fucking me up, she was never *safe*.

"Sim. Você fugiu." She spun on her spiky heel and stalked into the night, back toward the main road as a distant roll of thunder sounded across the sky.

I wanted to hit something, maybe punch a hole in the dumpster, but I just pivoted in the other direction, back into Vinny's to lock up and get the fuck home to the only one that truly mattered.

CHAPTER TWENTY-EIGHT

RAMONA

The rain was relentless, and as quickly as I ambled from the parking lot between Río's place, I was more than a little damp. Once I was in the semi-safety of the alley behind his building, I waved to Delaney who watched me run up the steps on the way to Río's door.

Again, I didn't have to knock, because he opened up as soon as I approached the apartment. Clad in a black cropped t-shirt and gray sweatpants of all things, Río looked a cozy dream with his hair falling in messy waves. His facial piercings glinted in the hall security lights, and I let him pull me by the waist into his home. My scent was becoming a central component of the space, and I wanted to crow in happiness that, once again, the only other scent was the fading trace of his sister.

"You already eat?" he asked after a greeting kiss to the forehead. "I brought some wings and fries from work and can warm 'em up if you're still hungry." I rolled my eyes at that because I could tell from here that the oven was already on and that he was warming the food anyway.

"Sure. But lemme change out of this." I stepped back and gestured to my damp clothing.

When I reached a hand for my bag that Río had taken and slung on his shoulder as soon as I'd crossed the threshold, he grinned lasciviously and wiggled his brows. "Need me to help you?"

I was already unbuttoning my shorts, not bothering to go to the bathroom or up by the loft. "You do that plenty."

He didn't deny it as he busied himself with our dinner in the kitchen, but I felt his eyes on me while I undressed. Today, I'd been a bit more self-conscious as I'd dressed, but shedding the hoodie now didn't fill me with dread, either. The soft cotton shorts and NYU t-shirt I'd packed were oversized and baggy, and I twisted my hair up with a clip from the front pocket of my bag to keep the damp strands off of my neck.

Río must've started on heating the food as soon as I'd texted that I was on my way, because he was already plating and carrying everything over by the time I sent a quick message to my brother and Sylvie that I made it to Río's okay.

We took our usual places at the couch, me on the cushions and him on the floor, while we picked through the wings and fries. He got them extra spicy, how I preferred, and my tastebuds were flooded with the delicious, sticky spice. The wings made me think of the family gatherings that we'd attended in earnest when I was a child, that dwindled and eventually petered out. They weren't jerk spiced, but the wings were good, and I cleaned the meat off with practiced ease, leaving nothing but bones.

Río's eating was much the same, and once we finished, I took up washing the dishes while he threw out the trash and straightened the counters for the night. It was pleasantly domestic, so much so that I didn't need to ask anymore where things went. I returned our two plates, now clean and dry, into the cupboard that was otherwise sparse.

Princess, I think I'm gonna have to keep you.

I let Río lead me up to the loft, and I wondered how quickly he would pack up his stuff when he was ready to move to wherever he was meaning to go. Would I have to hide out in a duffel bag to make absolutely sure that I went with him?

His bed was made, and a pile of books, including his sketchbook, rested on the floor. The rain was pelting the windows, giving a constant pitter patter and roll of lightening. Perfect cuddle weather.

Río gave me a funny look when I held up an arm and got to work, giving way to the urge in my chest by arranging the pillows and comforter to make a little comfy cocoon. He didn't have too much, just three pillows and the large cover, but my thoughts narrowed to this single-minded drive. I improvised with my t-shirt and his sweatshirt that he had thrown over the bed.

After a few final adjustments and pats, I got a soft enclosure for our night that I was pretty proud of. Not that I was used to doing this for two, but being wrapped in soft blankets made me feel nice, so this little half-fort would hopefully bring him some enjoyment, too. The sight of it filled my belly with a cozy rightness, and I hummed in satisfaction.

I climbed into it first, testing that the walls and base were all good, before turning to invite Río to follow.

Oh.

He was smelling like that again. Deep like chocolate and sweet fruit with his own spiced heat. His claws had descended, and an almost feral expression had replaced the easygoing one.

He pounced on the bed, so fast it made me jump. My Jaguar was careful to not disturb the blankets and pillows I'd arranged, all the while sucking me into his black hole stare. He knelt on the bed, knees nudging against mine, and took the corners of my jaw in hand. He tilted my head up to face him, and the tips of his claws pressed against the back of my neck.

"You made a nest for us." His words were almost hard to understand, infused with a low, feline growl. He nudged the side of my face with his, purring and licking, and a breathy, vibrating thrum started up in my chest. It reverberated with his, striking a harmony that filled the space and entire apartment.

Río pushed me onto my back, and I wrapped my legs around his waist. He snatched the clip out of my hair and snuffled in the curls—despite them being a frizzy mess, he seemed to love it. I ran my hands across his arms, rippling with lean muscle, and my breathing quickened as I felt the beginnings of short and soft fur emerge. His voice continued to distort, and his mumbling in Spanish made what he was saying impossible for me to translate.

"… tu eres maravillosa… princesa bella, mi cielito… mi otra mitad te amo te amo te amo." How he felt about me, though, I understood. It was the same as how I felt about him.

My own version of the cocoa and strawberries combined with his, wrapping us in sweetness that was emphasized by the bed I'd arranged. A nest, he called it. It obviously meant something, though I didn't know how to verbalize it. Río's cock was hard and pressing between my legs, and his arms now had long stretches of black fur. Another ran up his neck, stopping just behind his ear.

He pulled back, eyes yellow behind the plastic of his contact lenses, and opened his mouth. The ivory fangs were beautiful, and I trembled with the need for them to be buried in my neck. Not a desire—something I felt like I'd die without. "I'm not leaving without you, Ramona." The hissing snarl wasn't human at all anymore, and I mewled, nodding and baring my neck for him to do it. To claim me all the way.

He snapped to the sensitive curve of my shoulder, beside the bottom of my neck. Sharp teeth nibbled and pulled at the skin, eliciting a high-pitched yelp from my lungs. My hips pressed against his, needing to join in all ways. Now, now, now.

"Please, do it, do it."

He roared, the same noise that he'd given that day in the forest. Was that only a few weeks ago? It sounded like a saw cutting through wood, and my body vibrated again in answer. *Yes, yes, yes,* every part of me chanted and begged.

Río stilled, and I blinked up at the ceiling, worried that he was going to back out, not give us what we were both needing. A burst of thunder crashed outside, soon followed by a flash of lightning that cast his face in sharp relief. Some of his human voice returned, but the rest of him stayed half-shifted. "I'm not a good person, Ramona. I've... killed people. You're in danger. Being with me."

I pushed him up with a hand at his throat so that I could more clearly see. The anguish was creeping back over his features, the urgency around us retreating. Taking a note from him, I searched his eyes, let my senses stretch over him. By what he said the night he fucked me for the first time, I already knew that he wasn't innocent.

And maybe I wasn't either, because I didn't care. Life after my attempt to take it away was colored differently, but I was more than willing to let my non-human half guide me to where I'd been drawn all along. To my Río.

"You'll keep me safe?"

His grip on me tightened, and his lip curled in a snarl at the thought of something threatening me. "Always."

"You love me?"

His chest heaved, but he didn't hesitate. "I love you." The scent of it rained down on us, washing over me.

"I love you, t—" Río tackled me back into the blankets, and our lips smashed together. I pulled and grabbed at his hair to keep him on me, groaning as we met in a wild mess of clicking teeth and swipes of tongues. Purposely, I cut myself on his fangs.

The taste of my blood ramped the both of us even higher, and my own teeth itched to claim him. Everything outside of this nest was unimportant. Irrelevant, even. I'd almost left this world without ever crossing paths with this Jaguar that was made for me.

Like hell was I going to turn back now.

Río brought his hand between our bodies and ripped through my bra and the thin shorts I wore. My panties went with them, becoming strips of tattered fabric that he shoved out of the way. Red lines raised on my skin, where his claws had swept through but didn't break, and I used my own hands to tear at his clothes.

I didn't have claws, but I had the burning in my heart and my own heightened strength on my side. His shirt tore like tissue paper, his sweatpants pretty much the same, until we were naked flesh on flesh.

"Río Bernal, do it now, so help me god." I gasped into his mouth, blood coating my lips while I writhed beneath him.

He trailed wet and bloody kisses to the right side of my neck and stopped. I slapped at his shoulders, giving my own non-shifter version of a growl.

"You sure, baby? We don't have to."

"*Río*, make me your mate."

He groaned, and the flash of pain made my heart burst with a golden light that overtook every one of my senses. The thread that was spun the moment we met, the fibers of which that felt like they'd always been there, strengthened until it was a truly glowing and living thing.

Río's claws sunk into my hips, and I pierced the skin of his shoulders with my nails before sinking my own blunt teeth at the base of his neck.

With an inevitable thrust, he completed our joining in flesh and blood, and tears streamed down my eyes at the blanket of rightness and peace I felt. As he moved around me, inside of me, I knew that it wasn't going to *fix* my problems, but enhance the strength I had to face them myself. My Jaguar. My... mate.

Río released his teeth and licked over my new mark, plunging slowly with his hips while I answered his movements with my own. The storm outside continued to rage, making the moment between us feel even more tender and private. "I love you, Ramona. My mate. Mi alma gemela." He groaned and held me like I was a treasure.

And in his arms, I... believed him. This love was new, only

two months old, but the humming light filling both of us tran-
scended time and space. "My mate. My Río."

His eyes shimmered and spilled, creating joyous tracks down
his angular face. I licked at them, held him, while we made love to
each other and settled into the decision we'd made.

CHAPTER TWENTY-NINE

RAMONA

Río took the next three days off of work, and I stayed at his apartment. Texts from my mother, and less so, Sylvie and Orion, filled my inbox, but I only responded to the necessary ones. Telling Sylvie where I was. Ignoring O's reminders about his command.

I damn sure didn't tell them that my brother's prediction had already come true.

Number Fourteen. My mate, truly. Every time I thought of the word, the deep, fulfilled sensation in my chest would almost pulse, reminding me of its presence.

This time with Río was too sacred. My shifter side was fiercely protective of our mound of blankets and the tenderness with which we shared in them. I rebuilt it every time our fucking or lovemaking wore it down, and we lounged in each other's arms, kissing and laughing and adjusting to this new feeling of *more*.

We talked for hours, filling in the gaps and enhancing our matehood in the process. Giving it sustenance to grow and fill, and already, I was acutely aware of his solid home within my heart.

And he told me more about the danger he'd spoken of. When he tried to warn me away from something that was unavoidable. As we sat up in his bed, he filled the picture of his past. That his father ran his family with a viciousness that was far, far worse than my mother ever could be.

"I lived in Georgia with my mom until I was ten." That explained his slips into a Southern twang, at least. "My father demanded I come live with him and my sisters—Catalina and Xiomara—or he'd take it out on Mamá." I nodded, remembering the names of his siblings that he'd told me a while ago. I rubbed his bare chest while he recounted for me the memories that haunted him. "And…" he took a deep breath, "I couldn't let them find out about my younger brother. Javier. Or else our father would take him, too."

My gaze trailed to his torso, where the three cranes flew, and I traced the wings of the two smaller ones that followed the larger. I flicked my eyes up to him, and he nodded at my silent question. "So I made sure that we all got out." He smiled sadly, and a shallow dimple appeared on his left cheek. "Just wish we could've flown together."

The sprawling sadness interwoven through this memory and his words was heavy. Too much for one person. I kissed his nose while he caressed the scars on one of my arms. "I'm sorry."

"S'okay," he said, even though it wasn't. "He's grown, now. And Mamá is a fighter. I'll see them again, someday. And they'll both love you." I felt the blush flare on my cheeks, so I hid my face in the crook of his neck. Some of his resignation gave way to an affectionate chuckle.

The one boyfriend I'd had before Río was a stupid high school thing. We'd gone to the same schools together since we were small, and our parents had already been acquainted before he asked me to homecoming when we were thirteen.

That had been an immature and flippant relationship. A puddle too small for a bird compared to the expansive ocean that was what Río and I were, now.

Still, we'd gone about this a little lopsided. As we'd eaten ice cream in our nest, with our marks still a fresh and lively red, he'd snarked and called our path 'a little ass-backwards'. But then he'd grinned, his nose scrunching in happiness, and I couldn't keep mine from rising to match.

"Um…" I mumbled now over his skin, right into his mark that'd healed to a brown impression of my teeth. "So, my brother." Río traced the edge of my face, like he'd done on our first date —because it *was* a date, I now realized—and kissed my temple in encouragement for me to continue. "He wants to meet you. Properly."

He hummed but otherwise didn't react. "As Pack Leader or as your brother?"

"Not sure. Both? He said that he wasn't going to ask you to become pack, but he needed to know you."

Río gave me another kiss, and I relaxed into his chest, glad that he wasn't getting upset at the notion. It'd be a shock to everyone when I turned up with a mate, but I was also excited to have him by my side.

"All right, Princess. You just tell me when." I nodded into his skin and kissed his mark. He shivered, tightening his arms around me. "Who woulda thought that I would mate the most beautiful girl in the world?"

I groaned into his skin. "You are so stupid."

"Nah, baby, I think I'm the smartest motherfucker alive. As soon as I saw those honey eyes of yours, I knew that I had to have you."

My nose wrinkled. "Honey eyes?" I watched him suspiciously, but he just kept on smiling, like I was missing a joke, and we fell into each other once more. He allowed me to unfurl into a softer version of myself and open myself completely. Only with him.

We fell asleep sometime later, tangled and pleasantly exhausted. So much so that when I was awakened by a foreign distress in my stomach and the urgent blare of an alarm, it took me a moment to realize where I was.

The sky outside was already a bright blue, and, knowing that Río had an opening shift this morning, I figured that his alarm had been going off for a good while.

An elbow knocked into my ribs. The nudge didn't hurt, but it wasn't comfortable either. "Ow." I propped up on my hand and blinked to further clear my senses. Beside me, Río's muscles were past the point of tense, coiling as if he was facing an attack. But there was no one here other than me, so it looked more painful than anything. His features were twisted in outrage, beads of sweat ran down into his hair that stuck to his temples.

That was the feeling in my stomach. Whether I was truly experiencing it or just more attuned to him now, I didn't know for sure. What I did know, though, was that I had to soothe him.

"Hey, it's okay." I laid a gentle hand on his shoulder, feeling the burning and hard skin. "Río, it's just a nightm—"

His roar was loud enough to be heard a block away. It rattled my teeth, and if it weren't for my own dormant training, I would've been completely thrown on the floor by whatever was happening in his dream world. Instead, we fumbled back onto the mattress, destroying the outer edge of our nest.

Río's eyes were wild but unaware as he flashed his fangs at me, and my heart cracked for him. No, I wasn't scared, because even though his teeth and claws could easily tear my throat out, he kept the latter buried in the mattress beside my head. He snarled in my face but went no further.

He breathed heavily over me, gaze still unfocused. "Baby, it's okay," I tried, going for a lighter caress on his chest.

Bad idea, because he ripped his hand out of the bed, and, before I could flinch, slapped himself. It caused a reverberating smacking noise and bright wounds from his claws that welled with blood.

"*Stop,*" I cried and grabbed his wrists. Twisting both of our bodies while he thrashed, I flipped us, disturbing our pillows even further, and straddled his hips. He kicked uselessly at the bed as I used all the strength I possessed to subdue him. I kept

Río's hands bound to the mattress above his head where he couldn't hurt himself anymore.

In turn, he shredded the blankets, head whipping back and forth while he mumbled in a language I hadn't yet heard him speak. It wasn't Spanish—Portuguese, maybe?

"Río, honey, p-please. You're gonna hurt yourself. I love you, please stop." Fat tears plunked down on his cheeks, brushing into his lashes and arcing down to his ears. "You're okay. I love you, *please*." My lips trembled as a particularly harsh wave of resistance wracked his body, arching his back before he collapsed back to the bed.

His hands were still opening and closing, making a complete wreck of the covers and sending up a flurry of pillow fluff.

So at a loss of what to do, I bent forward. Still unafraid of his body's weaponry, I kissed at the side of his mouth. He growled but didn't bite, so I risked a brush of my lips at his lower right fang.

A barely-there touch of his tongue met my lip. "It's okay, it's okay, it's okay," I chanted while I moved up his face. When I reached the sharp edge of his cheekbone, I dragged the flat of my tongue up the skin. Tasted the salt of his sweat and my tears.

The sour scent of fear began to retreat from the air, so I kept doing it. I licked up his face over and over while murmuring about how much I loved him.

I was so lost in my efforts and prayer that I hadn't totally noticed that he'd stopped fighting me. Not until a hoarse croak halted my pleas. "Ramona?"

My grooming of his face became less frantic, switching back to kisses, but I didn't stop. "You're okay. You're safe."

"W—what—?"

"You had a bad dream, you, you hit yourself, and I had to make you stop, baby tell me what to do, I don't know how to make you feel better, tell me how to help." My voice broke, muddled by the torrent of tears that refused to stop.

"What're you..." He blinked up at me, eyes widening as he

took in my panic that he was surely seeing. When he shoved against my hands, this time, I let him go, and he scrambled out of the bed. He was hyperventilating while staring between me and his hands as if he didn't know what to be horrified by.

Then, he went from flushed to pale, and he dashed down the steps and to the bathroom. The door banged against the wall, followed by the sound of the toilet lid cracking against the tank and his vomit splashing into the bowl. For a moment, I was stuck, listening to him be sick and grieving over the ruined nest. It was silly, but my… my Wolf whined at the realization that our post-mating peace was over. Despite being so dormant that she would never fully emerge, she was part of me all the same.

I could kill his family, I cursed as I scrambled out of the bed. Río was coughing into the toilet, now, and I knew that they were the cause of his nightmares. Whether it was his father or sisters that scared him in his sleep, they'd all had hands in the abuse he'd suffered.

The acrid smell of vomit was wildly unpleasant, but I pushed through to hold back Río's hair while he emptied the rest of his stomach. In the white-tiled bathroom, my suicide attempt scars were illuminated in total clarity, but I barely gave them a glance.

"Go back to bed, Princess," Río said harshly and spat in the toilet. His words echoed within the roundness of the bowl as he clung to the side of it.

I stayed put. "No." His alarm was still ringing beside the bed, no telling how late he was going to be for work now. If he even wanted to go.

"*Ramona*," he barked, and I froze.

"I'm not leaving—"

"¡Escúchame!" He raised his voice, and I dropped my grasp of his hair. It fell in a tangled heap on his back. Río jutted his chin toward the door. "I gotta clean up and go to work. Put on some of my clothes if you need."

My chin wobbled, but I did as he said. He clearly didn't want me to bear witness to this, but why couldn't I see this part of him? What did I do wrong?

I swept my wrists over my eyes, clearing another welling of tears, and trudged up to the loft. I had to bite the inside of my cheek to keep from whining again at the sight of the ruined nest. Dismantling it made me sad, but seeing it all damaged was worse. Only one of the pillows survived the wrath of Río's night terror, so I set it against the headboard. I threw the ripped comforter and blankets onto the floor and shoved on his hoodie that was two sizes too big for me. Eight puncture holes in the arc of Río's hands were visible on the navy sheets, but I didn't have the energy to fully strip the bed. I pulled a pair of basketball shorts from his dresser and slipped them on. He was being a fucking asshole, but being in his clothes comforted me all the same. I ran a hand over my mark and breathed a little deeper.

Río came back up the steps and paused. His jaw ticked while he barely looked at the bed, his scent a churning wash of emotions. None of them were happy, and I wanted to cry all over again.

He sighed. "I'll buy more stuff for the bed later."

While he dressed for work, I sat on the couch, watching the cleared sky through the windows and tried to figure out what the fuck to do. Río's curdled shame and my own grief for our nest were making it hard to think, but what I knew for sure was that I wanted to be here for when we fixed it.

RÍO

I kicked the walk-in closed, balancing fresh ingredients to replenish what was empty on the line, only to have the shredded mozzarella topple to the floor. A scatter of white cheese dusted the floor and my shoes, but all I could do was sigh and trudge through it to set the rest down.

I had a mate for less than a week, and I'd already fucked up.

It was fucking Xiomara coming around, bringing me into our dad's bullshit. The night terrors used to be really bad, but through the years, they'd let up. And since I'd been with Ramona, they'd been nonexistent.

So, why fucking now?

I didn't even want to run anymore. I just wanted to forget the Serafim name, all that came with it, and just recall my adolescent years as a blank spot to skip over. Frankly, everything between leaving Mamá's house on my tenth birthday and meeting Ramona was pretty much irrelevant. Living with her, walking alongside my Princess, was what I wanted to do. What I needed. And why the fuck couldn't I finally have that?

My throat choked up while I swept the floor. I'd ruined the nest she made for us, demolishing the gesture and honeymoon bubble we'd been in. It was hard to even look at her, knowing that she sensed every pathetic thing I felt about her seeing me that way.

The rest of my shift passed in a blur of one annoying and fucked up hour into another. It still beat following my father's orders, no matter how brutal, but customer service was its own sort of hell. Even when I was a step removed as a manager.

I'd walked to work to give myself space to think, but when I returned home, the sight of my truck snagged my attention. How was I going to make it up to Ramona? She hadn't texted or called, and if I were her, I'd probably be hiding out at my brother's to get away from the problems I'd already caused. And she didn't know the full extent of the shitstorm Mara would bring when she learned about this.

Unless I got us out of here before then. Yeah, another thing to drop on my mate.

"Fuck," I muttered and unlocked my truck. The conversations needed to happen. I wasn't so much of an asshole to sweep what happened this morning under the rug.

But running to the grocery store felt much more tangible with the swirl of emotions I was already feeling. I wasn't a spectacular cook, but some of Mamá's more simple recipes were ingrained in me. Ceviche de camarón didn't involve using the stove at all, and tostadas were easy enough to make. By the time I left and returned to the apartment, I could smell Ramona's presence inside. Had she stayed the whole time? I'd been so worried when I got in my truck earlier, I was too scared to truly check.

Now, with arms weighed down by the guilty shopping I'd done, I felt like a dog with its tail between its legs.

Stepping inside the small apartment, I was hit with the scent of *us*. This wasn't just my home anymore, was it? We hadn't really discussed if she'd be moving in, but the spicy-sweet of our union was home. My muscles relaxed, my mind further cleared. Tears collected in my eyes.

Home.

And when Ramona poked her head out from the loft to peer down at me, I almost dropped everything to race up to her. Because *she* was the true home. This apartment and this stuff didn't matter as long as I had her.

She scowled down at me, but I saw the softness she held in her lips. The worry in her honey eyes.

I glanced around the apartment, noticing now that it looked pristine. The damn floor sparkled. Now, I wasn't a slob, but I damn sure hadn't mopped once since I moved in. The books I usually had scattered wherever I had been reading or sketching at the moment were in a neat stack on the coffee table. Even the fucking windows looked cleaned.

Oh, she was pissed.

I cleared my throat and headed to the kitchen area. "Hey, Princess." Why did I feel like I was standing before a firing squad? Or facing down with Mara, armed with everything she could do and her fucking katana while all I had were my claws. Nah, I braced myself as she descended the steps, and I busied myself with unpacking the paper grocery bags. This was much scarier.

She propped her hip on the counter beside me, crossed her arms. Taking out the Maseca was suddenly very interesting, and I gave the shrimp a few once-overs to make sure that they truly were deveined.

When it was evident I wasn't going to say something, Ramona huffed. "Are you okay?"

I felt about five inches tall. It was one thing for everyone else to know that I wasn't shit. It was far, far worse to have my mate see me that way. Too weak to handle some silly nightmares that I didn't even remember by the time I woke up.

"Yeah." I couldn't look at her and see the rejection in her eyes, so I started on washing the vegetables and limes. The action at least let me do something with my hands, and I felt Ramona staring at me as I dried everything and began to work on the shrimp.

I chopped them into smaller pieces, tossing them in a bowl. "Do you want help?" she asked, almost hesitantly, and I risked a glance in her direction. There wasn't anger rolling off of her, but I couldn't parse through the nuance of her emotions. She didn't *look* like she was about to demand we dissolve our matehood.

"You ain't got to, baby." My southern accent slipped to the forefront, and I frowned.

With a light touch on my shoulder, she stepped up to the ingredients I had laid out. "Just tell me what to do."

"Um. You can slice those limes? There's a citrus thingy in that drawer over there," I pointed my knife at the right one, "and all the juice goes over the shrimp."

She nodded, her big curls bobbing, and we worked in silence to get the shrimp marinating. It went a lot faster with her beside me, and soon, I was starting on making the tostadas while she chopped the tomatoes, cucumbers, onions, and cilantro. Kneading the dough had always been my job before my life went to shit, and my hands worked with instinctual ease.

The soothing nature of making tortillas gave me enough courage to apologize. "I'm sorry, baby. For fucking up." The words sliced up my throat, but I needed to say them. She deserved that much.

Ramona sighed and finished the last cuts through the cilantro. "I didn't like that you left."

I nodded, jaw working as I tried not to fucking cry. My princess had already been through so much. She still carried those dark feelings with her, and I needed to at least be mentally steady for her. Knowing I already failed was making it hard to not break down.

I didn't realize I'd stopped kneading the masa and was staring off into space until her touch on my back snapped me back to attention. She rubbed in small circles, right between the shoulder blades. When I didn't pull away, she stepped closer and rubbed her cheek on my shoulder.

I was shaking, trying to hold everything in, but she was sneaky this way. My mate. Her touch was reassuring and safe. When was the last time that I truly felt safe?

"What do you need, Río?"

"Beats me." My chuckle was far too shaky for my liking, but there was nothing I could do about it. Even with the best of intentions, she couldn't erase all the wounds I'd covered with my tattoos and years on the run.

"Does that happen a lot?"

What was she going to do when I gave her the depressing truth? Even if I wanted to, though, I couldn't lie to her. "Off and on. Haven't had one that bad in a few months."

She placed a kiss over my work t-shirt that I still had on, right over my mating mark. "What normally helps you? I wanna know how to handle it better next time."

"Princess. It's not on you. You've got enough—"

"Shut up. Tell me. I promise not to panic again if it happens."

I clenched my eyes closed and began moving again. Not enough to separate us, though. I'd set out the cast iron tortilla press I had bought after my second year on the run. The store-bought shit never tasted right, so I indulged in the unnecessary appliance. Part of the reason why I had to buy a truck in that same year was because I couldn't really stop myself from holding onto little parts of normal life. My Iceman and a small amp. Art supplies. The comal that I had already set up and heating on the stove.

"I..." The masa was warm between my palms as I pulled from the large ball, creating smaller ones that would soon be the tostada shells. After I'd made a few, Ramona jumped in, working slowly to make balls the same size as mine. "Just trying to calm me through it, I guess? If it looks like I'm—hurting myself. Wake me up like you did."

She nodded and finished off the last of the dough, and I started flattening the first in the tortilla press. "I can do that."

She accepted this so easily. Being mated to someone so broken that they couldn't even trust their dreams not to leave them puking and overwhelmed. "Thanks, baby."

Ramona hummed and watched me transfer the dough circle to the hot comal with a practiced turn of my wrist. I gave it a few seconds, letting the masa cook, before flipping it over with my fingers. Once it was done, I moved it to a plate and went to press the next one.

My mate already had it ready, a little thick, but not bad. I smiled in thanks.

We had a little assembly line going, and after the tortillas were all made, I moved them to the pan of hot oil. My initial intention of a low-effort meal had turned into a long process, but the quiet, concentrated time with Ramona was nice, and the result would be way better than eating our ceviche with tostadas from a plastic bag.

I showed her how to fry in the cast iron skillet, letting her take charge of the tongs while I instructed. The apartment filled with the aroma of my childhood, and I'd almost forgotten how this morning began. At least, until she deposited the last tostada on the baking sheet I'd designated for draining. "I'm still mad at you."

I sucked in a breath, forced it out of my nose. "How can I make it up to you? I don't really know how to get the memories to stop, but I don't want to scare you like that ever again, and—"

"No. I'm n—you *yelled* at me." Her bottom lip jutted out ever so slightly. If she were a different person, I would've called the expression a pout.

It was hard for me to remember everything that'd happened this morning other than the exhaustion, the fear that she'd call this whole thing off, and the taste of stomach acid on my tongue. "I... I didn't realize. I won't do that again."

She sniffed and leaned over to kiss my cheek. "See to it that you don't." And that was that.

The rest of the air loosened between us, and we finished assembling everything, all the way down to the slices of avocado to top our tostadas con ceviche de camarón. The first citrusy crunch wasn't exactly like Mamá's, but it was damn close.

Ramona was letting out happy little moans and hums as she ate, and my chest swelled with pride that she enjoyed *our* food that much. The dish was light enough that we both made it through an ungodly amount of food—her appetite rivaled mine, and I loved it—but I'd made sure to buy enough ingredients so that we'd have leftovers. Cleaning the kitchen also took half the amount of time with her beside me, and soon, the apartment was just as tidy as when I'd entered, scared shitless that she was going to break up with me.

"Go shower. I'll find us something to watch."

We went in separate directions, and I sped through my shower so that I could finally get to the good part of holding her. It motivated me to confront the place I'd claimed my mate right before I destroyed the nest she made for us. My hair was still dripping as I climbed the steps, towel wrapped around my waist.

I stilled as soon as I caught sight of the bed.

Ramona was sitting cross legged in one of my shirts and nothing else. Her shoulders were hunched, back slightly curled as she braided her hair over her shoulder. With one hand, she paused the laptop and looked up at me. She'd… she'd made a new one. There were new blankets, more pillows, and pieces of our clothes woven throughout to make a cocoon of our scents. "Princess."

I blinked back the tears—what was it about this girl that was making me fucking cry all the time?—and continued up into the loft. She smirked, looking mighty proud of the little masterpiece she created, and I rushed through drying off the rest of the way and pulling on a pair of boxers. When I climbed in, she scooted just enough for me to settle nearly on top of her.

My purr rumbled, and I nosed my way into her hair. "This is perfect, Ramona." Normally, I slept with my hair loose, but I decided to braid mine for the evening, too. Mirroring her posture, I combed through my hair with my fingers and got to plaiting. Her curls were a lot thicker than my wavy strands, so I quickly caught up and was tying mine off at the same time she'd reached the end of hers.

She smirked and fiddled with the end of my braid, and I pulled her fully into my chest. "I love you," I whispered.

She tilted her head and pressed it to mine for a light kiss. "Te amo." When I jerked back in surprise, her lips pulled back to reveal a full grin. I'd never seen her smile this wide before, her amber eyes sparkling. "That means 'I love you', right?"

I swallowed and nodded. "Te amo. My mate."

CHAPTER THIRTY

RAMONA

I finished getting ready in the loft while Río stepped into the bathroom to take a shower and put in his contacts. He'd grouched about my not allowing him to hop in with me when I'd taken one earlier, but we'd be fucking *late*, knowing what usually happened when we shared the small shower stall.

I smoothed a hand over my dress and twisted in front of the mirror. Delaney and I had gone shopping earlier today while Río was at work, and the short halter dress had caught my eye. The color was a pretty coral that felt summery, and the loose skirt might've been considered scandalously short if I'd been shapelier. But Río had commented on my legs enough that I wanted to highlight them. The neckline dipped into a lower V, but I didn't have much in the way of cleavage. Would Río like it? When we'd met up downtown for our little day out, Delaney had sputtered as soon as he caught scent of me and squeaked a noise that completely mismatched with his size. Then, he'd crashed me into a bear hug, swaying and chanting about how happy he was for me.

When I'd continued to come back to the dress as we walked

around the shop, Delaney had talked it up so much, I decided to try it on. With my arms behind my back, I'd exited the curtained stall to his enthusiastic applause that made me blush.

The chunky, black leather sandals felt more like me and waited by the door downstairs. I gave my hair, held back in a low ponytail with two curls framing my face, one last once over and grabbed the black denim jacket before heading down. The shower had been off for a while, so I figured Río was about done. It was late enough for the sky to be those final shades of magenta before darkness took over. How Sylvie convinced my brother to make this formal meeting a double date, I probably didn't want to know.

Just as I hit the base of the stairs, the bathroom door opened, releasing a thin cloud of steam left over from Río's shower.

I wanted to melt into the floor. We'd dressed separately, and he was giving himself one last glance in the mirror before stepping out to face me. He stopped too, and it really was the first time we'd gotten dressed up to go anywhere. Most of our time was in casual clothing or naked, so it took a second for my mind to make sense of what had me almost foaming at the fucking mouth.

Río was in the nicest pair of black jeans I'd seen from him—most of his usual wear was ripped or thoroughly worn in from skating—and the leather belt at his waist was smart and simple. His white t-shirt looked soft and was thick enough to obscure the collection of tattoos underneath. The black denim jacket looked like the masculine pair to mine, and as he straightened his collar, I homed in on the collection of chunky, silver rings on nearly every finger. His hair was half up, and the jewelry in his ears and on his face sparkled.

"Come here," he commanded, voice low and huskier than usual. My feet followed his order without me thinking about it, and when we were less than a few inches apart, he started both hands at my wrists and moved them up to my shoulders and neck in a gently possessive gesture. The warmth of his skin was a significant contrast with the cool metal that made me shiver. And when he turned me around, manipulating me to his liking, I could barely breathe. Río traced his touch along the bumps of my spine that were exposed before crowding my back and wrapping his arms around me. His nose traced the curve of my throat, and he kissed my mating mark.

"I love you, and if I wasn't trying to make a good impression, I'd bend you over right now."

"Well, you've already pissed my brother off twice. So."

His chuckle was raspy, taking on that feline hiss that my body was trained to crave. "You're right." So fast that my mind spun, Río grabbed the base of my ponytail and pushed us around to the back of the couch. Where we'd fucked for the first time.

I'd been so nervous then, but now, when he guided my chest to rest on the tops of the cushions, I was already moaning loudly at the kisses he dotted along my spine. He pulled down my panties, and I kicked them off as quickly as I could manage.

He swiped his finger through where I was already slick and caressed my clit just lightly enough to leave me screeching out and pressing back onto him for more. After all our pre- and post-mating fucking, he knew what rhythms brought me to the top the quickest, and he wasted no time teasing me there. His other hand was palming and firmly holding my left ass cheek, probably watching with satisfaction what he was doing to me. If his grunts and groans were any indication.

A few final swirls made ecstasy flash behind my eyes, making my body quake and liquify at the same time. Río growled a string of approving words, a mix of English and Spanish, and when I finally came back down enough to register what was happening, his bare cock was pressing into me.

Río took my hips in both hands, his claws out and poking into my flesh how I loved, and I almost choked when he plunged in a long, deep stroke. "Fuck, Princess. You're a fuckin' dream." His hips met my bare skin, and the fact that we were both fully clothed, too impatient to undress even though we were at home, made this even hotter.

With every slow retraction of his hips, I pushed back on him, wanting him to *move*, but he was stronger than me and refused to let my urgency set the pace.

I mewled an embarrassing noise, impatient to have him ruin me, but Río kept on, going slow and ending each thrust with a deep, bone-rattling circle of his hips. "You know better than that, baby."

Over my shoulder, with tears in the corners of my eyes, I glared up at him. "Fuck me. We're—" I gasped as he snapped his hips again.

"You said it didn't matter if we were late. You wanted my cock tearing you apart so bad that you smelled like sex the second you stepped down here. So, take what I give you." The last sentence was more growl than words, and he increased how hard he took me, but never the pace.

My lower back arched, and the new angle nearly had my eyes crossing. Was I drooling? He was such an ass, but he knew both of our bodies like we'd been doing this for years. It couldn't have been more than five minutes of him fucking into me, but the tormenting pressure of him inside my body caused another release that was thunderous with how long it'd built. I had to force my fingers to uncurl from the couch, or the fabric would've become shredded with how my muscles tightened.

"You feel so good, baby." My face heated, but Río's loud groan in response was fuel that kept me babbling and moaning. "Fuck me so good, my mate, *fuck*."

Río let loose a loud, scratchy growl and kept on for a few more pulses until he stilled, grinding his hips into mine while he came with a deep rumble that I felt all the way into the floorboards. Our breaths synced as we settled from the aftershocks, and my mate draped himself along my back again, giving sweet kisses to the base of my neck. He pulled me tighter onto him, emphasizing his claim.

I fucking loved it.

"See? You should listen to me more often."

"I should see how *you* like it being ordered around," I spat weakly. The reality was, Río taking charge was exciting and always resulted in this exact outcome. He didn't have to be a bastard about it, though.

"Oh, I already do." He smiled into my shoulder and planted one more kiss before he straightened the both of us. With a bracing touch on my hip, Río pulled out, and I couldn't hide the non-human hum of deep satisfaction at the sensation of his cum starting to drip down my thighs. Me from three months ago would think it was disgusting.

Me now seriously contemplated swiping my fingers through it and popping them in my mouth. Oh, god.

He walked back toward the bathroom, leaving me swaying in post-orgasm bliss until he steadied me once more and swiped a washcloth between my legs. Río bent on one knee, holding my panties out and guiding me to step into them. He pulled them up my legs, eyeing the brown skin all the way, and settled them back on my hips. His lips pressed into the curve of the hipbone before he smoothed my dress back down.

Río looked up at me, black eyes glittering like the night sky, and his smile wasn't cocky. It was full and loving in a way that left no question of how he felt about me. I cupped his cheek, slipping my fingertips into his smooth hair. He kissed the inside of my wrist, eyes on me, before he finally stood.

"All right. *Now* we're late."

———

RÍO

Mating my princess before we left the loft should've helped ease my anxiety for tonight, but, as I climbed out of my truck, my palms were fucking sweating. The restaurant Ramona and her sister-in-law chose resembled a house, and the large porch in the front had been converted to a seating area illuminated with small lamps on each table. I took a drawing inhale, scenting that the Leader and his mate were already here. Shit.

I rounded the front of the truck to open the door for Ramona, but she beat me to it, scowling as if daring me to say something about it. Normally, I would've, but any snark I usually had in abundance had retreated behind the wall of anxiety I fucking felt. This was bullshit. I had reduced Leaders to their knees with packs twice the size of his. I'd threatened rival crime family leaders with words and the razor tips of my claws without a second thought.

None of them were my new brother-in-law. Who, from what I could tell, already hated me.

I retrieved the bouquet of flowers I'd bought on my way home from work this afternoon, the pink counterpart to the red roses I'd bought Ramona. She'd let out a bemused chuckle when I presented them to her, but she promptly trimmed the stems and set them in a cup of water on the coffee table with a little smile.

Grabbing Ramona's hand, largely for comfort, we walked toward the restaurant and wordlessly followed the scent of her family. My new family.

To put it lightly, I didn't have the best experience with these sorts of things, so maybe that was contributing to my expectation for this to blow up in my face. Just as we rounded a corner, I saw our destination. Or my demise, depending on how you looked at it. Which, based on how her brother was staring at me, unamused and utterly unimpressed, I was thinking it was that second one.

Ramona squeezed my hand and went a step further by bringing the back of it to her lips for a quick kiss. When she let our hands fall back between us, I tightened mine in thanks as we came to a stop.

Both the witch and Leader stood, but she was the one to step around the table and bring my mate into a hug like she hadn't seen her in months. It'd actually only been a day, but my princess hugged back and blushed as the witch marveled her outfit. Ramona had put her jacket on before we exited the car, but she was slowly unfurling, and I was honored—and more than a little emotional—to see it.

While they embraced, I stuck my hand out to the Leader who was dressed in a simple dark gray t-shirt and blue jeans. His curly white hair looked freshly cut, and he eyed my outstretched hand with a frown.

Feeling like a fucking idiot, I let it fall, but Ramona nudged me with her elbow and stretched up to whisper in my ear like they wouldn't be able to hear. "O doesn't like shaking hands." And understanding dawned on me. She'd already told me that, too. When I'd low-key paced the apartment and demanded the basics of how to win her brother over.

So, he gave me a tight nod, but I immediately noticed the rosy blush that started on his cheeks. It was easier to see on his pale skin, but it was just like how my mate would blush for me.

Feeling a fraction more relaxed, I extended the paper-wrapped bouquet of roses and lilies to the witch. "For you," I said, and the big smile she gave in response was almost infectious.

"Wow, these are beautiful! Thanks!"

I didn't miss the very canine harrumph the Leader gave as we took our seats. Or his narrow-eyed glance at me. "Oh hush, baby." Sylvie, I tried to remember to use her name, gave the Leader a kiss on his cheek that only made them redder. She set the flowers on the wide patio ledge beside her and grinned conspiratorially to Ramona. "Now you'll know what it feels like to have a possessive mate."

"As if she isn't the same way." I slammed my lips shut and prayed that my smartass mouth hadn't gotten me in trouble. You'd have thought with all the punishments, the tendency would've been eradicated long ago. In every other situation, I liked to think that it was part of my whole charm.

The witch—Sylvie—snorted and nodded. "Looks like we got two protective Wolves. S'not so bad if you ask me." The Leader narrowed his eyes at me again, as if I was the one talking about him, and put an arm around Sylvie's chair.

He finally spoke after our server deposited glasses of water and took our drink orders. "So, why did this happen so fast?"

My eyes widened, but Ramona just settled into my side while leaning toward him. "No one else can have a mate besides you? Doesn't seem fair."

He rolled his eyes as if he expected these sorts of retorts from my princess. "You just met, so I'm trying to understand how this happened."

"I don't think you want the details, O," she said, and I winced.

Sylvie heaved a big sigh and massaged her temple. "If you two would stop this back and forth, I'd like to actually get to know him."

I sent her a grateful smirk and cleared my throat. "Sure. Shoot."

Before she could ask whatever question was in her mind, her mate cut in. "What's your name again?" Though he wasn't meeting my gaze, and I knew now from Ramona's debrief that it was to be expected, there was an underlying meaning to his question that sent alarm bells off in my head.

"Uh, Río."

"Last name," he demanded a touch more gruffly, and I was getting more suspicious.

"Bernal." I drew out the last syllable, trying to gauge why he was reacting this way about something he surely already knew. Though it wasn't a *lie*, it was only one of the surnames I'd been born with. He couldn't possibly know that, though. Right?

His responding grunt made me feel even more uncertain, but when Sylvie started asking me about working at Vinny's, I tried my best to focus in on her cheery demeanor. It made me feel a little better to know that she'd worked there for a time a few years back, that she and the Leader had met there, just as me and Ramona had.

Our drinks and appetizers came, and by the time we finished the charcuterie board filled with intricately plated meats and cheeses, the conversation had thawed a bit. My new brother-in-law kept sending me looks, but I truly didn't know what the fuck his problem was. Aside from his initial, curt question regarding the timeline of our relationship, I didn't get the sense that he necessarily had an issue with the idea of his sister being mated. It was *me* that was the problem, but what else was new?

I'd gone with a steak for my meal, as had Ramona. The two of them ordered two different pasta dishes that smelled pretty good, but at the first bite of my filet, I was happy with what I'd ordered. Our chatter died down a little while we ate, but apparently, we were all pretty speedy eaters because it wasn't ten minutes later that we were pushing our plates away. Only Sylvie had any food left, but I supposed that made sense.

We ordered another round of drinks, with which our server brought the check. I snatched it before the Leader could, and I counted it as a win, triumphantly slapping my card down.

At least, until he leaned back and opened his mouth. "I'm going to have to be frank." Was this what it felt like to watch the flash of headlights before a car hit you head-on? "What's your relation to the Serafim Group?"

The beer I'd been setting back on the table slipped from my hand. My heart dropped just before racing like it had the night I'd left that life. Racing off into the night on my bike, I'd been convinced my father would catch me, send Mara or Catalina for my head.

Ramona caught the glass before it could topple over and make even more of a mess of all of this, but I couldn't bring myself to thank her or take my eyes off of her brother's. I couldn't tell whether I wanted to bolt or be sick.

The Leader sniffed, tasting the air and, no doubt, the fear that was clouding all of my thoughts. How did he know about my family? But that was quickly answered. I felt so stupid, thinking that Xo had just been passing through or following me on her own personal mission. Why else would she be here if it weren't for business? After all, I'd been sent to territories to make deals with Pack Leaders more than a few times in my old life as an enforcer. And with the decisions I'd made in that role, I knew that whatever contact he'd had with my family had been unpleasant.

No wonder why he hated me.

I clenched my eyes shut, wanting this all to be a night terror that I'd wake up from with Ramona's arms around me, her licking my face and saying she loved me. Instead, I'd seen the confusion in her honey eyes. I felt the prickles of her growing suspicion in my chest like it was my own, and I fucking hated it. No matter how far I ran, I should've known that my father would always catch up to me.

After a tense silence, I gritted out the response, "My father and sisters run the organization." There was no sense in lying, now.

"And they come to town, just as you start spending time with my sister. You take her as a mate after your siblings sent me to return to my pack with the dismembered head of one of our own. A son of an elder. Sitting here with you now, I can't deny the scent of family you all hold." He spoke low enough to keep the conversation private but direct so that I couldn't escape.

Despairingly, I opened my eyes and looked to my mate. Her brow was furrowed, looking at me like she didn't know who the fuck I was, and that just about broke my heart. I should've known I wouldn't be able to have such a precious thing in my life. But, selfishly, I'd wanted her.

I swallowed and forced back the tears that were starting to collect in my eyes. "It's the reason why I left. I didn't want that life anymore. You may not believe me, but I love your sister more than anything, and my family has *nothing* to do with us."

I turned my head again, taking in the sight of my princess since it was looking like it was the final time. She looked so beautiful. Had I told her tonight how much I loved the curls that draped so cutely on the sides of her face? Or how bright she looked in that dress? What about the fact that with her, I felt… good. Like I wasn't the worthless one in a family of Shifters.

My princess raised her hand, and my old instincts had me bracing for her to hit me. *It's what you deserve, after all.*

Instead, a soft caress met my cheek, and I was helpless in keeping a tear from falling. I clenched my jaw, fighting the memories that flashed through my mind, and the adrenaline that was still pumping into my blood. But I wasn't going to attack or run. Even if this was over, I wouldn't do that to Ramona. Not after the last time I'd fled from her.

"These are the people that hurt you?" she whispered, and I cracked my eyes open again—when had they closed?—to find her meeting my gaze head on, searching.

When I'd been dragged to the Serafim compound, I'd tried to keep a brave face when I thought it was a great idea to enact a hunger strike. My father who, cruelly, looked so much like me, had stood in the room, arms crossed, while his soldiers took turns beating me.

I'd been ten. And left to heal in my room alone, without food for two days.

When, at fifteen, I refused to rough up a mother for lapsing on her loan from us too many months in a row. Secretly paying her balance out of my own account, Cata had ratted me out, as she was the main keeper of the family's finances. Pai ended up ordering the young Fox that'd reminded me of Mamá to be killed anyway. In front of me and right before he ordered Xiomara to shift and break my legs, along with the general beating that'd been meant for the Fox. But something about the combination of shock, head blows, and cracking my skull on the concrete floor in one of our warehouses had been too much for my shifter healing. When I'd woken to Mara sneaking into my room and setting my legs and smuggling me painkillers, the world was blurry.

I swallowed, snapping back to the here and now. "Yeah." I fucking hated how much my voice shook. Though the power being a Serafim enforcer brought was intoxicating, I wasn't cut out for that life. Not like my sisters who'd been snatched up by our father since birth. Our mother had started out as a fling and ended up meaning nothing more than a prized breeding source for my father's little army of Shifters. Even though I'd been born a disappointment, he'd decided after my tenth birthday that I at least had some use and trained me to be a killer.

Ramona nodded decisively and leaned forward. I'd have fully accepted her ripping out my throat, would have preferred it to her denying me, but, instead, she held my face and kissed my nose. Then my lips, followed by a little lick along the side of my face.

I grasped her elbows, forced myself to exhale. In my ear, she whispered, "I believe you, my Río. Te amo." Over her shoulder, she glared at her brother, lips pulling back in a snarl—on *my* behalf. "You apologize to my mate right now, or I'll never fucking forgive you." The bright venom was gone from her usual barbs, and a cold conviction stood in its place.

Her brother appeared less prepared to rip my life apart at the seams, but it wasn't looking like he was ready to fully back down, either. "Because I hurt his feelings? I have a pack and my *family* to protect. And in case matehood has made you forget, Mona, that includes you."

His green eyes flashed, and though I wasn't Wolf, I sensed the layer of Leader authority now lacing his words. Ramona stiffened around me, body called to obey, but she continued to snarl. "You don't know what they did to him, so shut the fuck up. Do you trust me?"

He grunted but nodded without hesitation.

"Well, I trust him. I love him, and unless you forgot, you can be born to a shitty parent without having to answer for their wrongdoings."

The Leader blinked and glanced in my direction once again. The tension between all of us was so thick, a knife through it would probably leave thick trails of blood. A low, raspy rumble started, and it took me a while to realize that it was my mate. Growling and coiled to defend me.

Finally, her brother came to some sort of conclusion. "I will not apologize for being suspicious." Ramona's quiet growls grew louder but not so much to draw notice from the tables nearest us.

"But I will for upsetting you, Mona. And for provoking any unpleasant memories for you. Jaguar."

"He has a name, you stubborn asshole," she hissed, and I would've swelled with pride at having such a fiery mate if I weren't already a combination of keyed up and fucking crashing.

The Leader glared, almost as viciously as my mate could. "Río. And you will give us all the information you can to help us deal with your family." Without so much as a goodbye, he stood, signaling the end of this train wreck of a double date.

The rest of us were slow to our feet, me most of all, but Ramona's steady hand around my bicep gave me support. I couldn't believe she still wanted me, now knowing full well how my family was. Naively, I'd hoped she would never discover the full scope of how terrible they could be and how I had been. I wished every day that I could forget, myself.

We followed the Leader silently to the parking lot, and it did cross my mind that perhaps he'd just try to kill me. However, when we came across their car first, he and Sylvie stopped to face us.

She looked me up and down, and Ramona started her low growling again. I pulled her into my chest and kissed the top of her head. "I can't speak for my mate, but I believe you. Don't make a fool out of me or my sister." With that, she slid into the passenger seat. Orion closed the door for her. "Tomorrow, you will come to the witch house to discuss all of this with me. If you don't, you'll no longer be given the benefit of the doubt."

I managed to nod. There was no love lost between me and the Serafim family, anyway. It'd been nothing to drop my father's name as soon as I'd left that night.

We watched them both go, and it was with Ramona's lead that we eventually made it back to the truck. She deposited me at the passenger door and told me to sit while she drove us back home. I didn't even have the energy to refuse, so I handed her the keys.

The rest of the night passed in a fog. One that kept me from the clarity that would've made me embarrassed at Ramona's careful encouraging me up to the loft and undressing me as if I were a child. I stood stiffly beside the bed, waiting in a haze as she quickly built another nest. And when she pulled me into her arms, whispering about how good and loved I was by her, underneath the exhaustion, I was eternally thankful that she'd deemed me enough to keep. I fell asleep with my mate's head on my chest, her kisses over my heart taping it back together.

CHAPTER THIRTY-ONE

CATALINA

The soldier, a shifter of some species I didn't care to recall, repeated the news that left me chilled to the core. We'd finally added air conditioning to the warehouse office—what the fuck was with places up north not having A/C?—and it droned in the background, muffled beneath my rage.

The Glock I had resting on the desk was in my hand in half a second, bullet hitting the soldier between the eyes in a perfect shot. He slumped to the ground, but thank god for concrete floors.

"One of you! Clean this shit up," I directed the command to the others who'd been standing off to the side. They'd been with us long enough to look unfazed at my disappointment. One darted out of the room, presumably to retrieve cleaning supplies, while the other hoisted the body in his arms.

Xo squeezed in the doorway while our employee moved the body. This was turning out even *more* irritating than the situation back home—why were all the Wolves we came across determined to give me migraines?

Xo stepped over the pool of blood before my desk and whistled. I could smell the blue raspberry sucker she'd chosen and declined an offer of one from the depths of who-knew-what in the pockets of her tailored trousers. One time, when we were children, dressed no different than we were now, she'd been carrying three ravens' beaks, a dragonfly, and bubble gum.

"And where the fuck have you been?"

She shrugged. "Doing what you asked. Tailing the Wolf whore."

"And?"

She waved a hand, as if this wasn't important to her. There was a reason I handled the logistics and money while Xo did the field work. When she'd told me she stumbled upon someone *very* interesting while strolling around town, I'd figured we could use it to our advantage. As always, it paid off to have her true form a closely kept secret from all outsiders that we dealt with.

And when this good for nothing pack of rabid *mutts* somehow blocked our business permits going through, I decided I'd had fucking enough. It made sense that they had influence in official places, but we'd dealt with enough packs that just fell apart or in line when we blew into town, I hadn't given it any real consideration. They were making *me* look like a fool, and I wouldn't stand for it.

"Well, since you don't wanna go for the Leader's house, I found the next best thing, prolly." Xo shrugged again and bit into her sucker. She threw the stick onto the pile of blood another soldier was now trying to bleach and clean up. Pulling another sucker out of her pocket, she pulled the wrapper off and stuffed it with whatever else she had in there. This one smelled like cherries, and she popped it right in her mouth. "When you wanna do it?"

I sighed and pinched the bridge of my nose. At times like this, I almost missed our sniveling brother. After reporting that she'd caught his scent, when Xo went out again, he'd apparently left town.

Pai had been bordering on disgusted when Río was born, but, in my opinion, he didn't need some impressive gifts to wield a fucking gun. Claws and fangs could come in handy—all that Xo could do was more than an asset—but even shifters could get real cooperative when you had a gun to their temple. Less blood splatter that way, too.

"Did you find out when their next pack run is?"

She pulled out her phone and started scrolling like I hadn't just asked a fucking question. I waited, vein on my temple feeling like it was going to explode, as she snickered at whatever was on her screen.

"Xiomara!"

"Eh? Oh, next full moon. S'three days from now."

"Well, get shit ready!" Only she could get me to raise my voice from the carefully cultivated calm. Even when I killed, the angrier I got only resulted in a colder precision. I pulled at the chignon that was too damn tight on the back of my neck, letting my loose, dark brown curls fall into a haphazard heap that brushed my shoulders.

My sister tapped her phone a few more times, gave a final snicker, and turned her screen around to show me a photo of some roadkill that looked a week old, at least. *Meu deus*, I was surrounded by *idiots*.

She pouted, like I was supposed to understand whatever the fuck she found so funny, but put her phone away. With an exaggerated solute, she clicked her heels and chanted, "Aye, aye, captain!"

RÍO

The Leader and I sat overlooking the garden, and this time, he'd offered me a beer to go with our little meeting. The first time, when I'd recovered a little from feeling like I was for real going to lose my mate, he'd been more than short and suspicious of me. He hadn't even let me in the small white house, making me stand in the drive and unload all the basics about how my family operated.

Now, on my third visit, we'd graduated to sitting on the screened-in porch. I'd already told him everything useful. How there hadn't been a pack that'd truly resisted the Serafim Group. Either they became part of the operations, or they acquiesced to them planting the legitimate businesses to launder the funds from the weapons and drugs. My father had started off as an aspirational loan shark and grown an empire—in both the supernatural and human arenas—within two decades. If he wasn't such an evil motherfucker, I would've been impressed.

"What you're already doing is smart. But I'd also make sure that Mountain's Peak Pack is absolutely ready to come help at a moment's notice. My sisters are good at what they do, and you pulling their licenses is only gonna make them angrier. My father might be removed enough to just transfer them elsewhere, but I can't be certain his motives for coming here are purely for profit expansion. Just keep watching *your* back, especially." I winced. "When we'd take down a group, the Leader was the surest way to wipe out the rest."

"Have they made contact with you again?" He stayed facing the garden and took a sip from his bottle. He'd been nursing the same beer since we'd come out here, but mine had been sitting empty for a while.

"No. Not since my sister came to talk to me that night at Vinny's."

He harrumphed, calling to attention the unspoken fact that it was also the night that I'd taken his sister as a mate. He'd backed off on thinking I was with Ramona as a way to ingratiate myself with him and the pack, but I could still tell that he wasn't a fan of me.

At this point, there wasn't any information left for me to give him aside from anecdotes from my teen years that were all kinds of fucked up or most likely unhelpful. He listened through them all, face never changing. But I was becoming more accustomed to how he spoke, and after my mate's speech before our first meeting, I was doing my damnedest to not take this personally.

"You're both the most important males in my life, so I need you to figure this shit out and get along. O, stop being a stubborn asshole, and Río, te amo. Don't say anything smart." With that, she'd given me a kiss and retreated into the depths of the garden to give us space. No doubt listening to our entire conversation in case she felt the need to intervene.

I fiddled with the empty beer bottle and checked my phone. Ramona and I were gonna have to head out soon, but I didn't want the Leader to feel like I was running. "Have they done anything else?"

He shook his head. "No. And the quiet worries me." He'd kept from me any plans they made to deal with my sisters, but, as far as I was concerned, we were all the better for it. If Xiomara decided to pop up on me again, I didn't want even the possibility of her picking up on me knowing more than I should.

"Río, are you ready to go?" Ramona hollered from the raised vegetable beds, and I turned in that direction. She was in just a sports bra and athletic shorts, long legs looking golden under the cutting rays of the sun. She pulled off the gloves she'd put on to handle the plants, and Sylvie stood, too. They were far enough away that the conversation I had with the Leader felt private, but not so much so to make me anxious he'd try something. Like punch me with that right hook again. Really, if I hadn't tried to barge in when Ramona had been in a bad way, we probably would be a bit further in our... truce. Than we were now, anyway. Oh, yeah, and if I hadn't smart-mouthed him when I brought Ramona home that first time with her breath no doubt smelling like my dick. Really shot myself in the foot there, now that I was thinking about it.

Trying to find some common ground, I surreptitiously ran my gaze over his side profile, the black ink on his arm catching my eye. The art was thicker, more intense than what I had, but I could tell the artist who'd done it was skilled. "Nice tattoos. Where'd you get 'em done?"

He didn't turn, but by the furrow of his white brow, I knew he heard me. "All on my arm were done by a member of my old pack when I lived near Cape Cod."

I nodded and tilted my head. "The old Celtic style is cool. Wait—was that all hand poked?" He nodded, and I whistled, impressed. I pointed at the wolf that ran along his arm, recognizing one of the symbols. "Is that a faoladh by chance?"

The Leader raised his brows, his expression shifting just enough to show the barest hint of surprise. "Yes."

Boyish excitement filled my lungs, and he wasn't looking like he wanted to shift and rip out my throat, so I pressed on. "The faoladh were always one of my favorites of lycanthropic mythology. Well, I guess they're not myths, obviously," I snorted. "Sure, some shifters can't keep their instincts together, but most of us just want to live and respect the land we reside on, right? I used to have *tons* of books on folklore and shit when I was a kid, and I remember this particular one about a farmer who unknowingly saves the son of a family of faoladh."

He wasn't saying anything, so I kept on. "Irish folklore is really interesting—you know that they used to have a shit ton of wolves until the last sighting in the late eighteenth century? Never been there, but I wonder if any Wolves still reside there. I'd suppose so."

I took a breath and realized that I'd been rambling. When I was knee-deep in my interest in these topics as a teen, I'd gotten made fun of by my sisters, ignored or punished by my father. But, sneaking a glance at my brother-in-law, his shoulders were the *tiniest* bit more relaxed. "My grandfather's family came to the states to get away from the persecution of wolves. I'd imagine that I still have some distant cousins that stayed behind, though."

My mate had apparently been listening to our conversation, and she wandered over and rested her hand on my shoulder. Before I could stop myself, I pulled her down into my lap. "No, I get that. My avó was a Jaguar, so the family packed up and moved from Brazil to start over. Not sure all the reasons, but deforestation and people hunting jaguars was definitely a motivator."

The Leader nodded, and his eyes fell to his son who'd walked over and was trying to get his attention. The Leader got up to let him in past the screen door and plucked something off his head. When I saw the large spider that he lowered into a nearby dahlia bush, I suppressed a shudder.

Orion pulled his son into his arms and kissed the top of his head. "Are you leaving now?"

I startled at the abrupt halt to the conversation, but Ramona just twirled a lock of my hair around her finger and answered, "Yeah, we gotta get ready for the show tonight." We were playing a set at one of the bars downtown, and even though my band responsibilities had taken a backseat to the shitstorm that'd been going on, Ramona convinced me to go through with tonight, knowing that being around my friends and playing would make me feel better.

The Wolf pup started grasping for the Leader's beer bottle, so he pushed it out of reach. Ollie, the kid's name was, shot me an affronted look, as if asking me if I could believe that shit, and I couldn't help but chuckle. I hadn't been around kids since my little brother, but drawing a little grin out of my mate's nephew didn't give me a wash of grief like I expected it to. More just aching nostalgia for the days when I helped Mamá take care of Javi.

I swallowed the longing to see both of them again and brushed a thumb along the curve of Ramona's knee. Her winter grapefruit scent was mixed with the aroma of earth and heat from working the garden where Sylvie and Dahlia were still harvesting.

"All right. Bye." The Leader said simply and stood, taking his son with him toward the rest of their family. The pup gave us a little wave over the Leader's shoulder, and I waved back, letting out my claws to waggle in a way that Javi used to love. Sure enough, the little boy screeched a little giggle before his sister snagged his attention.

Ramona cupped my jaw and kissed my temple. "I think he's starting to like you," she whispered in my ear.

I moved my head so that I could meet her lips to mine. We kept it PG since the kids weren't too far away, but desire started swirling in my gut with her support enveloping me and her cute little ass sitting right over my dick. "Or just decided I'm more use to him alive than dead."

She traced just over my mark, not even needing to see it to know where it rested beneath my shirt. It made a shiver ripple down my spine. "Trust me. He wouldn't have let the kids around you if he didn't like you. Wouldn't have talked about his dad's family. If he doesn't have to, he won't engage in any pretending. It was genuine."

I sighed and kissed the side of her neck, where I knew she was sensitive. She wiggled in my lap, and I chuckled, holding her tighter. "If you say so. Ready?"

She flicked the ring I had in my septum and smirked. "Ready."

CHAPTER THIRTY-TWO

RAMONA

The bar was beginning to fill, and I tried to stretch my senses to keep track of where Río was backstage. His oversized hoodie was a dress on my frame and kept a steady waft of his scent calming me, the trail of the real thing leading to the door where he'd gone through to meet the rest of his bandmates.

I fiddled with the beer I'd been nursing since he plopped me at one of the high-top tables with the best view of the stage. This was my first show as his mate, and bubbles of excitement popped in my chest like champagne. The last one I'd gone to had been the night I kneeled for him, but now, he was officially *mine*.

The last few days had been rough on my mate. But when we went back to the apartment, I could tell he was in better spirits as he started getting his show gear together. When he insisted on us showering together, I couldn't refuse him then or when he pressed me up against the tiled wall as hot water cascaded around us.

"Hey, Ramona!"

I turned toward the deep, excited voice and couldn't help smiling back. Delaney's golden waves fell in pretty ripples, just kissing the tops of his brows. With his size, the sea of people quickly parted, but he muttered pleasant 'excuse me's' along the way. My smile didn't fall, but my eyes widened at the sight of his outfit, which was a far cry from his Montessori teacher or gardening wear.

The black Arch Enemy shirt was cut in half, revealing his tanned and toned stomach that was dusted with a healthy amount of hair. The sleeveless top highlighted his toned arms. His gray jeans were baggier, but with the way some were staring in the direction of his ass, I assumed that they were just as flattering as the rest of his outfit.

Like he didn't sense any of the attention he was getting, he opened his arms, and I fell into them immediately. I didn't know where my usual bites or apprehension went, chalking it all up to the kind, puppy dog energy he brought with him. We patted each other's backs and separated.

"Do you want to sit with me?" I gestured to the other chair at my small table.

"Sure!" He clambered into the seat, and I worried for a moment about it taking his weight. Mine even seemed a bit wobbly, but he settled in just fine. "How are you?"

His eyes were a few shades darker than his hair, and a light flush colored his high cheekbones. The way he asked the question wasn't that of a passing pleasantry, equivalent to saying 'hey'. His attention was turned to me, waiting and truly caring about my answer to the question.

It was no wonder I'd immediately softened toward him when we met. "I'm good. Excited for the show. You?"

He grinned, his teeth slightly crooked in a way that added to his charm. "Same. My roommate invited me and bailed at the last minute. I'm so glad I spotted you!"

The tension in my shoulders from sitting alone had nearly disappeared completely. I pointed to his shirt. "Didn't take you for a metal fan." Though, I supposed the same might be said about Sylvie if you didn't know her too well. Actually, Delaney and Sylvie were similar in the bright kindness that surrounded them.

The difference, though, was Sylvie's smoldering wrath underneath. With my new friend, I suspected he was all sweetness. He blushed harder and continued to chat with me. Apparently, his roommate had introduced him to the genre, and after being wary because of his upbringing, he'd gotten into it.

"What about you?" He gestured toward the stage, where the lights had been turned on to full blast, and those around us had gone lower. People moved toward the stage, getting closer or making sure they were settled with an acceptable view. My heart pattered with the anticipation that I'd see Río in his element once again.

I shifted in my seat, recrossing my legs and throwing my braid over my other shoulder. "Um, yeah." I said as someone began to emerge and a round of cheering started up. A touch more quietly, I followed with, "My mate is one of the guitarists." Naming what he was to me felt so good, and Delaney's wide eye and squeal of delight made it even sweeter.

I was no longer just rich girl or princess. I was Río's. *His* princess.

Six months ago, I would've slit my own throat for wanting to gush about such a cringey term of endearment. But who knew that it would feel so amazing? Not just powerful and sexy but safe as well. And when he kissed my scars…

Río emerged from backstage with the rest of the band, guitar already slung over his shoulders. The little braids I'd put in his hair were brushing against his cheekbones as he took his spot beside Tyler, the vampire I was coming around to feeling was a friend, too. Well, a good acquaintance, at least. The darkness that surrounded him was death two times over, and though it was small on my now growing list of reasons, the thought of him handling my body if I tried to off myself again was enough of a deterrent.

I had to give it to Tyler, though. It worked for him as he

prowled to the microphone, grungy makeup hardening the baby-faced features I'd seen at the skate spot and his home.

The Concrete Executioners didn't introduce themselves to the crowd with words but a reverberating string of deep, growly notes from my Río.

The rest of the members joined in, filling the bar with harsh, heavy music that I felt in my bones. Tyler's low, scratchy voice started soft but turned into a commanding boom that melded so perfectly with Río, Brody, and Jess's playing.

Not that I was really taking in much of the music. Río's hands were their own work of art, flying and strumming with long fingers that'd been everywhere on my body. His foot, clothed in a thick black boot, tapped along with Jess's work on the drums, and with the chorus of the song swelling with Tyler's screams, Río threw his head back, letting the music pour out of him.

As it ended, he looked right at me, bottom lip clenched by his teeth. He winked and grinned at whatever expression I wore on my face. For all I knew, I was drooling or staring with my tongue lolling out of my mouth. Ass.

The song started to come to an end, and Delaney's playful shaking of my shoulder drew my attention. He leaned in and spoke close to my ear. "Oh my lord, is *that* your mate?"

His excited smile lit up his whole face, and I felt my heart flip with pride in my Jaguar. My lips quivered with my battling urges to beam and keep my face flat. When I nodded quickly, I knew I'd lost to the former. "He is."

Delaney gave me a happy squeeze before resting his arm on the tabletop. He gave me his attention while the band rolled into another song. "Tell me everything from the beginning again! I'm so happy for you!"

Hopefully the heat on my face wasn't visible. There was no way I could go into full detail of how we'd first got together with my sunny friend. No matter if he looked like sex on a stick at this event. The sultry curl of his lashes and lingering stares of people around us didn't change the innocence that shone in his eyes.

So, I decided to skip over the explicit stuff, starting in a stilted, gushing rhythm. When I glanced back toward the stage, Río was still watching me, but his sexy and carefree posture had hardened. I arched a brow, unsure what had changed. Maybe he'd messed up the song? Or been irritated that I'd been speaking with Delaney instead of directing all of my attention to him?

I sped through the rest of our story to Delaney who responded with enthusiastic noises and exclamations, and while I answered his follow up questions, I kept my body and eyes angled toward the stage. Unease churned in my stomach at the switch in Río's demeanor, and the urge to question him about it left me feeling antsy.

Luckily, there were two other bands playing the local show, so Río and Tyler's band's set was fairly short. Their last song garnered a resounding roar of cheers and applause, mine and Delaney's joining in.

I watched Río stomp off stage, his back so straight that I could almost see his muscles tight beneath the fabric of his t-shirt. What the hell was going on in his head? I'd witnessed some of his moments, but nothing this quick and without a clear explanation.

Bar chatter increased while people spoke or made their way to get drinks before the next set. I'd still been nursing my beer, and Delaney wasn't drinking at all. There was nothing to do but wait until Río came out here and I could pull him away to ask what was wrong. If he didn't leave altogether. Would he do that? *Shit.*

My friend sighed, chin resting in his palm. "You're so lucky, Ramona. A great family and a new mate. Maybe your good luck will rub off on me."

It took me a moment to catch back up to what he was saying while completely unaware of the turmoil that was whirring around in my chest. "Ah, I guess. It's still new, but—"

"Hey, beautiful." I knew that voice, but it was the wrong one. Tyler sidled up to our table, still shorter than Delaney even while he was seated. My friend looked back at me, frowned, then turned to Tyler.

His jaw clenched, and he straightened in his seat. The gentle guy surprised me again, features hardening in a way I would've never expected. "She's taken." Delaney turned back and blocked me from Tyler's view.

Oh good grief, he was cute. And so unaware, because Tyler definitely knew I was Río's, and his hungry eyes hadn't even been on me.

Though he was normally the quiet, brooding shadow to Río's more lighthearted one, he was completely undeterred. If anything, he looked even closer to eating Delaney whole.

Before I could inform my friend what was actually happening, Tyler did it for me. He leaned an arm onto our table, grabbed Delaney's jaw, and turned his head back towards him. "Not talking to her. Let me buy *you* a drink."

My friend's Adam's apple bobbed while his face pinched in confusion. Vampire scents were weird, less distinct than other creatures. Maybe because they were technically dead, I couldn't parse out Tyler's emotions, but I didn't really need the ability with the lust written all over his face.

"You want to buy *me* a drink?" Delaney squeaked.

Tyler smirked and caressed his thumb on Delaney's face. "That's right, baby boy."

"Um…" My friend glanced back at me with uncertainty, and I gave him what I hoped was a reassuring thumbs up.

He took another nervous swallow, but I didn't catch what he said when he tuned back to Tyler because hot breath and a harsh hiss ghosted down my spine. "Come here." The command was emphasized by a hand on the base of my neck, pressing into my mark. But instead of inciting fear, I leaned into the demanding touch.

"Are—" I'd been about to ask Delaney if he was going to be okay if I got up to leave, but Río's tightening grip made my words die on a pleasured whimper.

"Now." And he pulled me out of my seat. I let him guide us through the crowd that was preoccupied with the new band starting up. His hair swished on his back, his boots thumping against the dirty bar floor. He was pissed, that much was for sure, and while I was nervous for the reason why, I was also relieved that he hadn't done something stupid and left.

Río took us down a back hallway, opened a door, and took me inside. Old, beaten sofas and wobbly tables sat amongst walls decorated with show flyers. Bags and instrument cases littered the floor, but I didn't have much time to take in my surroundings before I was spun around and pushed up against one of the tables.

"Who the fuck was that?" Río's front crowded my back, and I sucked in a gasp when his teeth closed around the skin below my nape. Not close to breaking the skin, but it was close to how he'd made me his mate. I bit my lip and moaned.

"Wha—what?"

His hands snaked beneath the hem of the sweatshirt and found the edge of my underwear. On instinct, I widened my legs and braced my hands on the sticky tabletop.

Río squeezed my ass and took another nibble on my neck. "You were talking to and smiling at that fucker who just said you were taken."

Holy shit. He was jealous.

If I weren't internally squealing at the realization, I would've laughed in his motherfucking face for thinking that anything would come between us. My conversation those weeks ago with Sylvie proved to be true. The *thought* of looking at someone other than my mate just didn't happen. There was also the fact that my friend had no interest in females whatsoever.

I smiled over my shoulder, taunting my mate that liked to say *I* was the territorial one. Río's nostrils flared, and his eyes narrowed to thin slits. "He's my friend and a teacher at my niece and nephew's school. I thought he was hot when I—"

Crack.

He'd rucked up the hoodie and slapped my ass. Instead of outrage, I just moaned and arched my back even further. Río cursed under his breath and delivered another spank to the other cheek. "Give me a reason I shouldn't go back out there and kill him," he growled, and the sound of his belt tinkling and zipper lowering forced another anticipatory groan from my throat. I couldn't see what he was doing, but it made the moment even more loaded. We were clearly in one of the green rooms backstage, and anyone could walk in.

I wanted it all.

Except for him killing my friend, at least. By the sound of his voice and the way his claws dug into my hip, I believed his threat. He pulled my panties to the side, and I whimpered his name. The head of his bare cock nudged at my entrance, spread me wider, and I pushed my hips back on him even more. The tip slipped in easily with how slick I was and still being stretched from earlier today.

The small noises coming from my throat exploded into a grating screech when he slammed in the rest of the way. Río grabbed hold of the braid he'd put in my hair before we left the apartment and forced my neck to arch back. His other hand held my hip, pulling me back to meet his punishing thrusts.

My eyes were rolled back, breaths punching out of me. "Whose fucking pussy is this, Princess?" he snarled in my ear.

When I didn't immediately respond, mind slipping away to be completely overtaken by the pleasure we created together, he spanked me again. Which really wasn't the best way to get me to respond. I was already so close.

"I said, whose tight little pussy is this? Answer me." With a hand on my back, he pushed me down onto the table. He delivered a hard plunge into me, making my toes scrabble inside my boots and my fingers tighten into fists on the flat surface.

"Y—*fuck*—yours. Yours."

He slowed his movements to grasp the back of my left thigh, hoisting it up and onto the table, too. When he thrust into me again, I had to bite down on the back of my hand to keep from downright screaming. The music outside was loud, but I would easily become loud enough to draw attention. And Río was no better with his curses and grunts while he worked our bodies to the edge.

He gave a hard, biting kiss to the side of my neck. "That's right, baby. Mine. And whose dick is this?"

"Mine."

"Fuck right, it's yours. Don't fucking forget it. Now, come for me, baby." The stinging slap of his hand on my ass and fucking forward of his hips while he held me down nearly made me faint. The door opened, and there was a surprised choke, but it didn't matter. When I turned my head, mind distantly recognizing the horrified eyes of the person interrupting, I couldn't care less. My muscles coiled unbearably and released in a rush, my vision whiting out as I came on Río's cock.

Just a few moments later, Río's hips stilled, and warmth flooded inside of me as he came. Almost black-out fuck drunk, I nearly asked him if he had something to plug me up so that I could keep his cum in me.

He gingerly placed my foot back on the floor, and I hummed blissfully as he nuzzled into the collar of my hoodie and kissed my mark. Our breaths calmed together, our aftershocks settled together, and my thoughts began to solidify with his hands rubbing gentle circles on my sides.

The walls vibrated with the music and cheers outside, and after a few more minutes, Río slowly pulled his hips away. He slid out, and the wet trickle of his cum tickled my skin. Yeah, the idea of plugging myself up didn't feel as urgent, but matehood was its own sort of drug, because I still didn't hate the idea.

Río's footsteps and presence drifted away, as if he was searching the room, and when he came back, it was with the drying passes of napkins between my legs.

I heard the swish of him throwing them away just before he pressed reverent kisses to both my ass cheeks. Without a word, I lifted my hips at his tugging on my underwear. He slipped the soiled fabric off my legs, helped me step out of them, and guided me to straighten from the table.

I blinked, trying to refocus to the room, and the furious strain was gone from Río's face. Instead, he looked at me with amusement and fondness.

"Hey!" I exclaimed as he stuffed my panties into his back pocket.

He held his hands up, as if I didn't see with my own two eyes what he'd just done. "What?"

I cocked my fist and gave his arm a punch. He didn't budge. "You were being an ass. And that's gross—" My words cut off in a yelp when Río hoisted me into his arms and carried me to one of the sofas against the wall. We plopped down, me in his lap again, and my cheek found its happy place in the crook of his neck.

"I'm not gonna apologize for needing you to know that I don't share."

I huffed and stayed right where I was. "I didn't really need the reminder."

"No? Cause I'm still debating whether or not to sever that dog's spine. It'd be quick, too." Instead of bristling or chastising him, my shoulders shook with laughter. Río pulled back to look down at me, brow furrowed in exasperation. "What the hell is so funny? I'll do it."

I rolled my eyes. "Boys are so stupid. That guy is my friend. Remember me mentioning Delaney before? And he's one hundred percent gay. As in, not interested in me. Though, we should probably make sure Tyler doesn't eat him."

Río relaxed into the back of the couch and ran a finger around the curve of my ear. "Well then, I'm… sorry for overreacting."

"Like I said. Stupid. But I love you, so I guess it's okay."

He chuckled and kissed the tip of my nose, following it with a pass of his tongue up the side of my face. His purr tickled my skin, and I giggled like a fool. *This is what it feels like to be happy*, I thought to myself. A day in the sun with my family followed by an evening with a new friend and my mate.

"So, how did it feel—"

The door opened, letting in a flood of heavy metal music,

cheers, bar smells, and a scent that had my blood literally run cold. My mouth clamped closed, and my eyes widened. The blurry figure of the person I'd seen just before Río made me come was now clear as day. No, no, no.

"Ramona. What the fuck has gotten into you?"

CHAPTER THIRTY-THREE

RÍO

I stared down at Ramona, laughing and perfect in my arms, and felt that my heart was more intact and full than it had been in… ever.

Seeing *my mate* with that hunky looking male had almost made me throw down my guitar and storm off stage to rip out his spine. I'd fumbled my way through our whole set while I saw nothing but red.

Now, though, she laughed at my ridiculous possessiveness, unaware how close I was to doing exactly what I'd threatened. What was one more body amongst the sea that'd died at my hands? Sure, the past eight years had only involved those that threatened my own safety, but I still remembered what it was like to kill for other reasons. To carry out orders, out of anger. Out of cold blood.

Ramona opened her mouth to speak, and I focused back in on her pleasant weight on my thighs. I'd had to keep myself from half-shifting while I fucked her, just allowing enough for my claws to extend. It was hard with how comfortable I felt around her. How could I not when she let me so freely past the cold and sour exterior to revel in the sweet, too?

The door opened, but I paid the person no mind. This was the first place I could think of to bring Ramona in my haze of rage, but I knew it was only a matter of time before someone from one of the bands came back here to get their stuff or chill after their set.

But instead of drunken laughter, it was a harsh hiss that made the beginnings of a growl churn low in my chest. "Ramona. *What the fuck* has gotten into you?"

She went absolutely still in my arms, no longer loose and free from our fucking. Now, *that* pissed me off. They'd walked in earlier, but both of us were too far gone to so much as spare them more than half a glance.

Ramona was sure as hell looking now, though. "What are you doing here?" Her fingers tightened in my shirt, crushing the fabric with a panicked touch. It wasn't quite bone-chilling fear that wafted off of her, but I wasn't able to decipher the particulars of emotions like she and her brother seemed to be able to do.

What I could tell, though, was that this female was Wolf, and they both knew each other. "What am *I* doing here?" the female scoffed and gave me a disdainful up and down. My arms were still tightened around Ramona, back turned a bit to partly shield her from the onslaught of whatever this was. "I'm here to bring you back to your senses. But clearly you're further gone than I thought."

My brows rose at the apparent insult directed at me, and I felt the familiar coldness creep in. What was it with everyone not thinking I was dangerous? Maybe I wasn't as determined to shake my family's legacy as I'd thought, because this shit was really starting to piss me off. It was cute when Ramona rolled her eyes at it, but everyone else could go fuck themselves. Including this icy-blonde intruder.

I took a drawing inhale to further see what I was up against, and I felt myself go cold for other reasons. Oh, shit.

"Yeah, 'oh, shit.'" Had I said that out loud? "Now, get your filthy hands off my daughter!"

"Mom!" What should've been a petulant whine came out as close to a growl as my little non-shifter Wolf could muster. I'd grown used to the noise that she'd let out any time she felt like I was in danger, so it wasn't as shocking to me as it seemed to be for her mother.

Her mother. Dios mío, this was turning into a mess I had never anticipated.

"Did Orion tell you where to find us?" At least Ramona wasn't trying to get up from my lap or let go of me. I halfway expected her to, especially with the realization that her mom had walked in on us while I was asking her daughter who my dick belonged to. Shit, I'd never done it before, but I knew for a fact that this was not how you wanted to meet your mate's mother.

Had I begun to think of how I'd introduce myself to this female that Ramona had only briefly described as 'intense and judgmental'? Putting my hair in a neat bun or a braid, trading the jeans and t-shirt for the tailored suits I'd grown to hate so much— but maybe Ramona would like seeing me in one? I'd gotten rid of the silver cow skull bolo tie I always wore while working for my father, but I'd find another or one similar. No fucking way would I wear a normal tie. It was an act of rebellion I'd stood by since I was a child. But I'd bring flowers, dark-colored, beautiful ones with supple petals and bright greenery, and a bottle of wine for her parents. I'd use every ounce of the manners Mamá taught me.

And here I was, messing up another meeting with my mate's family from the jump.

Instead of maybe a little wary, her mother now had a very negative first impression of me. One with her daughter bent over a table. Well, if I ran away with Ramona, it wouldn't really matter anyway.

Her mother scoffed and took a disgusted look around the room, arms crossed. "No. Your ungrateful brother wouldn't answer the phone, and when I called his wife, she claimed to not know where you were. Just that you weren't with them." Did I mention how much I liked Sylvie? She almost ripped my face off that one time, but she'd very quickly grown on me.

Ramona's shoulders relaxed minutely, undoubtedly glad that her brother and sister-in-law hadn't divulged the information that they were privy to. "His mate. And the mother of your grandchildren, by the way."

Something flickered across the female's face, but it was quickly erased with more of that pinched annoyance when she looked at me again. As if being angry with me was easier than facing Ramona's words. Ah, was she one of those mothers that were weird about their son's female partners taking them away or something? There was no doubt in my mind that when we finally reunited with Mamá, she'd embrace my mate with open arms.

"Leave. I need to speak with my other ungrateful child."

I opened my mouth, but Ramona bristled and shot back. "He's not going anywhere, and neither am I." Her words were firm, but her breaths were picking up. Arms still against my chest, she started pulling at the cuffs of the hoodie. I gave her a reassuring pet on her back and kissed her temple. If I couldn't kill her mother for being one of the factors that'd pushed my princess into such a deep depression, I would at least comfort her during their confrontation.

"You let him treat you like a whore, you stupid girl. What has gotten into you? Your father and I gave you far too much for you to act this way. Have you completely lost your mind?" Her voice rose to a biting yell that grated on my ears.

And instead of biting back, I felt my Ramona let loose a tremble. I tore my gaze from her mother to find her jaw clenched hard enough to crack a molar and the beginnings of tears shimmering in her eyes.

All right, that was it.

I gently removed her from my lap and whispered in here ear, "It's okay, Princess." When she continued to cling onto the front of my shirt. The skin of the backs of her hands was petal-soft, and after a few coaxing rubs, she released me.

My own father's abuse had come with calm, quiet commands, hard looks, and blows. Yelling didn't trigger me, but I already knew it did for Ramona. I stood between the two of them, shielding my mate from view once again. She'd been through enough.

"You need to leave."

Her mother swallowed but stood her ground. "I'm her mother."

I gave a dry chuckle. "You are. But if you're going to continue speaking disrespectfully to my mate, I'll have to make you leave. And I'd rather not."

Instead of acknowledging what I said, she looked around my shoulder and settled those pinning blue eyes on her daughter. "You're not thinking clearly, Ramona. You have a whole life back in New York. An apartment and a fantastic school to go back to. Are you really giving that up for a boy you certainly have no future with?"

I growled, pissed the fuck off at her implication that I couldn't give Ramona what she deserved and the fact that she'd hit a little too close to the worries that'd kept me up more nights than not.

Ramona shot to her feet and stood beside me. "I didn't give up anything for anyone." Her voice trembled, but she pressed on, "I left because I needed to. Being here with Orion, Sylvie, and the kids has been good for me. *He's* been good for me." My heart gave an excited thump.

"This is ridiculous—" The female started toward Ramona, hand outstretched to grab my mate's arm, but I took hold of her pale wrist instead.

"That's enough," I snarled. "You don't touch her."

She struggled with my fingers on her. "And who the fuck are you?"

I could tell it was a question she didn't give a shit about the answer for, but it slipped out of me anyway. "I'm hers."

The door to the green room opened, filtering in the roar of cheers and glasses clinking, and a few members of the band that'd gone on after us barged in with wide smiles and panting breaths. They were too hopped up on their post-show adrenaline to pay us any mind, continuing to rave about the crowd and their set.

I took the opportunity to turn back to Ramona. "You ready to go, baby?"

Her honey eyes looked up at me like I hung the moon, and her back was no longer curling forward but straight and strong. The tiny nod she gave me was all I needed, and I dropped my hold on her mother and replaced it with my arm around her shoulders. I couldn't resist kissing her temple as I marched us back toward the bar.

Brody and Jess were in the audience, cheering on the band that was playing now, but Tyler and the Wolf I was still not opposed to killing were nowhere to be found. All of them were just a passing thought, though, as I led me and Ramona outside and back toward home. By the tightness in her shoulders, I knew that she wasn't in the space to be around others right now. The shit with her mom ran deep, so I would take her where it was safe to process. Whatever she needed from me, I'd provide.

CHAPTER THIRTY-FOUR

RÍO

I steadied my bike while Ramona climbed off and removed her helmet. I cut the engine and kicked down the stand, parking beside Sylvie's red car. The harsh, winter frost scent of her mother was heavy in the summer air, and I rolled my tense shoulders.

Last night, I'd sat, rebraiding Ramona's hair for bed, and listened to her run through the years of animosity between she and her mother. How she'd felt under a microscope while also shoved to the side. The female had gone from the Leader's father to living with her parents before meeting her current husband, all but renouncing her shifter nature. Even the idea of that made my fucking skin crawl, and if you asked me, that seemed like the main reason why she was so miserable.

And like Ramona, I'd grown up with money. But I had been as depressed as I'd ever been while living in a mansion with my father.

"You sure about this, Princess?" I set both of our helmets on the seat of my Ducati, and Ramona shrugged out of the jacket I insisted she wear, now that rides with me were a regular thing.

Underneath, she had on another dress, apparently borrowed from her sister-in-law. The spaghetti straps weren't something I'd ever seen her in before, but she looked more than beautiful. The burnished yellow color complemented her skin and hair that she unclipped now that we'd arrived.

Ramona nodded and shot a slightly nervous smile my way. She'd insisted that I not cover my tattoos or take out my piercings when I'd thrown out ideas to appease her mother, but I did have her tie my hair back in a tight braid at least. My clothes were basically the same ones I'd worn to the disastrous date with Sylvie and Orion, so hopefully that wasn't a bad sign of what was to come.

Because her mom had demanded a dinner with everyone before Sylvie and Orion went on the pack run. To meet me and catch up with her son and grandkids.

Whether out of courage, spite, or a little bit of both, my mate had decided she wasn't going to hide her scars from her mother, and I might've shed a tear or two when she told me. I locked our fingers together and kissed the back of her hand. "I'm so proud of you." And the shy grin she aimed my way made me weak in the knees.

We went slowly up the front steps, and when Ramona turned the knob, the door was unlocked. I'd grown more used to the particular flavor of congregated Wolves, but I still preferred the unique blend of Wolf and Jaguar that filled our apartment now that Ramona was staying with me.

I kneeled to untie my boots, but went for Ramona's sandals instead. The silver buckles were warm under my fingers, and when I freed her precious little feet, I watched her blush and bite her lip. I helped her step out of her shoes and nuzzled the curve of her calf with a smirk. A flash of desire lit her honey eyes, and her shy smile took a different edge. I wanted to run us back home and make a new nest to stay sequestered in all night.

A throat cleared, cracking the moment I was having with my mate, and, lo and behold, it was her mother. She was holding a squirming Ollie and glaring at me like I was lecher, contaminating her daughter with my touch.

But, based on all Ramona had told me, this female's opinion about me had little to no weight in my mate's eyes. Now that she'd grown old enough to get out from under her mother's thumb, it really was Orion and Sylvie I needed to impress. Her father wasn't here to smooth things over, so if my mate's mother was determined to hate me, I was determined not to give her any ammo but strive for nothing else.

"Mrs. Wells." I nodded and untied my boots. When I stood and toed them off, I wrapped my hand around Ramona's waist.

The female didn't respond aside from a purse of her lips while the Wolf pup continued to squirm and start to whine. His little hands pushed against his grandmother and stretched out toward my mate and me. "Oliver, hush," the female chastised her grandson. Far less harsh than she'd spoken to me, but it still rubbed me the wrong way.

It probably wasn't my place, but I brought me and Ramona closer to her and reached out for the little guy. He practically leapt out of his grandmother's arms and into mine, this time clinging to my shoulders.

"Hey, bud. You ready to eat?" That was something he understood, and he gave a happy nod and waved to Ramona.

Ramona tickled her nephew's belly while I bounced slightly in place, swaying with Ollie resting patiently in my arms. My mate squared her shoulders and faced her mother. "Hi, Mom."

"Ramona. Are you ready to explain yourself?"

Instead of crumpling in the face of her mother's intensity, my mate just sighed, years of exhaustion deepening the action. "There's nothing really to explain. I was done with New York and needed to take care of myself. I met Río, and we fell for each other."

My heart thudded with pride and love, but her mother just scoffed while crossing her arms. She wore an expensive looking sundress, not unlike what I saw my oldest sister wear in her downtime. My mate's mother's white-blonde hair was secured with a headband that matched the color of her eyes. "What the hell do you mean take care of yourself? You've been given everything you need your entire life. You should feel *grateful*. Not blow up your life and run to your brother, disrupting him and his family."

Ramona blinked, clearly wounded by her mother's words. Through our time together, Ramona had once told me that she feared she was inconveniencing Sylvie and Orion by moving in, and of course her mother was able to zero right in on that insecurity.

Keeping my voice even, I cut in. "That's enough. I'm trying to be respectful, but I won't have you talking to my mate like that." To Ramona, I nodded toward the kitchen where I could hear the sizzling of our dinner and Dahlia, Sylvie, and Orion lost in a conversation. "You wanna go help them out with dinner, Princess?"

"*You* don't tell her to do anything, you degenerate."

A light snarl, complete with a flash of her blunt teeth, erupted from Ramona and aimed toward her mother. "We will leave right now and never see you again. Keep trying me."

Her mother blanched but tried to hide her surprise with a huff, tossing her hair over her shoulder. But I was staring at my mate. God, she was the most perfect thing in the world, and I would take on any and everyone to keep her safe and happy.

"Meredith. You know that we talked about this." Orion came walking into the room, mouth noticeably pinched in a way I'd never seen. I turned Ollie towards his dad, and the pup went more than happily. The Leader paused for a moment before deciding on something and nodding at me in thanks. Ramona's words from yesterday coursed through my mind. Maybe I really was making some headway with my brother-in-law.

He definitely wasn't as cold with me yesterday as he was with his own mother.

Meredith narrowed her stare at her oldest. "You may be a

Leader, but you're still my son. And Ramona is practically still a child, someone I am supposed to *protect*."

Orion swept his eyes over all of us before a crash in the kitchen made him flinch, followed by twin yelps of, "Sorry!"

"You've never been mated, so you may not realize that insulting one of our mates will result in swift consequences. Should you wish to stay here and visit, you'll act accordingly." The female had never mated his father, either? I shook my head and grabbed Ramona's hand as we followed Orion back toward the kitchen and dining room.

I'd never seen this part of the house before, but it was a mix of cozy wood, stainless steel appliances, and a nicely crafted dining table and chairs.

"Auntie!" We were settling at the barstools that separated the kitchen and more formal dining area when Dahlia waved from her little stool that allowed her to reach the counter and help cook. When she turned to me, she wrinkled her nose. "Mommy said I could call you Uncle Río now."

Sylvie shrugged from her perch beside the girl, and I chuckled. Aside from Orion and Ramona's mother's determination to be outright combative, this night was already so different than any experience at my father's home. It reminded me more of how things felt when I lived with Mamá and my aunt. And at least, here, it seemed that Mrs. Wells's threats held no weight. How refreshing.

Somehow, I got put on dishwashing duty, and the females insisted I put on an apron to match Orion's. How I got saddled with the pink one with red roses instead of a far cooler one that was black with flames, I didn't know. Probably because when my mate held it out to me, I was so wrapped around her finger that I didn't protest.

Ramona put my jacket on the rack by the front door, and I soon was up to my elbows in soapy water. Apparently, Sylvie and Orion were the type of people to clean as they cooked, but it was preferable to have my hands busy, anyway. Ramona and her mother sat on the barstools, sipping from glasses of wine, but while her mother asked snipping questions to her son and Sylvie, Ramona and I talked enthusiastically with Dahlia whose job was to help roll the little balls of gnocchi across the back of a fork, giving them the characteristic indents. She often looked to her father for reassurance, and in between taking the brunt of his mother's attention for the moment, he gave Dahlia soft instruction and encouragement.

Ramona held Ollie in her lap as I washed the last few dishes and Sylvie brought the platters of food to the set table. When we all congregated in the dining room, my pink apron shed to the side until after dinner, I fell into a seat beside Ramona, with Dahlia on her left. Orion, Sylvie, and Ollie were across from us, with Meredith taking the head seat. Orion went first, serving his mate and children with helpings of gnocchi and chicken with pesto sauce, before turning to his mother with a sigh and depositing a small portion on her plate. I went next, putting food on my princess's plate and halting when she gave me a sweet nod that what I'd given her was enough.

I didn't often eat Italian food, but it smelled fucking good, so I loaded up my plate until it was a big green heap, and followed everyone's lead, digging in. The herbaceous sauce was just light enough to go with the heat of outside, the chicken perfectly cooked and seasoned. "This is really good. You can cook, dude," I complimented and continued to inhale my dinner.

Orion didn't respond, just acknowledged my words with that same nod, but I took that as a win, too. With most of my food gone within two minutes, I leaned back for a breath and rested my arm behind Ramona's shoulders. She shot me a look while hunched over her plate before rolling her eyes. Didn't miss how she sat back to settle into the bit of contact, though.

I made sure to swallow my food before giving my mate a kiss on her cheek and returning to my plate. I felt ice on the side of my face, where Ramona's mother was boring holes with her glaring, but I'd faced far scarier foe. Something also told me that if I were still earning a crime family enforcer's salary, she'd be a little more understanding.

"So, what do you do?" Ah, there it was.

A large part of me wanted to ignore her since she hadn't used my name to address me, but I also didn't want to *outright* cause more trouble. I chewed my last bite of food, swallowed, and took a clearing sip of water. "I'm a manager at Vinny's Pizza." Wasn't gonna lie. The unimpressed glare that pinched her done-up face was way harsher than any my Ramona had given me.

"I know what it means to get swept up in young love, but this whole thing seems very premature. Mating is a serious commitment that neither of you are in the position to decide on."

I patted my napkin over my face and continued to keep my posture relaxed. Over Ramona's head, I gave my most polite smile. "I'd have to disagree on that. But I'll respect your opinion. Loving and mating your daughter is the best thing I've ever done."

Meredith's cheeks flamed as Ramona stretched to nuzzle into my neck. I buried my fingers in her hair, just keeping her close, and redirected myself to ask Sylvie about her newest novel. She shot me a grateful look and launched into discussing her book that was close to being finished and ready to send to her editor. Orion monitored Ollie as he ate his chopped up portion with his hands, smearing green sauce all over his chubby cheeks.

Ramona reached out to the basket of soft bread that I was pretty sure was homemade, and I felt the air chill a few degrees colder. "*What* happened to your arm, Ramona?"

My princess froze, and I watched in real time as a tidal wave of emotions crashed into her. Fear, anger, resolve. When we'd dressed this evening, she'd fully expected an interrogation, but the reality of the thing was very different. Sylvie and Orion were noticeably tensed, as if waiting for Ramona's cue to jump in and shut Meredith down. My back further relaxed into my seat, ready to judge and react to whatever was about to go down, protecting my mate at all costs. She'd said she wanted to face this, knowing very well that there was a possibility she would further limit or cut off all contact with her mother after this visit. I didn't pull her any further into me, knowing that she wouldn't appreciate me giving her mother more reason to pounce, but I did add pressure to my arm around her. Letting her know that I was ready to step in at any point.

Ramona closed her eyes, took a breath, and straightened her spine. I wanted to purr in approval but held it back.

Before she could open her mouth, her mother's blue eyes blazed, glaring at me as if she could will me to freeze over. "What did you do to her?" Meredith's voice succumbed to her Wolf, reverberating and becoming rough.

Sylvie stood and waved Dahlia over, to which the little girl reluctantly abandoned her seat and plate that was long finished. Orion pulled Ollie out of his highchair and handed him to Sylvie. At the very least, Meredith paused long enough for Sylvie to lead the kids away before growing more vicious. "I will kill you for hurting her, you absolute scum."

"*Mom*," Ramona returned the growl. Still, she lowered her voice, should the kids still be in earshot. "I tried to take my life. Did you think to ask me *why* I left everything in New York? Did you check in with me for the past, I don't know, ten years or so while I was depressed and cutting myself?"

The female's sustained grumbling stopped while confusion flittered over her features, as if Ramona was speaking another language. "What are you talking about."

Instead of growing angrier, Ramona just sighed and shook her head. "I was in a really bad place for a long time. And I'm finally clawing my way out. With the help of my mate, and O and Sylvie. My friends. I have a… mentor, and living here has been good for me."

Meredith looked like she was short-circuiting, but I was more focused on how Ramona was relaxing like an anvil had been lifted off of her back. I nosed my way into her hair, I couldn't fucking help it, and drew in the thick grapefruit aroma. I pressed kisses into her scalp, and her body rumbled with a silent hum.

Finally, her mother found her words. "Why on earth would you think killing yourself was the solution, Ramona? You always have me and your father to speak with. We would've gotten you *help*." At least she had the decency to sound regretful and less accusatory. Slightly.

I shot her my own withering glance and waited for Ramona to respond. She locked her fingers with mine beneath the table. "At the time, I just wanted the hurt to stop. It was more about that than anything. And, no. I don't have you to talk to, and Dad only checks in with me when you convince him to make the time. I didn't trust you especially to remain uninvolved from any help I *did* try to get. It was probably the wrong decision, but it led me here, and I'm really, really happy now." I kissed the top of her head. My stomach still wanted to drop empathetically, knowing the never-ending despair all too well, when I imagined how Ramona had been in those days. How those sort of days would still crop up. The difference, now, was that she had support and stronger foundation within herself to be a soft ground when she fell or needed to rest.

Meredith didn't have a response to that, and Ramona had taken on a delicate shiver from the surge in adrenaline of finally revealing the truth to her mother. Her restlessness, I felt like it was my own.

I reached up and caressed the line of her jaw. "You wanna help me with the dishes, Princess? And we can go home for a movie?"

Orion, who had remained silently supportive through the whole encounter was watching Ramona, some kind of communication flitting between them, if the tiny shifts in his expression were any indication. A small smirk shifted his pale pink lips, and he shook his head as if Ramona had thought something amusing in his direction. Ramona let out a little snicker before turning to me. "Yeah." She grinned, like the sun breaking through the clouds of a winter day, making the snow glitter. My purr released of its own volition, and I kissed her plump lips softly. There was no stopping it.

When I turned to Orion, he gave an annoyed huff, but it sounded more of innocuous irritation, rather than true disapproval. "You sure you won't need us?" I left the other half of my question, whether he really wanted Meredith to babysit the kids while he and Sylvie went on the pack run, unspoken.

He stood and began to gather the empty plates and glasses. "I'm sure."

Meredith retreated somewhere in the house, and I heard the distant trill of an outgoing call before the slamming of a door. Ramona, Orion, and I cleaned the kitchen in a comfortable silence while Sylvie reappeared with the children. Dahlia looked like she was burning to ask questions about that happened, but even she seemed afraid of her grandmother, because she kept them to herself. They wiped down the table and collected the rest of the dishes, and soon, the dining room was sorted out, and the kitchen sparkled.

At the door, Ramona and I put our shoes back on, and I slid into my jacket.

"Bye, bye," Ollie said around the fingers he had stuck in his mouth. I released my claws to wave at him like I had yesterday, and his lips spread into a joyful grin while he leaned into his mother's chest.

Dahlia clung to the side of Orion's leg and stared up at us with her bright green eyes. "Are you gonna take me to skate soon?"

Ramona chuckled and crouched to be at the pup's level. "Sure thing. Do you want Río to come or for it to be a girls' day?"

Dahlia leaned into Ramona's ear and whispered loud enough for us all to hear. "Girls' day this time. Boys can come after that." I watched fondly as Ramona kissed her niece's cheek and agreed to their girls' day.

When she straightened, I took her hand in mine and nodded to Orion. "Thank you for dinner. Sometime soon, we can have you all for dinner, if you'd be willing." Hastily, I added, "No pressure, though."

Sylvie offered an encouraging grin and nod at her mate who sighed ruefully, just as I had when Ramona suggested I wear the pink apron. "All right."

I fought the urge to reach out my hand to shake his, remembering his reaction to the last time I'd done it. As if realizing we were having a peaceful moment, Meredith walked up the hall, and every person, even Ollie, stiffened slightly in anticipation. "Ramona. We'll talk more about this later." She looked between the two of us and waved a flippant hand. "What am I supposed to tell your father?"

"Tell him the truth," I supplied. My mate's mother looked at me as if I'd lost my mind. "Who knows, maybe he'd want to take you as a mate, too. I couldn't imagine keeping Ramona without fulfilling that part of both of us." I nodded at Sylvie and Orion and paused to see if Ramona wanted to say anything else. She didn't pipe up with anything, but she did give Sylvie a quick hug and offered a fist to Orion. He softly bumped it with his knuckles, and she gave a final wave to her mother.

We walked out of the cabin, the purpling sunlight speaking promises of more peaceful days ahead. Really, I was ready to take on anything with Ramona with me. After putting on our helmets, she took her spot as my backpack and locked her arms around my waist. The deep rumble of my bike was as comforting and familiar as my mate's presence, and I couldn't wait to be home and further wrap us both in the serenity of each other.

CHAPTER THIRTY-FIVE

RÍO

It wasn't like we'd done anything but eat and socialize, but as we made our way home, I felt bone-tired. How Ramona survived living in a home with that female, I had no idea. Her words were like blows, and the constant battle left a headache starting behind my eyes.

Luckily, though, with the space filled with the aroma of us, the pain was already lifting. I knew Ramona didn't need the lights, but they let my eyes feel a little less strained. The lamp in the living area was sufficient and cast a yellow-tinted glow. Ramona took meticulous care of the roses I'd bought her, but I was gonna have to get her a new bouquet sometime soon. I swiveled a look around—actually, I'd have to encourage her to put her stamp on this place. Now that I was helping Orion take on my family, I'd see it through. To ensure the safety of my mate's family.

Maybe we could keep this place *and* travel. This could be our home base while I showed my princess the world. Would she enjoy that?

Ramona wound her body around mine and braced her hands on my chest, breaking me out of my wandering thoughts. Her hair had a sweet indent from the motorcycle helmet, but her honey eyes looked darker, and I didn't think it was because of the low lighting.

"You were so great, Río."

My chest swelled. "Yeah?"

"Yeah, you did so good with my mom and family. The kids love you, and. Yeah. Just perfect. Good."

Well, if that didn't clear my headache and let loose a delighted purr from my depths. My cock took notice and hardened in my jeans.

"I'm so glad I met you, Río. You're the best mate. Te amo." My lids lowered as her words swirled around in my head and trailed down my spine like the light caress of her delicate fingers. Ramona was sweet in her own sour way, but she fucking did things to me when she said stuff like this.

Ramona worried her bottom lip with her teeth as I pressed our bodies together, fitting like two puzzle pieces. She caressed the corner of my jaw, and I felt her heartbeats pick up faster. The little smirk that ticked up the corner of her lips had me pausing in anticipation, now suddenly horny as fuck. "You're such a good boy."

I had to flex my fingers to keep my claws from ripping into her dress. I searched her face with wide eyes, the reality of her words and scent about to send me into fucking orbit. Or into a puddle, seeping through the floorboards. Fuck.

"Do you like it when I say that, Río? Tell you how everything you did tonight was right?"

Dios mío, she was going to fucking kill me. When had I gotten so hard? If she kept on, I was going to come in my jeans. But if she kept saying shit like that, I might not be too mad about it.

Ramona trailed her finger down the side of my neck, sweeping around the tattoo there before continuing down my chest where my heart was threatening to fly right out. "So, you said on our first date, that you'd maybe let me tie you up." Her brown skin had a bright red flush, but she pressed forth, "Was that a joke?"

Oh, god, I was rolling my hips against hers, trying to get more friction to find some relief. No, it hadn't really been a fucking joke when I said it to her, though I'd intended for her to take it as one.

"Because. You're so good to me. I want to take care of you, too." She snaked her hand between our lower halves, pressing against my hard dick that was screaming to be in our mate already. Or spreading open her pretty, full lips. Painting her face with cum.

I groaned at the mental image and more mumbled praises from my mate. When I was able to focus on her again, she was a mixture of shy and smug and excited. I was never gonna live this down. "Congratulations, Princess. You've discovered I have a praise kink. Don't start acting up about it." But, who was I kidding? She'd already won.

She led me by the fucking belt buckle up to bed, but I was more than eager to follow. She could've led us both over a cliff, and I would've gone happily.

We didn't turn on the lamp up here, so there was only a faint trace of light from downstairs. I was already shedding my jacket and t-shirt while she got to work on my belt and pants. None of it was fast enough, if you asked me.

Lifting the dress over her head was much quicker, and she shimmied out of the black thong. I'd have to steal that one, too. Sue me for wanting something to scent when I was away from her.

Ramona pushed me toward the bed, and I went more than willingly. My heavy cock plopped against my belly as I lay outstretched, and enough precum was dribbling out to start running down my front. I gripped my hard cock, staring at Ramona like the goddess she was, all long limbs and supple curves.

She bent to pick something up off the floor, and when she straightened and I saw it was my belt, I had to squeeze the bottom of my shaft to keep from busting.

My mate smiled nervously, and if that wasn't the cutest thing.

At least, until she climbed onto the bed, slinking over to me in a motion that was more jaguar than wolf. I was proud and nervous and so fucking horny, I couldn't think of a single snarky thing to say as she straddled my hips but refused to fully seat herself and press against my dick.

"Put your arms above your head, Río," she said, still chewing at her lip like she couldn't believe she was doing this. Taking the control of this moment when I was usually the one to call the shots. She'd soon find out that I was more than fine to give her the reins.

I did as she said, back arching slightly as I fumbled to grab one of the spindles of the headboard. "Good boy," she whispered, and my breaths released in a tender, crackling purr. The tightening of my belt around my wrists only made me harder, pulsing just far enough away from Ramona's pussy to feel its delicious heat but barely brushing where I wanted to be so badly. But she hadn't told me to do that, and I *wanted* to be good.

She bound my hands to the bed, though we both knew that it wasn't a true restraint. I could get out of these binds whenever I wanted, but it was that my princess trusted the both of us enough to do this. To unfurl even more.

"Okay, um. What's your safe word? We should do that, right?" She tucked her hair behind her ears and sat back on my thighs, waiting.

Honestly, I was more just trying to calm my breathing so that I could make this last. Still, all the blood had rushed to my dick that was now almost looking angry and weeping precum. "Uh..." I forced an exhale through my nose and wet my lips, trying to get my thoughts to coalesce. "Um, it's araña."

Ramona leaned forward, bracing her arms beside my shoulders and leaned down to kiss my forehead. Then the tip of my nose. But when she started at the corner of jaw and dragged her tongue to the top of my hairline, I almost lost my shit. An embarrassing whimper escaped, but there was no stopping it. I curled my toes and fingers, now tipped with claws, tensing and trying to think of anything that would keep my release at bay.

She pressed her lips in a soft, barely-there gesture to my earlobe and whispered, "What does that mean? I took French in school and was never great at it." She chuckled and it sent my entire body into goosebumps. My cock flexed, needy bastard, and flopped back down against my abs. That jostled my piercing, and I had to clench my eyes shut, whimpering *again.*

"Río?" She made her way down the side of my neck, finding home at her mark on my skin, the little minx.

I full on groaned, and my hips thrust uselessly, mindless for some sense of friction to help get me over the edge. "T-trying to be good and not come, Princess. W-what was the question?"

Ramona straightened a little bit. Her hair was like bounding clouds, shimmering with light that matched her honey eyes. They were liquid gold, and the mischief and adoration stole my breath. She smirked and dragged her finger in sweeping lines across my cheeks and around my lips. "I asked what araña means."

That was something to hold on to. It was my safe word for a reason. Even with my curious nature as a child, my admiration for living things big and small, the thought of one touching me still made me shudder. I could marvel at their form and all the variations nature created while still being weirded out by all the legs.

I managed a slight frown at the thought of it. "Spider. Creepy little things."

She stopped painting invisible patterns on my skin, blinking wide until her full lips broke into a wide, sweet grin. "I don't like them either," she said, and I groaned again, throwing my head back. Of course, because this Wolf girl had been made for me, and me for her.

RAMONA

The coincidence that didn't feel like one at all had me giggling, of all things, and Río continued to shake and squirm beneath me as he tried to keep a hold on himself. I didn't know what the fuck I was doing, but my suspicions about how he'd react to something like this had been building through the course of our relationship. The confirmation was better than I'd imagined, but I didn't realize it would turn me on *this* much.

I fought through the embarrassment threatening to halt the words coming out of my mouth, blush furious and commands halting. My mate seemed to like it, though. That was all that mattered.

"Baby. Look at me." It took a second for him to lower his head, but when he did, my mate already looked a wrecked, half-crazed mess. A large amount of his hair had fallen out of his braid due to his squirming, his black eyes were somehow hazy and frantic at the same time, and his body was shaking with held-back urge. Was this how he felt when he was over me? Contorting and working my body how he pleased to bring us both into ecstasy? I could already see the appeal.

I took hold of the end of his braid, removed the hair tie, and unraveled it until the long waves fell across his shoulder. "You look so handsome, baby. The most beautiful and sexy male in the entire world." His lush black lashes fluttered with the praise, hitching in a gasp before settling on a deep inhale. "I couldn't have picked a better mate. You're everything I need, my perfect Jaguar. Aren't you." His long, lean muscles were tense, beautiful lines of inked brown.

Río was a combination of coiled and melting at my praise, but more of the strain fell away as I ran my touch over his pecs that were hard and steady. When I flicked the barbells through his nipples, though, he jolted like I'd shocked him. He moaned a long, drawn out sound as I continued to gently flick and twist his dusky nipples and piercings. The black metal seemed to make him extra sensitive here, and I cursed myself for not doing this sooner. "You're so good to take care of me like you have. Such a good boy."

A steady stream of precum was running from the head of his

golden brown cock that looked swollen and painful. "P-princess, you're gonna kill me." His deepened, gravelly voice was a growl, whimper, and plea all at once.

"Well, you look like you'd come if I just look at your dick long enough, so we'll do something else first." I increased the force on my attention on his nipples, just a little. "Do you think you can taste me? And make me come first like a good boy?" I took a risk and blew a gentle breath toward the head of his dick.

I watched in awe as Río writhed and nearly screamed. Twin tears collected and started to fall from his eyes, but by the overwhelming swell of his hot and sweet scent, I knew that he was crying from pleasure and trying to do what I said.

On my way to his mouth, I bent down and dragged my tongue across the hardened nub on the left, careful to not press myself into his cock that was literally pulsing with need. I was already wet enough, nearly dripping, and this would be over far too soon if I made that slip up.

More tears were running down the sides of his face into the pillow, his teeth biting so hard into his lip that it would've probably started bleeding if I hadn't moved his hair out of the way and straddled his face. Mentally, I pulled my list out to take notice of this moment. Number Fifteen, with Río trembling from my praise, and his reaction sending us both into a new kind of heaven.

My mate's eyes opened, now completely blissed out and looking at me like I scattered the stars. He presented his tongue for me.

How I'd ever been shy about doing this with him in the beginning, I almost couldn't fathom. Because as soon as I sat on Río's face, he lapped and tasted like I was the most delicious meal he'd ever had.

My back arched, grinding even more against his tongue and lips, and I had to steady myself on the headboard, just above where his hands were straining within the binds I'd put him in.

Río breathed harshly through his nose but never tried to come up for a true deep breath, completely losing himself between my legs, and if I weren't trembling and moaning with every flick of his tongue, I would've been able to properly marvel how easily he slipped into this place. He alternated from attending to my clit, sending bright ripples up my spine, and fucking me with his tongue, truly eating me from the inside out.

He drew it out, let my pleasure roll until it was a big, undeniable thing, and I reached down, clutching one of his hands and locked our fingers together. He held on just as tightly, keeping me steady as my muscles shook and threatened to topple over or collapse. It was too good, too good, and I was mumbling a string of praises for my perfect mate and telling him to just keep going right there, because I was so close.

And then he purred, as if he was saving it for that moment where I was so close to falling into sweet abyss. The vibrations extended to his tongue, and I felt myself flood his face even more while tightening all over. Everything ceased to exist but Río's tongue vibrating between my legs and my hand in his. The light in my chest felt like it was never-ending, and I came with my jaw dropped.

Río settled his ministrations, but the purr continued, drawing out every pulse of pleasure my body was willing to give until my muscles twitched with oversensitivity.

I scrambled clumsily off of his face, careful not to catch any of his hair, and sat back on his chest. After a sniff of the air and a confirming glance behind my shoulder, I let out my own light hum of approval. It wasn't quite a purr, but the sentiment rolled through him just as effectively.

If I thought he looked wrecked before, it had nothing on him now, mouth and cheeks completely slicked, lips red and slightly swollen from his wet kisses, and sweat wetting the hair at his temples. He was barely keeping his eyes open, and there was a frustrated furrow between his thick brows.

My hand found his mark without even having to look, rubbing and petting hard into the muscle. "That was so good of you, baby. Now look at you. My good boy, I love you so much." I got choked up a little bit at that last one, voice growing a bit thicker as I saw how much the words affected him.

Another round of tears fell from his eyes, and I lowered to lick them away before resuming my descent down Río's body until I rested over his legs again. Between my thighs, I trapped his together and finally turned my full attention to his cock. It was flushed and throbbing, the vein winding up his shaft prominent. "Do you think you've been good enough for me to take care of this, baby?"

He blinked a few times, as if he couldn't quite understand what I was saying, and it took more time for him to form the words, his mouth trying to connect with his thoughts. "I d-don't kn—" I cut his insecurity off with another twist of his nipple, harder than I had before, and a groan of pleasure-pain punched out of him. It seemed to wake him up a bit, and when I let the sensitive peak go, he stammered, "If-if you think so. Please."

"I asked if *you* thought you were being good. Did you do what I told you to just now?" I shimmied a little lower, seated on his shins, now, and leaned over his cock. Instead of giving him the contact he was so obviously craving, I took little, kittenish laps at the precum running down his torso. It made the tattoos sparkle and shine, and I hummed as I tasted the salt and the warmth of his skin. "Answer, me, baby." I paused.

"I—I. Yeah, I made you come first."

"And what about as my mate?" *Lick,* "Have you been good to me? Loving me and taking care of me?"

We watched each other as I purposely got less than an inch from his dick that twitched but never connected with my face. "Yeah. I t-try." His voice broke, and he had to clear his throat, "I try my best."

I pressed a kiss into the bleeding heart inked on his skin. "Baby, it's more than try. You're beautiful and marvelous. You know that? And." I sighed and palmed his shaft. He sucked in a gasp and froze, waiting for me to finish. "You were right. I love your dick."

Puckering my lips, I let my spit dribble onto the head of Río's cock, watching the saliva trail down the curve of his cockhead while he groaned a pained, rough noise. My thumb nudged the black barbell through the slit, eliciting more sounds of pleasure from him before I moved my fist, making the rest of him nice and wet for my throat.

"You're such a good mate, my Río." I meant every word, so grateful to have him in my life, and thanked the universe as I swallowed half of him down in one motion. He cried out, yelling loud enough for the neighbors to have no question of what we were doing, and I hollowed my cheeks as I pulled back, only to plunge again. I dragged the flat of my tongue against his shaft, tickled the barbell each time I teased the head. Río's legs were bunching and shaking beneath me, but my body restrained them, too. His shouts and curses in Spanish turned to a string of what I guessed were pleas, and it didn't take long at all for him to stiffen even more in my throat. I pulled back until his slit rested on my tongue, just in time for Río to throw his head back and erupt, shooting cum into my mouth.

Trying my best to collect but not swallow, I breathed through my nose, lashes fluttering on my cheeks, and moved my fist to milk every last drop out of him. Deepthroating was still a skill that eluded me, but I liked to think I'd improved my dick sucking in the short time we'd been together.

Careful not to spill, I opened my mouth for him to see the cum I collected, tongue sticking out.

"*Fuck*, Princess." Río seemed to have a little more of his wits about him, now that he wasn't fighting back his orgasm to the point of tears, and his own tongue licked slowly at his lip as he watched me close my mouth and swallow.

CHAPTER THIRTY-SIX

RÍO

I used a light, hatching motion to shade the sketch I'd been working on in the moments Ramona and I had like this over the past few days. Where we lay next to each other in our nest, doing our own things together. She had a book propped up on her bent knees, while I leaned against the headboard on the side of the bed nearest the lamp, my sketchbook open.

The sleek Gray Wolf sat on her haunches, head turned to look over her shoulder at me. The stoic expression of her light eyes contrasted with the playful tail I imagined wagging when she bared her teeth. Her ears were pinned back on her head in challenge, and I smirked as I continued to shade the swaths of darker areas of fur on her back and face.

Ramona shifted beside me, sending a current of our scent my way as our nest moved beneath her. We both lounged naked, and the way she'd repositioned herself left the dip of her lower back arched just before the perfect swell of her ass. She crossed her legs at the ankle and left them swaying in the air as she propped up on her elbows to keep reading.

Her brows were pulled in the little frown she usually got when she was reading, and I abandoned my Wolf sketch for a moment to look over her shoulder.

Three sentences in, and I couldn't resist giving her a hard time. I set down my sketchbook and pencil and straddled over her, my half-hard cock resting between her cheeks. My hands planted on either side of her book, and my loose hair was a canopy over her head. "'He gripped her hair with an unflinching hold,'" Ramona sputtered indignantly, but I kept on reading with my grin evident in my voice, "'pulling at her hair just enough to draw tears while he thrust his cock to the back of her throat. She sighed in bliss'— Princess, you are a dirty girl, reading porn before bed."

She twisted around to glare up at me, shoving her book to the edge of the nest. "It's not *porn*. And how do you think I knew at least a little about sucking dick the first time we met?"

We'd been resting in our nest of blankets and pillows and clothing, recovering from the dinner with her mom and the sexy as fuck round of bondage, for a few hours, but the memory of my mate slipping so nicely into my command without even knowing me had my gut swooping. What could I say? I liked both submitting and controlling.

And though my princess liked it when I took over, I now had first-hand experience of how much she liked to exert her power over me.

I snarled playfully and shot down to her neck, nipping along her skin and making exaggerated grumbling noises. She batted against my shoulders and arms, and her surprised chuckles turned to full-out giggles as I brought my hands into my tickling. While I nipped along her shoulders and cheeks, my fingers danced along her sides and armpits, letting my mate's mirth fill the tranquil air.

"Río," she gasped, but my princess was as strong as I was. She held me close and didn't try to push me away. Even the annoying glass lenses before my eyes didn't obscure my view of Ramona, flushed and happy in my arms. Her hair was freshly braided and fuzzing as a result of her writhing. I loved it.

"What is it, baby?" I added a little more force to my biting at her mark while gentling my fingers fluttering along her ribs.

She was still smiling, but her eyes narrowed. "What happened to you being a good boy?"

My cock gave a happy jerk at the pet name, recalling *very* well what she'd just done to me, and I smiled cheekily. "Hmm, Good Río can't come to the phone right now, but if you leave your name and num—" The rest of my words were muffled beneath her hand clasped over my lips with her expression turning dry and amused.

I, for one, thought I was fucking hilarious, so I just took a good lick against her palm. She grimaced and retracted her hand to wipe it on the blanket beside us. My lips fell into a pout. "Come on baby, don't act like you don't like my tongue. You'll hurt my feelings."

Ramona rolled her eyes and stuck *her* tongue out at me like the delightful brat she was. Joke was on her, because I was a brat, too. I quickly grabbed at her jaw so that she couldn't escape as I extended my tongue to lick at hers. My sweet and sour persnickety Wolf didn't shove me away. No, she opened her mouth to lengthen the contact of our tastebuds that still held each other's flavor.

My mate whimpered under me, still allowing me to lick her, and the insistent cloud of arousal grew around us. But as mates now, the scents were so intertwined that it was impossible in our nest to decipher from which of us it originated. With my hand still holding her face in an immovable grip, I moved to her cheekbone, licking and tasting while she hitched a leg over my shoulder. "Baby." Her plea was breathy, and how could I deny her?

In her ear, I growled, half-shift already starting. "What is it, mi alma gemela? Do you need some help? Craving my dick in that tight pussy so badly already?"

I released my hand on her jaw and brought her other leg over my shoulder, bending her in half. She squirmed impatiently, making the sweetest little mewling noises of frustration. I'd bet that she didn't know she was doing it, and I wasn't going to draw attention to her wordless begging for what only I could give her.

Ramona bit at her lip and tried a weak glare up at me, as if she didn't wanna give me the satisfaction. But the first brush of my hard cock against where she had already gone all sweet and slippery had both of us groaning. "Fuck you, *yes*. Give it to me."

I angled my hips to nudge just the slightest bit into her, feeling her lips part around me. A full-body shiver shuddered under my skin. Even still, I tsked, trying to ramp her up even more. "Now, that's not how you get what you want, Princess. I'm in control again." I was thrusting shallowly into her, teasing the both of us.

Somewhere under one of her satin-covered pillows, Ramona's phone started ringing and vibrating against the bed, but we both ignored it. She hitched up onto her elbows, contorting her body even more and creating a delicious angle for me to fuck into. This time, she didn't glare or spit another demand. Her arched black brows drew up in the middle, and her slender throat worked in a swallow. "Please, Río. I want you so badly." She chewed at her lip, and I felt my restraints rapidly fall away. "Just hold me down and fuck me and take what's yours."

Oh, she was good. I wasn't a territorial Wolf, but my Jaguar reacted just as any shifter would to that taunt. Even if it was blatant manipulation, there was no holding myself back from sinking my teeth into her mark and bottoming out into my mate.

She screeched, ending the noise on a drawn-out moan as she let me take her with the same ferocity as I had in the tree. I pumped my hips and pulled my fangs out of her neck to suck and lick at the emphasized claim I had on her. Her toes dangled helplessly in the air as I fucked into my mate like we'd never get to do this again. She'd made me desperate for her then turned around and similarly showed her belly to me. She was fucking perfect, just whimpering with each thrust and holding on. She clenched tightly on me, letting my rough fucking take her up and over the edge. It was a dream, it was bliss, and my body was on fire with her shaking beneath me.

I kept on, chasing my own release, and Ramona petted my back through my fast and erratic movements. "Mm, that's it baby, you fuck me so good, Río, te amo, te amo." Her voice was hoarse but sated and full of love, and it was her use of my name and my first language that snapped the last string holding my orgasm back.

It almost hurt in the way the pleasure balled and exploded, where I couldn't see or hear, just *feel*. And as I filled my mate, her walls still convulsing and milking me, I was forever grateful that I'd decided that night during my closing shift to not bolt it out of town.

That I let my Jaguar instincts guide me the second I'd seen her honey eyes. If I knew the fucker at all, he'd been leading me to her all along.

It took a while for the world beyond the comfort of our joined scents and the warmth inside my mate to filter in. The taste of her blood still lingered in my tongue, and I took her jaw again, forcing her mouth open. Ramona was so fucked out that she just smiled and opened up, trusting me wholeheartedly. I spat into her mouth, demanding she taste us both, and she took it in, just as greedily, with a hum. Fuckin' perfect.

She rubbed her hand against my hips, reminding me that I still had her folded like a pretzel. I pressed up a little and gently guided her legs to the mattress, still unwilling to pull out of her. What would she do if I gifted her a plug for nights like this? So she could keep my cum in her while it was just us in the safety of our home.

The idea and her inevitable irritation but secret excitement about the notion had me grinning down at her and snuffling into her hair.

The insistent ringing over her phone jangled against the soupy bliss both of us were very much enjoying being lost in. With a grumble, I followed the noise and vibrations, pawing through the mound of us-scented fabric until I found her phone almost fallen off the edge of the bed.

A photo of her brother smiling softly while he tossed Dahlia in the air took up the whole screen. It looked like something she'd stumbled upon and took in secret. "Who is it?" Ramona mumbled.

"Your brother." I went to put the phone back on the bed, but she stilled and scrambled up.

Without resistance, I handed the phone to her, wondering what was so special about her brother calling, but sat back and waited.

She leaned on an elbow, and I half listened while still marveling at where we were connected. When she answered the call, however, I froze as I could hear crackling of chaos on the other line.

Over that, her brother growled a bone-chilling note. "Where the fuck is your mate? Is he with you?" Shit. Why did I feel like I was about to get punched again?

I didn't even need to try and remember how to get there. The smoke rising into the black sky was enough of a beacon. I ground my teeth, pushing my bike as quickly as I could go with Ramona clinging to my back. The house wasn't far from my apartment, and the smell of ash and doused flames was already stinging my nose and eyes, even beneath my helmet. Ramona's arms tightened around me, and I squeezed her hand reassuringly before returning it to the handlebar. Not ten seconds later, we were pulling into... what was left of the white house.

The fire truck parked out front had its flashing lights turned off. The firefighters almost finished packing up their stuff, now, and commotion of multiple humans and shifters assaulted my senses. But I fought through the cacophony to stay steady and strong for my mate. And to prepare for the onslaught that was sure to come my way after what my sisters had done.

The white witch house was a charred, smoldering mess. Wolves milled about like concerned citizens, but I knew that they were trying to catch any helpful scents that would aid them in their own investigation of what happened.

Ramona and I had just hopped off my bike and taken our helmets off when the Leader came around what was left of the house and stormed toward us. His green eyes were blazing, glowing in a way that was far from human, and I caught the scent of forest still strong on him. The pack had been on a run, and I knew immediately that Cata and Mara had planned this around the event. Knowing that the pack would be occupied.

The Leader's usual orderly curls were a mess about his head, and I suppressed a growl when his hands connected with my chest, grabbing at my shirt. He was shaking, trying to hold back his Wolf since there were a few concerned human neighbors present as well, but I wasn't going to fight back. "What the fuck do you know about this. Tell the truth, or I will fucking kill you."

"Orion, stop!" Ramona urged with her own growl. Seemed like we'd been through this scenario before.

I kept myself steady and open. Any type of defensiveness would set him off, and we obviously had bigger problems to worry about. "I assure you, Leader. I had nothing to do with this. And I will stand with you to get revenge." I let my Jaguar slip a little to the forefront, taking advantage of his eyes staring mine down to see the sincerity of my words. Ramona was my family, and by extension, this Wolf. His mate and children were all mine to defend, too, and the times I'd been here, I knew how special this place was to all of them.

He sniffed the few inches between us, claws ripping into the shirt I'd hastily pulled on when Ramona answered her brother's call. We'd dressed as quickly as possible, and I'd popped in my contacts so that my glasses wouldn't get in the way.

Orion's growl settled a bit, and when he eventually dropped

his hold on me, I surreptitiously released a long exhale. Ramona clutched my hand in hers. Her eyes were glassy with tears as she faced her brother who had calmed only a fraction. "How bad is it?"

He swept his hands up and down his face, before dropping them to his sides. Not only did his fingers and hands twitch, but his wrists jerked in agitated movements as well. "Bad. Whatever they did blazed right through the wards Sylvie and Josie had kept up over the years."

"And the garden?" Ramona croaked. We couldn't see it here, with the blackened skeleton of the house and smoke blocking our way. By the lack of hope in her question, I knew she already had a feeling of what his answer would be.

I brought a hand around her waist, bracing for her brother's response. "Destroyed."

My princess let out a little distressed whine, and I tucked her head into my neck while fighting back my instinct to take this on as my fault. Would they have still done this if I hadn't mated Ramona? When Mara interrogated me about my mate who wasn't even my mate at that point, I'd been tightlipped. As if the powers that be took some small mercy on all of us, her scenting was weaker than other shifters, so maybe not. But she could've still smelled Ramona on me. And the familial note that ran through her and the Pack Leader.

Orion went to go speak with another Wolf who eyed me suspiciously but said nothing, and I rubbed soothingly at Ramona's shoulders. She stayed rooted in place, unwilling to go closer and see one of her favorite places gone. My mate let me comfort her as silent tears spilled down her cheeks. My Jaguar grumbled, itching to retaliate against those that'd made my mate upset.

A flash of rage shot toward us, something I'd never experienced before, and it took too long for me to recognize Sylvie, rushing from where the garden once was. Her hair was down and wild, with twigs and leaves that'd probably been a result of full immersion in the interrupted run.

Her cherry-red painted nails resembled drops of blood, and they were like talons, aimed for my chest like she wanted to pull out my soul. Her brown eyes were glazed and wrathful, even as Ramona lunged between us.

"Sylvie!" Ramona snarled just as Orion wrapped a hand around his mate's waist to keep her from going at me. My princess held her sister at arm's length, muscles bulging as the witch continued to press forward. She was mumbling in a foreign language, using words that weren't of this world at all.

Fuck, I caused this. Right? My family had destroyed something sacred to my mate and *her* family, and I was the link in between.

I wanted to say something, but my words were more than just stuck in my throat. It felt like it was slowly closing, invisible hands circling around my windpipe while cotton was stuffed down my throat. Ramona was struggling in front of me, but I couldn't get my body to obey. My muscles were trembling, not unlike when I was about to shift, but it was wrong and painful. I clutched at the base of my neck, not knowing how or what to do to make it stop.

Sylvie's hands were trapped by Orion's arms, opening and clenching at her sides, and when she met my panicked stare with my mate still struggling in the middle, she smirked in a dark, possessed way that was nothing like I'd seen before.

Ramona cast a worried glance at me over her shoulder, and, through the black now creeping in on my vision, I saw her eyes widen even more as she took in my state, now kneeling in grass, mouth opening and closing uselessly. "No, Sylvie! He didn't do this! O, get her to stop! Where the fuck is Josie? Can you call her?"

A few more seconds of agony, just as I started welcoming in unconsciousness as a reprieve from this pain, it stopped. Well, the force causing it stopped, but I coughed until my throat was raw, and my limbs were still tingly and sore. Ramona collapsed by my side—when had I fallen completely on the ground?—and ran her hands over my face. Her whines of distress were nice and something to hold onto, so I let her cool citrus fill my lungs and calm my racing heart.

"She's still helping Juno—Sylvana, mo ghrá, I'm here…" The Leader was speaking low and urgent, and when my clearing vision focused on them standing just a few feet away, the witch was now weeping in her mate's chest. Great, big wails that grated on my ears, but I was just thankful that she was no longer trying to murder me with whatever fucking kind of magic that was.

A couple humans and Wolves jogged over, obviously seeing me on the ground, and asked if I needed assistance. With lame assertions that I just tripped and fell after arriving, they eventually backed off and continued to look over to the scene of smolder and ruin.

I sat up slowly with my mate's arms still around me, breathing through the lingering tremors. Witches could be particularly nasty, but the dark power off of Sylvie wasn't fucking human magic. How in the hell I hadn't realized until now that she was Fae, I didn't know. Now *those* were some vengeful fuckers.

Ramona kissed my face relentlessly, still making that very canine sound of distress. "Are you okay, baby?" She scented at my neck, and the gesture itself was bolstering my energy and making me feel better.

Slowly rubbing my cheek on her temple in return, I tried a deep breath, finding my lungs aching but otherwise okay. "I'm okay, Princess. Really thought I was gonna be killed by a faerie for a second."

But my mate was unamused by my try at humor. She shot me a look that was full of worry, relief, and irritation. "Don't even joke about that. If she weren't grieving, I would've had to knock her on her ass."

A warning growl carried over to us, and I shifted a little to see the Pack Leader still cradling his mate in his arms. Her sobs were calmed to little hiccups, and an older woman with fiery hair had wandered over and was rubbing Sylvie's back. Whoever she was, the combination of she and Orion's reassurances were working, and the churning rage was all but gone from the air.

"Watch your mouth, Mona," the Leader grumbled, and his face was sharp.

Ramona bared her teeth. "And you watch your mate. We're family, but I won't have her hurting mine. Especially when he had nothing to do with this."

I tried to sigh, but everything was still raw, so I coughed halfway through the gesture. Ramona rubbed my back in soothing circles, and I was eventually able to draw in enough air. "It's okay, Princess. I get—"

"*No.* Don't you fucking try and make excuses for someone attacking you, Río. I won't hear of it, so just be quiet if that's what you're gonna do." She punctuated her command with a kiss on my temple. There was no hope for me ignoring a directive like that, so I just leaned into her and tried to begin forming a plan.

Another car drove up, the engine growly and smooth. Confused about the scents that came with it, I looked over my shoulder to find Tyler shooting out of his challenger, along with that blond Wolf I almost killed.

"Oh my god!" The non-shifter Wolf ran over, rivers of tears running down his face. He dropped down beside Ramona, but before he could put his arms around her, I bared my fangs in warning. Ramona had assured me that he had no desire for her, but forgive me for being a little on edge.

The guy blanched, and *Tyler* placed a pale hand in his blond locks and *hissed* at me. What the fuck was going on? "W-we saw the smoke, and I just felt something was wrong. What can we do?" He looked from my mate and I to the Leader, his mate, and the older human.

Instead of answering that question, I turned back to Orion. "Where's the rest of the pack?"

His jaw tightened, and he looked over his mate's head on the scene before us. "Here. Or somewhere safe and protected."

I didn't comment on him keeping the details of their whereabouts from me. Instead, my mind was clearing and whirling with possibilities. What would I have done if I were still an enforcer when a Pack Leader refused to cooperate? Be irritated, for one. Intimidate, which was obviously what this was. Then, hit them where it hurt most. Which, for proud Leaders, typically wasn't threats to their own wellbeing.

"We—"

"Leader! We got one!"

CHAPTER THIRTY-SEVEN

RAMONA

"Leader! We got one!" Harrison ran from the forest over to us. His dark hair was disheveled, and he was missing a shirt, but he drew everyone's attention.

Orion nodded and looked down at Sylvie's face, held in his hands. She seemed to be back to her normal self, staring up at him with wide, trusting eyes, and he nuzzled his nose against hers. Roz, who I'd met once before, gave Sylvie's back a few more pats and started to back away. "I'mma handle these nosy neighbors while y'all take care of things."

As she marched over to the humans that were trickling away, I gathered to my feet and helped Río to stand. He leaned on me a little too much for my liking, but I steadied us both until he rose to his full height. I watched as he took a deep breath, and his face smoothed into a cold mask. His lids lowered a bit, his mouth became a flat line while his shoulders relaxed. Was this how he'd been in his old life? Where he killed and was abused by the people that should've been the kindest to him?

Our little group followed Harrison into the woods, running with Orion and Sylvie in the lead right behind him.

Up ahead, there was a circle of three naked Wolves with another shifter on the ground that was dressed in a suit and already roughed up. He smelled feline, like the pine and wind of a mountain lion. His lip was already busted, his eye already swelling and blackening, but he just smiled when my brother stopped and stood over them.

"Should've agreed to the terms, dog." His mousey brown hair was pulled back into a short ponytail that was dirty and bloody. Ana, the blonde Wolf Vera had tried to taunt me with those weeks ago, crouched and punched the mountain lion in his other eye, and his head thumped against the forest floor.

O raised a halting hand at her and the pack members that were snarling and ready to rip the shifter to shreds. By the barely-suppressed frenzied energy around all of them, they'd tracked this member of the Serafim Group down. Herding and hunting him and now ready to sink their fangs. Even I felt restless looking down at the mountain lion, wanting to join in.

Río, myself, Harrison, and Delaney and Tyler stood a few paces away, though.

Orion crouched, and completely in sync with him, the Wolves did too. They grabbed the shifter's arms and legs, holding him down so that there was no escape. "Where are Catalina and her brother?"

He managed to tilt his head, though. Around Ana, I saw his deep blue eyes land on Río. "The traitor? You have him right there." I tried to step in front of Río, growling at the accusation, but his arm around my waist held me at his side.

"No. The other one. Where are they?"

The mountain lion just grinned a bloody smile, which was met with the deepening of Wolf snarls and snapping of fangs. Río stiffened around me, and his voice cut through their rage. "Leader. Who is protecting your house?"

In confirmation, the mountain lion began to chuckle. At least long enough for the raspy sound to release into the air before my brother bent over him to rip out his throat with his teeth. Blood splattered over his pale skin and the bare forms of the Wolves that were still holding him down. Orion spat out a mess of blood and flesh while his pack was still waiting for his permission to take the spoils of their hunt.

My mouth watered as I watched the last twitches of the body on the ground, but Orion's Leader command snapped my mind to attention. Sylvie wiped a hand through the blood that dripped down his chin and muttered almost inaudibly to herself before dragging her tongue through the bright red.

"We're going to the cabin. We'll run faster through the forest." His glowing green eyes landed on me. "All non-shifters go to Tina's. Meredith should already be there with the pups." I wanted to object, but the disobeying words literally wouldn't form without a strong feeling of dread passing over my mind.

The Wolves around us started to shift, and the agitated air cranked up even higher. Río's arm unwound from my waist, and I watched, stunned, as he plucked his contacts out of his eyes and threw them to the ground. He handed me his phone and keys, and a jangling beside us proved Orion was doing the same to Sylvie. Not even taking the time to undress, my mate joined the others in shifting, the visceral sound of bones popping and skin rippling even louder, now. It made my own body jittery and frustrated. My Wolf recognizing her pack but unable to take part.

And I was fucking pissed.

Río must've sensed that too, because his Jaguar with fur dark like the depths of the forest around us nudged my chest toward Delaney and Tyler to my right. Orion was doing the same to Sylvie who was outright arguing with him. It should've been comical, her going back and forth with a Wolf that only grunted back at her, but they seemed to understand each other just fine.

Tyler spoke up. "We need to let them go. I'll drive."

Sylvie gave Orion one last frustrated kiss on his head, smearing blood on his white fur. Still simmering with anger, I did the same to Río's and whispered in his ear. "Be good, and don't fucking die. Te amo." He licked the scar on my right arm before darting toward the trees with the five Wolves, prepared to take on his family.

My heart felt like it was being torn in two as we followed Tyler back to his car. His small hand in Delaney's was something else to ponder, but my main, terrifying concerns were for my mate, my brother, and my niece and nephew.

When we all stuffed into Tyler's car, I tried calling Mom, only to have the phone ring until it got sent to voicemail. I tried twice more, and nothing. "Mom's not answering the phone." I glanced out of the window, where the city lights were dwindling and giving way to the more open road.

Sylvie's eyes were also set on the world outside of the car. "I told him the directions to take us to the cabin. Like hell are we not helping." She turned back to me and bit at her lip. "I'm sorry I almost killed your mate."

My Wolf grumbled, and it came out of my mouth as a weaker, human-stained version. "I would've killed you if it'd gotten any closer to that. Just put that scary shit to good use on the actual bad guys." My sister didn't fight back, and I watched steely determination settle over her face in the form of a small smile. She nodded.

"I'm scared," Delaney whispered from up front, and I saw the searching, desperate look he gave Tyler who kept his eyes on the road, more than breaking the speed limit.

The vampire sighed as we raced down the road that connected Antler Pointe to my brother's land. "I've never willingly gotten involved in shifter bullshit, but I agree with the witch. And I'll keep you safe, boy." Without turning his head, Tyler wove his fingers into Delaney's blond locks, drawing out a tiny mewl from my friend who was a full foot and a half taller than him.

"Okay." I ran my hands over my face while Sylvie was quietly reciting her fucking elf words to herself. "Once we're done with this bullshit, there are *many* explanations that need to be shared."

Tyler just chuckled, continuing to pet Delaney who, from where I could see, appeared to be in heaven with Tyler's hands on him. Thoughts of the dynamic that Tyler once admitted he preferred tried to step into the forefront of my racing mind, but I just shoved it back as the smooth road gave way to gravel.

The car slowed as we went through the trees, and my body vibrated. Even encased in the metal shield of the car, the scent of too many shifters made my mouth go dry and my heart beat even faster. There were Wolves, but also a smattering of other species, and—

The sound of gunfire startled all of us but Tyler. Delaney yelped and covered his ears, and the light up ahead wasn't just from the cabin. Multiple unknown vehicles were parked on the edge of the yard, and when I looked to the front porch, across the moonlit distance, I saw Mom.

She was half-shifted, gray fur winding down her bare arms and her fangs out with her snarl. A few other Wolves, fully shifted, stood beside her, as they faced a fucking line of people in suits with guns.

"Stop!" I shouted at Tyler who obeyed, just as one of the attackers turned their head, and my heart dropped.

They... looked like Río. At least, from the side. Their more feminine features, cheekbones and chin slightly softer slopes, were so startlingly like my mate's that I knew exactly who had just had a gun drawn on my mother. The black eyes weren't bottomless safety like Río's but all-knowing.

"Aside from the height difference, you'd know Cata from her sharpness and Mara from her smile. Both are fucking deadly in their own way."

Delaney started to release a stream of, "No no no no no no no," hands holding his ears and eyes clenched shut as if he could will everything to stop.

Catalina, I identified, waved her gun at us. "Get out of the car." The soft command was heard by us all, but it wasn't until she shot one of the headlights of Tyler's car, glass smashing, that we moved to comply.

Tyler was hissing, though whether his anger was about the car or Delaney turning into a sobbing mess, I didn't know.

As I closed the black car door, my own anger was eclipsing everything. Finally, I was faced with one of my mate's torturers. When would I get this chance again? My Wolf paced within my chest, wanting to exact revenge, but my more logical mind tried to remind us both that my niece and nephew were certainly inside and in danger. And where were Río and Orion?

Howls from the woods reached my ears, as well as a grating, sawing roar, just as I began to worry. How had we beat them?

The four of us stood beside Tyler's car, but it wasn't enough to make the Serafim goons lose their attention on Mom and the Wolves from the pack that'd probably been sent here to escort her and the babies to Tina's.

I sniffed the air, trying to get my bearings on who I was facing, but, who was I kidding? Even with the four of us—well, three, since Delaney was a trembling mass hunched into Tyler's side— how were we to take down a Shifter with a gun?

"And Cata is like my father. She can shift into pretty much any animal. I'm the only sibling that's limited to just one other form."

Catalina Serafim, my... sister-in-law, crossed her arms while still holding her gun. Her white silk blouse was tucked elegantly into her black trousers, her hair slicked into a neat bun at the base of her skull. "Well." Her brows rose. "Now, this is interesting."

Tyler and I both growled, and I cracked my knuckles down at my sides. Sylvie had gone quiet, and out of the corner of my eye, I noticed her expression taking on that eerie, witchy vacancy. The one that filled with darkness as she'd tried to go for Río. Here's hoping her grandparents truly taught her a thing or two.

"Now, how did the whore of Howl's Fury team up with the mate of the arrogant Pack Leader here? *And,*" Catalina zeroed in on me, "why in the hell do you smell like my brother?"

I felt the presence of Wolves around me, scented blood that I prayed wasn't theirs, and straightened my spine. Stretching my senses, I felt my mate not too far away, his calm heartbeat influencing mine to not be afraid. At least enough to speak when I had no weapon of my own but my fists.

"I'm his mate."

Sylvie's featherlight whispers reached my ears, but I kept my attention forward, facing Catalina's scrutiny. Hopefully it would buy Orion and the others time to get the babies out.

Río's sister tilted her head, appraising me like I was an abstract painting. Trying to understand what the appeal was when she just saw a bunch of paint splatters. "Hm. And the sister of the Pack Leader, if my scenting is to be believed." She continued to search, mind practically buzzing with calculations. She turned to Delaney. "And did you sleep with this entire pack too, Wolf whore? I guess anything to ingratiate yourself, right?" Tyler gave a louder, more grating hiss and stepped in front of my friend who was barely conscious at this point. My guess was that the Serafim Group had been brutally responsible for his old pack's demise.

"Mommy!" A scream sounded from inside the house, and it seemed to startle even Catalina. The Wolves on the porch, including Mom, growled at the guns trained on them, ramped up by Dahlia's call of distress.

Sylvie started forward, but Catalina pointed the gun at her. "Try anything, and I'll shoot you between the eyes."

My chest tugged, the distance of the golden thread shortening, and called to it, I looked to my right, where Río emerged, half-shifted. He was nude and held his clawed hands up. "Cata. Stop this."

She rolled her eyes and shot him an annoyed glance. Her sharp lip sneered his way. "Oh, perfect. Something else. Hello, Río."

My mate stepped even closer, but he wouldn't look at me. Why wasn't he looking at me? "You have the power to stop this. To leave and let these people be."

She watched her brother with everything but love and care. No relief after not seeing him for eight years. A nearly silent shuffle sounded to my left, but I fought not to react to Sylvie moving closer to the firing squad. Her mumbling was a string of fervent chants, tingling the air around us that seemed to grow even hotter by the second. The nighttime insects that were undoubtedly all around us were scared to silence with the volume of shifters congregated here. On my brother's sacred land.

"Of course, I do. But this is business, which you never had the patience to understand. And this pack has been uncooperative. So." She shrugged and started to turn her head back toward us.

"I'll go back," Río said, taking another step toward his sister and ripping my breath away. "Leave this pack and my mate alone, and I'll join the family again."

Catalina waved her gun, as if batting away Río's bargaining. "As if I care about any of that. Pai hasn't said anything about you in years, and crossing paths with you now is an unfortunate blip."

Almost too fast to see, her arm straightened, aiming the gun at me. Before I had time to gasp, Tyler materialized in front of me just as she pulled the trigger. The smell of vampire blood, like dead roses, tickled at my nose, and I stood, frozen, as Tyler dropped to his knees.

Delaney screamed and ran to Tyler to catch his head before he hit the ground. Río growled, fangs and claws drawn, as Catalina turned the gun on him. "Never seen a vampire trade their life for another before. What a waste of immortality." She shrugged, as if it couldn't be helped.

Río's Jaguar was pulling forward again, his features twisting and his rational mind taking a backseat to his desire to protect me. At the expense of himself when someone important to him was already lying bleeding. "I'm okay, baby. I'm okay." My voice trembled, but Río stopped looking like he was going to do something stupid that Catalina was more than prepared to counter as she stared him down. "Te amo, te amo."

I glanced back at Sylvie who was even closer behind the Serafim goons and caught her eye. She muttered something else to herself before nodding, just a minute tilt of her head, and turned to do the same at Mom and the Wolves on the front porch.

What the hell did that mean? Go, right?

Drawing on every class and training session I ever took, boxing, judo, and otherwise, I shot forward, swerved around Delaney and Tyler, reaching for Catalina's wrist that held her gun. Using all my strength, I forced both of our arms skyward, sending up her rounds in reaction straight toward the stars. Snarls broke out behind me, but no other guns sounded. Switching hands and wrapping my arm around her waist, I twisted my body. Planting my hip against the small of her back, I felt her tense, her muscles bunch, but I managed to send my own force up and backward. I flipped Catalina over my shoulder until she landed face-down on the ground.

She screeched, but I dove on top of her and wrestled the gun out of her hand. Her fingernails scratched at my skin, drawing blood, but I kept on until I was able to flip her over and pin her wrists. She was just as strong as Río had been in the throws of his night terror that *she* had a hand in causing, but what I lacked in ability to shift, my body made up for in adrenaline-boosted brute strength.

With the butt of her gun, I pistol whipped her face twice, as hard as I could, before cracking into her cheekbone with my elbow. My heart raced in my chest, but my rage, remembering the exact flavor of Río's terror when I'd witnessed his nightmare, made my vision a bright crimson. Catalina's head lolled to the side, her breaths shallow. I hit her once more for good measure, feeling her body go lax beneath me.

"Mommy!" Dahlia's voice cried out again, though this time, it wasn't from inside the cabin. Risking a glance to my left, I saw Sylvie amongst the flurry of Wolves and suited shifters that were fighting with fists instead of their weapons or other forms. They were quickly losing to my mother and the Wolves. Especially—I almost couldn't tear my eyes away—as Sylvie held one heart in her hand and was snatching another out of the suited chest of a felled shifter on the ground. She was a mixture of elegant and feral with blood staining her t-shirt and shorts, the lower half of her face dripping as she took bites of the still-beating hearts and muttered with each swallow.

Scrabbling footsteps stole both of our attention, and when I looked in the direction of the lake, I saw my brother, naked from shifting to human form and pulling Dahlia toward the trees. Where was Ollie? I looked and saw my mom, a silver-colored Wolf amongst the bloodshed at the front of the house. Sylvie was already starting over as Dahlia's piercing scream had me whirling back around.

To see Río pounce behind Orion, wind his arm around his shoulders, and grasp his throat, plunging his claws into his neck.

My body jerked in shock, and the second plunge was my mate's other hand sinking into Orion's torso. Blood spurted from his throat, and he dropped Dahlia's wrist, who kept running straight for the trees.

In paralyzing horror, not knowing what way was up or down, I opened my mouth to scream, but nothing came out as Orion writhed and shook in Río's hold.

My brother turned his head to the side, to look Río in the eye as blood spurted out of his mouth and ran down his front.

And he grinned a cheek-splitting smile.

CHAPTER THIRTY-EIGHT

RÍO

I let the scent of the Wolves, the sounds of their quiet and hungry breaths, guide me. While we ran, vaulting over fallen trees and winding around paths that they certainly were familiar with, I could only marvel at their coordination. How Leader didn't need to give orders—they moved with an innate synchronicity while I tried to keep up. And when we came upon the scent of a dozen and a half shifters hidden within the dense, dark wood, they fanned out.

As Jaguar, I was used to ambush hunting. Not this event of endurance. But, as Leader's glowing green eyes cut to me through the blur of my vision, I took it as a command to join the mob. In my own way.

I climbed while the Wolves cut a wide circle around the Serafim soldiers, some shifted and some not. My claws sinking into the bark of the tree was comfortable. Even when working within a group was new territory.

But they knew the land. And what I couldn't see, I could smell and hear. Quick, panicked footfalls. Harsh breaths of prey. My tail swished in my perch, waiting and observing until the twelve inched the enemies close enough to attack.

I felt my mate's distress, square in my heart. She didn't feel as far away as she should have, but before I could fully set my attention to her, the bloodshed started.

Wolves were messy. Intense. Cries of pain rang out into the night as they started lunging. No quick, killing bites, but ones meant to take down and incapacitate. Three of them went for a shifted Tiger, another one releasing a thick spurt of blood from a soldier in human form.

All kept me observing. Waiting for my time, and when a torrent of the Leader's scent, a warm winter's night, slashed into the air as someone landed a blow, I coiled.

And pounced. Leaping into the air with my destination a murky mix of white and red and black.

More soldiers were biting at Leader, trying to take him down, and I landed on the first one's back. Opening my jaw to crush the back of their skull was quick. The spurt of blood and tissue I barely even tasted as I pounced on the next one.

We were outnumbered, but they were the unarmed shifter reinforcements. They were unprepared on the pack's home, and once we finished off those that'd attacked Leader, it was a frenzy. The Wolves pulled at limbs, silencing screams and death gurgles like afterthoughts.

Until a shrill cry rang against the treetops. "Mommy!" I felt Leader tense near me—we all did.

We were close to the house, and with a few yips, we split off, leaving some behind to stand guard while we inched closer to the Leader's yard. Where the scents of my mate and sister made me want to growl.

Instead, I went back to that place. Where I knew my sisters and that they'd shoot first and not bother to ask questions later if we tried on them what we did to their soldiers.

Hell, I half-shifted, *they'd probably shoot me anyway*. "I'll protect them," I whispered at the white Wolf, whose out-of-place coloring was easier to see than everything else. "Wait here, or else you'll be their first target." He grumbled, tension thick around him, and not just because of his injuries. But he didn't follow as I broke through the trees with my hands up.

And if I thought my sister had any soft spot for me, that was quickly erased. I tried urging her to leave, still unsure where the fuck Mara was, but when she shot my best friend who took a bullet for my mate, I saw more than red. Her spine shattering beneath my fangs, body giving last twitches before stilling for good. Fuck everything, I'd kill her and not regret it in the slightest—

"I'm okay, baby. I'm okay. Te amo, te amo." Ramona. Her voice, shaking a little but alive and strong pulled me away from lunging on Catalina and blowing all of this up. It wouldn't take much for her to keep on shooting instead of toying with us.

My nose picked up on a shifting cold, like a harsh winter wind, but it was coming from the wrong direction. My mate lunged at Catalina, the witch and shifters near the porch clashed, but my instincts forced me to relax. To watch. And as my head turned, finding what was so important that kept me from helping them, I sprinted. Where what looked like Orion leading his daughter away from the bloody confrontation filled my chest with sharp panic and dread.

Dahlia screamed for her mother, and I pounced again. I directed Dahlia to the trees and kept the pressure of my claws and arms, refusing to let the jerking body go. With a confirming glance to the forest where Dahlia had gone where I commanded, I returned to the bright green eyes that were switching back and forth from an endless black.

More dark red blood spurted and drenched my wrists, but this was going to fucking end. Now.

Voice deep and gurgling, my tormentor somehow grinned even wider. "Oi, Yoyo."

My mate's distress—hell, the distress of everyone around me —threatened to pull my focus, but I kept true. If there was anything to stop this, to make sure Pai left all of us alone, it was to use his greatest prize to bargain for our lives.

Xiomara's body was dueling with itself, whether to heal, shift, or both, but I just sank my claws further into her neck, her side. Through it all, my big sister stared at me, her eyes that I knew like my own, were easy to recognize through the blur of my vision. She didn't try to fight, nor did either of us react when the rest of the Wolves started to emerge from the woods. Fabric and bodies rustled over the ground as the pack members carried in their kills. I sensed the Pack Leader, pretty wounded but okay from fighting the shifters that'd been hiding as reinforcements.

When I'd scented an uncanny copy of his winter aroma emerging from the cabin with a Dahlia that tried her best to dig in her heels, I just reacted.

Now, Mara's scent was slippery again, intangible and impossible to completely grasp. To my surprise, with Orion's voice, Xiomara whispered, spraying blood on my face with her words, "Te quiero, Yoyo. Hazlo."

Incredulous rage coursed in my chest, tightening my squeezing her and forcing up more blood. What fucking trick was she playing? Though I couldn't truly see it, the please was an unspoken supplication in her eyes that were inky pools.

"Everyone's different, but I try to relate the scents of emotions to things that are familiar to me. So that when I encounter them, I have like… an internal catalogue to refer to. If that makes sense?"

On my inhale, I was flooded with the surrounding blood and rage and… and the stale, damp of despair that I first noticed on Ramona the night we crossed paths at Vinny's.

The wrath that'd been carrying me flagged—had Mara always smelled like this underneath the elusiveness of her scent?

As Orion, Xiomara had some height on me, and with her feet still on the ground, she jerked, twisting our bodies just before I had to steady us against a punch of pressure that released a fresh torrent of her blood.

I blinked furiously, trying to make sense of what just

happened and clear my vision in a futile effort. Using the blur of shapes and scents, I quickly took in my mate on the ground, rubbing her face and surely glaring up at Catalina who was no longer fighting unconsciousness. She held two guns, now, one pointed at us and one at my mate.

My roar shook the trees, and I fought to keep myself from trembling. If I made a move, she'd kill Ramona before I could truly take a step. If I killed Xiomara as I'd intended, she'd kill us both.

"Déjala ir, Río."

"*Déjanos ir a todos*. A mi alma gemela, esta manada, a todos nosotros. O voy a matarla."

Cata was usually composed, even when she was raging, but I caught the telltale hitching of her breathing. Xiomara was already flagging, her heart slowing with the wounds I inflicted and Catalina's gunshot.

"Ya tu perdiste esta pelea. Tu puedes explicar algunos tratos de negocios fallados, ¿pero la muerte de su arma sagrada? No."

Mara wheezed weakly in my arms, her legs no longer holding her up and leaning into me to do it for her. There were some words there, too, but she was fading too fast for even me to hear them. The satisfaction I always thought I'd feel for slaying this particular dragon that still haunted me didn't have the kick to it that I'd hoped. All that filled me was determination and exhaustion.

Everyone around us was bracing, waiting for one of us to move. Either to end all of this or fully push us toward bloody chaos where fewer would leave the cabin grounds alive.

Mara's true form started to appear, darkening the Leader's pale skin to tan then brown. Her limbs began to shrink, forcing me to hold her in the air. Her body was giving up the struggle to heal her and keep her shift at the same time.

Catalina cursed. "Fine. We'll fall back."

"*No*. Fall back, leave town, and never come back. No retaliations, no hunting down me or anyone I care about. Say whatever you have to say to Pai to make it stick. That's the only way you're both leaving here."

She growled, something that she rarely ever did. "I should've fucking killed you when I had the chance."

The words barely grazed me. She'd said way worse when I truly accepted her vitriol as my fault. Now, I had the love of my mate to hold me steady. I felt it inside of me, undeniable and breathing. I was doing this for us. "You're running out of time." And it wasn't a bluff. Mara was fully in her true form, now. Unconscious and blood dripping into the grass at my feet.

More tense seconds passed, and I felt the Wolves that fully surrounded us, now. They didn't come too close, lest they tip Cata over the edge, but their presence was its own unspoken threat. My mate and I stayed still, holding in the balance as Mara continued to slip away. Had I judged Catalina wrongly?

Through her teeth, cold and hot at once, she gritted, "Fine."

I didn't let myself relax. "Drop your weapons. Command your soldiers to do the same. And fall back. I'm not releasing her until then."

With a grumble, Catalina did just that. I watched her form shift into a crouch as she left her guns on the ground at her feet. I didn't even have to ask for Ramona to grab them both and point them at my sister. Did she know how to use them? Sure fucking hoped so.

The Wolves pressed further, herding the surviving soldiers past their vehicles and toward the trees. The tide appeared to have fully turned, and the Leader handed an uncharacteristically quiet Dahlia to Sylvie. He was limping, that much I could see, but I also smelled the blood of at least eight others on him.

Once all those in the Serafim Group were accounted for and pressed to the perimeter of the land, I walked forward with Mara, lying in my arms as her heartbeat still struggled to steady.

I still couldn't make out Cata's features when I finally stood in front of her. No doubt, they were filled with disdain at being bested. Only time would tell if she'd stay true to her word. But, I resolved, I would make sure to be here if she ever went back on it.

I let my arms fall, dropping Mara into a heap at her feet. My little big sister, a true shifter like Mamá and Javi, landed with a thud. Tonight had been the first time she'd told me that she loved me. Invoking the nickname that she only used when she would comfort me in her own twisted way when our father and sister had their backs turned.

Whether the words and her taking a bullet for me were another ruse or not, I was too drained to care. As Catalina ordered one of her soldiers to pick up Xiomara, I remembered the scent of my sister's depression that rode the wave of her evasive scent.

I wouldn't feel the rearing grief of her sorrow until later. Until I wasn't so angry and still ready to deliver what she'd asked me to do.

Orion stayed half-shifted and ordered a number of his Wolves to follow him as they led Cata, Mara, and the rest of their posse through the forest. They didn't allow them to retrieve their fallen comrades, nor did they let them flee with their vehicles.

For a stilted moment, I wondered if I should go with them, to see that the danger of my past was truly gone, but a familiar, grounding hand caressed my back. Goosebumps swept across my skin and fur, and the enormity of what we'd just endured hit me like a fucking avalanche.

I took her in my arms, holding her head tightly into my chest while I shook with my purr and fear that everything could've easily gone the other way. Could it really be true that we'd survived?

Ramona let me hold her for what seemed like an eternity, her tears soaking my skin as mine did into her hair, as there was movement around us. I listened to the comforting whoosh of air entering and leaving her lungs, and eventually, the Leader and Wolves returned.

They confirmed that they'd chased my sisters and the Serafim soldiers to the nearest edge of the Antler Pointe Pack territory and notified the already awaiting neighboring pack to further chase them south. Apparently, Harrison had been sent to communicate with the Mountain's Peak Pack and had been waiting with their Leader who followed through with the collaboration.

The world spun for a second, until I was slumped in the grass trying to catch my breath. It was done. Over.

Ramona cradled my head into her chest. "I've got you, Río. It's okay. You saved us."

My mind replayed what'd happened, running over every piece. "Wai—Ty—" How could I have forgotten? My best friend took a bullet for my mate, I needed to go to him, to respect—

"Shh." Ramona licked at my temple, tightened her embrace. "He's alive. Delaney's taking care of him over there. Just breathe, baby. You did it. You're free."

I tried to do as she said, tried to breathe, but only a sob came out, a downpour of tears. "You did so good, my strong mate. You saved us, and you're free."

CHAPTER THIRTY-NINE
THREE MONTHS LATER

RAMONA

The buzz of the tattoo gun had me taking a nervous swallow, but I kept my arm outstretched and steady. The lights of the shop were brighter than I thought they'd be. "Ready, baby?" Río dipped the cordless tattoo gun in a small pot of ink that I knew was enhanced for the non-human customers. His hair was up in a messy bun, and I used his calm smirk to ground me. The idea had been mine, to have him do this now that he worked for Vera. When I'd formally introduced them, letting Río meet the one who'd given my Wolf the external validation she'd never had before, they'd actually hit it off well. And once I not-so-subtly mentioned his previous apprenticeship and evident skill, she agreed to take him on.

Now, my mate scooted a bit closer to me and the arm I had laid out, facing up. Before he descended, Río pecked a quick kiss to my lips and got to the first line on his stencil.

While he'd sketched and workshopped the design with Vera, I'd purposely avoided the details. Wanting to put my faith in him completely. I entrusted him with my heart and body, so this wasn't really a hardship.

The first vibrating scrape of the needle had my back releasing a bit of the stiff apprehensive tension. The leather of the reclining seat was comfortable, and I focused on Río's face as he worked. There was no furrow between his brows, just a smooth and relaxed expression where his black eyes were sharp behind his contact lenses.

"You ready for everything, baby?" His low voice above the buzzing was meditative, and I hummed for a moment as I thought through the question.

It was still hard for Río to not be constantly looking over his shoulder, even though it'd been months now since the pack had driven his sisters and what was left of their employees off of Antler Pointe territory. And true to their agreement, there business ventures had been abandoned, as had their interest in the region.

But, from what Río told me, as expansive as his father's reach was, it wasn't unreasonable that he still felt on guard about it. Hopefully, Catalina would keep her word. I could only assume that Xiomara had survived—surely if her wounds had been fatal, we would all be dead by now at the hands of his father's vengeance.

The nightmares still happened, but they were more intermittent and less violent. The nights I'd wake up with him tossing or mumbling frantically in his sleep, I would just cuddle his head into my chest and hold him through it.

He never remembered them, but it would still take a few hours for him to bounce back to his usual self. Working for Vera, though, along with band practice, seemed to help a lot. So, when he asked me last month how I felt about doing some traveling, to share in his favorite places and explore any that I wanted to experience, I wasn't exactly *surprised*, but it was still unlocking a new part of us, too.

"Ready like logistically or emotionally?"

He smirked, knowing full well which one was more difficult

for me. He lifted the needle, wiped at my skin with a paper towel, then continued drawing over my scar. "Both."

"Well, we don't need to bring anything tonight. And pretty much all my shit's packed and ready for when we leave. But. I'll miss everyone." The last part stuck in my throat a little bit, but I focused my mind on the adventures we were about to have.

Río got to a particularly sensitive patch of my skin, and he paused, gaze flicking my way as he sensed my rise in discomfort. I nodded for him to continue. "We can always not go, Princess."

And chicken out of the opportunity for dedicated time with my mate? Unlikely. Since he'd been working hard at the tattoo shop, I'd taken up managing Sylvie's socials, website, and basically become her personal assistant for all things related to her books. When her last one moved on to another job, I'd hesitantly thrown my hat in the ring.

We sat on two folding lawn chairs, overlooking the lake and the small ripples on the surface. I was finally putting that new swimsuit to good use, now, and we baked under the warm rays of the sun. "Um. Well, I know I didn't finish. But I could put my marketing classes to good use. At least, until you find someone new."

My sister turned, beaming at me excitedly. It was such a luminous expression that I could almost forget how she'd crouched over bodies, pulling out hearts. "Uh, first. You're a lifesaver. Second, you're hired! And third, the job is yours for as long as you want it."

I opened my mouth to fight back on her automatic agreement to the idea, reminding myself what Vera and I had talked about the last time I'd seen her. Among other things, accepting the positive view of others instead of immediately trying to dismiss them was something that was especially hard for me to fully take in. "Sweet." I forced myself to swallow my protests and concessions. "Thank you."

She waved away my thanks as the babies' squeals caught our attention. Behind us, Dahlia and Ollie splashed in the little inflatable pool as my mate and brother engaged in their imaginary play. After that night, when we finally had the space to assess casualties—two pack members and all but a handful of Serafim soldiers—we discovered that Orion's left leg had been broken in two places, in addition to the scrapes and bite marks that littered his skin. Mom had been miraculously uninjured and uncharacteristically concerned about my brother's recovery, turning into a damn hovering hen that refused to go home for another week.

But he was long out of the woods, focused on his family, pack, and career shift that was much more calming.

I turned back to Sylvie. "By the way, right before shit got scary there for a second, what kind of spell were you casting?"

She continued to watch our family play, grinning at my brother when he and Río looked over and waved. "Protection. Did you notice all the ones by the porch couldn't use their guns or shift? My magic was still a bit drained from—when I went off on your mate." She sent me a guilty look. "But there was enough bloodshed to push the odds in our favor. Once the bodies started to drop, it was easier to draw from the death around us." She shrugged like that was no big deal.

I was also realizing that she probably hadn't been joking about the blood sacrifices. "Uh. Cool."

"No, I'm excited to go. To spend that time with you."

Río smirked and kept his eyes on my arm. We discussed more of our travel plans and itinerary. At first, we'd planned on traveling via his motorcycle, but we'd ultimately decided against it. This was the first trip he'd taken that wasn't a result of running from his family, and we wanted to treat these next two months as a honeymoon of sorts. Hard to pack all we'd need for that long in a few saddlebags.

So, in the truck it was.

Río finished with my left arm before requiring me to take a break for the lunch he'd packed for the longer session. That also hadn't changed, my mate's concern for whether I'd been fed or not. After I inhaled the leftover tacos we'd made for double date night at our apartment, we sat again so that he could complete my other arm. Time slipped by with my mate's careful hands on me, and when Vera walked past, she watched him for a while, smelling of approval as she nodded.

"And that's it, baby." Río took a last swipe of the paper towel at my arms and straightened. "You ready to look?" His wide grin gave me the courage to exhale, stretch my neck, and look down.

And, okay, yeah, I started crying. Big, fat tears that I had to blink past to take in the fine linework details of Río's art that now lived on my skin.

"So," he pointed, "it's lavender, sage, and rosemary. For healing, protection, and love." I nodded and swept my gaze over the tactfully placed sprigs and flowers that incorporated the lines of my scars instead of truly covering. Turning them into something beautiful. The designs were slightly different on each arm, but the pair of them together was a garden I would take with me always. The resting monarch butterfly on my right arm sent me into another round of tears that dripped down my chin.

Río rolled his stool closer to me and took off his black gloves. He swiped through the rivers on my face with his warm thumbs. "Do you like it?"

I connected our brows and held onto his wrists. "I love it. And I love you. Thank you, baby."

He kissed me, firm and sweet.

And then, that evening, I stood with plush grass between my toes. The gentle lapping of the lake sounded against the peaceful hush that'd taken over the gathering on my brother's land. After pack meetings where we healed from the bloodshed that fertilized the ground we now met on, this moment felt simultaneously impossible and inevitable.

"Delaney Warner, former member of Howl's Fury. Your insight into the downfall of your old pack has been essential in protecting this one. You have proven to be kind, loyal, and brave, and we have unanimously voted to make you pack." My brother looked Delaney in his wide, brown eyes, and his voice was laced with Leader authority. "Do you vow to respect and honor this land and pack to the best of your ability in this life and after?"

"I-I do." My friend was crying, but his voice only trembled slightly.

Orion nodded at Delaney before turning to me.

The wind rustled his pale curls, and his green eyes shined. *I am so proud of you,* they said. "Ramona Wells. My sister. You are fierce, you are caring, and you have fought to defend this very land at risk to your life. We have all watched you grow and see your Wolf. That is why we have voted to make you pack." Through my own watery vision, I flicked a glance to Vera, standing with the other elders behind my brother. She smirked. "Do you vow to respect and honor this land and pack to the best of your ability in this life and after?" *I love you.*

"Yes. I do." My brother smiled. Properly, with eye crinkles and everything, and I couldn't help my tear-choked chuckle. Sylvie and my niece and nephew grinned from their place with the other pack members as they all faced us. My pack.

And then O moved to the last of us. "And you. Río Bernal, mate of my sister. Despite the bonds of blood, you stood with us against a great threat." I took in Río's form, standing tall with his arms relaxed at his sides. The braid I wove for him at home hung straight down his back, and his facial piercings sparkled under the sharp rays from the setting sun.

Healing from the altercation with his family, not to mention all the years he faced at the mercy of their abuse and then on the run afterward, was a slow and steady pace. But this time, he was not alone. My mate faced my brother and this group that'd tentatively taken him in. Bit by bit, meeting by meeting, Río was able to settle into this group of people. From being uncharacteristically shy and never once leaving my side to letting Harrison pull him into playing pranks and getting roped into tag with the pups.

O continued with no hint of the wariness he'd once held toward my mate, "You've killed for us and have proven yourself a shifter more than worthy. That is why we have voted to make you pack. Do you vow to respect and honor this land and pack to the best of your ability in this life and after?"

I braced myself for my mate to make a joke or some nonchalant statement to cut the seriousness of my brother's words and stare. But, instead, when I looked at Río beside me, he was no better than Delaney. Two tracks of tears wound down his face and around his wide grin. He met my gaze, and I didn't even need his scent of joy, relief, and love to know what he was feeling.

Only until I returned his expression, beaming at him while the heat of the sunset warmed my bare arms, did Río respond. "Yup. I do."

And, as was customary, the pack recited their own vow to us in unison, "We see you, we welcome you, and we vow to respect and honor you as pack. In this life and after."

So, how could I not start crying, too? With my face wet and my heart fluttering, I smushed into my mate's chest. Well, until I was passed to Delaney, then my brother, Sylvie, Vera, and the rest of the people that were now an extension of my foundation.

Pack. Number Sixteen.

We grilled, ate, and played, watching the lines of orange and yellow deepen across the sky, like scars of the sun. And when the moon rose in its stead, I watched as all those that could shift turned into their other forms. Most were Wolves in a variety of colors and sizes, though there were others as well. Río's Jaguar and an Ocelot named Stacy ran along with the Wolves while us non-shifters walked and laughed among them.

It was one of the runs where the pups were in attendance, and the merriment, the *freedom*, was sweet and cool like a spoonful of sorbet on my tongue. We tread the grounds of my brother's land and answered the call that we all felt. To be together with nature pulsing around us. Grounding and breathing life with every step and rolling breath.

RÍO

"All right, all I'm saying is, it's not a bad idea." I went back and forth with Tyler about new lyric ideas with my arm slung over Ramona's bare shoulders. Her mark was a dark brown arc of my teeth, set just at the juncture of her neck and shoulder. The lights in the pool turned it an even brighter turquoise than it appeared in the daytime, and our friends' chatter illuminated our last night with them before we set off.

After taking a bullet that'd been meant for my mate, Tyler had healed slowly but completely. Serafim weaponry was made for supernatural beings and humans alike, but where my mate would've likely not survived Cata's shot, with Delaney's blood, Tyler's body had been able to fully recover within two weeks.

My mate's best friend was seated at Tyler's feet now, looking in fucking heaven as Ty absently petted his head. The issues they'd been having the past few weeks were hopefully resolved, now. "I don't tell you which riffs to use, do I? Leave the lyrics to me."

I took a sip of my beer. "Ain't this supposed to be a democracy?"

He rolled his eyes. "I get in the middle of shifter bullshit, save your mate, *and* agree to housesit for *two months*. I think I've acquiesced to enough of your requests."

"Hey, I thanked you for all that!" Ramona piped up, and the look he sent her was noticeably softer than his no-nonsense expression with me.

"Be that as it may. You won't be here anyway. Just be glad we're taking a break on performances until you get back. We could easily replace you." I just laughed that off, not concerned in the least that he was speaking the truth. He gave side-eyes and sneers, but my friend cared far more than he wanted to admit. I fully expected him to incorporate my suggestion into our next song and act like it'd been his idea all along.

I leaned back into the pool lounge, pulling Ramona with me. She craned her head, caressing her scalp against the curve of my throat and kissing the healed scar of my mating mark. It sent a shiver of delight through my body and soul while I ran my hands across her flat stomach and tickled the piercing in her navel.

The gathering tonight was small, just the band and Delaney,

but that's what made it perfect, too. The sun was behind the trees, the sky giving way to the black and stars.

"We're leaving a list of what all needs to be taken care of on the counter, but it's basically her plants and collecting the mail." My mate and I had fully adjusted to living together, now, and with that, the space looked more and more like ours. Though the witch house was no more, Ramona still gardened at her brother's home every day she could manage it, and the indoor garden of potted plants now lined the windows of our apartment. She took meticulous care of them and had already gone through every detail of their maintenance with Delaney who agreed to watch over them.

Tyler and his new pet also agreed to get our new house ready in the meantime. Signing off on the shit I'd already set to be delivered and making sure it was all clean for when we got back.

I'd been thinking for a while about how I could surprise my princess who was now talking happily back and forth with Jess who was propped on the edge of the pool. And every time I dropped her off and picked her up from Vera's, her head always did a little turn when we passed a small cottage a few doors down. It was a brick house with two bedrooms, one and a half bathrooms. But the yard held a beautiful oak tree and more than enough space in the back for her to start her own garden.

When it had popped up for sale, I'd jumped on the opportunity, happily digging into my nest egg now that I'd found somewhere to stay. If someone had asked me at seventeen, when I set off on my bike with no destination besides *away*, I would've never fathomed having the most wonderful female as my mate or being a member of a fucking Wolf pack. I glanced around at my friends, *Now, the band stuff I would've totally believed.*

I turned Ramona's head, taking control of the pause in her conversation, and planted a kiss on her lips. She molded hers to mine, and the caramel and sweet cream scent of our love swelled between us. It was a full, golden thing that I'd never truly thought I deserved until now that I had the space to feel safe. The itch to move was still there, but now I had a mate to explore with, new cities a vacation instead of a place to start over yet again.

The hours passed, where we ate and laughed, and when Ramona got up to use the restroom before we packed up to go home, I tracked her ass in that skimpy black swimsuit like I had no other choice. The way her hips swayed and her hair bounced around her shoulders, there really was no alternative. *And those legs?*

I adjusted myself as I stood and quickly gathered our shit. When she returned, we said our goodbyes, and I rushed us both to put our gear on and ride off on my bike.

The vibration from my Ducati and my mate's body against my back had me fighting the urge to pull over and have her on the side of the road. But no, instead, I got us safely back to the apartment and hoisted her over my shoulder, which unsurprisingly forced an indignant shout from her.

She grumbled to herself but didn't fight to get down as I ran us up the stairs, nodding at one of our wide-eyed neighbors on the way. Really, they should've been used to our shit by now, anyway.

Once we were safely inside, I deposited Ramona right in front of the large window. Two large houseplants bracketed our legs and came all the way up to our hips as I caged my mate in. Her back and my hands smudged the glass, but the sight of the sleeping city behind her made up for it.

"God, I fuckin' love you, Princess." I let some of my Jaguar slip to the forefront, voice twisting into a half-snarl. Eager to finally get a taste of her, I dragged my half-shifted tongue up her cheek. Sweet and sour, grapefruit and sugar.

She pulled me even closer to her, fingers rested on the waistband of my swim trunks. "Te amo mucho, mi Río," she whispered before giving me a long lick of her own. She ended it with a flick against the piercing through my brow, and really, I couldn't be blamed for what I did next.

My claws tore easily through her clothes. The t-shirt and

shorts and the bikini top and bottoms underneath. And before she could even fully draw a breath to start giving me shit for it, I crouched and sucked one of her nipples into my mouth. So, instead of cursing me out for ruining her new swimsuit, Ramona held my head to her chest, toes squirming against the floor while she moaned my name.

My cock was completely hard, all the blood rushing from my head and only leaving behind the desire to please my mate. To get her to screech and come and then fill her until we both found ecstasy together.

I swept my tongue to the other nipple, biting with my sharp teeth and flickering until the air was thick with her release inching closer and closer.

My knees cracked against the floorboards, but I was past caring. Just needed to taste, to bury my face between her beautiful and strong legs. And Ramona was right there with me, resting her thigh on my shoulder so that I could eat to my heart's content. Ignoring my cock, I took my mate the rest of the way, groaning and purring while she whimpered a string of nonsense. I flicked and swirled my tongue through her orgasm, feeling the pulse of her clit against my tastebuds until she squirmed with oversensitivity.

When I stood, I took Ramona into my arms like how I had in the tree. It wasn't the Antler Pointe Forest, but we were high up enough to give me the same sort of thrill as I braced her against the glass. And when her honey eyes met mine, my princess, mi alma gemela y mi cielo, I knew once again that she was everything I'd been searching for. All those years of facing the terrors of the world alone were worth it. Working a stupid closing shift on a dead night on a random day in May had absolutely been fucking worth it because of her. And I was the luckiest motherfucker in the world to have her for the rest of my life and after.

RAMONA

I'd been licking myself off of Río's lips, but when he thrust into me, my body went limp. His claws and fangs held me at my hips and throat while the both of us were stripped of everything but each other. Where the golden thread shined brightest.

These months with Río had been the focusing of the blurry picture of my life. My tattooed arms clung to him as the slick sounds of our joining filled the apartment and our harmonizing chants filled my ears. His were half-shifted, black and furry and round, and I caressed the outer shell before holding my palm over his heart. It hammered as quickly as he fucked into me, as my breaths escaped my parted lips.

I pinched his pierced nipple between my fingers, and he somehow fucked even harder. If I weren't drunk with lust and the hazy midpoint between releases, I would've worried about the window cracking under the force of it. That with both of our strength, the glass shattering and us plummeting to the street below was probably far more likely than it would've been for two humans.

What did it say about me that I didn't care? That if I fell, I would be more than happy to fall with him.

The trembling and nearly panicked feeling of pleasure almost broken made me cry out and curl into him, my mate. I sank my blunt teeth into his neck, reopening his mark, claiming him again. And again and again, for the rest of my life and after, I would claim him.

He did the same, razor-sharp fangs splitting my skin like butter, and I could see nothing but the kaleidoscope colors of our matehood. Of our love that was spice and warmth and sweet and sour. Decadently spiced chocolate and brightly tart berries.

Río and I groaned into each other while I came just before he did, and my Wolf grumbled in pleasure at our mate filling us. Something I would never, ever get tired of.

He pulled back to kiss at my mark while I licked at the blood welling from his. "Mm, Ramona?"

Our chests pressed against each other, and my back was still plastered to the window that was now warm against my skin. "Yeah?" I pecked his ears that were cuter than they had any right to be. When I'd asked once why he didn't have to take all of his piercings out each time he shifted like he did his contacts, he'd just smirked. *"You think your sister's the first faerie I've ever met? They're vindictive things, but they make good shit."*

Río pulled back so that he could meet my gaze. His yellow and black eyes took in nothing else but me, and never would I have imagined being so grateful to be seen. "You want me to get the plug for you?" I scowled as heat suffused my cheeks, and I shifted, legs still around his waist and body still swallowing his cock.

He grinned, flashing his fangs at me. "Let's get it. I'll carry you." And he peeled me away from the window with a kiss at my temple. I buried my face in his loose hair as he led me to bed.

EPILOGUE

The concrete floor under my ass had long ago become uncomfortable. The walls were much the same, but I gave up on my days alone being restful.

Or was it weeks? It all slipped through my fingers like dry sand, and the few rocks in there that were something a little more to hold onto were getting harder and harder to catch. Maybe there were jewels that could be found, though? Or scuttling crabs looking for their home.

I'd never been a crab before. Non-mammal minds were confusingly simple, the different appendages an adjustment, but if I were a crab, I'd be a king crab. Then I would take the name to heart and lord over all of my subjects. Be the queen king crab, ruler of the beach and command my lesser crabs to do my bidding. Like terrorize littering beach goers and kids that liked to piss in the water.

Could crabs swarm over people? Like in that mummy movie with the scarab beetles. Now, that would be pretty interesting. Flesh eating, hive-minded. Pretty sure that was fictional, but maybe Yoyo would know for sure—

Yoyo. My brain got stuttered up again. Water filled my eyes, and I put my fingers up to them, collecting the drops. I popped them into my mouth, sucking on the salty wetness. Everything was dry here, but I was used to it.

Uncomfortable. I could deal with discomfort. Wasn't so bad when you accepted that it'd come to you and that it was there to teach you something. What was I here to learn?

I reached into my pocket, but there was no fabric. Oh, yeah. No clothes. That was okay, too, though. Running my hands against this body helped. No candy, but it let me remember. How did I get here again?

Elephants have good memories. "Did you know that?" I used my fingernail to scrape against the concrete floor. Using a bit of energy and feeling it zap against my heart, I made it a claw so that I could gouge into floor. Bad, bad, bad, I grinned. Grinned so wide that it hurt my cheeks. Elephants had good memories, and I liked being big.

Big or tiny, medium was more boring.

Yoyo had been so small when I broke him. Snapping his legs was fun, the crack like breaking sticks. "Crack, crack, crack." I took my claw and pricked my thumb. The blood tasted kinda sweet, though it was mine, and I sucked my thumb like how Yoyo used to when he was a baby.

I didn't really mean to fuck up his eyes, but he was always looking like that, so I'd started wailing on his head. He was a shifter, he could take it. Small.

That pup was small, and I'd known she was hiding that baby, but there was no fucking way I was running myself, a pup, *and* a baby through the trees. Fuck what Catalina ordered me to do. Wasn't even sure she knew what she wanted to do with the kids. Bargaining chips or just more collateral because she was pissed? Whatever. If it came to the second, I would've done it quick. Snuck her some flan and watched a movie or some shit and waited until she was asleep, maybe. I wasn't opposed to killing a child, but I also knew there were fates worse than death.

The sound of footsteps was different than those of the soldiers.

My ears perked up, and I scooted over to cover the writing I'd made in the floor. I smiled again. "Bad, bad, bad, bad."

The metal door opened with a creak, and I blinked against the flooding light. I felt my eyes shift to a form that could more easily take in the bright—there, yeah, that was better.

I hugged my knees to my chest and crossed my ankles, rocking to feel the rough lines I'd gouged in the concrete against my skin.

But he was here, and my chin raised to follow his slow advance toward me. *He* was the king crab, and when he crouched in front of me, his scent was like spicy, hot rain. I let it fill my lungs and my belly that'd long ago stopped cramping.

"Xo." His hair was like rippling, shiny chocolate, while mine and Yoyo's was like coal.

"Papai." I grinned and showed him every one of my teeth. His eyes were the same color as his hair, and his stare on me felt nice. Like the sun, and I was a flower. If only I could be a pretty flower. Plants were too different, but that seemed like the easiest thing. To just take what was given by the earth and let it control my fate. I'd like to die that way. Under the sun until it burned me right up.

Pai didn't say anything, but that was okay. It was hard sometimes to keep track when I was like this, alone with everything, and I didn't have my—

He reached into his pocket and pulled out a Jolly Rancher, the blue kind. He put it in the palm of his hand and extended it out, but I wasn't so far gone that I forgot how to really be good. I knew how to be good.

"Pode comer."

I kept myself from snatching and took the piece of sugar gently. When I popped it in my mouth, I kept the wrapper clenched in my fist since there wasn't a trashcan in the empty room. Just me and Pai.

I hummed through the sour taste. It wasn't as good as a blue sucker, but it was okay. I clacked the hard candy against my teeth and moved it around my tongue. I ran my eyes over the room again, took in the soldiers that hung back near the door and in the hallway. But I'd never fought back, so it really wasn't necessary. I knew that I'd done wrong when I let the little girl slip through my fingers. Or when I felt at peace with Río's claws in my skin, making me bleed.

"You know the rules, Xo. And still, you decide to break my fucking heart."

"Desculpe. Eu posso matar ele para você." *Crack.*

But Pai shook his head and started to unbutton his shirt. He wasn't wearing a tie, which meant he was done working for the day. How many days had it been? There weren't any windows in here, so tracking the sun was impossible. I hadn't had a meal or water in so long, so there were no mealtimes to gauge the passage of the hours. The world could cease to exist outside of these walls and this hallway, and I'd never know unless he told me.

Pai was good like that. Telling me. Cata would probably just let me rot. Yoyo would—

No, he was gone now. Escapou.

"Não. Você vai fazer outra coisa para mim."

He was wearing a black t-shirt underneath, and I sighed as he put his nice one over me like a blanket. "Qualquer coisa, Papai."

"Good. It's very important. But you're going to have to live somewhere else for a while. With someone else."

The candy was getting smaller as I sucked it down, but Pai knew. He reached in his pocket again and pulled out a cherry one this time. My second favorite. He gave me permission, and I took that one, too. "Okay." I was used to traveling, going on assignments. But this one sounded a little different. "What will I have to do?"

He smirked, now petting my head in the way that I loved. His fingers in my hair made me purr. "To be good. To still work for me."

"Okay." I grinned. I knew how to do that. "Do I get my sword back?"

"Of course. You'll need it. Now, come along." Instead of

helping me stand, Pai took me into his arms. He was tall, and this form was not, so I fit easily into his chest while my legs dangled in the air. He kept the shirt around me, but his body was more than warm enough. He walked me into the light, and the soldiers parted in a coordinated wave. But they were nothing, and we were everything. "Let's get you ready for your wedding."

ACKNOWLEDGEMENTS
AND A NOTE

Thank you so much for reading *Scars of the Sun*. This is my third novel, and though I never anticipated writing it, I probably had the most fun so far with this one. Río's POV was especially funny, so I hope you enjoyed it too.

As always, I wouldn't have finished this book without the support of my friends, family, and kind readers and authors who I've met along this journey.

Again, to Darcy and Alexia, thank you so much for your feedback, fun conversations, and willingness to always read these long ass romance books. We all know by now that I can't be brief to save my life. These characters and these novels would not be what they are without you both. Thank you.

To Maria, I'm so glad that our paths crossed online. Thank you so, so much for your encouragement and help in polishing this book. Writing a trilingual character is *not* easy, and you helped me refine this story as well as Río's Spanish and Portuguese so that he could be the character I envisioned.

To Rosie and Bella, thank you so much for taking the time to literally go line by line and help me edit this book. And just when the words were blending together in my brain, you helped me tweak and tailor it to what it is now.

ACKNOWLEDGEMENTS AND A NOTE

To all the readers who have posted, reviewed, and interacted with me thus far, I most certainly wouldn't be here without you all.

And to my husband. *My* guitar-playing skater boy. Us meeting in the summer eight years ago directly inspired this book, and you are always multiple numbers on my list. Thank you for always being my cheerleader. For listening to me vent and gush and always being down to get a little treat with me. I love you.

So, what's next?

Seeing as how this book and series started as a fun little side quest, this is just a guesstimate. But! You can probably expect Xiomara's book sometime next year (I envision Fall 2025).

Want to read Tyler and Delaney's love story? Read their novel, *Bloom in Darkness*, now!

And if you haven't already, might I tempt you to read my vampire romantasy, *Twin Blades*? Because I'm still working on that sequel!

Wanna know how Ramona reacted to her and Río's new house? Sign up for my newsletter to find out! You'll also receive access to bonus content, art, and more!

And lastly, if you would be so kind as to rate and review this book, I would greatly appreciate it!

ABOUT THE AUTHOR

Noelle Upton is an indie author and lover of fantasy, romance, and dark tales. When she's not writing or reading, Noelle enjoys dancing, chatting with friends over good food, and laughing with her husband. Her three series, *Twin Blades, A Light in the Dark*, and *Demons & Cryptids* are ongoing, and *Scars of the Sun* is her third novel.

www.noelleupton.com

ALSO BY NOELLE UPTON

Twin Blades

**The Warrior Queen, the Protector of Innocents… fights in seedy taverns
and picks pockets for the highest bidder.**

But her people have been rebuilding from near eradication. And after a
century of running, Meline returns home at the request of the only family
she has left. They've built a kingdom from ashes and connected with
other leaders to give them all a fresh start, but they are still under attack
with the threat of another slaughter on the rise.

So, to atone for her sins, Meline agrees to travel to faraway lands and
persuade more to her family's cause. Even if the agreement demands she
take a personal guard. But not all is as it seems, and her Shadow is hiding
a secret of his own.

Through homecoming and redemption, Meline finds herself leaning on
her companion as they face tense negotiations, assassins, and the
mysterious powers of a dark Goddess. But will it be enough to confront
the person she once was and conquer Death? Or will it lead to the ruin of
those she loves most and the future of her people?

Shadows & Flames

He is blessed with Fire.

She is cursed with Death.

After years apart, a new contract brings Meline and Elián face to face
with both each other and a mysterious new enemy, more powerful than
these immortal assassins could imagine. While they travel to a new
world, the spark between them burns even brighter, and back in their
realm, an old foe has been stoking the flames of war.

Shadows and Flames follows two immortals with Goddess-given powers as
they rebuild what was broken between them, rescue a dear friend, and
shed light on secrets that could break them all over again. It is the second
installment of the Twin Blades series.

In the Light of the Moon

Sylvie, a twenty-eight-year-old undergraduate student, has recently moved to Antler Pointe following the death of her father. She's committed to finally finish her degree in English and to learn her family craft under the tutelage of her grandmother. One night, while closing up at her part-time job, Sylvie stumbles upon an injured man. After helping him on his feet, and watching him shuffle off into the night, Sylvie goes into her last year of college with an enthusiasm to finally set her life back on track. What she doesn't expect, however, is to quite literally run into the man she helped, now fully healed. He's curt and suspicious of her but is committed to settle the debt of her kindness.

Orion is a literature professor who has settled in his hometown after years of trying to find his place. After a disastrous attempt, Orion has resolved himself to live a quiet life on his family's land with nature and books for companions. But once a witch with kind eyes saves him by caring for and generously gifting him with her smiles, he starts to hope that he may not need to remain alone.

However, there is something sinister happening in Antler Pointe, and while they're eager to explore a peaceful life with one another, Sylvie and Orion are quickly swept up in a string of disappearances that culminates in a bloody showdown. *In the Light of the Moon* is a paranormal romance with a fall backdrop where witches and shifters meet, fight, and love. All under the light and shadows of a living forest that calls to both groups with very different songs.

Bloom in Darkness

In the small New England town of Antler Pointe, **Delaney Warner** is finally living his dreams. He's in his last year of college for his teaching degree, he has a brand new pack that is *so* much better than his last, and he's got more friends than he ever imagined. After his tragic upbringing, Delaney is now determined to try new things and thrive. So, when his roommate suggests he attend a metal show downtown, he dresses up and wiggles on over. If there's one thing Delaney has found, it's that life is full of surprises, and when the lead singer of the Concrete Executioners calls him beautiful and buys him a drink, he may have found the best surprise of them all!

Tyler Lee has the weight of his family's hopes on his shoulders. After moving away from Antler Pointe in the seventies, he returns as a jaded vampire and takes over his family's funeral home so that his elderly parents can finally retire. Now back in the town his younger self was so determined to escape, he's mentoring his nephew, managing his brother's recovery, and counting down the days until he can live for himself again. That is, until he sees a sweet boy with golden hair and pure soul through the crowd and can't resist spending a night with him.

One night turns into more, and Delaney and Tyler form a bond that feels a little too much like fate. Even still, Tyler worries that his darkness is too much for his boy, and Delaney's past threatens to rip them apart.

Bloom in Darkness is a standalone novel featuring characters from the *A Light in the Dark* series. Prior knowledge from *Scars of the Sun* (ALD #2) is recommended.

Love Always, From Antler Pointe

Welcome back to Antler Pointe, a town filled with humans, shifters, vampires, and faeries. This time, we catch up with Sylvie and Orion for a special moment, Río and Ramona as he tries to make up for some oversights, and Tyler and Delaney as the former showers his mate with an unexpected surprise.

After their own celebrations, the Antler Pointe couples convene for an "Intimate Palentine's Day Extravaganza." Hosted by one very excited Jaguar and his mate who would do anything to keep that goofy smile on his face.

This Valentine's Day novelette is filled with a few spicy moments, a lot of sweet ones, and a special night for this found, supernatural family.

Prior knowledge of the previous *A Light in the Dark* series books is recommended before reading this story.

Wicked is the Night

Xiomara is the head enforcer of the Serafim Group, the best shifter family business in the world. She gets called in to collect heads or make sure people get with the program, but this new assignment is different. When her father tasks her with taking down their biggest rival from the inside out, Xiomara is all too eager to sign the marriage contract. Her husband turns out to be a stupid workaholic, but the job gets harder the longer she's out from under her father's thumb.

Boone isn't new to this. At one hundred and twenty-five years old, he's been in the business since he was running moonshine in the North Georgia mountains. Benicio Serafim has been a thorn in his side for the last few decades, and when the opportunity arises to get close enough to stab him in the back, Boone doesn't hesitate. His new wife is a ball of chaos, claws, and hidden knives, but he slowly grows used to his kitten.

Will Xiomara be able to end Boone Albright when the time is right? Will Boone be able to take down the Serafim Family? And who the hell is stealing from them all?

Wicked is the Night is a paranormal romance standalone novel and is book three of the A Light in the Dark series. Prior knowledge from the previous books is helpful but not required.

How I Became a Succubus's Pet

Daniel, a college junior who somehow found his way in a History of the Occult class, is trying to keep his scholarship. With a degree he may not even want hanging in the balance, he decides to go all-out for this extra credit paper. But conducting a ritual from an old, forgotten textbook isn't one of his brightest ideas.

Not when it ends up being real.

After summoning a succubus and accidentally binding his soul to hers, Daniel is dragged to Hell where he waits for his demon to find a solution. He works in her shop, meets new friends, and builds a new life for himself while Feronia's allure grows by the day. One that asks him to submit.